ALEXANDER GALAXUS

Book I

Alexander of Terra

A novel by

Christopher L. Anderson

iUniverse, Inc.

New York   Bloomington

Alexander of Terra
Voume 1 of Alexander Galaxus

iUniverse books may be ordered through booksellers or by contacting:

iUniverse
1663 Liberty Drive
Bloomington, IN 47403
www.iuniverse.com
1-800-Authors (1-800-288-4677)

Because of the dynamic nature of the Internet, any Web addresses or links contained in this book may have changed since publication and may no longer be valid. The views expressed in this work are solely those of the author and do not necessarily reflect the views of the publisher, and the publisher hereby disclaims any responsibility for them.

ISBN: 978-1-4502-4119-9 (sc)
ISBN: 978-1-4502-4120-5 (ebk)

Printed in the United States of America

iUniverse rev. date: 7/30/2010

To my parents who instilled in me the desire to create new worlds

PROLOGUE

"Come now child it's time for bed," Kvel Mavec told her daughter.

"But Momma, can't I stay up and watch the Circus, please?"

"Etris, you know you're too young to watch the Circus Pantrixnia broadcasts! They're far too violent for one of your age. I'm none too pleased your Father allows you to watch football. Did Father let you watch the Circus?"

"No, I saw it at Tria's house, Momma, at her sleep-over. They had one prisoner who was on his third day before he got eaten. Three days! Tria's father says that's almost a record!"

"Well, I'll have a talk with Tria's parents tomorrow. Now, that's enough. On your knees child and say your prayers."

"Yes, Momma," the girl sighed, folding her sprightly silvery form at the side of her bed. She looked up through her bedroom window, through the clear climate controlled skies of the planet Kempec Primus and crossed her arms over her breast. Her beautifully luminous pupil-less eyes closed and she recited the same litany repeated a trillion times every moment by trillions of galactic children.

"Bless my world my life to keep, bless my people as they sleep. Slumber sweet, yet slumber light, lest Alexander evade our sight. For the Conqueror shall never cease, on that day I'll make my peace. Beneath Alexander's throne, I pray, rather Death take me away. If I die before I wake, I pray my God my soul to take. Amen."

"Amen, my sweet," Mavec said, tucking the girl under the covers.

"Is Alexander coming tonight Momma?"

"Not tonight, dearest. I would have heard something."

Etris smiled, as she always did with her mother's reassuring answer. "But why does Alexander want to come here, Momma?"

"He's a Terran, he's a conqueror. That's what Terran's do my love."

"But why?"

Mavec sighed, and said, "Because long ago, Alexander the Great united all of Terra under his banner—a banner of conquest. Terrans yearn for unity, and one day they will unite again under the heir of Alexander. When they do they'll follow Alexander's call to the stars, for though he is dead, his philosophy survives. It's their religion; it's their way of life."

"Will he make me part of his harem?"

"Gracious what a thought!" Mavec started, and then she sighed, stroking her child's head. "It's alright Etris; I remember having the same thoughts as a girl of your age. We'd sit around the light of a lumen and talk about the terrible Terrans and what would happen to all of us when Alexander finally came—oh the morbid thoughts of school-age girls!"

"But why does Alexander want to hurt us?"

"I don't know if it's anything personal, dear. That's how they are. Terrans have hurt and killed countless millions of their own people in this centum alone. We can expect no mercy from them. They are an adolescent race of uncivilized barbarians. Now, enough of that, Etris, if you really want to know, ask the school-computer about Terran history. The night is no time for such talk."

"You're a Senator, you'd tell me, wouldn't you?" she asked again, clutching her covers around her. "Alexander's not coming tonight is he, you promise?"

"No, the Terrans have not found the heir to Alexander; they are far too fractured after the last great war to unite. There is no cause to fear tonight or for many to follow!" Mavec kissed her daughter tenderly and turned off the light.

"Good night, Momma!"

"Good night, dearest!"

Chapter 1:
The Pain

"I am Alexander! I am Alexander! I am Alexander!"

Desperately Alexander fought the alien probe trying to control his mind. Instinctively, he fought back in the most elemental way, repeating his name over and over. It was a basic form of identification, but the harder he fought the rising tide of pain the deeper he sank into its molten embrace. The pain started in the hollows of his temples. From there it spread along his nerves, tunneled through his skull, and rode the subterranean rivers of his blood until finally it spilled into his cortex and flooded his thalamus, permeating every fiber of his being. A malignant surging force pushed aside every shred of self awareness leaving Alexander blind, deaf and frozen in the agonizing moment. He wanted to writhe, to kick, to scream, but he couldn't move. A weight crushed him, as if he was under water too deep for his muscles to overcome, too deep for him to force air though his throat and too deep for him to concentrate on any thought but the pain.

As a helpless observer he watched the ephemeral glow of the pain grow in his mind's eye. His brain became a fiery thing. The pain transformed each neuron into a tiny inferno as it sped like a sentient torrent of fire through the hemispheres of his mind. It advanced in its merciless search, ratcheting along every neural path, deeper and deeper into his psyche until his mind swelled, throbbing with an acerbic, delirious ringing of titanic bells. The pain entered the core of his memory, rushing through the gates, clutching and ripping at the tendrils of his thought. There it gathered, as if the pain found what it sought—it surrounded the citadel of his past. The assault trebled. He fell into a sucking whirlpool of anguish. Alexander's fury rose in a last desperate rebellion against the mind rape of the pain.

Revulsion churned within his spirit; revulsion against a crime so horrific to his identity that the debilitating power of the pain dwindled noticeably. He fought. Yet even as he grasped for a way to combat the pain a lock turned, a door opened, and something within his being was now naked, open for inspection.

The gate to his memories burst, and a deluge of repressed events shrieked through his consciousness, exposed for all to see. They distracted his effort, and involuntarily he witnessed the images of his own existence.

There, along a lonely stretch of road, he watched himself, the victim of a kidnapping by strange frail beings with shark's eyes. The eyes latched upon him; they were black as pits and devoid of feeling. The beings put him in a coffin-like prison. The interior glowed with a sickly hue. It was bare metal, comfortless, cold, with skeletal ribs dripping with condensation. There was no sound, no movement, no sensation of touch; his only companion was the pain. The coffin opened, and under a battery of bright lights he saw the operating table. He was looking up at the lights. The table was like a slab of ice. He couldn't move. Out of the corner of his eyes he saw instruments, probes and equipment standing out in brutal relief. The frail beings bent silently over his naked form. Then there was the pain.

He was back on earth amidst the mind numbing normalcy of existence. Time marched on—years it seemed. Then events repeated themselves: a kidnapping, another coffin and the pain. They returned him again and normalcy settled in until the cycle began all over again: a kidnapping, and now—in the present—the ever-present pain.

Alexander reeled, screaming, "Oh God, not again!"

Anger replaced helplessness, and he focused on a single motor activity. With a battery of thoughts roused by fury, each more resolute, more insistent than the last, he attempted to open his eyes. His first try earned no result, but he felt the sensation of pain fade. A glimmer of gray light tingled his optic nerve. He redoubled his effort, feeling as if he lifted massive steel doors with his will, not the insignificant hoods of flesh that hid his sight. The gray turned green with areas of fuzzy light and dark patches. Two of the dark patches moved and grew. They were small and thin. Were they people; the captors of his memories? He concentrated on one of them, but his sight was inexplicably dim. Try as he might he could not resolve the shapes. Frustrated, he sent a command to his arm. A buzz of sensation ran through the limb. Ah! His nervous system was reacting to his commands! He reached for the shape.

It moved away suddenly, and the pain returned tenfold, overwhelming, incontestable. He cringed, expecting to collapse under the onslaught. His mind almost gave up, but his body automatically resisted the pain, tensing to weather the storm. The wave of pain passed and he remained conscious—though drained to the point of death.

Through narrowed eyes he watched two strange beings at work on him; at the moment he was unable to do anything about it.

CHAPTER 2:
EXPERIMENTS

In the narrow confines of the ship's laboratory Alexander convulsed and went limp. The two slight figures standing alongside exchanged meaningful, but silent glances.

"Extraordinary," the Scythian, a telepath, thought to its companion. "I cannot recall ever seeing one cognizant of the probe at such a high level. Was that level five as anticipated?"

"It was," the other replied. It scanned a series of screens, shifting the patterns with thought keys. At length it thought, "We have nine millennia worth of data on this species, but I have no record of any cognitive activity for Terran subjects above level four, however, this is the Terran male's third capture. It's possible the male is developing resistance to the probe."

"Impossible," replied the first. "Many Terrans are captured dozens of times without any increased resistance to the probe. Still, it is unusual, and this is one of our profile cases, not a random subject, is it not?"

The second Scythian watched a series of lights wink in response to his mental commands, and the screens displayed a new set of data. "Yes, the Terran caught the attention of the profile protocols. Prior to the initial capture the subject was a gladiator in one of the more violent entertainment spectacles." The Scythian pointed to a screen with a long thin finger. The screen showed Alexander in purple and white armor, with horns on his helmet, battling other gladiators in silver and white.

Alexander stood in the snow over his fallen foe, bloody, muddy, with his breath smoking from beneath his helmet. He raised his arms to the adulation of thousands.

The Scythian keyed the computer, and the scene shifted to a series of warplanes. "After a short period in the games it became an officer in the atmospheric arm of one of the nation states. That is where the protocol made the first identification." The Scythian turned to another screen that displayed personality categories and their scores. "As you know the protocols routinely scan the Terran's battery of intelligence and personality tests. The information is primitive, but still useful in tagging those individual Terrans which, under the right conditions, could cause significant upheaval on a planetary scale."

The Scythian left the displays and returned to the prone body of Alexander. "This subject fits many of the alarm categories. Strangely enough it is considered highly intelligent, even by galactic standards. Although its education is understandably primitive, the subject held advanced degrees in the sciences including physics, mathematics and astronomy. The subject's unusually high level of aggressiveness, demonstrated leadership skills and its high intelligence flagged the subject. From the protocol's point of view there was great potential in this individual."

"Where does the Terran's career stand at this time?"

A mental note of surprise emanated from the second Scythian. "It is in transition. The Terran is no longer in the military, but there seems to be no particular reason for its departure in the Terran records. Records indicate a swift rise in positions of responsibility—as our observers expected. The Terran had considerable expertise and command experience, as noted by its superiors, but in the end he failed to advance to the upper echelons of command." The Scythian stepped away from the screen, his thin arms spread wide. "I cannot interpret this data."

"I can interpret this for you," the first Scythian thought as he looked over the data. "I have seen this before. This particular Terran meets the classic personality profiles for times of conflict. In its career no conflicts of significant scale occurred. Often Terran military institutions quietly discourage aggressive strong willed officers during such times. Apparently, the more politically oriented Terrans are threatened by this aggressive type of Terran. This Terran, which thrived in Terra's gladiatorial games, only aggravated its situation. Events have already quelled what potential it had, without our intervention. What else is pertinent in the Terran?"

The second Scythian changed the data displays, and thought, "The Terran is consistent with its personality profile. Records indicate it is an expert in physical warfare, as well as with assorted weapons. It is highly intelligent, as mentioned, possessing degrees in advanced science. Interestingly enough, its work focused primarily on space travel. The subject is well above the average in size and as expected it is physically quite powerful. There is, however, a noticeable decline in physical capability primarily due to age and various injuries. If you will address the medical scan we've highlighted the major areas of difficulty."

The second Scythian moved over to the table where Alexander lay. A blue swath of light enveloped his body and he rose about a foot off the table. Portions of Alexander's structure became transparent down to the level of the damage. Symbols floated in the blue air next to the injury explaining the extent and nature of the problem. Slowly, as if on an invisible spit, Alexander's body rotated while the second Scythian studied it.

"There is major connective tissue damage to nearly every joint. There is evidence of primitive replacement surgery on the right knee. The artificial joint is a metal alloy, heavy and crudely manufactured, but apparently serviceable. The Terran has multiple injuries to the spinal column. There is a significant amount of scar tissue in the extremities. Incredible! A Scythian would terminate its life cycle rather than endure such physical difficulty."

"The injuries undoubtedly originate from the Terran's career in the games. Perhaps that is why there was a change in careers. That is enough on this subject; do we have access to the Terran's memory patterns? Good. What do the previous core scans reveal?"

"This is interesting," the second Scythian thought, moving in a short clipped motion as if unused to unsettling events. "Normally we gain access to the memory core of the brain on the initial study. It is noted, however, that the Terran's resistance to the probe on the previous two studies was significant enough to bypass the memory scan routine. This is then our first memory scan for this individual."

"Really, that is quite unusual," the first admitted.

Images came through on the screens. The pictures were incoherent at first, but after some telepathic adjustment the Scythian announced success. "I have accessed the portion of the memory with previous personalities."

"Find the oldest coherent fragment," the first ordered.

"Identified, and stimulated," replied the second. Screens previously dark sprang to life within the room. The two beings glanced at images of mountains and the sea. There was a woman with hair of gold, and lovemaking. Multiple scenes of primitive war followed, all in different locales. The Scythians witnessed dozens of towns burned, towers stormed and the great crush of steel clad men savagely hacking away with blood drenched blades. There were gray skies and mountains. There was the sea. There was the woman and his children.

The second Scythian said, "It is an older persona, by Terran standards. But there is nothing extraordinary in the observations: the particular mate, mating and offspring are constant themes amongst the Terrans."

"That is a failing with the two sex species. I see no relevance to these images," the first replied with repugnance.

The images shifted to the woman again, as if the memory was taking a long last look at her. A cold fog enshrouded morning replaced the woman. A growing battle scene erupted out of the glooms, this time in greater clarity and detail than ever before. It swiftly formed into an image of the man, his beard red with blood and his armor rent. He stood alone on a bridge while a horde of enemies tried to cross it. His notched ax rose and fell amongst the ranks of his foes leaving a mound of tangled dead.

"This must be the death memory," the second noted.

"Shocking, make a note of it for the Bureau of Information. I can think of no better example of Terran ferocity."

"As you wish," the second said. The image went on, giving an interminable sense of time, until finally another warrior stabbed him from underneath the bridge. The image faded, but before it went completely dark there was a dim picture of two women dressed in glowing metal scales. They came to the fallen man. Beyond them a huge red bearded Terran waited. The image disappeared.

"What was that last portion?" the second Scythian asked.

The first answered, "Possibly a primitive ritualistic belief. Often the Terrans attempt to explain the unknown with a set of beliefs based on identification—I believe they term the concept religion. It is prevalent in all of the thalamic driven races of the galaxy. Catalogue it and move on to the next."

The Scythians continued with the memory scans. The life memories of Alexander varied, and they grew sharper and more complex as they climbed into recent Terran history. The exercise took some time, and by the end of it the first Scythian was disinterested.

"Catalogue what we have, then prepare the male for return."

The Scythians' colleague, however, appeared agitated, thinking, "I believe there is something noteworthy in this Terran."

"What do you mean?" asked the first, its thoughts perturbed. "The memories were not so different from the thousands of others we have catalogued."

"I believe there is something else," the second replied. "The computer has run its correlation scan against recorded Terran history and has found matches."

"So the Terran has been noteworthy in their history on more than a singular instance. I admit it is unusual, but,"

"You do not understand," the second thought, interrupting his superior—a highly unusual act for a Scythian. "The significance is in the consistency of this Terran's affect on Terran history. These are not insignificant life events. The Terran is linked in all of its life memories to Terrans identified in their own recorded history. In other words this Terran made a significant impact upon his world in every lifetime."

"All of them?" the first Scythian thought, stiffening perceptibly.

"All of them," the second Scythian replied firmly.

"We have seen this before. Certain Terrans, as did Alexander the Great, make their presence felt in each life experience. Is this one of those Terrans? What do his current life memories tell us? How do they compare with our current observation of Terra?"

"There is nothing which correlates this Terran with records of present history outside of his performance in the gladiatorial games. That facet of his life is insignificant and can be discounted. Gladiators of this world are lauded and admired, but never remembered. However," the second Scythian thought, but there was a lapse, and an incomplete thought.

"Well?" the first pressed.

"There are many images of what they call dreams," the Scythian replied. "The empathic charts also show extraordinarily high readings of frustration. Apparently, the subject is agitated over his lack of signature success. Although there is evidence of significant accomplishment associated with the gladiatorial games the Terran appears to views these glories as irrelevant. There are also images of events that have not occurred. There is a great deal of mental energy expended on these pseudo-memories. There is one other thing I feel I must point out."

"Proceed."

"You mentioned with great accuracy that such a being as this could not succeed in times without conflict. He is ambitious, aggressive, intelligent, and a leader. I've run a comparator protocol. The subject does compare quite favorably with the personality profile of the Alexander of two millennia past; that is, Alexander the Great."

"Comparisons are one thing, however intriguing; association to past personalities is another. There was no indication in the memory scan that this being even had an ancestral personality in Alexander's time."

"That is not unusual," the second said. "We ran only a surface scan to the oldest coherent fragment. If there were a memory pattern dating to Alexander's time it would undoubtedly need to be rebuilt. That could be done with an in depth catalogue of the core. Of course, such a scan would take time."

"Yes, we would undoubtedly spend more than the allotted time on this individual," the first thought uncomfortably. "Without further proof of identity I cannot justify the deviation."

"Yet his first cognitive thought trigger was an identification of self. It was identification not of Alexander Thorsson, but simply of Alexander!" the second thought, uncharacteristically and earnestly pressing its point.

"Meaning that even if this is not a continuation of the personality of Alexander the Great it could very well be a being who at least sees himself as the next Alexander. It is a lengthy supposition, but one with merit."

"Shall I set the scanners for a prolonged study then?"

The first Scythian hesitated. It turned, and in a very unusual display of physical agitation—for a Scythian—it paced. Round and round the laboratory it went. Finally, it stopped, and thought, "Set the scanners for a fragment search. Often old psyches can be identified from a fragment of a pattern; a single visual cue momentous for a particular life cycle will identify the general time frame of the psyche. We might investigate a dozen such visualizations in the time it would take the scanners to catalogue a single memory pattern. Proceed."

The second Scythian did as he was told. They ran through several images, each of some import to its owner, but none enlightening. Then a silhouette of the man appeared on their screens. He looked over a darkening landscape from the vantage of a high mountain pass. Beyond the stars shone fitfully over a slumbering world.

The Scythians stiffened bolt upright as if hit by an electric shock, but any further inspection was interrupted. Their screens went suddenly blank and flashed on again. When they brightened the image of one of their own people appeared. Its thought-expression instantly demanded their attention. A telepathic carrier wave addressed them.

"This is the Scythian High Council with an urgent update for all Scythian citizens, especially those outside the home territories of Scythia. After lengthy negotiations with the Chem, we regret to inform you that the Chem have thus far refused our calls to open their borders. As you know Chem is the only civilization completely outside our sphere of influence. Our only protection from this thalamic race is through self imposed Chem isolation, which has lasted since the termination of their wars of expansion thirteen millennia past. There is increasing doubt as to Chem reaction. At this point in time, there is any number of possible Chem reactions, including punitive action. However, our calculations view this possibility as remote.

"Heretofore, our approach with the Chem has embraced the logic of our proposals as the central reasoning behind acquiescence. The ineffectiveness of this direction of negotiation can be blamed on the Chem weakness of linking emotion and reason in policy. The over-emphasized sense of honor the Chem hold as their primary dogma makes them jealous of incursion and has been particularly difficult to overcome. We therefore conclude that we must invigorate our approach with an emotional argument.

"Our ambassadors are approaching the Chem with the intention of using the Terran stratagem. As you well know we used this technique of negotiation on the Golkos, who are our closest approximation to the Chem. We experienced markedly successful results following an initial negative reaction. The Chem are expected to react with extreme emotion to the threat of Terran mercenaries being used against their empire. We predict such a reaction will be short-lived with no serious repercussions.

"Despite this assurance all Scythians are to be on the alert for aggressive Chem activity, especially along the Scythia-Chem frontier."

The message went on, but the first Scythian commanded the ship's computer to send the tapes to the Homeworlds. "We must inform the Council of our findings. This particular Terran, if his records are manipulated correctly, could be used against the Chem . . ."

✠   ✠   ✠

The two beings turned away from him, watching another of their kind on the view screen. Alexander saw his chance. He felt ill with exhaustion, but he had no choice. Carefully, he slid off the table. His legs were rubbery and it took a concentrated effort to stand, but the aliens were still engrossed in their communication. He took an uncertain step, then another, creeping up behind them. Alexander was going to take their two melon heads and smash them together. He doubted if he had the strength to kill them, which was just as well—he might need them alive.

He reached for their heads.

A hammer blow shook the ship, jarring Alexander painfully. He reeled across the metal deck, careening into the instruments and sending them crashing onto the floor. Alexander tried desperately to extricate himself before the aliens saw him; he needn't have worried.

The shock sent the aliens skidding across the deck as well, crashing violently against instruments and bulkheads. Their little round mouths warbled hideously, as if they were terrified animals not sentient beings.

Alexander found the irony momentarily intriguing.

He didn't have time for further reflection; something was happening to the ship, and he had to at the very least maintain his freedom. Alexander scrambled up through the tangle of metal, screens and cables and headed for the aliens.

One of the aliens saw him. It howled in a high keening way, eerily in synch with the ringing hull. It reached for something in its belt and aimed it at Alexander.

Another blow hit the ship, and the alien's blue beam sailed wide. The gun flew out of the alien's slight hand, and instinctively Alexander snatched it out of mid air.

Alexander reached the alien and backhanded it across the face. Despite Alexander's weakened condition the alien cart wheeled across the deck. It crashed into a wall of screens, and Alexander froze.

The images on the screens were unimaginable. They were all of him, or so it seemed. It was as if he was watching movies of himself in different times. He saw his football days; he saw himself as Viking warrior; he was a general; he was a king; and in the center plate he saw himself looking over a broad valley from a high pass—lights twinkled in the distance.

"Have mercy, oh Alexander!" said a high sing-song voice, breaking his reverie. He looked down to see the one alien helping the other to its knees. It prostrated itself before him.

Before Alexander could say or do anything a loud hissing noise began behind him. The aliens covered their faces.

He looked back to see a red light force its way around the rim of the chamber's hatch. A bright flash erupted, blinding Alexander, and a shot split the air as the clamps gave way. The hatch spun off its mounts and whirled across the short space, crushing one of the Scythians' against the wall. A dark pool of sluggish blood spread from underneath the twisted metal.

A menacing figure stepped into the chamber. Though almost as tall as Alexander the being was markedly slighter in build.

"Alexander save us!" cried the remaining alien.

"Who the hell are you?" Alexander demanded.

The new alien stood scarcely three yards away. He drew what looked to be a pistol and shot Alexander.

Alexander twisted away at the last second, but the shot hit him on the right side of the chest anyway. It whirled him around, burning his chest and shoulder with a sharp electric sizzle. His head swam, and his eyes lost their focus, but he fought to stay conscious. Going on pure instinct, Alexander bull rushed the new alien. He struck the lighter alien with his shoulder, knocking him easily aside. Alexander headed for the glimmer of light that must be the hatch; he had to get out of there.

His vision started to come back, at least enough to see that there were two other tall dark figures entering the hatch as he was trying to leave it. He plowed through the bodies as he used to do with the behemoths of the NFL. There was no resisting him. He burst through, staggering down a bright green corridor, bouncing off the walls like a pinball.

Alexander's vision began to clear. There were hatches on either side of him. He passed by several closed hatches, then he stopped. A hatch on the right was open. Within, on a huge screen, was the unmistakable horizon of the Earth. He ducked in and found a long curved panel on which were groups of controls, lights and displays. It had to be the bridge.

First things first, he muscled the hatch closed. He didn't know how to operate the automatic mechanism so he forced it closed, spun the latch, and locked it. Then he turned to the control board.

"Alexander, if you can't figure out the door how are you going to fly the ship?"

He'd just started to scan the displays when a familiar hissing sound turned him around. He leapt out of the line of the door as the hatch came free. It crashed into the control board. Alexander rushed the figures beyond the open hatch, but three bright blue beams hit him in mid stride. Everything instantly went black.

The Chem warrior stepped onto the bridge and stood over Alexander. He wore a mottled suit of metal-like armor and a close fitting helm. Luminous blue eyes stared down at Alexander with satisfaction.

"So this is a Terran in the flesh," he said, rubbing his jaw where the Terran struck him. "Impressive. Signal Lady Nazeera. We've accomplished our mission. Bring him and let us go!"

Chapter 3:
The Legacy of Alexander

Sixty-seven parsecs away Ambassador Kvel Mavec of the Kempec Empire entered the marble halls of the Galactic Senate on the neutral planet Roma. Mavec, as she always did when first arriving in the Senate, toured the upper galleries before descending into the pit of the Senate chamber. There, looking down from niches in the gallery, were the marble statues of figures renowned throughout the known galaxy. They were the builders of Roma; beings of nobility, destiny, peace, war, and even betrayal. Not all the beings were glorious in their lives, and some recalled the darkest failures of a civilized galaxy, but they earned a place on the gallery overlooking the Senate, nonetheless. Their unseeing eyes gazed down upon the rulers of the galaxy so that the lessons they taught in history might never be forgotten.

Mavec could recite the particulars for each of the statues in the gallery, and she stopped for some time beneath the noble artifice of Novus Novek, the Conciliator, of her Homeworld, Kempec. She was tall and spare, as were most of her people, being of the same galactic family as the Chem and the Golkos, but the marble did not reveal the dusky glisten to her flesh or the luminous eyes. Still, Mavec was impressed with the likeness, and reveled in the honor of having one of her people in the gallery.

Novek's inclusion with the famous of history was no mistake. She mediated the final peace between the Golkos and the Chem, ending the millennium of brutality known as the Chem Wars of Expansion. That was thirteen millennia past, and since then peace reigned in the civilized galaxy beneath Novek's gaze. Next to the Kempec was the likeness of Terumaz of Chem herself, the great lady with whom Novek brokered the lasting peace. It was a triumph of memory that warmed the heart of Mavec.

Yet even as she enjoyed the flush of satisfaction she felt a burning gaze on her temple. Involuntarily she cast her glance across the gallery to the most infamous of the Roma's builders.

There, set aside from his peers in a solitary niche at the end of the gallery was the most disquieting being in the galactic company. It was not that the figure was malevolent in form or composure, quite the opposite. The statue initially recalled glory in its most basic form. Heavy musculature characterized the being as a Terran warrior, but from the gilded cuirass to the flowing shock of marble hair the being was still beautiful and awe inspiring. Such was its peril; for the genius of the artisan revealed the true character of the man. He was a conqueror.

The blank stare of the far seeing eyes looked up to the heavens, caring not for policy, advancement or benevolent prosperity, only conquest. Mavec walked over to the statue, even as she had every time since, as a young woman, she entered these hallowed halls. She stood beneath the powerful being; her breath caught in her lungs.

"Alexander the Great," announced a silken voice behind her, startling even the composed Kempec. The announcement came from the Hrang ambassador, a tail-less saurian of stout frame, whose people were remarkably adept at galactic intrigue. Mavec knew the Hrang over many periums, and though she respected her peer, there was always a level of suspicion to be dealt with. The Hrang were master spies, using dermal implants to amplify their native chameleon-like attributes, and they normally knew quite a bit more than was good for them.

Ambassador She-Rok bowed stiffly in apology, and told her, "This has always been one of my favorite places. I suppose I am fascinated by the dreadful. I can never ignore Alexander when I come here. Almost as a punishment I peruse his words and imagine their ultimate effect on our civilization."

He pressed a switch at the base of the statue. A golden glow enveloped the effigy, and suddenly the marble took on the olive tone of flesh, and the harsh gleam of bronze beneath ruddy gold. The eyes took on life and looked out to a darkening landscape from the vantage of a high mountain pass. Beyond the stars shone fitfully over a slumbering world. A strong magical voice cried out to them.

"How may I look to the horizon and be satisfied with past victories? The conquests of the past matter not; it is the striving forward which feeds our restless hearts. So it is that we must move onward, never ceasing, lest we stagnate and grow rank in spirit. To that end shall I seek that which lies beyond, and verily shall I have it, then on to the next. Behold the vistas of the universe! In it there is enough to sate even my yearning spirit, aye, even to the spirits of my descendants. From this pinnacle I look afar and I see countless worlds to conquer, even to the everlasting and innumerable stars."

The monologue ended, and the statue's newfound life returned to cold distant marble. The Hrang smiled nervously. "No words ever spoken in this galaxy of ours have ever borne so much weight, or ever entailed so much dread. Is it not strange that Roma should play host to a being who could not imagine its existence? Certainly even Alexander could not have foreseen how far his words would carry, or how many empires would tremble at his name. Yet it is always the same, no matter the number of times I listen. I cannot rid myself of the oppression which hangs over me, or the thrill which courses my limbs when faced with the semblance of Alexander. The terrible and yet awe inspiring Alexander! Is the sensation similar for you, Mavec, or do the Kempec have a lesser opinion of Terra's God-king?"

"Why ask when you know the answer?" Mavec replied. "Who of the Galactics may ignore Alexander's boast, or the burden which it delivers? Not the Kempec, at least. Not the prideful Golkos. Not even the vaunted Chem. Alexander affects us all, even to the ideal of this city, this world, and the Galactic seat of government."

Mavec turned away from Alexander and walked to the gallery rail. Below was the pit of the Senate where the twelve civilized cultures of the known galaxy labored at the mechanization of coexistence. It had worked for thirteen millennia, but ever since the rise of the Terran God-king there was a pall cast over the gleaming marble city. Mavec addressed that very thought and wondered aloud whether Roma of the

Galactics would ever bear the same fate as its progeny: the Eternal City on Terra, Rome.

Mavec shook her head, and said, "Two millennia past, shortly after the death of Alexander, we covertly founded the city of Rome. The city prospered; growing upon a political model we formulated to encourage coexistence as the overpowering goal. Secretly we molded the philosophy of the city, stressing service over ambition, citizenship over discrimination, prosperity over luxurious sloth."

Mavec left the rail and walked back to Alexander. "Surprisingly, there were many completely Terran ideals to draw from, not the least of which was Alexander's example of a true multicultural empire. We ensured that Greek and Egyptian philosophers, magistrates and artisans found their way into Rome. An empire grew from Roman ingenuity and their extreme desire for order. In the span of a few centuries it encompassed most of Alexander's former empire."

Mavec sighed and returned to the rail. "There was a time when it seemed we achieved what we sought. Yet despite the massive Galactic effort Rome was a completely Terran city, and a Terran empire. Terrans are an adolescent race. While the ideals of Rome drew them, their attention was soon diverted to the possibility of using Rome's power for gain. The security provided by Rome's legions became a tool for expansion, glory and conquest. New names arose amongst histories generals, all vying to be the heir of Alexander. For a time, even in its distinctly Terran flavor Rome was a stabilizing factor in Terra's progression."

"Yet then Rome slipped into sloth and greed," She-Rok said. "The Empire fell, and it took Terra into darkness and barbarism."

"We failed," Mavec admitted. "When the Roman Empire was no more, we accepted our defeat, and relegated the uncontrollable, unalterable Terrans to strict Scythian quarantine." Mavec turned her luminous eyes on the Hrang, and added, "Yet like the Roman experiment, the quarantine of Terra was not handled exactly as we envisioned."

"Rome was not such a failure as you might think, Mavec," She-Rok said, joining Mavec at the rail. Less morose and more practical than his counterpart he could conjecture dispassionately. "Even the Terrans, from Scythian report, glorify their version of our city. I do not think it was a mistake for us to found it. It was a risk, but not so much of one. The Terrans had already proven themselves capable of prolonged empires by that point in their development, and even of idealism. Rome was meant to harness the constructive energies of a potentially dangerous race within a carefully constructed framework which would promote order, prosperity and mutual respect. In many ways it was successful."

"Rome still failed, She-Rok," Mavec said sternly. "It was successful so long as it followed the Galactic model and was not too Terran. That was our mistake. We did not realize that so far as the Terrans are concerned the legacy of Alexander is all consuming. Alexander touched a nerve in their psyche; his philosophy still resonates after two millennia.

"How long did Rome last before a warlord seized power intent on following in Alexander's footsteps, two, maybe three centellia? In the end Alexander's will held sway. Despite all the advantages we offered the Terrans turned Rome into a more efficient and vastly more superior destructive power. We would have been better served to leave well enough alone."

"Perhaps, but I still do not accept our complete failure," She-Rok replied. "In many ways Rome has served to mentor the Terrans into our systems of law, citizenship and morality. These are apparent, even if they are not dominant. We have, I admit, failed to change the core Terran philosophy of cosmic domination. That may be too much to expect, however. Alexander is as much a legend to his own folk as he is to us. It is difficult to change the words of your once and future lord. The Terran situation, for better or worse, is set. The Terrans have their dreams of galactic conquest, but they cannot reach us, yet. The Scythians still hold the keys to Terra's shackles. Without the ability to leave their planetary system the Terrans are dangerous only to themselves, and they may very well succeed where we fear to tread. The last centellium has been very encouraging!"

"Encouraging?" Mavec exclaimed. "She-Rok, what is encouraging about it? They've progressed from a planet bound people to the outer reaches of their solar system in less than half a centellium! When has another culture in the known galaxy presented us with such volcanic technological growth? Two centellia past they used beasts of burden for transport! Even given the technological capability to match such growth we could never adapt to it. Galactic culture and its technology are linear. We change with exquisite sloth. Our technology has remained at an equivalent level not only through the last age, but three hundred millennia prior to the Chem Wars of Expansion. I cannot even fathom such growth, such chaos. How can we know what to expect?"

"We do not need to know, so long as the Scythians' keep the Terrans where they belong."

"The Scythians, Terra's ever-present keepers and protectors," Mavec said, her angular face framing an expression as close to a smile as her demeanor would allow. "Whenever Scythia desires a new trade agreement, lower tariffs, or anytime there is a resolution in the Senate protesting Scythian ownership of extra-empire commercial interests the Scythians threaten us economically. With their vast holdings in financial institutions and their monopoly on trade we cannot answer their demands in an equivalent manner. The only recourse we have is military. We have a great stigma against using force as an instrument of policy, but even considering we deemed such a horrendous step necessary there is always Terra to stop us. In recent history both the Seer'koh and the Golkos threatened the Scythians only to retreat under threat of unleashing the Terrans. It is stupefying and simple: if any state threatens Scythia, they will unleash Alexander and his legions upon the galaxy. What recourse do we have then? We accede, and thereby feed the bloated Scythian juggernaut, making our position all that much more untenable."

Mavec pounded her slight fist on the marble rail in a rare expression of emotion. Her voice was bitter. It was a marked departure from her diplomatic demeanor.

"They are remarkably adept at reminding us of that particular bit of blackmail. They have Terra, and the Terrans wait upon them for their opportunity. Terrans are nothing more than Scythian mercenaries, but even in that they present their keepers with a deadly danger. Though they prod us with a Terran threat, could the Scythians actually control the Terrans once they were loosed upon the galaxy?"

"Certainly not," the Hrang said with steadfast certainty. "Greed and profit drive the Scythians, but they are not fools. They have a wonderfully developed sense of self protection. I would think, and all our observations support this theory, that the Scythians would do almost anything to avoid an actual relationship with Terrans which might lead to their expansion into the galaxy. They are far too dangerous."

"I do not disagree with you, She-Rok, but still I wonder just how far they are willing to push that particular bluff. I wonder whether we have the strength and fortitude to actually answer such a possibility."

Mavec sighed, gazing down into the pinnacle of galactic civilization: the pit of the Senate. Normally she would recall with pride their accomplishment of ordered civilization, for here even amongst the layer upon layer of galactic intrigue even age old enemies like the Chem and Golkos met with civility. Passions remained, but they didn't interfere with the workings of the galactic bureaucracy. She looked about the Senate at members of the twelve civilized cultures, seeing in them a growing homogeneity. True, they still considered themselves members of twelve separate empires rather than citizens of a single galactic entity, but there were certain inarguable ideals which bound them all together.

"I wonder She-Rok, for all that Roma and our Galactic Senate have accomplished, have we succumbed to the inevitable apathy of success? For thirteen millennia we've been at peace. Precious little has changed in technology, customs or people."

She-Rok shrugged, and joined her at the rail. "You're right, of course. Peace on a galactic scale for such an extreme period of time allows for unprecedented prosperity, but there is always a price. Expansion and exploration ceased as our cultures recovered from the catastrophic wars. When normality returned stagnation came with it, and matters of debate are now relatively petty. No one is willing to risk war for pride or policy."

A loud gong sounded in the cast chamber. All eyes turned to the center of the Senate pit where a huge holographic image brightened. It showed the graven features of the President of the Senate, a Golkos. His voice instantly commanded the attention of the audience.

"My fellow Senators an event is transpiring in our galaxy that has not happened in decands. Fate stands upon the knife's edge. The next few moments will write history. Behold!"

Mavec moved to the rail, and She-Rok was right beside her. She waited impatiently for the face of the President to fade, and the follow on image to clear. There was some problem with the transmission, as if it were being beamed from some remote corner of the galaxy.

"What in the world can this be about, do you know anything She-Rok?"

"On my word, I'm as surprised as you Mavec."

The image cleared to the view of a single planet, blue and white, floating like an iridescent marble in a sea of velvet.

"This day on Terra history is being made," the President said gravely. The scene narrowed to a gathering of thousands of thousands of Terrans, their voices raised in a deafening roar. The Senate shook.

"By the stars, they've discovered the heir of Alexander!" Mavec breathed.

CHAPTER 4:
THE TERRAN GAMBIT

The hologram in the central pit of the Senate panned down to the scene below the enormous crowd—it was a green field painted with parallel white lines. On one side of the field was a group of gladiators in purple, on the other side and equal group in white.

Mavec and She-Rok sighed with relief. The Kempec felt as if she could breathe again; indeed, so terrible was the moment of anticipation that her chest hurt with a sharp cramp.

"I invite you all to enjoy the first session of overtime warfare in the pinnacle of gladiatorial games: the Super Bowl!"

She-Rok cursed, "Damn him, I was going to watch this after today's session—now it'll be ruined for me! Minnesota and Pittsburgh are playing, the Vikings are my team and they're going for their first Super Bowl since the days of Alexander the Great."

Mavec looked at him in amazement.

"Not the true Alexander, of course," She-Rok smiled. "This was a defensive tackle that played for the Vikings, I don't know, maybe fifteen periums past. He was a joy to watch, absolutely ferocious to the core—but somehow honorable. He was the Most Valuable Gladiator in their only win. They haven't been back to the Super Bowl since."

"How ironic is it that we now find our entertainment amongst the very people we're deathly afraid of," Mavec sighed, watching the contest because no matter how terrible it was she was fascinated by it. Not only was she mesmerized by the spectacle, every member of the Senate put aside their business to watch the gladiators.

It was a damning sight. Mavec knew that her people, whether they be Chem, Golkos, or Kempec were not the people of an age past. They'd lost their edge, and it was obvious every time they beheld that most immature and fascinating species, the Terrans. True, Terrans were barbaric, single minded, and utterly without compassion, but there was a ferocious love of challenge which she could not help but admire. Terrans dared to live, always changing the rules by which they existed; Terrans challenged the very universe to keep up with them.

Mavec knew with a profound sense of loss that her people had no such aspirations. The Galactics discovered long ago that singular formula for living within the universe, and their intention was not to stray from it whatsoever.

"Damn!" She-Rok cursed, as one of the players in white kicked the football through the white uprights of the goal posts. "Lost again—they should really send the kicker for Minnesota to Pantrixnia! Ah well, at least they made a game of it this time. Unfortunately, I'm not nearly as adept at picking my gladiatorial teams as I am at political intrigue. The Vikings haven't won since the days of Alexander. I wonder whatever happened to him."

"I can't imagine why I would care," Mavec said. She couldn't get away from the fascination of Terrans quickly enough. "Whatever became of that particular gladiator can't be nearly as inauspicious as what's going on in the pit below—look."

The match was over, and business returned to normal.

The Scythian ambassador approached Nazeera of Chem. The Chem kept an ambassador in Rome. It was a traditional role, for the Chem as a rule offered little advice and asked for none at all. Recently, however, the Scythians had been pushing the Chem to open their borders. The people of Terumaz, the old galaxy's proudest and sternest people, sent a member of their Triumvirate in response to the amazing solicitation. Nazeera of Chem, tall, powerful in mind and manner and honorable to the core of her being, answered only to the venerable Elder of Chem. She came to Rome to discover why the Scythians should make so bold a request, and then to issue a final inevitably negative response.

Mavec liked Nazeera, and admired her for her steadfast resolve. As she suspected, Nazeera's review did not take long, and she rejected the Scythians' out of hand. The Chem, she told them, had no need of Scythian trade and no desire to open Chem space to Scythian convoys. With that issue resolved Nazeera felt the subject was closed irrevocably, but the Scythians apparently thought otherwise. For the past several decands the Scythian ambassadors poked and prodded other Ambassadors, including Mavec, trying to gain support for their cause. The endorsements were half-hearted at best, but as Mavec told them in her steady diplomatic voice, "While we are sympathetic to your over all goals the Chem are, after all, the Chem, and my people are not willing to openly antagonize the people of Terumaz."

It was a veiled reference to the Chem's more militaristic but still recognizable past. Frustrated, the Scythians upped the ante, actually including the reminder of Terra in their dialogue with their fellow ambassadors. They did not use this tact directly with the Chem, for who could know how the Chem would react to such outright threats? The intent got to the Chem anyway, even as intended. The result was inconclusive, but it was obvious that the Chem did not like what the Scythians were saying at all.

This was the cause for Mavec's concern. The slight Scythian in drab gray-green stood out in stark contrast to the exotic Nazeera, dressed as she was in her ceremonial armor. The Chem planted her long nailed fists on comely hips, daring the Scythian to interrupt her privacy, but the slight being approached nonetheless and addressed her. Mavec couldn't hear the conversation itself, she didn't need to. She shook her head in the universal gesture of disapproval, muttering, "Here we have a scenario which fleshes out the difficulties we have been speaking of She-Rok. The Scythians of pre-Alexander days would not consider breaching Chem isolation for any reason. Yet here they are, and quite sure of themselves, mind you. Nothing good can come of this."

"Indeed, Kvel Mavec, you appear struck with apprehension at the sight of our Chem and Scythian friends in parley. The Kempec are well renowned for their skill in diplomacy. Why would you be dissatisfied with dialogue?"

"No doubt you already know the answer to your query, She-Rok," she chuckled nervously. "Should I disappoint you with the truth or allow you to gauge my opinion with your misconceptions. What do you think?"

"The truth is always more fascinating than the most fanciful supposition, my friend, and I hope you will not rob me of the pleasure. In this case, however, your distress is not unique, either to the Kempec or to yourself, Mavec. I would not be surprised if we shared many of the same concerns regarding the Scythians. Therefore, I have no objection to opening my mind to you, in exchange for your honest opinion, if such is the price."

"You need not buy my honesty, She-Rok. I will tell you plainly and bluntly my opinion: the Scythians are overplaying their hand. I can see nothing good coming of this."

"Have you informed the Scythians of your opinion? After all, you know the mind of Nazeera of Chem perhaps better than any other politician, or have I been misinformed? Rumor has it that you've been heavily tasked these last decurns to ease the growing tensions between the two states."

"Your information is quite correct, as usual, She-Rok. Unfortunately, the facade which you see before us—the Chem and the Scythians in rational dialogue—is just that: a facade and nothing more. The Scythians have told me repeatedly that although they appreciate my efforts they are their own best counselors. I was cautioned in the most strenuous way not to interfere with their negotiations and especially not to build a consensus decrying the Scythian attempts in Chem."

"Indeed? I assume that the Kempec government conveniently found itself content to be of any use it could for the Scythians. After all, when seventy-five percent of your trade and sixty-three percent of your financial institutions are controlled by the Scythians you must take care not to tread on their all too delicate toes."

"Your data and your assertions are unfortunately accurate, She-Rok. It is all the more distressing when we represent the status quo as far as Scythian influence is concerned. It presents us with a very difficult problem, and we have precious little capacity to affect the outcome. On one hand the Scythians are steadfast in their contention that Chem must at the very least open routes through their space for Scythian traders, if not open up their empire to free trade. That the Chem shall never do, they prize their privacy most jealously."

"There is no compulsion whatsoever for the Chem to deal with the Scythians," She-Rok added. "They are unique among the civilized cultures in that they have no need of the Scythians. They did not need Scythian aide to rebuild after the wars and are thus completely autonomous. The Scythians, of course, would like to change that slight oversight. There are vast markets in Chem, or at the very least, if they win free passage that would improve the efficiency of their freighter traffic by approximately thirty-five percent. That would be pure profit."

"Profit—one hundred and thirty-five percent of infinity is still infinity! The fools are risking another galactic war based on incalculable profit! They have no idea who they are dealing with."

"Do you really think the Chem will go so far?" She-Rok asked, showing surprise at the level of Mavec's concern.

"My dear She-Rok, we have here a classic example of two bulls going up against one another. That in itself wouldn't trouble me so much. If this were a Chem-Golkos problem neither I nor any of our galactic cousins would care one way or another. The general peace would continue, and the two parties could quarrel amongst themselves. Our particular problem is that the Scythians, unlike the Golkos, have neither the inclination nor the capability of defending themselves. Yet they don't need a military when they can coerce support from the rest of us. The Scythians have established an economic hegemony over most of the civilized galaxy. This economic power directly translates into political power, of course, and it doesn't take many whispered threats for even the Golkos to be cowed. Balk at Scythian leadership and Golkos would be without power, food and money in a decand! A galactic civilization with roots a ki-millenium past would be back to barbarism."

"We've all received communiqués from the Scythians expressing their desire for political support, Mavec, and we have all acquiesced. Why shouldn't we? Certainly the Chem are not going to launch another war of expansion over this issue. The Chem wars were long ago, and I cannot think that even Nazeera, despite her well established image as a soldier, would be so keen as to begin a war over trade routes."

"Do you actually expect Nazeera to accept Scythian demands?"

"Of course not, and the matter will end there. The Scythians will be disgruntled, but unlike the rest of us they have nothing to hold over the Chem. Despite thirteen millennia of peace the tradition of Chem militarism is still too vaunted to illicit any aggressive response on our part. Even the Scythians cannot expect that level of cooperation."

"I do not think that will be the end of it," Mavec told him sternly.

She-Rok shook his bullet head, unfazed. "Mavec, you read too much into this. Even the Golkos, whom I admit may be tempted by the idea, would not go to war with Chem over such an insubstantial issue in their interests. Despite their bluster they remember all too well their disaster at Koor-tum, where the Chem destroyed half their fleet. The Chem are their betters, and they know it. They will not support such a scheme, no matter the Scythian threats, and without the Golkos there is no chance of militarily competing with the Chem. There the matter will end. Our states shall perhaps disappoint the Scythians, but no more."

"You do not understand the Scythian mindset, She-Rok. They consider the Chem their last great challenge to uncontested power in the galaxy. Remind yourself why we as advanced cultures have allowed such growth and influence within the Scythian Empire at the expense of our pride and sovereignty? The Golkos and the Chem are not the only military states in the galaxy, and they may not be the most dangerous."

"Alexander? Do you really believe the Scythians would consider threatening the Chem with Terra?"

"Yes, haven't we been talking of this very thing? Whether they know it or not the Terrans are no less than Scythian mercenaries. For two millennia, She-Rok, the Terrans have fought the galaxy's bloodiest wars amongst themselves for dominion. They search for that singular being that will fill Alexander the Great's glorious throne, and lead the Terrans to the stars in search of endless glory and conquest. The "Legend of Alexander" is studied in every school, college and university. We know their motives, and by constant report we know the veracity of their barbarism. Yet as we all know the Scythians, and the Scythians alone, hold the key to Terra. We dare not make a move without fear of a Terran legion landing on our Homeworld; a legion transported by the fastest ships in the galaxy and armed with the most modern weaponry. I shudder to think what would occur if Terrans ever set foot on Kempec! After witnessing the slaughter they impose on themselves imagine what they would do to another race! The thought is too terrible to comprehend!"

She-Rok sighed, nodding, "In the last centellium alone they've killed over one hundred million of their own brethren. I do not think even the Chem would wish to face such barbarity."

"That is the central question in my mind, She-Rok. What will the Chem do if the Scythians openly threaten them with Terra? We have always backed down in the past, but the Chem, who knows what they will do?"

"They may well call the Scythians' bluff. The Chem prize honor above all. Yet were I to wager between a Terran warrior and a Chem I would call it no contest. Could you see it any other way? Terrans are the pinnacle of the sentient warrior. A Chem may be quicker, but Terrans are half again as large, hardier and far, far stronger than any other sentient. That does not even consider the fact that Terrans are born and bred in a warrior society. What the Chem recall as a distant memory Terrans experience in everyday life. Normally, nothing, not even death, would cause the Chem to give in; but who can say what a race will do when their empire is at stake?"

"It depends entirely on just how great the Scythian offense is," Mavec answered. "This is Nazeera of Chem we speak of, probably the most prideful Chem since Terumaz herself, and by all accounts her equal. Nazeera will not take well any amount of Scythian meddling, and I can only imagine her reaction if the Scythians threaten Chem with Terran legions."

"I am of like mind, Mavec, but there is only one way to find out," the Hrang told her, and he dialed in a setting on his disk. A red light flashed on the circumference. She-Rok pressed it with his thumb and another hologram materialized above the disk. The hologram featured Nazeera of Chem and the Scythian ambassador. She-Rok cut off Mavec's protest with a wave of his stubby hand, "This situation is far too important for Kempec prudence, now listen!"

Even in miniature they could see the luminous blue orbs of Nazeera flicker with concentration as the tiny Scythian waited upon her. The eavesdropping Kempec and Hrang missed little of the confrontation; however, as Nazeera was wholly absorbed in an incoming communiqué on her secure etherlink. When the link was complete, she gave a short, wry smile and tucked the comm-pad into her belt. Glancing up, she found the Scythian still there, patiently awaiting its audience. A flush of anger raced across her darkling chiseled cheeks. Placing her hands on her armored hips only served to expand the perilous nature of the Scythian incursion, but if the being took the hint there was no sign of it. The volume of She-Rok's hologram was low, but the perturbation in Nazeera's voice was unmistakable.

"What is it now, Scythian? You have my answer, and that of the Elder of Chem. There is nothing to debate. We will not, now or ever, allow you access to our space. Nor will we allow Scythian freighters passage through Chem space. What could be clearer? I see no reason for continued discourse, and as such you should do well to avoid trying my patience!"

"We are painfully aware of the jealousy to which the Chem regard their territory, Nazeera of the Triumvirate," the Scythian answered in its high sing-song voice. "Yet I think you still mistake our intentions, and that, more than all else, demands our attention." It cocked its over-large head, as if giving a lecture and began a litany all too obviously rehearsed. "The rest of the galaxy is indelibly connected by the bonds of economic dependency. This interdependency has created a peace too final to be broken. The Galactics have finally turned to the answers which drove Terumaz the Great to end the hostilities perpetrated by the noble Chem. You have grown and blossomed for it. Do you feel no desire to share your experience with your brethren? Certainly the Galactics, and the galaxy as a whole, cannot but help to build upon the structure of civilization with the Chem as their guides. How can self imposed isolation further either the cause of Chem or her Galactic cousins?"

Nazeera was in a towering rage, but the decorum of the Galactics oldest establishment restrained her. In a tightly controlled voice she told the Scythian, "You may dispense with such fantastic inventions of idealism, Ambassador. There is no Scythian altruism behind your facade; there is only your search for increased profit and power. I find both motives irritating in the extreme. Chem does not need you, Ambassador, nor does Chem desire your presence in her space. Understand this, ambassador: we will not subjugate our sovereignty in any manner to Scythian desire for profit. Do you understand? There is no other purpose for continuing this discussion. Good day, Ambassador!"

"I had hoped for a more rational approach to the problem, Nazeera of the Triumvirate. At the very least let me apply to you again for license to run our freighters through a limited number of corridors across Chem space. The galaxy is a vast place, and even a small number of these corridors would bring our cultures closer together. Though you disdain profit I am certain that we could come to some agreement whereby the compensation would be equitable. It is not just for Scythia that I ask this. Your galactic cousins support us fervently on this particular issue."

"Once again you dissect the meaning of dialect with a cut of your own flavor, Ambassador. I have indeed received position papers from your fellow Ambassadors, all lauding the possibilities. Hear you nothing of what I say, or are you deaf to all that does not meet with your approval? We do not care. Send all the leaders of all the cultures to Nazeera's doorstep and have them plead on your behalf, it will fail to alter my mind. Chem will do as Chem sees fit. The hand of Scythia may be heavy without our borders, Ambassador, but in the empire of the Elder of Chem it is inconsequential at best."

"The policy of Scythia is many things, Nazeera of the Triumvirate, but it is never to be ignored," the Ambassador told her. The Scythian stood stock still, and though its voice was constantly pleasant, anything but threatening, there was exactness to its words, which made it more keen and dangerous than a lion's roar. Nazeera's eyes took on a deep purple burn, but the Scythian pressed on. "We have explained the advantages of our offer numerous times. Our patience wears thin. Perhaps it is time to consider other options. If the Chem are unwilling or unable to grasp the opportunity Scythia and her galactic companions offer, then she must be left behind. We can no longer afford to slow our evolution as a galactic community because Chem prizes the ancient ways. We would, of course, rather have the Chem as willing companions, and cherished protectors of our traditions, rather than leaving our brethren behind to dwindle and fade into insignificance. Yet if we must leave you behind, then that shall be a loss, and a lesson, to our community."

"Very well," Nazeera smiled, "if that is all to your offer then by all means leave Chem behind. Why should we desire your company? Chem has kept a representative in the Senate since the days of Terumaz, and despite our well guarded sovereignty we have attempted to be a calm steady influence on galactic growth. If, however, the galactic community is so devoutly supportive of Scythian jealousy and desires our advice no longer then so be it. We shall withdraw today, this moment!"

"Believe me, Nazeera of Chem, nothing would so pain Scythia, but for one distressing eventuality. For our community is growing, and needs space. Peace! I speak not of our established community, for who among us would be so bold, and foolish, as to have designs on Chem territory? We have too much respect for Chem to wish it as a possibility. Yet we are not alone, and of this we poor Scythians know too much. For two millennia, we have borne the hardest tasking: to maintain the incarceration of Terra and the heirs of Alexander. Unfortunately, the Terrans are far too potent a species to keep isolated for all time. When presented with a difficulty they have the unnerving habit of stubbornly seeking for a solution until the problem is solved. This is the eventuality we feared, and the reality we now face. The Terrans are on the verge of breaking out of their system despite Scythian efforts to prevent this possibility. Once they are out we have no way of controlling them, unless it is to present a constant front to them. The Galactics must speak as one voice, Nazeera of Chem, for only in that manner may we turn the legions of Alexander into the empty cosmos and away from our homes. Do you then still wish to stand alone? With the Galactics Chem may grow and prosper, as Terumaz the thrice renowned no doubt intended. Without us you stand alone against the legions of Alexander. Which way shall Chem go?"

"You dare to threaten the Chem with your Terran mercenaries! You worms! You have not the courage to openly challenge your betters, but rather use a mythical confederacy to justify your endless greed. That is subterfuge too deep, Scythian, even for your people! I shall not stand by and hear more of it! Prepare yourself, Scythian. If you can truly commune with all of your folk during times of import then do it now! For the next time you see Nazeera of Chem it shall be after she has settled with Alexander once and for all time. Then, my treacherous friend, you shall see me on the smoking husk of your Homeworld, where I shall sentence you to Circus Pantrixnia for your crimes!"

Nazeera promptly left the field of the hologram. She-Rok turned the image of the lone Scythian off and said, "Dear me, that did not go well at all!"

CHAPTER 5:
TURNING LIES INTO TRUTH

The group of five Scythians gathered around the low metal table was misleading. Though only a limited number of Scythians were present in the Spartan council chamber the entire cognitive consciousness of the race was present. There was no spoken dialogue, no visual presentation and no animation whatsoever. There were only the silent figures, but they belied the mountainous decision before them. Thoughts flew around the Empire with uncharacteristic speed; unsettling thoughts born of a rising and perilous tide.

"Our Ambassador to Roma delivered the Terran strategy exactly as prescribed by our behavioral calculations. We accounted for every variable; however, there was no way to plan for psychotic emotional reactions. There could have been no way to predict Nazeera of Chem's actions. Still, the information gained from our operatives in the Terran System may well prove valuable, and the directness of our threat may well buy us time.

"We now enter a dangerous and unplanned phase. If the Chem are indeed sincere in their warlike stance, as they seem to be, then they must believe we are just as determined in our defense: i.e. the Terran Stratagem.

"The miscalculation of Chem intentions has placed the Empire in a precarious position, however. By our calculations, the possibility of Chem overreaction to our probing was negligible. Yet Chem attacked nonetheless. In the decurns since the Chem incursion, we have noted no new activity along our frontier, but we cannot be overly comfortable. The Chem gave us no reason to expect their aggression prior to the destruction of our experimentation vessel. We must now decide whether Chem aggression will expand. The Chem are a thalamic race with ancient codes of emotional restrictions governing their behavior. These emotional codes limit rationale and logic in Chem actions, making them very difficult to predict. After our initial failure in estimating Chem reaction we must now come to a conclusion based on limited data. The central question to our dilemma is this: will the Chem escalate from murder to genocide?"

There was a long pause in the train of thought.

"Is it necessary to discard the socio-economic model all together? Admittedly the database for the Chem is as limited as is our historic contact with them, but it is hardly non-existent. We have free access to Chem ethernet broadcasts, and thus an accumulation of their socio-economic communication information over the last twenty millennia. Why would the model be so unreliable? There is no obvious reason for such an error. Can we conjecture, perhaps, that the failure of the model may be due to an individual's interference as opposed to the calculated reaction of a culture at large? It is well understood that the socio-economic mathematical models are very accurate in estimating probable cultural actions, but virtually worthless in estimating individual actions. It could be proposed that Nazeera of Chem, with whom the final negotiations were brokered, has manipulated Chem policy by her own opinion and not through cultural evolution. In that case we must assume that we face an individual of great power and ruthless character who acts on personal opinion and not for the good of the whole."

The original thought replied after a short pause.

"That line of reasoning is well worth noting. We note as well, however, the discrepancy of time in Chem actions. Certainly even the socio-economic model for the Chem showed an increased level of risk after the Terran strategy was introduced, but our experimentation ship was boarded, its crew murdered, and the Terran subject kidnapped immediately after Nazeera of Chem refused our overture. It takes at least seven decurns to travel from the Chem frontier to the region of Terra, and even then it would take a Chem scout ship some time to ascertain the correct coordinates. Terra's position is not known without our empire inside one thousand cubic light years. Therefore, if Nazeera of Chem gave the order to send a scout ship into Scythian space then that order occurred in the midst of our negotiations. It is a small point, but it paints her as an individual capable of pro-active decisions as opposed to reaction. We must take this into account."

"Point taken, but considering this individual's characteristics is it your conclusion that Nazeera of Chem has formulated a complete plan of action consistent with her threats and that this plan has already been implemented?"

"That is our estimation. There is no data to support it, however. Our profiles are built upon the Chem culture and not individuals. The Chem are the most historically violent race in the known galaxy outside of Terra, and extraordinarily jealous of their ways. They are not above mimicry, however. The Chem are perhaps more fascinated with Terra than any of the other civilizations. Recall the Chem re-creation of Roma Terra's gladiatorial games. The Chem have cultivated this bastardization of Terra's Circus Maximus on their prison planet of Pantrixnia. The Chem revere Terrans, to a certain extent, as brother warriors, but it is also apparent that they fear them. Even the Chem would not breach intergalactic law so blatantly without some real concern."

"That is, then, to our advantage, and it is our tasking now to increase that concern. Inaction is no longer an option."

"It is then your opinion that Chem will pursue their threats?"

"They must, as the threats were issued in a public forum and are now common knowledge. Even considering the past failure of our model there is no rationale that results in the Chem reversing their position. We reiterate; they rule themselves with the irrational emotions of honor and pride. Nazeera of Chem and her people cannot now retract their threat. We face certain cultural genocide with inaction."

"There remains only one option then. We must awaken the people of Alexander and unleash their legions on the foes of Scythia."

There was a long silence.

"Is it within our capacity to control these beings?"

"Ours is the superior intellect."

"Agreed, but the question remains."

Another silence.

"At the moment we have no choice."

CHAPTER 6:
THE TRIAL FOR TERRA

A blur of gray light signaled Alexander's return to consciousness. The flash of cold metal on his flesh snapped him awake. Instinctively, he recoiled at the memory of the cold operating table, but upon opening his eyes he realized he was somewhere else. The dim light was barely sufficient to reveal a cylindrical dull metal room. Seamless metal plates clad the walls, distinguishable from each other only by grain and shade. There was an alien texture to the metal. There was a different feeling in the air; it was a feeling he couldn't explain but it was obvious in the smell, the weight of the air, and the temperature. This was a different ship, and considering his past experiences that was all to the good.

Beyond this simple observation, however, there was nothing to enlighten him. An injury shortened five year career as a defensive tackle, a nine year stint in the Air Force, and four years in the airlines didn't prepare him very well for this predicament. All he could trust were his instincts, but all they told him was that he was far, far away from home.

Alexander sat up and shivered. He was naked and cold—so cold the chill settled in the marrow of his bones and radiated outward into his flesh. The chill was worst in his metal knee, and it made the fused attachment points in his femur and tibia ache. It was a familiar sensation, though—he went through it every winter—and strangely enough that sense of familiarity made him more at ease. Other than the cold, his only discomfort was being hungry, and a slight pain behind his left ear.

Alexander reached behind his ear and found a minuscule lump. Beneath his skin there was a small hard substance; it felt like a granular sliver—irregular like shrapnel. He shook his head, unable to explain what was going on. He struggled for a moment, a profusion of thoughts and memories sporadically bombarded him. Making sense out of the deluge was impossible. Was this one of those dreams within dreams; where nothing made sense and every event twisted in its own strangely irrelevant direction, or was this reality? The former struck him as somehow disappointing, while the latter caused a buzz of trepidation in his stomach.

He stood up stiffly, grunting at the ache in his knee. Laboriously, he moved around the room; he desperately needed an activity, a goal or at least a purpose. It was not through any training that he accomplished this leap from languid apathy; rather it was the instinctual response of his nature to do something, anything constructive.

His movements, albeit slow and careful, were nonetheless painful. He stopped, and slowly methodically stretched the muscles in his great frame. Every muscle in his body was excruciatingly stiff; it was evidence of a long confinement. There was otherwise no sense of time for his captivity, but for the first time he had conscious memories of his internment. As he haltingly paced about the room examining the walls he felt his memory returning with more order. The strangeness of the memories attacked him, and everything he'd learned from institutional Earth told him to reject them out of hand. But Alexander trusted himself more than his teachers. In doing so a paradigm shift took place. As Alexander accepted his memories for what they were, he expanded his universe exponentially.

The shock of his ordeal with the aliens struck him with horrible clarity. Each capture, imprisonment, experiment and return was indelibly branded into in his mind. In fact, he had a clear memory of the Scythian Council's message, his subsequent escape and the boarding by the Chem. That he could remember anything of these strange encounters was surprising. Certainly he'd remembered nothing of his previous abductions when he lived on Earth. The Scythians habitually repressed his memory before returning him to Earth, but they obviously had neither the opportunity nor the inclination to do so after being boarded.

The Chem killed the Scythians, but he knew nothing of what happened after they shot him on the bridge. He must therefore be under the Chem's control. The slight deductive victory made him feel better, but beyond that, his reason failed. He still had no clear answers as to the basic questions of who, what, where, and why.

Those answers, he felt, would come eventually whether he wanted them to or not. The very memory of his previous abductions helped to steel him against the unwelcome sense of panic that now festered in the pit of his stomach. He at least understood the nature of his predicament. Events still controlled him, but he had his wits about him. He was still a prisoner, but he was conscious and unrestrained. In general his circumstances had improved considerably.

Alexander walked around the room a while longer—the strength returned to his body. He felt better. Now he had to think, to concentrate. He sat down in the center of the room, assuming the closest approximation of the lotus position he could manage. He needed calm.

With a determination to prepare for the future, Alexander recalled every memory of his abductions from the first occurrence over ten years ago to his present situation. Reviewing them in minute detail, he became convinced that this situation was markedly different from the previous abductions in more ways than its interruption. He was cognizant of something unique about himself that troubled or excited the aliens considerably.

He took some comfort in the change of events, for two reasons. First, he was conscious, and that alone meant he'd have at least some control over things. Second, it was apparent that he had some value if, as it seemed, this other group of aliens had gone to the trouble of capturing him. Before, he was simply an object of study, now whoever had him would not so easily discard him, or so he hoped.

Suddenly he found himself laughing out loud. The action caught him off guard, but it was healthy. He attempted to remain calm and in control, but deep inside he was still deathly afraid. His instincts told him he was in deadly danger and completely out of his experience. No rationalization could make his circumstances better. He was afraid, and he'd every right to be. In admitting that fear he prevented it from controlling him. He couldn't remove his fears, but he didn't have to give in to them either. He laughed again, and this time he found comfort in his own voice.

"Well, Alexander you always wanted to get into space, but you weren't prepared to make the political sacrifices to get there by a more traditional route. That would have meant selling your soul. You've been frustrated time and time again by a tedious existence where you didn't make a difference. I don't know what it is that drives you to the expectation of something more than the ordinary lot in life, but here it is. You've gotten what you wanted: something more exciting than the rat race everyone else has to deal with. Make the best of it! Fretting over it certainly won't help."

He'd always envisioned his life with a greater purpose than the institutions of Humanity could somehow provide. Now his mind cleared and a thrill of anticipation coursed through his sinews. His instincts told him this was what he'd been waiting for all these years. All remaining stiffness and discomfort faded, and his muscles filled with warm blood, swollen, tensed and ready for anything.

A voice filled the room. Initially it was absolutely unintelligible, but in a few seconds words formed in his head, even though his ears made no sense of them. "Terran, can you understand me? Terran, can you understand me?"

A look of consternation crowded his face, as the conflict between what his brain heard and what his ears heard caused a wave of nausea to wash over him. The speaker continued and he grew accustomed to the sensation. His ears and brain reached some form of agreement.

"Yes, I understand you," he answered eventually, standing up and waiting for a door to open.

No door opened. Instead, the floor trembled, and then slowly rose. Looking up he watched the ceiling open. The floor rose through the hole, and a bank of lights flashed on, bathing him from above. The glare blinded him, and the old urge to panic returned, knotting itself in his throat. His mind raced to prevent his newfound courage from disappearing. He shut his eyes tightly and saw himself as his captors must: a naked blind Human, completely at their mercy, at the point of cowering in fear of his life.

Revulsion and anger rose in response, and the momentary fear left him. He told himself, "If these are your last moments Alexander don't spend them as a quivering lump of flesh! You've lived proud and well, if to no purpose. You can die just the same!"

Alexander drew himself up, once again strong and resolute. Crossing his arms defiantly over his chest he flexed every muscle in his frame. He almost laughed at the attempt to look intimidating, thinking, "If Hollywood is right, then every other alien, excepting the ones who captured me, are bigger stronger, faster and smarter than me!"

The thought put a scowl of disdain on his face. His eyes smoldered under knit brows daring anything and anyone to challenge him. The harsh lights finished his transformation, cutting deep shadows into his body, amplifying the athletic build into the graven image of a gladiator. The lift stopped, and after a long silence a resonant voice came out of the glare.

"Terran, as Warlord of Terra you stand accused of acts of aggression towards the Galactic peoples! What say you?"

Alexander stared in the direction of the voice, astounded. The indictment was curt, damning and incomprehensible. Warlord? Terran? What was all this? They thought he, Alexander, was the Warlord of Terra? Terra? Earth! Warlord of Earth? Earth didn't have a warlord, and never had, unless one went all the way back to Alexander the Great.

How could an advanced civilization ever come to that conclusion? He hated to admit it, but Alexander was as anonymous a Human Being as could be found. As for planet-bound Earthling's threatening a space faring empire, well that was so farfetched it didn't even register.

There was no way of answering the questioner, but he accepted the statement as their opinion—what else could he do? He didn't trust his diplomatic skills so he made a demand instead. Drawing himself to full height Alexander lowered his voice to a forceful growl.

"I do not answer to thieves in the dark, nor do I answer to derogatory labels. I am Alexander Thorsson. If you wish to parley with me then let me see my accuser. Then I shall respond!"

"You are in no position to issue ultimatums, Terran!" the voice told him. "You will answer, and then you and your race will face punishment!"

The last statement held no room for argument, but it also held out little hope for reason. Alexander, by his own hastily formed opinion had nothing to lose, so he chose to retain the aggressive tact to the end. Pleading with unreasonable people never worked on Earth, so he had no expectation of success here.

He recalled the final moments on the previous ship. These were presumably the Chem, his new captors. They appeared strong and warlike, while the Scythians were anything but that. He played on the contrast, using his seeming ignorance as a dagger.

Shaking his head and putting contempt into his statement, he replied, "Enough of your games! Do not try to intimidate me! You Scythians, or whatever you call yourselves, have had your way with me in your experiments. That's the only way you can face Terrans: in the dark with your technology as your shield. Well I grant your science gives you an advantage. You're right to use it. With your puny bodies and technocratic ways I don't expect you to have the courage to face me!"

There was a wrathful roar all around him. It was deafening. Then two sharp concussions, metal on metal, turned the cacophony into an uneasy silence.

The voice said, "You dare to mistake the glorious Chem for the worms of Scythia? With that you forfeit your life Terran, and the existence of your race!"

Alexander jumped upon the Chem's response, trying to restrain the concern in his voice, but his words quavered just the same. He spread his arms wide and addressed the darkness behind the lights, his strength undiminished but rationality became the dominant tenor of his voice.

"You say to me I'm now in the hands of another captor? How should I know that? Moreover, you ask me to see a difference, how so? I am a captive, blinded, immobilized and subject to the basest treatment imaginable for an intelligent being: a subject for experimentation! Now another race has me, and rather than dissecting me with your machines you put me on trial. You bring me naked and blind to judgment for myself and my race? I ask you, as a civilized being, if you were in my position what difference would you see in your captors?"

The Chem met his answer with silence. The lights dimmed and the Chem revealed themselves to Alexander. They stood above and around him on the raised steps of a semi-circular chamber. Their blue eyes glowed from long angular faces. The Chem were a lean race, bipedal and in all obvious respects humanoid. They were almost as tall as Alexander, but not nearly as heavy in build. Ropy muscles cut through varying shades of tawny flesh, and their clothing accented their somewhat wild and warlike nature. The Chem wore metallic cloth of dull amber, red or purple beneath ceremonial armor. Alexander saw both male and female representatives in the audience. The dress of the two sexes was similar, though it differed in very Earth-like qualities. The male dress accented the arms and shoulders, while the female's accented the breasts and hips. The commonalty between their worlds almost amused Alexander, but the expressions from the assembly, though alien, were obviously hostile.

"I am held captive by a race of warriors, as unlike to the worms of Scythia as a dead planet to the glory of a star," he said quickly, and then he let his voice rise and become more demanding again. "But why then, people of Chem, do you treat me thus? If you have complaint with me or my race why did you not face us openly with your questions? Why this covert kidnapping, for it seems to me to be beneath you?"

"A fair question in appearance," answered a smooth voice, and Alexander's eyes darted to a female in the foremost ranks. The new speaker was exotic in her alien beauty; she was lithely built, with long blue-black hair sweeping back from her dark crested forehead. The vibrant blue eyes, strange in their absence of pupil or iris, but intent on him nonetheless, glowed under finely chiseled brows. Nobility marked her sharply cut cheeks and her aquiline nose. Her chin, providing a narrow base for such a proud visage, was almost delicate. A fantastic array of crimson-purple armor and clothing did nothing to conceal her strong but graceful form; rather, it accentuated her in a wild unrelenting air. With her arms clasped before her she lost none of the power or strength of her male counterparts, but she added a perilous feline ferocity to her presence. She continued her question in a dangerously venomous tone.

"Why should the Chem stoop to such tricks? Come now, Terran, we are not children. Is it any wonder you, of all beings, should demand stealth? Who else but Alexander himself should we expect to find communing with the Scythians? Who else would be so bold as to usurp the appellation of the legendary conqueror, and the privilege of the son of your God of War?"

She stepped down from the stands and walked around Alexander in a wide circle. "Look at you! Victories lay upon your breast, battle-scars upon your body, and blood upon your hands. There is dread upon you and within you; so much so that you enticed the intervention of the Galactic worms, and fell into our fortunate hands. It is now our part to play the inquisitor, Alexander of Terra, retrograde though that may be to your life experience." She stopped in front of him and planted her hands on her hips. "This should prove an interesting test of adaptability, for what manner of being is Alexander, but one accustomed to command, or demand? Still, you are right to demand such an accounting from us, aren't you?"

"Am I?" he asked, feeling that she expected a brutish answer from a brutish race—beneath their contempt. Alexander had no idea why they considered him a warlord of Earth, or what their beef was with his planet, but they thought so, and he didn't get the impression that arguing the point with this woman would get him anywhere. He accepted the fact, and his responsibility—and it was surprisingly easy for him to do so. He didn't have the time to hone his crude words into eloquence, but he sensed that at all costs he had to make her understand that he, and Humanity, was worth consideration and respect.

"Am I right to demand a reason for my kidnapping, and for these charges levied against my race and myself? Why should I wish to know the reason I'm suddenly plucked from my home and put on trial? Is it any wonder why I ask such questions or make such demands? If the Scythians did the initial theft and you, the Chem, merely took me from their laboratory then I may have some cause to thank you. I find that difficult to do under the circumstances. I find it doubly difficult to believe that you should rescue me from the Scythians and then put me on trial for such capital charges."

He looked around at the tiers of Chem, and spread his arms wide. "You tell me that I stand accused of complicity against your empire, but that is a broad statement, my dear Chem. I find it a difficult concept to imagine considering our ignorance of you, and the superiority of your technology. What manner of threat can Humanity be to the Chem? The idea is fantastic but impossible!" He looked back at the woman, and said tersely, "We know nothing of you; you are not being reasonable. Can you explain any of this?"

The woman turned to her people and raised her arms, and Alexander had the unsettling feeling that she was telling them, "You see, just as I expected!"

She turned around and approached Alexander. She moved like a cat, with a silky deadly grace. She glared directly into his eyes. He returned her stare with conviction, but could not read her intent. The blue orbs of the Chem woman were almond in shape, but there was nothing that told Alexander she focused on him, unless it was the almost imperceptible and universal power of the stare. The eyes presented no clue as to her mood, or her soul, and that alone made him stridently uncomfortable.

She passed close by his shoulder, went behind him and came back around, as if stalking him. Alexander stood still, though he followed her with his eyes. Finally, she halted by his side and smiled. The effect of her sharp canines resting on her full lips increased his agitation, and his fascination, but he merely narrowed his eyes to grim slits.

"You are a wily one, Terran," she told him, laying a sharp nailed hand on his shoulder. She smiled broadly now and looked about to her peers, saying, "Behold the innocent Terran, stolen with nefarious purpose from his Homeworld and charged with heinous crimes! Oh, ignorant Alexander of Terra, whom we plucked like a flower from his scholarly studies of wit and altruism!" She smiled again, and sauntered to stand directly before him. Brazenly she looked him up and down, and then she reached up and grasped his shoulders. She tried to shake him, but though Alexander endured her gaze and her advances, he barely shuddered as she tried to move him.

She nodded, stepping away with her arms spread wide, and announcing, "Behold the body of a scholar! Have we not seen, oh members of the Assemblage, the scholarly activities of Terrans through the millennia? Their many clever wars based upon reason and carried out through debate, where the victor beat the opponent in a battle of wits and words? By this Terran's reasoning his mentor, the inestimable Alexander the Great, conquered Terra with his potent parables of philosophy! Look at this Terran and note the proportions of a thinker! Of what use are those shoulders and arms Terran? Are you brawny from lifting books? Where does your chest spring from, the tilling of flowers? Why are your legs so knotted and bulky? Is it from the chasing of women? By the looks of you they may need the chasing; I'll warrant they'll not come to you willingly!"

The assembled Chem laughed, and the Chem woman finally turned back to him. "Really, Terran, what would you have us believe? You are no scholar! If this is not the body of a warrior then what are you? I ask you, Terran, what are you?"

Alexander withstood her chiding, and her anger, stoically. It would do no good to rant or argue; he'd not win that battle. He was no orator, he was not gifted in debate but he thought he understood something of the woman before him; people, it seemed, were people after all—no matter where they might come from. He played on that. With no anger in his voice, and just a touch of sadness, as a teacher would a pupil who still didn't understand, he asked simply, "What's your name?"

The immediately identifiable question shifted the woman's thought, for it was as if he heard nothing of what she just said. In seeming frustration she threw up her arms and stated, "There is no profit in this! Either the Terran has no understanding of his position at this moment, or he's mad. I see no use in continuing this interrogation."

She began to stalk off, but Alexander stopped her by saying, "I might very well be both you know."

She turned around and stared at him.

He allowed a silence to develop and then he slowly began to make a circuit of the pit, as if lecturing a new assembly of college students. "Has it ever occurred to you and your fellow Chem that I might very well be wondering exactly the same things? What is it you really want of me, you Chem? You make sport of me, and bait me, but you don't ask reasonable questions. I might eventually take such actions as a purposeful attack on my honor, but I don't know you. So, for the moment, before I give in to any irreconcilable and unfortunate opinions, I shall give you Chem the benefit of the doubt." He let his gaze sweep over every member of the audience before letting it rest with finality on the woman. "I assume you tempt me through your own ignorance and trepidation, but I warn you my patience has its limits."

"Does it?" the woman smiled, approaching him again. "What would those limits be, I wonder?"

Alexander crossed his arms over his breast. "You have been walking upon their borders for quite some time now."

"What happens if I cross that border, Terran?" The Chem prodded him.

Alexander's brows furrowed, and his sigh of frustration rumbled from his chest like a discordant organ. The Chem woman actually leaned away from him, though she did not step back. Alexander shook his head. "What have I done that you should mock me so? Am I so far beneath you as a being that I should not be worth the slightest amount of your courtesy?"

"What would you have of me then, Terran?" she asked, relenting in her scorn somewhat.

"My name is Alexander," he said forcefully.

"Very well, Alexander of Terra. You've earned that title on Terra—and we the Chem know how laudable that is. I will no longer admonish it, though I condemn you for it."

"May I ask your name?" Alexander requested.

"For what purpose," she asked, her manner at least partially decipherable to him: an irritated but amused puzzlement.

"If you want to start a dialogue then it would help if I knew your name—you, after all, know mine. It's only fair."

"We did not bring you here to begin a dialogue, Alexander of Terra," she told him. "We brought you before the august body of the Chem Assemblage to answer charges."

"Then you are my accuser," Alexander told her. "Among my people it is the right of the accused to know one's accuser. No person of name or rank should be charged by the nameless or the anonymous."

The woman paced in front of him for a moment, cocking her head as if in consideration of his words. At length she turned again to him, and told him, "So it is with us. Very well, I am Nazeera of Chem, of the Triumvirate of Chem. Does that satisfy you, Alexander of Terra?"

"Thank you, Nazeera of Chem. For what crimes do you accuse my people and me?"

"Now you try my patience," Nazeera told him, her eyes growing somewhat brighter.

"We are two new races, completely unfamiliar with each other, Nazeera of Chem," Alexander told her quickly, following directly with a question. "Isn't it reasonable to make things plain, instead of assuming they are understood?"

"Your understanding is of precious little importance to me, Alexander of Terra," Nazeera told him curtly, but she added, in a matter of fact voice. "It is part of the Galactic record that Scythia subtly threatens her neighbors with forceful invasion by Terran legions to gain economical advantage. Terra has been at Scythia's beck and call for over two millennia; that is not a matter for debate. What is a matter for debate is the particular threat Terrans pose to Chem. That is why you are here. You are here, Alexander of Terra, so that we may learn all that we can of you. Then we shall end your threat to ourselves and the galaxy."

"This is a matter between Scythia and Chem, not Chem and my people," Alexander told her.

"You are Scythia's might, and so you are Scythia, Alexander of Terra," Nazeera told him harshly, adding, "It is beneath your warrior's nature to plead a separate innocence from your masters!"

"We recognize no masters but ourselves!"

"And you are justifiably damned for it!" Nazeera retorted. "You validate the Galactic legends then, and the Scythians' threats! Terra has waited all this time to find the means of unleashing her power on the galaxy and continuing her conquests! Terra is the aggressor, and Scythia holds the key to her cage. You dare not cross your words now, Alexander of Terra. You've caught yourself in your own web!"

Alexander realized the utter futility of pursuing that tact further, and he felt he'd lost a valuable opportunity to his temper. He'd let a chance for reason, slight though it may have been, disappear for the moment at least. Still, he'd learned something: the Chem and the Galactics feared Earth, or to be more accurate, Terra. He had no idea why, but the name of Alexander the Great and the fear of Terran legions ready to advance upon the galaxy weren't lost on him. The Scythians, his original captors, were involved in some way, but he had no time to figure out how.

The reality of the Chem conviction remained, however, and it was a more powerful tool than he could have hoped for. Returning to his former tactic, he told her grimly, "I can see your mind is set, and that no amount of truth or reason will sway it. Very well, think what you will, Nazeera of Chem, as your prejudice will prevent you from believing anything but what you wish to hear. Mark this, however, and mark it well! Terrans are a breed best left to themselves! Leave us alone and we will respect you in kind. Threaten us and we will respond in kind! Mark me, it is better to have Terrans as a possible threat on an isolated planet, than Terrans set in a desperate war against you. Do not make that mistake! The Chem are an honorable and admirable people, but take care. To declare us a renegade race is an offense of the first order. Measure your actions accordingly. We do not easily forgive treachery!"

"You speak proudly, Alexander of Terra, as one would expect from the mercenaries of Terran legend. Look, Chem warriors, how cunning the Terran is to demand answers from us, appeal to our justice and reason and then threaten us with defiance! I see through you Terran, as we all should. I will waste no more time bandying words with you. You are a common mercenary guilty of plotting with the Scythians. We shall treat you as such. You deserve no better."

"Do you therefore favor execution Nazeera?" a heavy, white bearded Chem asked.

Nazeera bowed to him, saying, "Such a question, noble Elder of Chem, may perhaps be best directed to our prisoner." A dangerous smile curled on the face of Nazeera, a face that Alexander, under other circumstances, would have called beautiful. There was a lilt in her raspy voice which translated across any distance, and she turned to the Terran and caressed his cheek with one razor sharp nail. Blood sprang from beneath the edge, but Alexander did not move.

"Well, Alexander of Terra," she purred, "what would you have us do with you? Would you desire a death swift and painless? We can be merciful in that way. You will simply slide into a deep sleep with no pain, no discomfort. Or perhaps you would wish imprisonment instead. You could live out your days, alone, confined, but alive and comfortable. What do you say to that, Alexander?"

CHAPTER 7:
THE BIRTH OF ALEXANDER

In that moment Alexander knew who he must be. The Chem saw him as a warrior of a warrior race. They would never believe otherwise. Therefore, that was what he must be with every fiber of his being. He must present Terrans as a race too formidable and dangerous to be meddled with. He couldn't afford reality. He couldn't afford feelings. He had to focus on the perceptions of his audience—the Chem. That's all that mattered.

Alexander didn't have the luxury of lengthy reflection or even reality. He drew upon himself, his past, his beliefs and those of his ancestors to flesh out his new persona.

The need of the moment balanced on the point of a knife, and he realized the dangers of a false step. He was a single Terran out of almost five billion beings, but before the warriors of Chem he spoke for all, and this guided his words. Fortunately, the Chem game was transparent. These beings detested weakness, as was obvious in their view of the Scythians. They were contemplating conflict with Terra, and he was here to confirm their suspicions of a warrior race too brutish to be given respect or consideration. He must change that view.

The Chem must think that conflict with Terra would come at too high a cost. There could be no weakness in his demeanor. He would have to dredge up every bit of the ruthless cunning that enabled Terrans to ascend from woefully armed gatherers to the masters of one of the most fantastic planets in the galaxy. The failure of his performance could spell the doom of the Terran race or at best a horrible thralldom under unyielding masters.

Finally, certain of his situation and his course, Alexander smiled. Slowly he reached up and took Nazeera's hand from his cheek. Her flesh was firm, but with silkiness to it. Her blood was as warm as his, and he felt her thrill at the alien contact. He held her hand for just a moment, firmly but without threat, then he gently kissed it, saying, almost in a whisper, "If this is how you wish things, Nazeera of Chem, then so be it."

Alexander released her hand, addressing her directly, and forcefully. "There is more to your question than words, Nazeera of Chem. You insult me brazenly, for what is imprisonment but a lingering death? What is execution but slaughter fit only for domesticated animals? My ancestors roved the wild seas in search of war and plunder. They feared only to die in their beds of old age without a sword in their hand. How have I wronged you and so warrant such a sentence? My ancestors should laugh me out of Valhalla as a coward!

"You have your opinion of me; words alone will not change it. I hoped for more from advanced beings. Very well then, you shall see that we are not so trite as to beg for our lives, but we shall not give them up willingly." He turned from Nazeera and addressed the entire Assemblage. He raised a threatening finger to all of them. "Do what you will with me, if you can. I defy you to the end. Yet gauge well what you see in me, for it will return to you five billion fold! It will come to you with fire and revenge, as in your unwarranted actions you forfeit the respect and kinship we might have offered you as friends. Think carefully about your next steps concerning us. I am one Terran, and my death may be excused, but you shall rue the day that you threaten all of Terra! Think carefully on it! You do not yet realize your peril!"

The Elder Chem addressed Nazeera, "Alexander of Terra speaks as if he were a warrior of Chem, Nazeera, what do you say now?"

When he turned back to her there was a strange expression on Nazeera's face, and she held the hand Alexander kissed as if bemused by the act. She nodded, as if impressed by Alexander's words, and said, "Let us test the mettle of this incarnation of Alexander, for we all know how well Scythians weave their words. For a mercenary he is eloquent and clever. So much may we expect of a Terran warlord. Yet what lies behind the title? Let deeds be the test of him. Pantrixnia has Terran beasts upon it, so he should not feel so far from his home. Send him to the prison planet!"

There was a roar of approval from the assembled throng, and Nazeera, regaining her full composure, climbed back on the first step, an evil smile lighting her exotic face.

The floor began to descend. Nazeera called to him, "We shall see if you fight as well as you speak, Alexander of Terra. Farewell, and remember that I shall be watching!"

Alexander pointed a threatening finger at Nazeera, saying in a commanding voice, "Mark what I have said concerning Terra! If wronged we will come to you with fire and fury, and shall never stop until the thirst for vengeance is forever sated! Take what you need from me and leave my planet to itself! As for myself, I forgive your trespasses, and bear you no ill will."

Alexander smiled and bowed. "It was an interesting meeting, Nazeera of Chem. If my words had no effect on you then maybe my deeds will bear me out. I shall make every effort not to disappoint you. Farewell, I look forward to our next meeting!"

Darkness enveloped him as the metal ceiling slid closed over his head.

✠   ✠   ✠

Nazeera folded her lithe arms over her bosom and cursed, "Impudent Terran!"

"Have a care beloved sister, I think he likes you," noted a handsome, and large, Chem male next to her. He simply laughed at her responding scowl. Nazeera's husband, a shorter heavier Chem standing behind him found no humor in the remark.

"You speak disgusting thoughts, Nazar," he growled, his light skin blushing. "I do not wish to hear such things spoken before myself, or my wife!"

Nazar grinned, showing all of his brilliant platinum teeth. His elongated canines snapped together as he laughed, "Why I almost think you sound jealous, Bureel! Don't pursue that charade, or make any false claims of affection in front of me. It's no secret that your father arranged this marriage because of my sister's place, and my own, in the Assemblage. My father would never have agreed to such a union if he did not owe his life to yours. That's no debt of mine, however. I tolerate you, no more, and would gladly have traded my seat for my sister's happiness, but such was not our father's final wish."

"Your opinion matters little to me, Nazar," Bureel replied. "I only voice my revulsion to your thoughts, as much as to your opinions."

"Oh, I don't know, he was rather handsome in an alien sort of way," Nazar said. "Leastwise you wouldn't mistake him for a female! He certainly held himself well. Much better than you would have Bureel."

"You dare to insult me!" Bureel started, but Nazeera cut them both off.

"Cease this bickering, both of you!" she ordered. "We're on the brink of war with a race that may very well be our equal and you two are busy chattering nonsense! You will cease and desist at once."

Bureel flared with manufactured anger, saying, "Our equal? Think what you say, my wife! Let me sport with him in mortal combat and we shall quell this fear of Terrans in your heart."

Nazeera instantly confronted him, placing her angrily contorted features inches from those of her husband. Her voice was barely above a whisper, but Bureel backed away. "You will not address me as wife in the Assemblage. I am your senior in this chamber, Bureel. Tread with care. I will not remind you again!"

The male Chem drew back with a snarl, but he said, "I stand corrected, Nazeera, but what of my charge? Bring the Terran and myself together in equal combat, and I will end this discussion here and now! Why do we waste our time with probing and evaluating these Terrans? If this Alexander is any example then the Scythians exaggerated every quality of their persons. He is a lout, without brains enough to bear me service. I daresay he has the courage to match his wits, and faced with a challenge to the death he would crawl upon his belly for mercy!"

"From the looks of his arms, Bureel and those saurian eyes, I would hazard to say that Nazeera would be free to search for a new mate of her own choosing, and not our father's," Nazar told him.

"You dare!"

"Enough! Enough!" Nazeera exclaimed. "I'll hear no more of this discussion. Bureel, I will not sponsor your request, and since you must have one of the three Triumvirates to sponsor a bill from a lower level of the Assemblage-I doubt if either Karel or Puriezia would go against my wishes-your challenge will go unfulfilled. Without my support, I don't think your scheme for glory will come to much. Now, I must attend to the Chamber, where the Elder and the Triumvirate will discuss the particulars of this unpleasant situation in detail. I therefore take my leave of you."

Nazeera turned on her heal, her black tresses whipping behind. The two males bowed as befitting junior members of the Assemblage and left in opposite directions.

Alexander settled himself once again in the gloom of his cell, exhausted. The enormous effort of self control and debate that characterized the most important half hour of his life, and possibly of Terran existence, drained him of all energy. He had no illusions as to the import of his actions, and as ill an ambassador as he thought he was Alexander couldn't afford the luxury of failure. He sat on the metal floor and gathered his thoughts. He won a small victory. The Chem would send him to a prison planet, he couldn't remember the name, and there test his "mettle." The situation was turning out to be logical, if not desirous. The Chem wanted to know what they were up against.

His task now, his only task, was to put forward such a powerful image of Humankind that the Chem would have second thoughts on attacking Earth. His personal survival and safety were secondary now. He was an actor assigned to play the role of a Human as he should be, and not necessarily as he was. His only regret was his condition. At thirty-nine he was past the peak of his physical powers. He'd seen too little of the gym or dojo in the last years, and old injuries made themselves more apparent. Still, he told himself, he wasn't completely without physical ability. At six foot two, two hundred and thirty pounds he was somewhat pared down from his playing days in Minnesota. A black belt in the martial arts could be thanked for his not "ballooning" in weight when injuries forced his premature retirement from football. His short career in the trenches of the NFL, although saddling him with an artificial knee and a suspect back, still endowed him with a commanding physique and a sense of fearlessness in personal combat. In the military he became an expert marksman, and had the benefit of annual survival training.

With his experience and remaining physical powers he'd no doubt he could live off the land of this prison planet. He could handle himself, unless it came down to a test of tooth and claw. In that arena genetics hobbled him, and so it did not warrant his concern.

As he pondered his position Alexander was unaware of the changes that came over him. His entire being centered on his task. The cold of the floor disappeared because it was unimportant. The discomfort of his physical position didn't reach his brain because it was trivial. Imperceptibly, all that was dominant for survival asserted itself. The brutal endurance and cunning of the primitive Homo sapiens combined with the skill and intelligence of modern man. Without his knowledge, he advanced as a being, even as parts of him regressed to their most primitive. It was the secret to survival for the Human race throughout the millennia, to somehow reach their full potential when nature demanded it. He sat and he thought, waiting with the stamina of newfound patience.

He drifted off to sleep. How much time passed he couldn't say, but his mind was busy with a swirling avalanche of dreams and thoughts. Finally, he awakened. He was sitting on the edge of a bed—his bed. He felt groggy and disoriented. What was that dream he had? It was like a book. Muttering to himself he got up and went into the bathroom. He relieved himself, brushed his teeth, lathered his face and began to shave. It was then, as he looked at the bathroom in the mirror, that he realized this was his apartment in his Air Force days.

The thought struck him, "I'm not in the Air Force anymore—this must be a dream."

The bathroom disappeared, and his eyes snapped open. He was still in his cylindrical metal cell, but a panel was open revealing a lighted corridor.

CHAPTER 8:
LITTLE GREEN MEN

"Bloody hell, what the devil does this mean?" growled Admiral Sten Augesburcke. He stared incredulously at the message Captain Buckminster gave him. The Captain ordered flank speed, and the acceleration of the "Starship Enterprise" through the Atlantic swells forced the Admiral to steady himself against the rail.

Augesburcke read the message twice, again breaking into swearing heavily laced with his Australian accent, belaying both his temper and his background. Augesburcke was an Australian exchange officer now in his second tour of service with the U.S. Navy. He was so well thought of that the Navy enticed him with the opportunity of a lifetime: the "Enterprise" battle group.

They were steaming back to Norfolk for a well deserved rest when a classified message from the Pentagon interrupted the ship's routine. The flush of Augesburcke's temper reddened the already swarthy features. He ran his hands through his short cropped silver-white hair and pulled at his mustache. None of his aboriginal ancestor's patience, however, seemed to touch the Admiral at moments of ill or, as in this case, mysterious news. After a third perusal of the message the Admiral demanded, "This was it? They sent nothing else? What kind of order is this?"

"I have no idea, sir," the Captain reported, adding, "But the orders are quite specific. There's not much room left for interpretation."

"None, I would say!" Augesburcke agreed, reading the message aloud as if to assert to himself it was true. "To all USN vessels—proceed at flank to nearest friendly port. Break formation. Readiness status *Alpha*. Await further instructions. To Enterprise: B41 will transfer Adm A to new post as CINCCODOTS. Congrats. Urgent, no delay."

Augesburcke glared at the paper, ignoring the broad context of the message for the moment. "CODOTS, what the blazes is that supposed to mean? I would have sworn we thought up every possible nonsensical abbreviation possible, but this is a new one. And what's a B41? Is that a ship or a plane?"

"Neither of those designations is in the book, Admiral, and they're not codes that I know of. We received an alphanumeric code immediately after the clear text confirming the validity of the message. I've already ordered all ships to *Alpha*. All decks are sealed, and we are in the process of moving ammunition from the magazines. Our aircraft will all be loaded and ready to go within the hour. The first fully armed patrol has already been launched. Each ship in the battle group has its orders."

Augesburcke crossed the bridge and glared down at the deck. The "Enterprise" anti-submarine helicopters were in the process of launching, and fully armed fighters and bombers were taking their place on the vast armored deck. The "Hornets" rose from the bowels of the ship bristling with needle-like air-to-air missiles, but on some of the aircraft the weapons were fatter, longer, and with larger fins. The latter weapons were not the conventional olive in color, but a dangerous shining white. Augesburcke stared in disbelief.

"My God has it come to this? Why no warning? Is it terrorists or the Russians gone mad? I can't think of anything but that the balloon's gone up, John, can you? Why else would we be loading nukes? But this is damn strange. We're heading to port and not to open sea; we're splitting up the battle group and ignoring standard submarine defense; we've got nukes on our jets and there's no mention of who or what we're aiming these things at. Is this for real? Let me see that code!"

The Captain showed him the alpha-numeric message which followed the clear text message already read by the Admiral. Returning to the bridge the two officers decoded it, although it had already been through numerous iterations by the Captain and the bridge officers.

In the end Augesburcke simply swore, "Goddamn it, that's a fine how do you do! Clearance to unlock, arm, and launch, but at who, they haven't given us any damn targets?"

Augesburcke took out his pipe, lit it and puffed savagely away. After a moment of reflection he left the bridge, Captain in tow, steaming like a freight train. Once outside he leaned over the rail, the wind whipped by at over seventy miles an hour with the "Starship Enterprise's" speed. A froth of white foam boiled from the "Enterprise," and her escorts were fading fast towards the horizon.

"Damn strange!"

He puffed savagely at his pipe. The wind tore at the smoke, sending it off over his shoulder and out to sea. The thrill of the big ship's speed broke the Admiral's temper, and he suddenly grinned, shouting over the wind, "Look at that, John! She's still the fastest ship afloat; even the new "Aegis" ships can't keep up with her when she's got her steam up! Damn, but it's good to have this feeling again! John, I don't know what's going on, but it's hot! This is no bluff and bluster. My dad used to say he'd get a bellyful of shrapnel before engagements. I've missed my wars, except for chasing these damned 7th century zealots around. Not anymore. This is big; I can feel it."

"I hope you're wrong, Sten, but here's my problem: when I got the initial message I asked our communications people what they'd been listening to. I mean, there's got to be something going on. They've got nothing, absolutely nothing. It's as if the world communications nets had all gone off the air."

"How did we get our message then?"

"There was a window of one minute where all of a sudden every military channel worldwide came alive. We called our people, the Russians called theirs, the Brits, etc. Then everything went dead again. Even the French shut up. If it's radio silence then everyone's in on it."

"Well it won't do any good to worry about what we can't control; we'll just have to wait. Maybe this B41 that's coming to get me will have some answers."

An hour later, still two thousand miles off the coast of Virginia, a solitary aircraft announced itself on radar. Captain Buckminster informed the Admiral, "It's your bird, sir and he's coming in hot. We clocked him at mach three-seven."

"Hell, I didn't know we had any carrier plane that went that fast!"

"We don't, at least as far as I know. The "Hornets" will join up on him as soon as he slows. We're turning into the wind. I gave orders for the deck officer to bring the pilot to the bridge as soon as he's aboard."

"How long will that be?"

"About five minutes," the Captain said. The two men waited outside, and in a few moments they spied the sleek shapes of the fighters escorting a long angular aircraft half again their size. As the aircraft entered downwind Buckminster called it out, "I'll be damned, it's a "Vigilante" with a NASA/DARPA tail flash. I didn't know there was any still flying."

"Someone's in a hurry," Augesburcke nodded. "Make ready to fuel him as soon as he shuts down. The big guns don't let their toys out in public without good reason. You may not know it, John, but NASA and DARPA don't put their flashes on the same bird unless it's a *Dreamland* airplane. Area 51 and all that super secret squirrel stuff. Don't bother getting the pilot out, like as not he's under orders not to leave the cockpit. Just get me suited up."

Buckminster did as the Admiral asked, and as the "Vigilante" touched down they came out on the deck to meet it. The flight deck crew expertly released the cable and guided the pilot directly to the port catapult where a fuel line waited for it. The pilot shut down, but only the aft canopy of the aircraft rose. Without hesitation Augesburcke scrambled up the ladder and squeezed into the aft cockpit. The Admiral plugged his communications cord in immediately, asking, "What's this all about?"

"Just strap in, Admiral, I'll explain on the way," a female voice answered.

"We're just sitting here, and it will take at least a few minutes to get gas. Can't you give me anything?"

"Admiral, I don't know the full picture," the pilot informed him. "There is a briefing file in the back there that you are not to open until we are airborne. I'm afraid that's all I know. I just drive these things. Now sit tight, whatever's not in your file will have to wait until we get to New York."

"New York, why the hell aren't we going to D.C.? Strike that, you wouldn't know would you? Well, when will we get there?"

"Less than an hour, sir," the pilot told him. "You better strap in, Admiral, we've got our gas, so we're out of here!"

"Roger," Augesburcke answered, motioning to Buckminster, who was on the ladder strapping him in. The Captain raised an ear of his headset and leaned into the cockpit to listen.

"I don't know what the hell is going on John! They're bugging me out to New York-who knows why-little green men from Mars are probably trying to take over Wall Street and they need an Aussie who can drink them into negotiating!"

"Drink a few for me then, Sten! I don't want to hear that some half-pint put you under the table! Good luck!" Buckminster laughed, shaking the Admiral's hand. He hopped down the ladder to the steel deck, and gave a final wave.

Augesburcke strapped on his Oxygen mask and felt the cool flow of air. His canopy came down, and now he was trapped in the aircraft, like a sausage in a can that was slightly too tight. He fought the feeling of claustrophobia that tightened his gut and made the sweat pop out on his forehead. The "Vigilante" shuddered as the engines started, and the sickly sweet odor of exhaust and jet fuel permeated the cockpit. He switched his mask to "100%" Oxygen, and the all he could smell was rubber and plastic—it was an improvement.

A roaring grew in his ears. The jet rocked violently.

Almost too late he saw the deck officer give the go signal. Augesburcke planted his head against the seat just as the catapult fired. Despite his readiness the acceleration threw him back into the seat. The deck of the ship disappeared and all Augesburcke saw was the bottle green windswept Atlantic. It looked dangerously close, so close the streamers of spray whipped up to grab him. Involuntarily Augesburcke lifted himself in his seat—away from the water. It was a mistake.

The pilot pulled back on the stick. The g-force plastered Augesburcke back into the steel seat. In his dimming vision all the Admiral could see were the thick Atlantic clouds.

The mystery of the file was forgotten. All Augesburcke wanted to do for the next few minutes was to keep his lunch where it belonged. He'd never particularly liked flying, and though he'd logged more "cats" and "traps" than he cared to remember this flight was particularly nasty. The "Vigilante" punched its way through layer after layer of cumulus clouds, bucking the Admiral like he was a doll. The ascent lasted ten interminable minutes. When they finally found smooth air above the clouds, and Augesburcke was about to breathe a sigh of relief, the pilot pushed the nose over. The maneuver allowed the aircraft to accelerate more rapidly, but it sent the Admiral flying against his straps, his stomach rising with him. In a desperate bid to retain his dignity Augesburcke threw the oxygen switch to "Emergency." Immediately a welcome stream of cold Oxygen splashed his face, and in a few moments he could concentrate on something besides trying not to heave.

With a momentary respite from the nausea Augesburcke tore open the envelope. In the space of a moment every symptom of airsickness was completely gone.

"Mother of God," he whispered. The document at the top of the stack was the most incredible piece of paper he'd ever seen. The letterhead was from the United Nations Security Council. That was not so unusual; Augesburcke received taskings and status reports from the council before. It was the first line of the communiqué that drew his attention.

"On January 2, two days ago, official contact was made with representatives of the extra-terrestrial Scythian Empire. Contact was initiated by the Scythians after their representatives landed on the front lawn of the United Nations. A Scythian delegation has been in constant dialogue since first contact with representatives from the Security Council. The purpose for Scythian contact is twofold: a desire to warn the population of Earth (Terra in galactic standard) of possible hostile actions to be taken against our system by another extra-terrestrial empire, the Chem; and the establishment of a mutual defense agreement between our two cultures. Substantial evidence, (contained within this briefing package) exists to substantiate Scythian claims. The United Nations Security Council, working at the behest of the governments of the member nations and in cooperation with civilian and military working groups from member nations, has created the Council of Defense of the Terran System, CODOTS, for implementation of terrestrial policy. This council will be limited in membership to twenty-two representatives of various backgrounds. The membership selected comprises people of civilian, military, political and academic experience from six continents. The CODOTS council is a streamlined working group which shall formulate and implement a plan of action appropriate to our present circumstances. CODOTS shall wield the equivalent of executive planetary authority during the current crisis with the United Nations Security Council acting as a legislative governing body. As Commander in Chief of the CODOTS council, you shall have all the respective powers as commander, manager, etc. All information relevant to this position is contained herein. You will brief the Security Council on your initial impressions of the situation and your plan of attack on arrival at the United Nations. Good Luck."

Augesburcke let out a long whistling sigh, paging absently through the thick stack of papers behind the cover letter. There were dossiers on the twenty-one other members of the CODOTS council, dozens of photographs of the Scythians, and a file on the Chem. At the back was a photocopy of star fields showing the relative positions of the Scythian Empire, the Chem Empire, and buried in the midst of Scythian space a circled star: the Terran System. He shook his head, thinking of that small circled dot amidst the hundreds upon hundreds of like dots.

"What could anyone possibly want with this place?" he asked himself, and then he turned back to the cover letter and read it again. He stopped at the last part and shook his head again.

"It looks like I've got an hour to become the expert. Not expecting much are they? Ah well, I suppose one way or another something's got to be done about it. I must admit, though, this would go down a lot easier with a bottle or two of brandy."

CHAPTER 9:
NAZEERA

Nazeera exited the Elder's chambers exhausted. The meeting of the three Triumvirates of the Assemblage and the Elder of Chem took nearly a fifth of a decurn. The "Legend of Alexander" had everyone on edge, even the eldest members of the Assemblage, but the debate tried her patience.

Nazeera was a creature of action. The limited scope of Chem action thus far comprised only the boarding of the Scythian experimentation ship and the taking of Alexander. That took place only after the insistence of Nazeera. There had been a debate for some time in the Assemblage concerning the anticipated Scythian demands, which were as unacceptable in their hypothetical status as when Scythians made them formally. The nebulosity of the issue centered on the Terran question, and what the Scythian threat would eventually mean to Chem. Nazeera was vehemently against any concession to the Scythians, but she was also aware of their complete ignorance of the Terrans. True, they had many millennia worth of Scythian distributed data, all of which was authentic. Yet data could easily be edited to maintain a particular view, and Nazeera wasn't willing to accept any Scythian authored viewpoint without contention.

If the Chem had an innate distrust for the Scythians then Nazeera personalized it. The visceral philosophies of the two peoples were diametrically opposed. Their relationship fell from the diplomatic pedestal of cordiality to open hostility in one fatal step. Unfortunately, from Nazeera's point of view, what should have been a swift response to the Scythians dissolved into another quagmire of endless debate. Though they now had Alexander there were no plans for military action. The Chem Armada was to be mobilized, but beyond that there was only talk.

The dominant member of the Triumvirate stalked out of the council chamber to find Nazar waiting for her. She stopped next to him, taking a deep breath before she trusted herself to speak. Her shoulders rose as she slowly took in the moist heavy air of the Chem Homeworld. With excessive control she allowed her breath to whistle through her sharp teeth, releasing her tension and clearing her mind. Shaking her leonine mane she was now ready to address her closest confidant and friend. Nazar was dear to her, and all the more so since the death of their father, but she betrayed little warmth in her greeting.

"Waiting for news I suppose?"

"Waiting for you," Nazar smiled, handing her a regenerative drink. "I owe you an apology. You have more than enough on your mind without my baiting Bureel. It was rather callous of me."

Nazeera threw him a half hearted grin, "Yes it was callous, but more so for Bureel. Therefore, it was not without amusement. Your baiting of him, my dear Nazar, is somewhat of a tonic for me. As his wife," she spat out the word as if the concept were pure poison, "I have no right to speak my mind in public, despite my repugnance of him. An arranged marriage has its elements of chance, but that I should mate with a dog such as Bureel is unthinkable! I wish I could forgive father for that."

"He's bringing up the subject of an heir is he?" Nazar asked cautiously.

"He is most insistent on it, and I have little recourse," Nazeera admitted, tossing the drink down and stomping down the hall—her anger apparent. "It is not only time honored tradition, but it is in my marriage vows, and so it is law. I can delay, as I have, but I have no right to refuse."

Nazar followed, staying close on her shoulder. His voice was insistent, but it sank to a harsh whisper.

"Maybe you can't legally refuse him, but there may be another way, Nazeera."

She glanced at him without stopping. "Go on."

"It is somewhat eccentric, I admit, but then again we are approaching desperate straits aren't we? Oh, I've seen that look of yours before, but hear me out. I propose we allow Bureel to make good on his boast to combat the Terran. He is a brawny fellow with pluck. I daresay he could solve the problem of Bureel quite permanently."

Nazeera stopped quite suddenly, staring at the floor. The image of Alexander throttling Bureel brought a momentary smile to her lips. Then duty intervened, and she felt the responsibility of the Empire on her shoulders. "No, I can't use this for personal gain, that's going too far!" she thought, but to Nazar, she said, "You tempt me, brother, you sorely tempt me, but we have already decided the dispensation of the Terran."

She started walked again, but at a more measured pace.

"I hope you weren't serious about executing him," Nazar said. "I realize Terrans are a possible danger to the Empire, but I'm not certain executing their warlord is the best idea. I wouldn't deal so ignobly with even a Scythian without due cause. At least allow him to die in battle. Terrans could understand that without enmity. My advice is for you to allow Bureel's challenge. This would be to our advantage."

Nazeera laughed, "You are a simple schemer, sweet Nazar. You are right, it would be to our advantage but it would not be to the advantage of the Empire. What if Bureel killed the Terran? We would have lost a wonderful opportunity to study a potential adversary. There isn't time enough to return to Terra and abduct another. No, we can't use him to our own advantage, but we won't dishonor him with execution or Scythian style experimentation either. That avenue was taken out of our hands with the discovery of his unique status. We will send him to Pantrixnia, as I suggested. There I believe we will find out much more about our adversary than any battery of tests, or even a combat with Bureel. He does have pluck. I think he might survive quite a while longer than many envision."

"Pantrixnia, I thought you were jesting at the Assemblage!" Nazar replied. "I can't think of what you can learn of him there. The most pernicious Chem villains don't last a full decand, and I can't imagine the Terran doing that well. Terrans may be the most physically powerful Galactic sentient, but there's more to Pantrixnia than brawn. He didn't look particularly swift and his strength will not help him against the beasts of that planet!"

"Nonetheless, that is what we decided. His cunning interests me more than his physical prowess. I studied the information our scouts retrieved from the Scythian data banks thoroughly while the Terran was enroute. Thus, I knew a great deal more about him than he could have guessed during our tête-à-tête in the Assemblage. The Scythian tapes contained a great deal of piquant information, including past life memories. He's a warrior that one, always has been. There are indications of an extremely savage past, and much of that in positions of power. This being is hungry for notoriety, and his past lives indicate a willingness to take great risks to accomplish his goals. This particular life cycle is remarkably devoid of any great accomplishment, and it galls him. It is somewhat remarkable, as his accomplishments in this life cycle are considerable when projected against the norm. He was a gladiator, Nazar, rewarded for his exploits in the arena of football. He was promoted from the pit of Terra's most savage game to full citizenship and the post of a military officer in one of the premier factions on the planet. There he became a field commander and an expert at unarmed and mechanized combat, but somehow failed to advance any further. Politics seemed to play a part. In that respect, at least, Terrans may not be much different than us. He left that faction embittered. It was a mistake."

Nazeera led Nazar outside the building, past the guard, and into the forest surrounding the Assemblage compound. No other buildings were apparent. She took a path that wound through the jungle.

"Considering the Terran caste system and its volatility I'm surprised he was allowed the freedom of departing his faction, I would certainly never have allowed such a defection! Alexander is frustrated with his position in life, and considering his past he may have reason for it."

"Then what is this about his status as Warlord of Terra?"

"I'm getting to that. Alexander is one of those rare figures that are dangerous if left uncontrolled, and true to form his aspirations did not die after his dismissal. It's difficult to sort out fact from fantasy when dealing with memory, but we know for a fact that the Scythians had multiple contacts with him. It's obvious now why. Alexander had the aspiration and the ability, and the Scythians were intent on tackling the Chem problem. They found the heir to Alexander."

They walked for a while, listening to the birds in the jungle. After about five minutes they came to a waterfall. Brown foamy water slipped over an outcropping of black rock to fill a muddy pool. It began to rain.

Nazeera stooped to wash her hands, fully aware of tenseness in the jungle. This pool was set apart from the Assemblage compound. It was the perfect place for an assassination, or an ambush—she heard the parting of undergrowth and instantly leapt aside. Out of the corner of her eyes she saw Nazar leap the other way.

A vibrant green body several times her size landed on the mud where she'd stood. It was a small carnivore, a purla, and it scrambled at the bank, its six legs trying to keep it from toppling into the muddy water after missing Nazeera.

She laughed, drew her pistol and shot it.

The purla jumped into the air, flipped around, and landed with a heavy plop on the muddy bank—dead.

"Nice shot," Nazar smiled, holstering his own gun.

"He'll make a nice business suit," Nazeera said, holstering her gun and pulling out a long knife. She squatted over the dead animal and began to skin him.

"It's intriguing that we found Alexander in a state of communion, possibly with the Scythian Council, when we boarded their ship. I can't say what their negotiations were about, but it seems clear that the Scythians identified him as the heir to Alexander, possibly even the genetic descendant of Alexander himself! The Scythians needs fit Alexander's desires perfectly."

"Then what's the problem?" Nazar asked, cutting several long strips of flank meat and roasting them on branches with his gun. "I mean, if we know who he is, and we know what the Scythians want to do then what's the mystery?" He handed her some roasted meat.

"We know so little about Terrans in the flesh," she said, squatting like some primeval cavewoman and ripping at the roasted meat while she talked Galactic politics. "We've known what the Scythians were up to all along, but now that it's happening we need to know more. I'm not convinced Alexander is the only warlord of Terra, there's too much dissatisfaction with this life cycle. For a being like that anything but the pinnacle is empty. Whatever his motivations were on Terra he now has his opportunity at notoriety as the de facto representative of his race. This is what he's been waiting for. I want to see how he uses it."

"Remind me never to perplex you. I don't want you trying to find out what makes me tick."

Nazeera just smiled and finished her snack.

"I wouldn't want the fate of Chem resting on my performance on Pantrixnia," Nazar grunted, finishing his meal. He wiped his greasy lips on his sleeve. "I'd give myself two decurns. The second night would find me with no luck left to draw on."

"We'll see," she nodded, as she finished skinning the purla. She rolled up the pelt, washed her hands and tucked it under her arm. "Ah, now that was a refreshing lunch. Now back to business." She headed back down the forest path. A scavenger was already pulling at the purla's carcass. "The challenge on Pantrixnia will answer many of our questions concerning Terrans, but I have many more I want to pose to Alexander in particular."

"Such as whether or not the Terrans are massing even as we speak?"

"Amongst others," she said. "The spy ship didn't see any signs of that when they took Alexander, but what they may have in mind I don't know. We're finally mobilizing our Armada, and I can't imagine the Scythians being able to transport millions of Terran warriors into our space before we're ready. We're not as lax as our brethren, though we're not as strong as our ancestors. It takes a lot to motivate us out of the Empire, Nazar. I spent the last hours persuading the Elder to take even these meager steps. We've become a contented people. Our empire building days are in the past, and now we sit and enjoy the luxury of our ancestor's gains. We're proud and haughty, but we're slow to anger. Perceived threats don't concern us, at least they didn't concern us, until now. The Scythians' affronts finally pushed us to action, but there is a great amount of inertia in the Chem."

They reached the compound. A door slid open and they entered the corridor. Nazeera led Nazar into an elevator. She pressed the button for the lowest level. There was a slight bump, and then the lift whirred as it took them deep into the bowels of the compound. "We can and will deal with Scythia, but we know so little of Terrans. Have we finally met our match in this galaxy? Can Terrans actually defeat us? Do they even wish to? We don't risk the Empire of our ancestors without careful consideration."

Nazar shook his head, saying, "I can't argue against your logic. You've won the point, dear sister; very well, but what do you wish to accomplish concerning this particular Terran? Pantrixnia may well settle issues of cunning and mettle, but it does nothing to answer questions of motive."

"You're quite right, Nazar, and maybe we can expect nothing more than dissuading some of the myths. Whatever we find out will be more useful than the whisperings of the Scythians which like as not, make the Terrans more than they are. We shall not let all our information be dependent on Pantrixnia, however. On that point you demonstrate remarkable foresight. The Elder agrees with you, Nazar, and has therefore assigned me to interrogate the Terran before his departure. He's given me three decurns within which to form a personality portrait of the Terran independent of Scythian data. I don't know that I expect to find anything special, but perhaps he'll let down his guard more so with me, than he would before the entire Assemblage."

"The plan has merit. Beautiful women have historically been more successful at wheedling secrets out of men, and this fellow doesn't look as he'll be intimidated. You mean to see him alone then?"

"I do. Now is the best time, as Pantrixnia will forever prevent any further interrogation."

"That is, unfortunately true," Nazar agreed. "It's a pity though. He impressed me. Yanked from his Homeworld to the Assemblage, that's not the way I'd like to be introduced to interstellar travel."

"Why Nazar, you speak of him as if you thought him ignorant of the Scythians and the galaxy at large!" The lift stopped and the door slid open. They were in a metal corridor. Luminescent panels on the ceiling were the only thing breaking up the monotony of metal. "Galactic history has always placed the Terrans firmly in the Scythian camp, waiting only the time when they acquire the means to reach the stars and begin their conquests."

"I didn't get that sense from him," Nazar told her. "He's intelligent, more so than I expected. He chose his words very carefully before the

Assemblage, and as you so deftly pointed out he deflected our questions with his own demands. That tells me two things. If he's a Scythian mercenary he's intelligent enough to avoid problematic questions. If he isn't, if he is indeed ignorant of all that's going on out here in the cosmos, then there was no answer for him to give, and he thought quickly on his feet. If Terrans are that intelligent, and they've known about space travel for two thousand of their years, then I defy the Scythians to keep them planet bound. I am, therefore, undecided. It seems then, somehow wrong of us to send him to place where we put criminals to die."

"You are growing an appallingly large conscience, my dear brother. I'd agree with you if the stakes weren't so high." They came to a blank wall at the end of the corridor. A small panel slid open. A silver baseball sized sphere with a single red lens floated out. It took their retinal scans and disappeared back into its hole. The wall opened onto another metal corridor.

"Isn't this the time we fall back upon our principles?" Nazar asked. "Aren't times of doubt and decision when we define ourselves as a culture and a people?"

"You raise difficult points, Nazar, and there are truths in them, but we're running out of time. The Armada will take at least six decands to mass. It is enough time for us to launch the invasion of Terra and the Scythian Homeworlds, but hopefully not enough time for the Scythians to arm the Terrans to any great degree. We face a difficult task ahead, and the future of our civilization may depend on the smallest scrap of insight we can gain from this Terran. It's not at all a desirable situation; compromises are inevitable."

"What are you going to ask him?"

"I haven't gotten that far. Maybe there is no right question. He is alien, and I do not know how he thinks. We'll sit down and hopefully have a nice little chat."

Nazar smiled that evil grin unique to the Chem. "You're going to have a nice chat, maybe a cup of tea, and then you're sending him to the most infamous planet in the galaxy, specifically cultivated over millennia to affect the honorable execution of all who enter its confines. My beloved sister sometimes you can be deliciously cruel."

"Spare me the observations, brother, are you coming or not?"

"Oh, I wouldn't miss this, except possibly for Bureel's hanging. Lead on," Nazar told her, an unsettling laugh erupting from his thin lips.

They came to another set of security doors. This time there was a vibrant red band coursing across the floor, walls, and ceiling. Nazeera stepped through it, and it scanned her. As the crimson band of light passed over her body a tiny object leapt out from beneath her armor. It was metallic, hardly the size of a pea, and it intelligently avoided discovery. Silently it swirled into the air behind them and sped, unseen, down the hallway.

CHAPTER 10:
BUREEL

In his personal office high in the central spire of the Assemblage Bureel pushed away from his desk, growling. "Damn them! I'd like to hear the interrogation of that accursed Terran."

"Unwise, my lord," Gurthur, Bureel's lieutenant, told his master. "The security screens would pick up the bug."

"True enough," Bureel frowned in an unpleasant way and moved over to the window. It commanded a sweeping view of Cherumaz, the capital of the Empire. The city was as much jungle as it was structure, and even then the buildings were of shades of jade, purple and ochre according to the colors of the Chem landscape. The beauty was lost on Bureel. His conniving mind was scheming.

"The Terran's trials on Pantrixnia will give us a wonderfully humiliating death to watch, though unfortunately too quick. I would that he could die slowly, preferably in the company of my brother-in-law! That grache! Bait me will he? Well, I am a patient Chem. There is always opportunity awaiting those who look for it."

"Have a care though, my lord," Gurthur cautioned. "Do not wear your intentions in public lest they undo you. Nazeera has powerful allies who love her as much for herself as for her father's memory. The people love Nazar as well. He is a young lion who recalls the memory of his noble father."

"That noble father paid his debts to my own with this hellish marriage!" Bureel reminded his companion angrily, but then he thought better of it complaint. "Still, I have wealth, a title, and a seat on the council; none of which my lesser father could have left me. Miserable favor though it is I shall work it to my likes in the end."

"Then have patience," Gurthur advised him. "Wear a mask of long suffering and noble silence in public while we work your future plans in private."

"An intelligent approach, certainly," Bureel replied. He returned to his chair and leaned back, popping a live beruba into his mouth. The beruba was a frowned upon worm-like delicacy with subtle hallucinogenic powers. The drug enhanced Bureel's daydreams as he ticked off the possible scenarios that might result in his continuing fortune and increased power.

He laughed.

"You know, Gurthur, this Terran may have more use for us than I originally anticipated. Certainly he will play his part cooperatively and die swiftly on Pantrixnia. That should settle the doubts of the Council and encourage them to push on with the plans to make war on the Terrans and Scythia. Now if the Terrans prove to be stubborn enough to put up some semblance of a fight, well, the safety of my wife and brother-in-law would concern me greatly. Nazar, unfortunately, cannot be dissuaded from rushing headlong in search of glory in battle. There are many strange fortunes in war not the least of which is a knife in the back."

He chuckled greedily, slurping up another of the worms which chirped in distress as it slid through his lips.

"My noble Nazeera is of similar mind. I shall curtail her adventurous nature, though, until she produces me an heir. I must press that suit quick and hard. Once we settle that issue I shall have no right to keep her from her destiny. She is a reckless one, if only she was more domesticated! It would be unthinkable if I should become an aggrieved widower due to her insatiable quest for glory. Alas, it's unthinkable that I should be left alone with my heir, her lands, her wealth and her title to carry on as best I can."

"Unthinkable, my lord, absolutely unthinkable," Gurthur smiled evilly, knowing his master's mind as completely as his own. "Might

I suggest, as an initial step, that we inform the networks of the coming spectacle on Pantrixnia? I'm certain that they could ensure a live broadcast of the Terran's adventures, with some help from your influence, of course."

"A subtly ingenious idea, Gurthur," Bureel agreed. "We can have the most positive effect on the Council if we pre-empt their policy and sway the people's desire to war and expansion over these upstarts. A live broadcast should keep everyone on the edge of their seats, for a limited time. Meanwhile we shall loudly proclaim a strategy of renewed expansion, first Terra and the Scythian Empire, and then those interloping cultures who sought to shield them!"

"And as the author of this policy the laurels will fall upon your shoulders, my lord," Gurthur reminded him.

"Possibly, though it would be a mantle of popularity that would need a pulpit. As a Fifth Level Member of the Assemblage my voice would be too silent, considering the import of my words."

"Should an unlooked for vacancy at a more powerful level occur, however, what option would the Elder have but to appoint you even if it were to the First Level itself?"

Bureel paced in mock agitation, "The Triumvirate! For instance, if my beloved wife were to fall in battle what better tribute to her could I make than to continue her work in her seat?"

"A noble sacrifice, my lord," Gurthur said. "Although you would of course initially wish to retire to private life . . ."

". . . In my grief at such a sudden, but not unforeseen tragedy."

"It would be a short retirement, as you could not ignore your call to duty from the people, and the legacy of your wife's unfinished work."

"Just so, my selfless devotion to my duty would break my grief. The avenging Chem, I would continue our conquests to their logical completion, as a tribute to her. Should I succeed then there would be nothing in the Empire outside my reach."

Satanic glee clouded Bureel's face. He laid a nailed hand on his lieutenant's shoulder. "Let us begin. Go to the networks and advise them of the coming attraction. I will publish my position on galactic expansion. With luck I shall beat the Terran into the evening broadcasts, but either way I shall certainly outlast him!"

CHAPTER 11:
HAUNTED BY HIMSELF

Alexander eyed the open door with suspicion.

He got up and walked over to it. Peering inside he saw a small chamber. There was a plain cube about eighteen inches to a side in one corner. In the back was a small area with a lip on the floor and what appeared to be a drain. He stepped inside.

A small waterfall flowed from a slot in the wall into the area with the drain. It was a shower. Alexander moved over to the cube and the top lifted off to reveal a seat with a large hole in it—a toilet. Alexander took immediate advantage of the discovery. When he finished showering under the waterfall he simply stepped out of the area and a rush of air dried him off.

Alexander stepped out of the bathroom, still naked and hungry, but feeling somewhat refreshed.

"Now what?" he asked aloud. "I assume you're watching me. Well, Nazeera, I'm ready for the next round." There was no answer. "Probably testing my patience," he grumbled. Truth be told, that was a problem. After winning his inner battle Alexander was ready to get on with whatever the Chem had in mind, so long as it wasn't immediate execution.

His statements to the Assemblage were at worst exaggerations of his personal views, so he wasn't worried about his story. His personal survival was a moot point, as quite frankly Alexander was too far from any kind of rescue to make longevity a concern. It was a grim point of reality, but once he unloaded this emotional baggage, it gave him a remarkable feeling of freedom. His concern was now that of putting the best possible face on Humankind as a species, and not with individual survival. He was ready; he wanted to get going.

He decided that if the Chem weren't going to play along then he'd at least keep up appearances. As his racing mind spun through the last hours Alexander began a choreographed routine used in martial arts. The slow movements focused his concentration, eating away at his self doubt, and leaving him calm with strong willed resolution. After fifteen minutes he got the desired response.

"Terran, I desire your attention," announced a strong female voice. It was Nazeera.

Alexander continued his routine. When she repeated her demand, he answered, "You can call me by my name, Nazeera. You know it well enough, unless the Chem have excessively short memories or no tape recorders."

There was a lengthy pause, then she said, "Very well, Alexander of Terra, I will let you have this small victory. I do not wish your subjugation, only your attention."

Alexander stopped. "You have my attention."

Another door slid open in the curved wall. "Enter; it will bring you to a chamber where we can discuss your situation in greater comfort. If you are obstinate, Alexander, let me assure you that I have several unpleasant ways of forcing you to do my bidding."

"That will be unnecessary," Alexander told her. He went through the opening and into a short hall of the same gray metal. After ten paces he entered a small Spartan chamber. There was a chair placed before a large plain metal desk, and behind that desk stood Nazeera of Chem. As soon as he saw her he was suddenly, and uncomfortably, self conscious of his nakedness.

"Interesting," she said, her brow rising. "Modesty? Why? You showed no such reaction in the Assemblage, and you seem to be well made. I do not see anything to complain of."

"I thank you for your kind observation," he said sarcastically, "but I had other things on my mind during my trial. Being alone with you is somewhat different. Besides it is not the custom of my people to go without clothing."

"Nor mine. Here, this is fitting—from one carnivore to another." She threw him the purla pelt.

Alexander caught it, trying to mask his surprise with a grimace. The pelt was still warm, and his hands were red with blood. "We usually tan our pelts on Terra," he said. "Is there some hidden message in this? Am I to dress like a caveman because my intellect and manners are so primitive?"

Nazeera laughed, and to Alexander it almost sounded like she was sincere. "A warlord with a sense of humor—you surprise me, Alexander." She snapped her fingers. A black sphere the size of a basketball appeared from within a niche in the wall. It had various appendages, several rows of winking lights, and a large red eye-like lens.

It flew over to Alexander, hovered for a moment, and then said, "Excuse me, please!" and snatched the pelt from his hands.

"Stand still!" it ordered, and a swath of blue light scanned him up and down and all around.

Alexander shuddered involuntarily.

Nazeera's eyes narrowed. "Does the automaton cause you discomfort?"

"No, it simply reminds me of something the Scythians did," Alexander admitted. "Their presence, even their memory, makes me patently uncomfortable."

"I know what you mean," Nazeera said.

"You're huge, how am I supposed to tailor proper clothing for someone this size?" the automaton asked. "There's not enough material to fit him into the current style."

"Do the best you can," Nazeera said.

"The things you people force me to do," the automaton whined. "Promise me he won't go out in public—I won't have my work ridiculed!"

"That won't be a problem," Nazeera smiled.

The ball went to work. It let go of the pelt, which floated in the air under the scrutiny of a reddish-orange beam of light. Alexander smelled roasting flesh.

"Sphere's with personalities, a gay tailor by the sound of it, fantastic," Alexander said.

"You don't have automatons on Terra, I assume?" Nazeera asked.

"We prefer to work with our hands."

"And this makes the tailor gay?"

Alexander smirked, and said, "Not necessarily."

"How strange, that a warrior race such a Terra should allow for a tailor," Nazeera mused, making a note on a small rectangular pad.

Alexander realized he was letting his wit get the better of him, this was business. He recovered, saying, "Who else would make the armor? You can't just let anyone forge it."

"Of course."

The worker finished tanning the pelt and proceeded to cut it with amazing speed. Every once in a while it stopped working to fly over to Alexander, measure him again, mumble to itself, and then go back to work.

"How long is this going to take," he asked.

"First you mock me, and then you ask me when I'm going to be done! Miracles take time!" the automaton said.

Alexander sighed and turned away from Nazeera.

"I have had plenty of time to see your nakedness, Alexander. It does not shock me, nor do I find Terrans as strange or ugly in the flesh as I would have thought."

"I'm glad I'm not revolting to you on that account."

"You are beyond my likes and dislikes, Alexander of Terra," Nazeera told him. "Personal matters are beyond my purpose here."

"And what is your purpose?" he asked, turning toward her and crossing his arms over his breast.

"Simply put, to find as much about yourself and Terrans as I can."

"There are better ways of doing that then sentencing me to death," he told her. "History on Terra teaches us that incarceration and intimidation are the least effective ways for people to communicate. Different races, different species, even men and women have found more practical methods of understanding one another."

"Do you insinuate sexual activity? I can't see that as appropriate or desirable in this situation. Certainly a Chem male wouldn't think so. Is this a particular obsession with Terran males?"

"It is an obsession, certainly, but that was not my meaning," he replied with a genuine laugh. "I meant something more innocent such as a sporting event, a concert or dinner—something more representative of normal life than imprisonment. I'd have to be clothed in proper attire, of course."

The automaton flew around to him, saying, "Well, this is as proper as it's going to get, time and materials permitting. Go ahead, put it on!"

Alexander shrugged the pelt on. It was cut as a tunic that reached to just above his knees, but the automaton fashioned a collar, sleeves and even a belt. It fit to perfection and allowed him absolute freedom of movement.

"There is a short cape, just in case it gets cold or you have to go formal—please don't use it for that, my reputation is at stake."

"It's amazing," Alexander said, and he meant it. "You made this out of a fresh pelt in only five minutes? Amazing!"

"Well then, that's quite kind of you," the automaton said, and it whirred away apparently quite pleased with the compliment.

"So what do you say, Nazeera?" Alexander said, turning back to the Chem woman. She looked on with what might be termed interest, he couldn't tell. "I'm now properly clothed. Would you like to take a walk in the park, or better yet how about dinner? I'm starving, and I promise to be talkative while I eat."

"Circumstances prevent us from enjoying recreation at the present time, Alexander."

"Why is that?"

"Can you be so ignorant, or are you just being obstinate?"

"I am ignorant, Nazeera," he told her forcefully, but calmly. "I am ignorant of you, of where I am, and why I am here. I am ignorant of everything about this entire ridiculous situation."

"You were read the charges by the Elder," she reminded him. "Terra, whom you represent—"

"I cannot claim to represent my world without the consent of the population—"

"Nonsense, Alexander of Terra, it is the right and duty of every being to represent their race wherever they may be and under any circumstances. You are here, alone of your race, therefore, you are the de facto representative of Terra. You will be treated as such."

Alexander sighed with resignation.

"We accuse Terra of complicity with the Scythians in planned acts of aggression against the Empire of Chem. What do you have to say to these charges?"

"Exactly what I said before the Assemblage: nothing. I know absolutely nothing of the charges, and until I met your Assemblage I had never heard of the Chem, or any other extra-terrestrial race. At this point in time the accepted view on Terra is that there is a possibility of intelligent life elsewhere, but that is all. We have no evidence that even suggests that the Chem exist, and that alone should rule out an act of complicity in aggression."

Alexander's voice lowered to a growl, his head tilted down, and his brows knit together. "As far as the Scythians are concerned, Nazeera, all I know is that I've been a subject for their experiments on three occasions. I'm not in league with them—rather the opposite! There's certainly no dialogue between us, and if there were I doubt very much whether it would be amicable!" Alexander shook his head, trying to rid himself of the memories of Scythian experimentation.

He sighed, running his hands through his hair, and admitted. "My personal experience tells me nothing beyond that. We Terrans have fictional stories of such things, but there's nothing factual. That's pretty much it."

"An interesting story," Nazeera said, sitting down behind the desk and motioning for Alexander to do the same. "Unfortunately, there is little to base my trust in you, especially when the stakes for Chem are so high. You have in the past, Alexander, proved to be vicious and untrustworthy. What has caused you to change?"

"What have I done in my past that gives you that indication?"

"Really, can you be so bold as to seduce me into your ignorance?" She inquired, her brows knitting and her eye's increasing in brightness. "I have the data records from the Scythians. It's obvious to me that you were important to them. They themselves admit as much. They singled you out for attention. Why is that?"

"Maybe they like football. I have no earthly idea."

"Really," Nazeera smiled, at least Alexander took it as a smile but it was feral, threatening and enticing, like a tigress slowly stalking him. She punched a switch in the desk. A small screen flipped up from the surface. She touched the surface of the screen, apparently punching in commands, and said, "This may help loosen you tongue."

Alexander jumped up.

He wasn't in the metal room anymore. He stood in the mud on a stone bridge under a cold misty sun. He could feel the chill of the moist British air. Britain, how did he know that? He looked himself over. He was wearing a chain mail hauberk, carried a round shield painted with a purple wolf on a golden field. In his right hand was a long handled axe. He gazed at a line of Saxon soldiers through the Viking goggles of his conical helm. Alexander took an involuntary step backward, but Nazeera's voice stopped him. She stood next to him, smiling.

"The Scythians compiled memories from your past lives, Alexander. This is one of my favorites. You called yourself a "Viking," and you spent your life pillaging the civilized world. You amassed quite a fortune before you finally fell on this bridge, holding an army at bay."

Alexander felt a chill rush through his body. The tramp of booted feet engaged his attention. The Saxons advanced on the bridge, a solid wall of spears and iron five men abreast. Alexander glanced behind, there stood King Harold Hardratti, and two faces he recognized—his sons. Like the rest of the army they were without their armor, caught by surprise by King Harold the Saxon's unexpected advance—they were doomed.

"See to the King, go now!" he heard himself yell in the Norse tongue. "Tell your mother I'll see her in Thor's hall at Bilskirnir!"

Without thinking, Alexander the Viking threw himself at the Saxons and his axe reaped heads and limbs as wheat on that bloody morning.

It was like a movie, except every movement, every breath, every sensation was too familiar. He couldn't explain or comprehend it.

"I daresay your namesake, Thor, would be proud, but that wasn't enough for you, was it Alexander?"

He glanced at her between strokes, a twisted grimace on his blood spattered face, having no idea what she meant.

Nazeera snapped her fingers and the afternoon at Stamford Bridge disappeared.

Alexander found himself standing on the battlements of a lonely castle. He wore a long purple cloak and a crowned helm. The helm dug into the flesh of his brow, as if it belonged to someone else. Below in the glooms he watched an army advance on his walls. They carried the hewed branches of trees so he couldn't tell their numbers—it was as if the forest itself moved. He laughed grimly, again as if this were scripted and not because he found anything amusing about it.

"You had a taste of riches and power," Nazeera told him, putting her hand on his shoulder as if she was the narrator for his past lives. "You wanted more. So in your next life you murdered your kinsman the king and took his crown. Your conscience and your enemies caught up to you eventually, though, and again you died nobly in battle. It's ironic that during the next life you are the pinnacle of honesty and honor."

"What do you mean, these were my lives?"

Nazeera snapped her fingers.

The castle disappeared, and Alexander found himself kneeling on a small platform next to a dirty brown river. Around him was an ancient city. The place smelled of turbid water, weeds and sewage. Alexander craned his neck to see a small circle of people looking down on him.

"What the hell is going on here?"

Some one behind him pushed his shoulders forward, forcing his head onto a stained block. He turned his head to the side; his cheek against the sticky wood. A large man swathed in black took his place next to him. He held a great axe.

Alexander struggled, but his hands were bound behind his back and a pair of hands held him down.

"Show some decorum, Gov'nor, you'll ruin my stroke and that won't go easy for you!"

There was a whistle in the air, and the executioner grunted. Something cold hit him in the back of the neck. There was a dull painful crunch as his vertebrae crushed his windpipe. His vision grew hazy, and the world twisted and turned. For a moment, his eyes focused and he saw the circle of people looking at him. To his horror Alexander realized the executioner was holding his severed head aloft.

Nazeera's face appeared in the crowd, and she asked, "What's next, Alexander?"

The vibrant heat of the Caribbean replaced the gloomy quays of London. Alexander was whole again and dressed in a burgundy frock coat with a pair of pistols in his belt and a cutlass in his hand. He stood on the swaying deck of a sailing ship, his free hand grasping the rigging. The smell of burnt powder and salt was heavy in the moist air. The sound of guns and shouts of men roiled around him. Through the smoke he saw another ship barely a yard away.

Alexander walked steadfastly along the deck, ignoring the whizzing shot and the splintering wood. He squinted through the smoke and calmly dictated the order of the battle.

"It's back to your old ways," Nazeera said, dressed in the outlandish gear of a buccaneer. "As a pirate you become infamous in the persecution of a king that wronged you. I could go on. Suffice it to say, Alexander, that you have a telling and appropriate name. Can it be by chance that you bear the name of Alexander the Great, the mightiest of Terra's warrior-kings? A warrior race such as your own does not bestow laurels without reason. Why were you named for Alexander the Great, whose name reaches the council chambers of every galactic culture, even the Chem?"

Alexander didn't answer, he couldn't and he was still trying to come to grips with what Nazeera was showing him. Were these really snippets of his past lives or were they nefariously manufactured films meant to cause a response? He couldn't tell, but they seemed horribly real, and his instincts told him these events actually happened to him.

"Do you still claim ignorance?"

Alexander was silent.

"You've been a pirate, a general, a king, and maybe more—we haven't delved as deeply as we might. What remains? You are thus far devoid of the accomplishments of your former manifestations. By the Scythian data tapes you yearn for something more, don't you?"

Alexander glowered at her, and ordered a broadside of grape. The guns thundered one after another. Screams and howls cut the air. He could hear the shot ping through the Spaniard's steel cuirasses, thump into the wood and give a horrible succulent plop as they penetrated flesh.

"I don't need your answer; I see it in your eyes. What is it? What can quell your spirit? What accomplishment in this life will gain you satisfaction? You are the representative for your race at this moment in time, Alexander, but will that be enough? Or, do you aspire to greater pinnacles? For two millennia dominant Terrans have vied for the honor of Alexander's mantle. Even I, alien to your race and culture know their names: Caesar, William the Conqueror, Genghis Khan, Attila, Napoleon, Lincoln, Hitler. Do you wish to add your name to this list of warlords? Are you intent on being the next Alexander?"

Nazeera walked behind Alexander. Laying a sharp nailed hand on each shoulder she spoke in his ear. The feeling of her breath upon his neck caused him to shudder, but not with concern or revulsion. He caught himself enjoying the touch of her hands on his body even the midst of the melee—even against the shock of his reincarnation.

"Is there reason for Chem to fear you? Did the Scythians discover your ambition? They've wanted passage through our space for a millennium, but we do not bow to their jangling of coins. They hate that, and us. You would be a perfect opportunity for them. You have all the skills they need: brutality, a lust for power, intelligence, even charm. Tell me truthfully Alexander, if the Scythians offered you the means to make the stars your kingdom would you refuse them?"

"I'm not interested in galactic conquest," he told her, trying to catch up with the realities of his past lives, his responsibility to Terra, and the reality of this beautiful alien woman.

Nazeera let him go but stalked around his mountainous form to put her face inches from his own. "Not interested in conquest?" she said sharply, her eyes turning dangerous lavender. "Look all around you! You base your entire existence upon conquest! Were everything you've said here to be the truth I should still condemn you for your past as a danger to the future of the Chem!"

Nazeera stalked to the opposite end of the ship and whirled on him. There was a gun in her hand. It was unlike anything Alexander had ever seen, but there was no mistaking its purpose, or her intention. She pointed it at his breast, and said, "There is nothing in your history that tells me that you can either change or be swayed to alter your opinion or your goals, Alexander. Well, what have you to say?"

CHAPTER 12:
AN INVITATION TO DINNER

Alexander growled like a cornered wolf. His own lives overwhelmed him. He knew too much, too suddenly. It was more than any Terran was prepared to learn about themselves. But he knew himself, and he trusted himself. He thought of himself as an honorable man, not the madman Nazeera saw. He drew a pistol and climbed onto the rail.

"How can a man fight himself, Nazeera?" he asked, and he leapt over the gulf and onto the deck of the Spanish ship. He shot the closest man to him and then lay about with his cutlass. The heavy blade beat the slight rapiers of the Spanish Officers easily aside, and he cut them or pistol whipped them into submission. "If I am who you say I am, the next Alexander, and an intractable, ruthless conqueror then you may have every reason to shoot me," he shouted over the din of battle, the glee of bloodlust twisted his face with a wicked wolfish grin. "If all you've shown me is true I'll be back in a hundred years, two hundred years, when Terrans are more capable and then complete my conquest of the Chem, and whoever else stands in my way."

Alexander fought his way to the afterdeck, tossing aside the pitiful Spanish sailors who barred his way. The Captain waited for him. Alexander charged him. He parried the Captain's cut, and clubbed him in the face with the hilts of his sword.

The Captain fell to the deck, staring up at Alexander with sweat running in rivulets down his red face and fear in his eyes.

Alexander pulled his other pistol and held it over the Captain's breast.

"Yield to me; lower your flag and I'll spare your lives!"

The Captain dropped his sword and yielded.

A cheer went over the ship, but as the pirates celebrated Alexander turned. Nazeera stood behind him, still holding the gun on him. He shook his head and walked up to her so that the muzzle rested on his breast. "We Terrans don't recall our past lives Nazeera. Until you showed me this I couldn't tell you whether I ever had a previous existence or not.

"You ask me if I'm the next Alexander. I'd like to be, but not by conquering other worlds. Oh, we Terrans dream of glory and battle, but when I look into the darkness of space I don't see worlds to conquer—I see worlds to explore.

"Does that sound enlightening? Sorry. Terrans aren't that simple. We're a paradox; we're magnificently benevolent one moment, and cruel the next." As if to punctuate the point the pirate crew picked up a Spanish sailor, and much to his distress, they heaved him overboard. They went to another Spaniard who held up his hand in fear.

"Don't worry mate," one said. "Your partner was done for—we did 'im a favor. What you've got is naught but a scratch. Do as we say and the Cap'n will let you live."

They helped him up, took him to the center of the deck and gave him water.

Alexander laughed, and said, "You may well fear us, Nazeera but I tell you, Terrans are just as likely to risk their own lives to save yours, without knowing you, as they are to attack you."

Alexander went back to the rail and looked out over the impossible blue sea that was the Caribbean. "After this your concern may grow. But let me add this to what I've said, it is another quality which defines us: we take a back seat to no one. We will not subordinate ourselves to the wishes of others. We don't desire superiority, but we demand equality. That's where your Scythian conspiracy falls through. As a planet Terrans would never accept such a yoke. We are proud, sometimes too proud, and we do not play the part of the pawn well. We like to think we control our own destinies."

"You are eloquent, Alexander of Terra," Nazeera said. "Despite the evidence of your own lives you speak well, but I fear you, and I fear Terrans. For the sake of the Chem I fear you now more than ever."

"You have nothing to fear of me, Nazeera," he told her. "I am an insignificant man of a planet bound people. The Chem have no cause to fear us, for the Chem have in no way wronged us. Were it in my power the only race that need fear retribution would be the Scythians."

"You are vindictive, and ambitious," Nazeera told him. "Your lack of notoriety in this life frustrates you no end. You are vengeful for the wrongs you believe the Scythians have inflicted upon you."

"I will admit to all. Would you feel differently?" Alexander said, pacing the deck. He ignored the ongoing business of plunder that began all around him, engrossed in a search to allay Nazeera's fears. Every word that came from his lips sounded artificial. A sense of defeat encompassed him. He climbed back onto his ship and headed aft. He passed a door and walked down a short, dark, cramped corridor to his cabin. He opened the door and stepped inside.

It was like coming home. He knew everything there. Alexander couldn't help walking around the cabin and gazing at all of his old things. Then he realized with an absolute assurance that this was his memory. This was once his world.

"I'm all that Nazeera. I plead guilty to wanting to make a difference in the life of my planet, hopefully for the better. I'm guilty for wanting to lead my people from this," he gestured to the horrific scene in the cabin windows. The dead and nearly dead were bobbing in the water. The sharks were already upon them. A single boat filled with the living prisoners bumped through the grisly obstacles.

"I don't want this as the future of my planet. I plead guilty to the desire to redress my grievances on the Scythians, but beyond that I've never meant to expand our strife to the stars. Unfortunately, the Scythians destroyed the same thing for me as the Spaniards did back then—something very special for my people and me."

"What is that Alexander?" Nazeera asked with new interest.

"They destroyed a dream. They destroyed an innocent adventure. Just as the sea was then, Space is our final frontier." He fell into a high backed leather chair, exhausted. "We dreamed of exploring its vastness even before we took our first tentative steps beyond our atmosphere. But the Scythians, by their slander, have turned space into a life and death struggle. It no longer beckons us. It threatens us.

"I've dreamed of the possibility of meeting someone from beyond Terra, and now here I am. I'm in the company of an extraordinary being, and a lovely woman. I feel as if I should be asking you to dinner, but instead I'm attempting to disprove slanderous accusations which may spell the end of my civilization. This moment should not have happened like this. We weren't meant to meet this way, but somehow the Scythians got a hold of history and twisted it out of whack. That is what I blame them for."

Nazeera's expression seemed to lose the inquisitorial harshness. "You speak of dinner as a ritual. Does the consumption of nourishment have some social significance on Terra?"

Alexander smiled, and some of the energy returned to his limbs. He stood up and went over to his personal cabinet. Using a small key he found still in his pocket he unlocked the door. Alexander knew what he was looking for, and there it was—a bottle of French wine. He opened it and poured two glasses. "On Terra when a man and a woman meet for the first time, and there is an interest on each side, the first social event they share is often to have dinner together." He handed her a glass.

"Why should you desire this of me?" Nazeera asked, taking the glass in one hand but still holding the gun on him with the other. "Alexander, I'm responsible for sentencing you to Pantrixnia. Why don't you hold the same level of anger against me, as you do the Scythians?"

"I can't hold you responsible for how they've twisted history," he said, tapping her glass. "To our health and to Terra and Chem!" he toasted, sipping the wine. The taste caused him to break out in a joyful smile, and exclaim, "Still excellent after all this time! Even if it's only a memory it's worth it. Go on, have a sip. It's called a toast, and I doubt the memory of my wine can poison you!"

Nazeera tried the wine. "It's excellent."

"This "Legend of Alexander" does indeed have its base in reality. Terrans have, I am afraid, given you ample reason to believe the Scythians. Still, it's the Scythians, and not Terrans, who manipulated the Chem. It is unfortunate, because, as I told you, it was not supposed to be this way."

"That's an irrelevant statement," she told him. "From what I've seen of your past, you are proud and vindictive. You should hate me by now. You're plotting something. I'll not end up like your kinsman the king, Alexander. Despite your charm, your words do not change my mind about sending you to Pantrixnia."

"The answer would be apparent, Nazeera, if you understood Terrans," he told her, leaving the cabin and climbing back on deck. He laughed grimly as his crew heartily waved goodbye to the marooned sailors, and began stowing away the plunder. "This is not our best moment," he said, "but it was reality. The Scythians, on the other hand, dealt with us in a devious and underhanded way. Treating us as inferior beings fit only for study. That grates against every sense of honor and honesty I have. You, on the other hand, have been open with me. I appreciate your candor."

Nazeera cradled her wine, sipping it again before shaking her head, and saying, "Alexander, I'm sending you to Pantrixnia and you will undoubtedly die a violent death. That is the reality of this life. Do you still feel no malice toward me?"

"Disappointment, yes, malice, no," he told her. "We both know why you are sending me there. It is not because of some personal animosity of yours."

"No Alexander. It is not that."

He leaned against the rail, almost losing himself in the moment of this previous life. "You need to know what you're up against, and this is your best way of accomplishing that. It's not how I would have wanted my first journey into space to end up, but there it is. You have your responsibility, and I have mine."

"What is yours Alexander?"

"To show you what Terrans are capable of, and hopefully persuade you that we are not worth the fight," Alexander told her bluntly. "It's a simple purpose, I admit, but if I've won your respect before I die, Nazeera, I'll have accomplished my goal."

"You have already done that, Alexander," she said, letting her gun fall to her side.

"Good, let's have dinner. In fact, let's dine in my cabin. We can have roast pork, bananas and oranges. I think I remember some dainties that were in that Spanish galleon's hold—they'll make a fine desert. We'll also get a chance to finish this wine." He raised his glass and drained it. "Who knows, we might even enjoy it."

"I'm afraid my answer is still the same, Alexander," Nazeera said, and she raised her gun and shot him.

CHAPTER 13:
CODOTS

The United Nations in New York, USA, was a veritable beehive of activity, as was every international institution across the planet. People rushed hither thither, seemingly without purpose, but even in the labyrinth that was the vast circulatory system of information gathering, processing and decision making a certain order reigned. The vast organization of Terra was emerging, and though not without its stresses and strains it was, nonetheless, single-minded in its purpose. At the head of this purpose was the Council of Defense of the Terran System, or CODOTS.

The title of this exclusive group of twenty-two Human Beings, drawn literally from all over the globe, was significant. The adoption of the archaic place-name Terra identified a planet and a people, once solitary and unique in their experience, as a star system; as a system they were common, insignificant, and very, very vulnerable. It was a paradigm shift of extraordinary magnitude, with a physical sensation akin to a slush ball down the neck, but it was necessary.

It was vital that Terrans as a race recognize and accept their own unimportance and get on with the labor of survival. To this end the nations of Terra agreed to the creation of CODOTS and gave the group almost sovereign powers over the system. Governments agreed to unquestioned use of everything from military resources to economic secrets. It was a total and unimaginable nationalistic capitulation, but the overwhelming evidence of the threat swayed nearly all the narrow minds within the realms of ancient Earth.

That the power of all of her nations now emanated from a tiny group of people was a necessity. The vehicle of the United Nations was not intended, or designed, for swift authoritarian action. They could, however, coordinate the implementation of decisions, and that is what they were relegated to do. In the CODOTS council was the power of decision making, brainstorming and strategy.

This awesome responsibility centered on the Commander in Chief of CODOTS, Admiral Sten Augesburcke. The Admiral was the perfect choice both politically and practically speaking. As a man of mixed heritage, he could represent all as easily as he could represent none. As a military man from the Australian Commonwealth, he avoided the suspicious distinction of an American dominated world government. As a leader, he could understand both the military and the scientific side of the dilemma, being a recognized expert in both professions.

Still, the greatest argument in favor of Augesburcke was his bullish, hard charging habit of attacking a problem and coming to a solution, whatever the cost. This manner was not easy for some of the CODOTS membership to endure, and it was nearly impossible for the Scythian Liaison, but results were all that mattered now.

In the bowels of the United Nations building the Scythian Liaison and two of its aides were in the process of enduring one of Admiral Augesburcke's long glowers of dissatisfaction. He'd quickly adapted to his new position, and Terra's new situation. It was an adaptation born of his own tendency to pursue challenges with a "full speed ahead, damn the torpedoes!" attitude; and an understanding that he didn't have the luxury of gradual acclimatization. The world's politicians made that apparent over the last few days.

So with his usual bull-headed nature spurring him forward he tackled the job as he did any other problem: personally, with a slow burning fury that the dilemma existed at all.

"Your proposal is not entirely unacceptable, Liaison, but it is nearly so. That you appeared one week ago with a fleet of merchant vessels loaded to the gills with weapons and equipment is one thing. I don't like it, but I accept it if for no other reason than I have no choice. Our own examination of Chem and Galactic ethernet traffic, with equipment supplied by you, has led us to the same conclusions concerning Chem intentions."

"What is the problem then, Admiral, if you have independently reached the same conclusions as the Scythian leadership?"

"Simply this: the Scythian situation and the Terra situation are not comparable. Chem has threatened to attack and subjugate the Scythian Empire in retaliation for an assumed Scythia-Terran alliance . . ."

"An alliance of Chem imagination, Admiral," the Liaison reminded him. "The Scythians are perhaps guilty of threatening to appeal for Terran aid, as we are now, but the Chem ultimatum is in the end economic in its origin. It is an attempt by the Chem to isolate and then destroy the peaceful Scythian Empire by using Terra as a target of convenience. As you now know, we've been watching your race primarily because of the Terran propensity for violence at the slightest prodding. Galactic legend has it that your warrior king, Alexander the Great, looked to the stars and saw there more worlds to conquer; and the sole objective of your people since that time has been the fulfillment of Alexander's dream. This is the thinking the galaxy has of Terrans, despite what Scythian report has indicated.

"We have watched you benignly for many millennia, and though our opinion of Terrans is far less paranoid than that of our neighbor's even Scythia began to fear the development of Terra. The explosion of your technology in this last century is without equal in this galaxy, as is the destructiveness of your nature. The Chem have long seen Terrans as a menace to their sovereignty. Their intent is to stop you before you acquire the technological capacity to leave your system. As Scythia has stood against the Chem in the Galactic Forum, often alone, we gain her enmity. The tie between us is Chem propaganda, justifying their desire to accomplish two differing goals simultaneously.

"As intelligent and benevolent people we cannot condone genocide. We have, however, no military means with which to deter the Chem, or defend ourselves for that matter. That is the crux of our offer. We can help you defend yourselves from almost certain extermination. In return we ask for enough Terran troops to serve as a deterrent to Chem aggression. The Chem are a warrior race who prefer planet bound contests, and not ship based stratagems. The presence of a large number of well armed Terran troops should ensure our safety, and your own."

"I will not contest the truth of what you say, Liaison," Augesburcke replied evenly, holding his doubts silently. "Nonetheless, though Scythian sovereignty is threatened its civilization is not. There are ample havens for a Scythian government in exile in the ten other galactic civilizations. You may become wandering gypsies, but your heritage will be preserved. Terra, on the other hand, faces extinction, and in that light the strategy you propose is pure suicide."

"On the contrary," the Scythian objected, but Augesburcke cut him off.

"Liaison, you are a political being. I am a military man. Your request for several million Terran troops is reasonable, and will provide reasonable deterrence in concert with Scythian defenses. A passive system of defense for Scythia is logical, but the same defense is completely inappropriate to Terran needs. Despite your protestations of Chem honor, no race, honorable or not, will submit themselves to a pitched battle in a war of genocide when there is an alternative which is easy and painless."

The Liaison was emphatic in its opinion to the contrary, its voice box emulating an irritatingly high pitched whine. "I assure you, Admiral, the Chem prize glory in battle above all. Their entire existence is based on honor, and it would be unthinkable for them to act in any manner of infamy."

"Again I remind you, by your own admission, that you are not a people experienced with military matters. We Terrans, unfortunately, have dealt on a small scale with the concept of genocide. It is, under the most lenient of descriptions, not an action within the capability of a folk entirely given to honor. There is no honor in genocide; there is no glory. The Chem may sing songs of their past conquests and their many wars. They will not sing of their destruction of Terra. If they are intelligent and practical, which I conclude they are after having watched their broadcasts on the ethernet, then I can come to only one conclusion: they will stand off Terra and pound us to dust. The planetary projector batteries you promised us will buy time, but not enough of it. In a matter of days if not hours it will rain bombs, and we will cease to exist."

"You forget the population on our home planets," the Scythian protested.

"Liaison," Augesburcke barked, his anger rising to the Scythians' cold hearted ignorance, "I'm not willing to allow almost five billion beings to vanish. Do you understand? Let me be perfectly clear. Before you see a single Terran warrior embark on one of your ships I want to see more. You've offered much and brought much, but your supplies are based on an ineffective defense. To protect Terra we must meet the threat. We need our own fleet."

"Impossible!" the Scythian started. "Even if we gave you Scythian vessels they are wholly unsuited for combat. Their design is based on the most efficient means of transporting large masses extreme distances at great speeds. Even if you mounted weapons on them they would be ineffective platforms. Their surface area alone would mark them as extraordinarily vulnerable."

"I do not speak of using Scythian vessels," the Admiral told him.

"Then where will you get the ships?" the Liaison asked triumphantly. Knowing the impossibility of answer it added, so as to underscore the benevolence and cooperation of its people, "Certainly if some avenue of mounting a fleet were possible we would be only too happy to lend any and all aid. You asked for a complete inventory of Scythian equipment, and we graciously acceded to your request thinking that the Terran propensity for ingenuity might in some cases lead to some practical use of a portion of the equipment. Indeed, had we the proper ships to offer you we might outfit the Chem fleet twice over! Unfortunately, such a scenario is impossible. We have, as you initially requested, sounded out some of your neighbors concerning the possibility of "leasing" suitable warships. Those requests were summarily denied. Therefore, we must logically return to the strategy of planetary defense. It is the only rational recourse."

Augesburcke spun through the inventory files of space borne equipment on his computer. The main viewer in the room repeated the Admiral's screen. "It is a considerable hoard of fleet equipment," he ventured. "How did you accumulate it, if I may ask? It seems an impractical inventory for a merchant race in a galaxy at peace."

"It was not always so, Admiral," The Scythian told him. "Our military inventory is not in so much demand as once it was, but there is no reason to discard it. We built our current military stores during the Chem wars of expansion, thirteen millennia past. That may seem a long time to you, Admiral, but I assure you the equipment is not only serviceable, but also up to date. There is little or no difference between equipment now in use, much of which dates to that very same period, and our inventory. What we have is a combination of spare parts meant for the fleets and armadas of the wars, and equipment salvaged from the wrecks. Unfortunately, there are few surviving parent vessels for this equipment; otherwise, we would have many more options to offer. We can provide you with perhaps half a dozen vessels for reference, but that is not the basis for a fleet."

"If we find the vessels would the equipment be of any use? By this I mean are the same principles of modularization applicable, or is this naval equipment unique to its purpose and platform."

"Not at all, it is simply equipment intended for warships, Admiral," answered the Scythian Liaison, somewhat phased by the inconsequential nature of the Admiral's question. Thinking that the Terran could not yet understand the basic theory behind Galactic technology it pointed out, "The principles are the same regardless of the purpose of the technology or piece of equipment. Please understand that this technology is extraordinarily old by your standards, and quite well developed, by our standards. It follows the same form and function used one thousand millennia past. Galactic technology breaks down into modular segments of power, control, transfer and usage. When we deliver a planetary projector, a surface to orbit energy weapon of great magnitude, its complexity is in the advancement of its simplicity, not in its function. There is a self contained power generator, the gun and a control board which governs both. After delivery the equipment takes little time to set up, using anti-graviton lifters and very little time to learn to use."

The Admiral looked doubtful. "Even to aim it? We've studied your proposal, Liaison; for clarification please reiterate the concept of tying such a weapon into a planetary surveillance system."

With expressive patience the Liaison told Augesburcke, "The concept of each discipline is universal. All Galactic equipment is able to interpret information from other Galactic equipment. The elegant practicality of the technology is in the generic coding of the signal. At this moment you already have a system wide surveillance system. That system automatically transmits information, which is pre-encoded to describe its source. When you receive your planetary projectors they will recognize this code and display the information automatically and appropriately."

"The same is true for fleet type technology?" Augesburcke asked. "In other words if we had an air tight ship that could host equipment we could plug and play: add engines, power generators, atmospheric generators, blaster batteries, and the works."

"Admiral, if you wished to we could attach all of this equipment to a steel sphere, and transform it into a superluminal capable steel sphere armed with blaster batteries. While it meets theoretical rigors it lacks practicality."

Augesburcke smiled, "Practicality be damned! Liaison you get on the comm to your superiors. I want every piece of equipment which was ever intended for a warship, and I want it yesterday! You do that and I'll get you double the number of troops you're asking for!"

"But Admiral, this is ridiculous! Without a specifically identified use for this equipment we are wasting valuable cargo space, and time. If your concern is the survival of your race we can evacuate enough Terrans from Terra to ensure your species survives. It is a difficult concept to accept I know, but it is all that is possible!"

"The evacuation will be necessary, I agree, but Terra's not giving up without a fight. You worry about that equipment, Liaison; I'll worry about the fleet to put it in!"

"Very well, Admiral, I foresee no difficulties in supplying you with the equipment at the cost of Terran troops. You will find, however, that it will be a waste of time and effort; of which you have little enough as it is. Think of it: to build a fleet capable of withstanding the Chem Armada in the space of a few of your solar months? Impossible!"

"That's what Terrans are best at, Liaison," Augesburcke grinned.

CHAPTER 14:
SHIFTING PERCEPTIONS

"You shot him!" Nazar said, bursting onto the deck of the pirate ship. The pirates ignored him.

Nazeera stared down at the enormous heap of Alexander with a grimace on her face. "I only stunned him, Nazar," she said, and she stopped the hologram. They ship disappeared and they were back in the nondescript metal interrogation chamber.

"Why?"

Nazeera walked over to Alexander and kicked him in the ribs.

He didn't move.

She took out her scanner and pointed it at him. He was alive. Nazeera was more relieved than she should be. She kicked him again.

Nazar sighed, and said, "Either you really detest him, or you're beginning to like him."

Nazeera ignored her brother and called for the automaton. "Take him back to his cell. Inject him with an appropriate sustenance booster, and see that he gets some nourishment when he wakes up."

"Yes Lady Nazeera," the automaton said. It illuminated Alexander with a blue beam of light and the Terran rose off the floor a half meter. It then towed him through the corridor and back to his cell.

"What was that all about?" Nazar asked.

How could Nazeera tell him the truth? Alexander somehow made her care about his fate, the bastard. That was enough. Instead, she said,

"He was growing impudent—acting like an equal. It was time to put him in his place."

"Well, he is the Warlord of Terra, and quite possibly the heir to Alexander. Maybe he was just being polite, speaking to you as an equal."

Nazeera simply growled at him.

✠   ✠   ✠

Alexander awoke with every nerve in his body buzzing. It wasn't exactly painful, but it wasn't very uncomfortable. He rolled onto his side, and grumbled, "If that's how Chem women say no, then it's a wonder they can procreate at all!"

"You must have made an impression on Lady Nazeera," said a voice.

Alexander looked up to see the black automaton floating next to him.

"I made an impression all right, are you here to finish me off?"

"I have no idea what you mean," it said. "On Lady Nazeera's instruction I'm here to supply you with nourishment." The automaton floated over to the wall. Two metal plates slid out of slots in the wall. One was the height of a table; the other could be a chair. A panel over the taller one opened and a tray slid out. On it there was a drink of blue liquid, a joint of meat, and what might have been an ear of corn—except that it was orange.

"Probably poison," he growled, but he sat down and took the drink anyway. He was famished, and he downed it in one gulp. It didn't taste all that bad, and it filled the void in his belly better than he expected. He consumed the meat and corn in short order.

Alexander felt much better now, except for a small patch on his left breast that was tender to the touch.

"I'm glad the Chem have a stun setting."

"Alexander, I'm waiting for you," said Nazeera's voice.

"Then you'll have to wait a bit longer," he said irritably, and he stepped into the lavatory.

"I'm not accustomed to waiting for anyone."

"So I gather," Alexander said, as he went about his business. "I'm not trying to be difficult, Nazeera but do you mind a moment of privacy? If you want to press the issue you can shoot me when I'm done."

"Hopefully that won't necessary."

She left him alone.

Alexander showered, but there was no comb, no mirror and no razor. "I don't know why I should care considering she shot me," he thought, rubbing the whiskers on his face. It had to be at least three days of growth. "Is that all it's been since my abduction? That doesn't make sense."

"Nazeera, you wouldn't mind giving me a razor would you?"

"I would rather you make your tone less familiar, Alexander."

"I'm not going to grovel for you, if that's what you want."

"Use a bit less cheek in your tone then."

"Very well, may I please have a razor, a comb and a toothbrush? I want to be presentable for you; that is, unless you're going to resort to torture—then it's rather moot."

There was a long pause.

"Hello?"

"I'm here, Alexander. I was accessing your memories on torture, specifically, your life as a pirate. No, I can allay your fears on that account. We don't use such primitive means of extracting information."

"You don't need to. I'm willing to talk, so long as it's with you."

"Why with me?" she asked, and her voice sounded curious.

"Look in the mirror."

"And what am I suppose to gain by that?"

"You're easy on the eyes."

"I don't understand."

"You're quite beautiful, Nazeera, and I enjoy looking at you—there, does that translate acceptably?"

"You're getting cheeky again, Alexander."

"Sorry."

"You'd get along well with my brother." A small panel slid open revealing the toiletries Alexander requested. "Come back into the interrogation chamber when you're done. Be swift."

Alexander finished and joined her. Nazeera was seated behind the table viewing the screen. He couldn't see what was on it, but she didn't appear to even glance up at him.

"Good morning."

"Sit down."

He sat down and waited.

Eventually Nazeera looked at him. "I trust you rested well? I gave no orders to provide you with furniture. I ascertain that such luxuries would be considered a sign of weakness, and beneath you. I hope I did not err?"

"We do not, as a matter of course, allow such slight matters to sway our opinions one way or another. It is of no consequence, Nazeera, though I thank you for the thought. That is of more importance to me than luxuries."

Nazeera refused the bait of conversation, and betrayed no sign of interest in Alexander's comment. Stonily, she said, "We talked in the Assemblage of Alexander, and the Legend of Alexander. Tell me your own thoughts on your namesake."

"I have very few thoughts on the subject," Alexander replied truthfully. "Certainly I know of Alexander the Great, and I will readily admit to admiring his accomplishments. Beyond that I have not pursued the subject in any vein but that of historical interest. I'm regrettably not an expert on the subject."

"Elucidate your desire to be the next Alexander, as you so eloquently put it to me previously," Nazeera asked.

"I don't think those were my exact words, and certainly my meaning was not in a military context, which I believe I also stated."

"Alexander was a conqueror. That was his place in Terran history. That's how he won his notoriety. There's no other context within which to subscribe imitation. Now, please Alexander, explain to me your meaning."

Alexander sighed. The remainder of the session's questioning was similar. Nazeera's interrogation continued along parallel lines to the day prior, but never quite the same. It didn't take long for Alexander to realize that Nazeera was looking for any inconsistency with their prior interview.

Although disappointed, he didn't know why, Alexander could not help but smile inwardly; having told what he thought was the truth before he had no trouble maintaining the consistency of his answers.

Nazeera failed to shed her impassive coat of armor. It made the session tedious and frustrating as she refused even to acknowledge his sidelong comments and attempts to fence with her. After several hours, made longer by his own curiosity, she left him to his meal-she refused to eat with him-only to return a short time later.

Lunch, as he called it, allowed Alexander to consider Nazeera and her new line of questioning. She was all business today, and though their previous session was not a social occasion by any stretch of the imagination it struck him as much more informal than this morning's session. This morning she probed and prodded with words, just as the Scythians did with their instruments. It was altogether a more comfortable form of experimentation, but Alexander felt his gorge rise at the thought of playing the docile guinea pig. Pantrixnia was one thing, being a cooperative and talkative prisoner was quite another.

Alexander was not unwilling to commit to a dialogue, but it would have to be on more equitable terms. She'd won the morning round, but if she were still curious about him the rest of the session would have to be on more equitable terms. He, despite their intentions, was just a curious about them. The more he understood them the easier it would be to dissuade them from their present course against Terra.

When Nazeera returned she asked politely if he'd enjoyed his meal. Alexander waved his hand, absently. "It was tolerable. It would have been better if you had joined me. If that were unacceptable in the Chem code of etiquette, I would have settled for eating outside, or at least with a view. Metal walls are somewhat lacking in ambiance."

"I thought Terran warriors relished solitude. The lack of distraction is perfect for contemplation."

"We are not quite as single minded as you may think, Nazeera."

"Then what are you?"

"We are explorers, by nature, and not simply warriors. Is it then so surprising that I would like to see some of your world? Terrans are a planet bound people. Now here I am, on a strange world with a new race of people. I want to explore it. And while I can't complain of the company, I would like very much to see some of your world."

"I will allow you no such convenience. Although you will never be able to pass on what you learn I see no advantage to Chem in furthering your freedom."

"You say that with great finality, Nazeera. You almost make me regret my compliment."

"Your regrets are beyond me, Alexander, but you do open an interesting subject. Tell me, if you were allowed more freedom of movement what would you observe on Chem?"

"It's a fair question. I'll answer, on a condition."

"Alexander, you are in no position to name conditions."

"Of course I am, Nazeera. I'm in an extremely powerful bargaining position. I have something you want: information." He smiled, and crossed his arms over his breast. "Now, the Chem are too noble to stoop to acts of torture."

"You infer the more basic forms of torture, such as you endured in your lifeline as a pirate?"

"I am unfamiliar with the occasion," he frowned.

Nazeera smiled, and consulted her view plate. "You are consistent with your story, at least, Alexander. I'll grant you that." She punched a button and the chamber became a dungeon.

Torches illuminated the dark confines of a steaming dungeon. The sounds of whips, screams, the hiss of irons and the squealing of wheels echoed off the dank stone walls. It was dark, and full of smoke, but Alexander recognized the place.

They strapped him naked onto a table. It was already wet with blood, sweat, and the filth of the prisoner before him. Hunkering over him were two gnarled torturers with glowing irons. Perched by his contorted face, like a carrion creature, was a pale caricature of a man swathed in vibrant red. The scene moved at a dreamlike pace, and the colors, sounds, and even smells were so distinct that Alexander reacted physically to them. Still, the scene was somehow unreal.

Nazeera stood between the man in red and a torturer, and she told him, "This is from your memory, Alexander. It is the root, shall we say, of your adventures as a brigand. Your career began with your capture and torment by a religious sect called the "Inquisition." This moment, of course, is prior to your escape. I think, by your reaction, that it is safe to say you remember this now?"

An iron burned into the flesh of his stomach. The pain was sharp, but almost as bad was the smell of his seared flesh. Alexander tensed against the straps, and the memories of the entire horrifying experience engulfed him, complete with the attached emotions: despair, fear and above all hatred. He gripped the edges of the table to keep from trembling before Nazeera. The veins in his arms throbbed, standing out over his forearms, biceps, neck and temple.

The torturer burned him again, while his partner flogged his loins with a short whip made of leather straps.

Against the pain, he growled, "Aye, it be real enough! I remember the heat of the irons now, as I can feel them! I remember you too, Guiseppe de Gaude, you dog!"

The man swathed in red only smiled at him and read blasphemously from the bible. "I'll return your treats in my own way when the time comes you bastard!"

Alexander started, almost forgetting the pain and the fury, for the words pouring from his mouth were thick with a Scottish brogue. More of his memory returned with a rush, and he realized everything that happened in that dungeon and everything that would happen. This was a different experience from the holograms Nazeera took him through before. Then the heat of the irons and the sting of the lash brought him out of his reverie.

"Damn it, you don't need to resort to this type of torture—not if a man's got it in his past!" Alexander growled, staring furiously at Nazeera. "What's the matter, you don't want to get your hands dirty?"

The hologram ended, and Alexander found himself panting in his chair, sweating profusely. He straightened up, and said, "I congratulate you on the realism of your holograms."

"I'm sorry, Alexander," Nazeera said quickly. Did she actually mean it? "I had no idea you would experience the torture as reality. I apologize. For most beings it is more of a detached experience, but for you . . ."

"I was back there, in that dungeon, it was visceral. Why didn't the other holograms of my past have the same effect? I remembered things, but this was so much more, I don't know, complete." He cradled his temple, and said in his own voice, half to himself, "All of it just came back, suddenly, like a bludgeon. What just happened? You showed me images before, but those were movies; they weren't quite real. This was, I don't know how to describe it, deeper. But it was too real in some ways. The sounds were too sharp, the pain too poignant. Was this manufactured to illicit an emotional response? What did you do, Nazeera?"

Nazeera seemed almost as surprised as Alexander at his spontaneous and violent reaction. Her expression was sympathetic; at least that's what he thought. Her words supported his observation.

"Alexander, I did nothing to you," she told him. "What you did was to yourself. Your reaction is to a completely suppressed memory. If it causes you discomfort you have my apology. That was not my intention."

In a calmer manner he asked, "Why wasn't I affected this way when you showed me images of my previous lives before?"

"I don't know, but I expect it's the level of reality of the image," Nazeera told him. "This is a core image. The other samples were summary versions, edited if you will, of superfluous data. The hologram I just accessed is as close to that of your actual memory as we can come. You will notice that it is still somewhat artificial. The colors, sounds, sensations etc. are all somewhat out of balance. This is due to the source, and not the technology. That is, the information source, you in this case.

"You're biased, Alexander, whether you know it or not, and therefore the information you record as memories is biased. This particular event, for instance, has certain points about it which are more important than others. The sounds are skewed. There are many loud sounds we can identify in the background, yet above all, far above the expected auditory level a machine would record, are the whispered words of this Guiseppe de Gaude. Those words were more striking to you than any other sound, and therefore your memory amplifies them. At least that is what we surmise. I cannot be precise as this is a Scythian data tape. You correctly and wisely speculate that the Chem do not use this type of methodology for interrogation, but we do use it for psychotherapy. It is common knowledge amongst all galactic cultures that most if not all psychological abnormalities which are not physical in nature are due to repressed trauma. The memory scan is an essential instrument in discovering trauma inducing events and ensuing therapy."

"What did your psychologists discover in reviewing my tapes?"

"Many interesting, but contrasting things, Alexander," she told him, a slight feline smile tugging at the corners of her mouth. "I shall not enlighten you, however. I would much rather find out or myself. Let us then return to our questioning."

"I'm willing to bargain."

"We're back to that are we? I don't think your bargaining position has improved, Alexander. You would do best to simply answer my questions. There are not many pleasant alternatives."

"There certainly are, in my mind at least," Alexander told her, settling back comfortably, now more sure of himself than ever. He was right. An interesting thing happened when Nazeera showed him the hologram of his torment in the dungeons of the Inquisition. Not only did the memories of the torture return, but so did the memories of an entire lifetime. The trials and tribulations of one Colin MacAndrews, a Scottish noble turned pirate, were now a sentient reality and not a history. He knew that life, but moreover he experienced it as his own memory. It provided a much wider view of life and experience than the narrow confines of Alexander Thorson's interesting but plain world.

He continued to press his point, now having an idea in mind for his own advantage. If the sudden revelation of the memories of one lifetime could be this enlightening what could he gain from his other lives? To this end he pointed out, "No doubt you realize that you can't coerce me into cooperation simply through threats, Nazeera, as what can you use against me that I will not endure beyond your prison planet? You will not stoop to Scythian subterfuge or Terran torture. What can you sway me with? I'm going to Pantrixnia, and whether it's now or several days from now it makes no difference. If I can fight for my existence there then it is a far cry more than the Inquisition ever intended for poor MacAndrews. You want to find out more about me, and in a certain sense I want you to know more as well, but not without a price."

Nazeera crossed her lithe arms and sighed, "You seem to have this all worked out, Alexander. I find myself in an unaccustomed position, but not an unenviable one. True, I could pack you off to Pantrixnia this moment, but it would gain me nothing to do so. I'm willing to be reasonable, and even magnanimous. What is it you desire?"

Alexander chose his words carefully. He didn't want to give Nazeera the impression that he coveted the memories or experiences of his past lives, though in reality he did. Nor did he want her to know that he wanted to find out just how much the Chem had learned about Terra. His core purpose still remained to manipulate the Chem's opinion of Terra and the possible dangers of conflict. If they had access to his past lives it was imperative that he put as much positive spin on those tapes as possible. He felt that he now had an opportunity to do just that. There must be a great many holes in the Scythian data, or at least memories vague enough to demand interpretation. If his memory tapes were as all encompassing as one might first assume then there would be no need for Nazeera's interrogation. They needed corroboration. If that was so, then Alexander wanted to be the one who gave it to them, with his own spin on it.

"These are my terms: I will not give you any information regarding current Terran military capability, nor what Terrans might do to defend themselves and their world against Chem attack. That goes without saying. However, I am willing to discuss Terra and Terran culture in detail if you so desire. I have no qualms about you getting to know us, so to speak. Ignorance of other people has always been the easiest path to war and hatred. I will even go so far as to give you my opinion on my own memory tapes. If you or your psychologists have any questions to ask concerning my past I will do my best to answer them. In return, for every hour we spend in here I would like an hour outside my prison. I would like to see Chem, and I would like you to answer any questions I have concerning the Chem. Non-military questions, of course"

"Of course," Nazeera smiled.

"You may continue your interrogation during these times, if you so wish, so that you may lose as little time as possible. That's only fair."

"Is there anything else?" Nazeera asked, looking more inquisitive than perturbed.

"Yes, as a matter of fact there is," Alexander answered, a rare smile washing his face of all tension and care. "The most important condition is that all such forays will be in your company. I will not answer to any other interrogator but yourself."

Nazeera laughed, and shook her head, "You are a consummate schemer, Alexander but I can't see any reason to dissuade you. I'll accept your proposal, but we must limit your forays to one per decurn, that is your day, and that being three of your hours in length. You will have a limited experience of Chem, but enough, I hope to satisfy your curiosity. More I cannot do. Time limits me, not my patience or ambivalence."

"Fair enough."

"Very well, may we continue? How much do you remember of this previous life now that your memory has been awakened?"

Alexander shrugged. It was a difficult question, for he didn't want to shock her into reneging on their agreement. On the other hand he would be asked his perceptions on other experiences, and he knew or guessed too much about Nazeera to think he could get away with lying.

"It's difficult to gauge how many experiences I should recall about a lifetime," he told her, truthfully. "Certain things come readily to mind, and other experiences may be recalled when I see them. It is much as my present life. I remember what I was, what I did, places, people, great events. Some of it's distinct, but most is still buried I think, waiting for a question or a picture to dredge it up."

"What is foremost in your mind in connection with that life?"

Alexander smiled, "I think of that life and I see the wide swells of the ocean. I smell the salt, the powder, the blood. I feel the long crush of boredom, both at sea and in retirement. I see my children, kin, my friends and especially my wife. Countess Eliza Orionez! I can see her eyes, feel her hair and hear her words. She was striking!"

He looked hard at Nazeera, cocking his head unconsciously to the side. The expressions on Eliza's face were strikingly similar to those of Nazeera. Alexander smiled thoughtfully, and said, "Eliza was strong and fiery; she was absolutely indomitable. You remind me a great deal of her, Nazeera. There are the mannerisms, yes, and your carriage, but most of all I think it's something in the eyes." He looked at her closely, now conscious of a growing blush under her tawny skin. "Yes, it is in the eyes. You share something of the same soul, I think."

CHAPTER 15:
THE COUNCIL OF FEAR

The mood in the Senate Council Chamber on Roma was somber. It was not a large gathering. There were only ten representatives, one for each of the civilized cultures outside of Scythia and Chem. There were no aides, no reporters, not even a recorder automaton. An opaque blue security screen shielded the counselors, making it seem as if they held their meeting within a bubble in time. Even the Hrang would have been unable to gain any data on what went on inside if their ambassador chose to be silent. At this moment She-Rok, the Hrang representative, simply listened alongside his counterpart Kvel Mavec to Grand Admiral Guenuel Koor of Golkos. The Golkos as a rule were not affable, but today the Grand Admiral was positively offensive.

"The situation is intolerable," she told the council. "The Golkos went along with your game, putting off Scythian requests for a deployment of warships to their space, and what do we get? The Scythians have cut off all traffic with the Golkos Empire. Within a decand the Golkos markets are in a panic, there are runs on foodstuffs, power cells, emergency supplies and armaments. There have been riots in the capitol. We have lost total communication with two of our frontier worlds, and five others have been forced to declare martial law. The Empire is in chaos. What happened to the slow calculated response of the Scythians? We underestimated their resolve, and it resulted in disaster. Even were they to re-instate trade the recovery period will be measured in periums!"

"What of it," hissed the Seer'koh ambassador, Sheer'nhak, twitching his serpentine tail irritably. Only half as large as the gaunt two meter Golkos the saurian nevertheless accosted the Golkos' view of the situation. "Are the Golkos alone in their quandary? No. We're all part of this. Rather than whining at the loss of our precious luxuries we should revel in newfound freedom. How many millennia did the Golkos stand alone before the sniveling Scythians sapped your will? The very trade you speak of was once Golkos strength."

Sheer'nhak's head bobbed up and down, a sign of his agitation. His sharp claws drummed on the hard surface of the table, clacking in a fusillade of irritating staccato shots.

"It is the same with all of us. Little by little we've sold bits and pieces of our empires to the Scythians and they've always called us to task for it. Were it not for our very rational fear of the Chem we'd have repeated our past cowardice and caved in again. I celebrate the Chem's stubbornness. The balance has been out of joint for too long in the galaxy. Now, painful though it may be, we have a chance to right it. Our civilizations have weathered worse in our history, and I daresay we will again. There's no point in complaining about it, so we might as well stick together and see it through."

"See what through, Sheer'nhak?" Koor asked. "It is all well enough to take the bitter pill of self sufficiency and swallow it, but is that all we face? Our empires are in crisis and we face the possibility of a Chem coming out, or worse the explosion of Terra into our galaxy? That's what this means. The Chem are pushing the Scythians to the brink, and don't think the Scythians will ignore the fact that not one of our fleets is deployed to Scythian space to protect them. Are we about to face Terran legions landing on our Homeworlds during this vulnerable period of chaos?"

"All the more reason to get our houses in order, and that quickly," Sheer'nhak said forcefully, his artificially altered voice rattling insistently.

"It would take even the Scythians time to deploy Terran legions," She-Rok said, breaking into the debate. "At this time we've intercepted a great deal of coded traffic on the Scythian net. They are deploying their merchant fleets throughout their empire, and it seems apparent that they are indeed arming Terra. The Scythian habit of efficiency and documentation is noteworthy, and consistent. Despite the possible misuse of data the Scythians continue to catalogue and schedule their convoys to the minutest detail. To be certain they do encode their ethernet traffic, but we broke that code long ago. The Hrang can provide a detailed accounting of which ships have entered the Terran system and what their cargo is. A comprehensive list would be exhaustive, and beyond necessity. Suffice it to say that Terra is arming for war, but there is at this point no indication of Terran troops leaving the Terran Homeworld."

"That will change," Koor told him.

"No doubt it will," the Hrang agreed, "but at this time the ethernet traffic only addresses plans for a Terran defense force to be moved to the Scythian Homeworlds, not beyond them. That is the Scythian plan. There are some interesting indications that the Terrans may have ideas of their own, ideas which may have implications for us all."

"How so," Koor inquired.

"From the ship's manifests we have discovered that the Scythians are supplying Terra with equipment for planetary defenses and troop deployments—that's to be expected—but that's not all. The Terrans demanded the Scythians supply them with their entire inventory of fleet spare parts and weaponry. The Scythians are cooperating in a most vigorous manner. We're not certain how, as of yet, but there can be no doubt about it: the Terrans have a fleet of warships and they are busy modernizing it."

"Impossible!" Koor exclaimed.

"You are quite correct, Grand Admiral, but I'm afraid it is true nonetheless."

The Council table erupted in pandemonium. Apparently, the news was too much for members of the Council. The prospect of Terran legions transported by their own fleets was worse than any Scythian threat.

Admiral Koor couldn't get the Councilors to come to order. It wasn't until she pulled out her gun and shot the communicator out of the hand of the Syraptose Ambassador that the Councilors emerged from their panic. The Syraptose turned his pudgy face to her in shock, unable to utter a single word of protest. The rest of the table turned to her.

Admiral Koor holstered her gun, and said, "That's better. We'll get nothing done with this yammering. It's exactly what the next Alexander wants. He will play to our weakness; that is, he'll divide us and pick us off one by one. Our only hope is to maintain a concerted front." She turned her hard eyes on She-Rok. "Ambassador, would you please elaborate. We're acting as if Alexander himself is on our doorstep. Is he?"

"No, Admiral, he is not. Before we get too caught up in this hysteria let me ease your minds somewhat. We know Terra has indeed been in the first stages of exploring their solar system. Our conjecture is that this effort is a desperate attempt to modify their primitive intra-system vessels into defensive systems. They have correctly surmised that if the Chem come they will not land on Terra and engage in a terrestrial war, which would be much to Terra's advantage. Rather Chem warships will stand off the planet and bombard it to dust. All the planetary projectors in the galaxy would not change the outcome of that engagement. Therefore, they are doing anything and everything they can to make the Chem pay dearly before they come into bombardment range. In our considered opinion there is nothing in this to be overly concerned of. Any Terran fleet which results from this enormous expenditure of energy will be wholly defensive in capability, and just as tied to the Terran system as their exploratory ventures. They simply do not have the time to build a fleet capable of threatening us."

There was a murmur of approval and relief at She-Rok's conclusions, and the Hrang continued.

"There are other developments which will be of interest to all of us. We have been keeping track of the Chem build up as well, and in doing so we have discovered that the Chem attacked and destroyed a Scythian vessel. In the process they captured a Terran from the vessel. We don't know why the Terran was on board, but it's very probable that he was a military liaison of some kind. Whatever his previous role he is now under the scrutiny of the Chem. Their obvious intent is to study their foes and so have a better understanding of what they will face when they attack Terra. In fact, the Chem consider this Terran to be so important that Nazeera of Chem herself took charge of the interrogation on her return to Chem from Rome."

"How do you know all of this?" Sheer'nhak asked. "The Chem are usually quite secretive about matters such as these."

"We had a bit of fortune," the Hrang answered, "and it turns out that won't be secret for long. We gained access to a tape which was meant for broadcast sometime in the future. The Chem sentenced the Terran to Pantrixnia, their prison planet. As all of you know it is not so much a prison as a place of execution. We've all seen the broadcasts. They are a Chem version of the Terran gladiatorial games."

"Yes, yes, what of the tape? How does it explain Terran intentions?" Koor asked impatiently.

"I will play the tape presently, and you may see for yourselves. Please excuse the poor quality. It is a hurried copy of a copy provided by the Chem Assemblage to one of their ethernet broadcast companies."

In the center of the table a holographic projection began to play. It was a copy of Alexander's trial before the Chem Assemblage. She-Rok allowed it to run its full length, and a nervous silence followed every word. When the tape finished the ambassadors glanced at one another, dread in their expressions. She-Rok addressed the obvious question, telling them, "It is a strange coincidence that the Scythians had on board their ship a Terran claiming to be none other than Alexander, or more properly his heir. It may also be coincidence that the Chem seem to accept him as such.

She-Rok consulted a handheld screen for a moment, then added, "We can't know for certain, but it's obvious that during the questioning the Terran is bothered by the distinction. He attempts to dissuade Nazeera of Chem that he is the representative of Terra, and even goes so far as to plead ignorance for his people. When these attempts fail to move Nazeera he shows his true self. Let me repeat the latter section for you all." She-Rok pressed a lighted switch on his console and the projection zoomed in to show Alexander pointing a threatening finger at the Chem. In a commanding voice he said,

"Do what you will with me, if you can. I defy you to the end. Gauge well what you see in me; for it will return to you five billion fold! It will come to you with fire and fury, and it shall never stop until the thirst for vengeance is forever sated!"

"Thus did Alexander of Terra show his true self," She-Rok continued, "and in doing so reveal what his intentions are. The Terrans know of

Chem's plans, obviously through our friends the Scythians. Alexander's plan may have been to strike at the Chem Empire. Fortunately, the Chem interrupted his preparations, striking when the Terran Overlord was off-world negotiating with his Scythian allies. The Chem now have Alexander, and they shall take care of him before he could lead his people to the stars."

She-Rok looked around the room for confirmation of his conclusion, but all he saw was nervous skepticism.

"I sense you are unconvinced with the evidence. It is sketchy, I admit, as we have no concrete data concerning the current Terran political situation. There is some history on this particular Terran, he was a famous gladiator but there are no records of his political career. The last power struggle of note on Terra was fifty periums ago between the warlords Kennedy and Khrushchev but that resulted in a stalemate. According to Scythian report, conflict on Terra has been continuous since that time, but without resultant unification. It is probable that the Scythians mislead us as far as the rise to power of the Terran formerly known as Thorsson, now Alexander Thorsson."

"Probable? She-Rok it is not a probability but a certainty!" Koor swore. "I will hazard to say that none of us doubt that he is none other than Alexander, the heir of Alexander the Great. Terra has been unified beneath our very eyes and we knew nothing about it until it was almost too late!"

"The Chem are to be congratulated for their watchfulness, even as the Scythians are to be damned for their treachery!" Sheer'nhak spat, beside himself in indignation. "To be so duped by the Scythians that they conspired with the Terran Overlord without our suspecting is detestable. My only joy is that the Scythians will more than likely pay for their double-dealing with their civilization. If the Chem leave any of them un-skinned the Seer'koh will make it our duty to finish the job!"

"If they have the chance," Koor reminded her comrade. "The Chem will have to triumph over the Terrans first."

"But the Terrans will be without their Overlord," She-Rok reminded them. The rest of the table looked to the Hrang, and the reptile smiled. "My friends it took the chaotic Terrans two millennia to find their Overlord, and the heir to Alexander's legend. Now he is in the safe keeping of the Chem, and soon he will be nothing but a short lived spectacle on the Galactic ethernet. Alexander shall die on Pantrixnia for all to see. With him will die Terra. Without Alexander there is no cohesive Terran threat and the Chem will do what the Chem do best: conquer and destroy their enemies. Terra will cease to be a civilized world, unless the Chem seek to settle it. Chem ardor will be spent on Terra and Scythia, saving us from them and extinguishing forevermore the Legend of Alexander."

CHAPTER 16:
A WALK IN THE PARK

Alexander peered down the dark undulating tunnel. The comparison to being inside someone's intestine couldn't be more uncomfortable, or more appropriate.

A short way ahead the passage widened somewhat, but in the midst of that larger space the warm sour air sparkled with flashes of light—like blinking Christmas lights. They didn't cast any illumination on the passage, and he knew that he didn't want to touch them. He approached them carefully, meaning to slide to the side of the passage and pass them by. There was plenty of room to get through them, but as he approached the lights Alexander heard a multitude of chimes. The sparkling lights moved toward him.

He froze.

The lights stopped, but one stopped so close that he could feel it's brilliance on his skin. It was still inches away, but it roasted him as if the light were a small inferno.

Alexander stepped slowly, carefully back.

"You're sure this is how I get my memories back?" Alexander asked Nazeera. She stood behind him at a safe distance.

"You should be cognizant of the concept of association, Alexander."

"Yes, like I associate Nazeera with peril," he growled. He stooped low, being careful to make no sudden movement. He took a round rock and rolled it along the rough floor ahead of him. The sparkles flurried around it, emitting a plethora of pops and zaps. When the rock stopped they took up their positions in the middle of the passage again.

Alexander took another rock and eased towards the sparkles. When he was within a meter of the dangerous cloud he tossed the rock back whence he came—toward Nazeera. The sparkles took off after the rock, and Alexander moved forward, taking care not to walk faster than the rock rolled. After moving beyond the spot guarded by the sparkles Alexander stopped and glanced back.

The rock stopped at Nazeera's feet, but she stood there unconcerned as the sparkles attacked it. When they were finished they began to float back to their station. Nazeera stepped smoothly up to them.

Alexander grinned as the sparkles moved toward her.

Nazeera simply smiled and raised her hands. She moved them outward and then back in as if weaving on an unseen loom. Half the sparkles followed one hand and half the other. They went out and rushed back in, out then in. Each time they rushed in the sparkles crossed paths and some collided. When they ran into each other the emitted a flurry of angry sparks and went out. After doing it a half dozen times only a single sparkle remained. Nazeera drew her hands apart and it split in two. When it crashed back together it snuffed itself out with a plaintiff sizzle.

"That was a much more elegant solution than mine, I'll admit, but how does it get my memory back?"

Nazeera touched her sleeve.

Alexander was in the cockpit of his purple fabric covered Fokker Triplane. Ahead of him was a Bristol Fighter—a two seat Tommy scout with a dangerous rear facing gun. Without thinking Alexander jinked to the left, but stopped the plane before it traveled more than a few meters.

The rear gunner tried to lead his target and shot a burst wide.

Alexander jinked to the right and down.

The gunner missed again.

Alexander jinked up and to the right, then down and to the left.

The gunner shot a steady stream around the sky in his frustration. His gun jammed.

Alexander was in range. As the gunner pounded on the breech of his gun, Alexander sent two short bursts into the Bristol's engine. Smoke poured out of the Brit plane. Alexander smelled the unmistakable odor of burning oil—and the sickly terrifying stench of gasoline.

He was back in the tunnel, and a profusion of Prussian memories flooded his mind. He shook his head, and muttered, "So this is what passes for therapy on Chem."

The rest of the morning was similar. For Alexander, it was like an Indiana Jones obstacle course with short breaks for movies. It was hard work, and more dangerous than he'd have liked. It wouldn't look good if he got himself killed before they sent him to Pantrixnia.

At last they exited the tunnel onto a path which led through a dense jungle. Nazeera had to tell him the session was over, and this was Chem proper.

"So Alexander, what do you think of my world?"

"It reminds me of the tropics of the Spanish Main," he said, as a thousand bits of memory and experience whirled around in his head. Four hundred years past he attacked ships and towns on the steaming coast of South America, and the Chem woods carried the same heaviness in the moist air, the same all pervading heat, and the same buzz of insects in his ears. Alexander found a multitude of memories awakening at every turn. They demanded his attention. He was finding the reality of his past lives wasn't as advantageous as he anticipated.

"Are you finding the memory recall protocol helpful in identifying your past lives?"

"It's hard to say, at the moment," he answered truthfully, stooping to dip his hand in the cool water of a small stream that cut across their path. The jungle brought a score of episodes too interesting for his twentieth-century mind to ignore. At the moment they were not experiences he could draw on, but experiences which intruded upon him nonetheless. The act of conversation became a management struggle, and he had to push the intriguing memories aside so as to dwell on the present. Maybe Nazeera knew this, if past life memories were so accessible in her world, and maybe that was why she didn't balk at giving Alexander such access.

He didn't regret his strategy, but like many things that look good on the surface he had to have patience with his newfound awareness. The old adage of taking one step back for every two steps forward applied perfectly here, but at the time he could ill afford going back at all.

"I see you spent much of your adult life in this same climate when you were a pirate," Nazeera mused, reviewing an electronic notepad built into the sleeve of her coat—she wore it regardless of the heat because, as she told Alexander, it was an environmental garment that kept her warm or cool at need.

"I find it strangely coincidental that your career as a pirate catapulted you into the echelons of nobility; it's rather like your advancement from gladiator to warlord."

"You have an active imagination, Nazeera."

She made a note with the tip of her finger.

"So what did you think of our session this morning?"

Alexander rubbed his shoulder, which was still sore. "I didn't think memory recall would be so—so painful. Do all the Chem go through such trials?"

"No, trials such as those are reserved for a select few."

"You've been through them then."

"I have."

Alexander nodded, "I thought so, but I still think you did a masterful job. I was thoroughly impressed."

"May I remind you that you're the one being evaluated," Nazeera told him.

"You just keep thinking that," Alexander smiled.

Nazeera allowed Alexander to eat in a clearing with tables. His lunch waited for him. She did not share his meal.

"You're going to waste away if you don't eat something," Alexander complained. Nothing he could say changed her mind.

After lunch they continued to walk down the path. Here and there the forest thinned and Alexander saw Chem buildings soaring out of the jungle like enormous metallic trees. Canopy-like platforms sprouted from branch-like arms, arches and trunks. The buildings were purple, jade, rust, and crimsons—all the colors of the vibrant Chem landscape.

"It's amazing and beautiful—much like you."

Nazeera glanced away, and then she laughed, and said, "That's an ancient interrogation technique, Alexander, but thank you for the compliment anyway. Do you have the same opinion of Terran cities; do they reflect their inhabitants?"

"Too much so, I'm afraid," he said, telling her of the sprawling, teeming, concrete canyons. He followed her up a rope ladder and into the lower branches of a tree. A narrow, swaying, seemingly flimsy bridge of rope and branches swung from the tree into space. Nazeera started onto the span. Alexander swallowed hard and struck out after her, trying to appear calm. He stole a look down. The green carpet of the forest was at least thirty meters down.

"You were saying?" Nazeera prompted him.

"What?"

"You were describing Terran cities, Alexander. What's the matter is your memory that short or are you agitated over something?"

"What in the world would I have to be agitated over?" Alexander growled to himself. A hundred meters in front of them was a sheer gorge wall. A hundred meters below a boiling brown river flowed through the jungle. Alexander clenched his jaws. He hated heights.

"Are you alright, Alexander?"

"Of course, I'm invigorated is all. I've been cooped up in cells and ships for who knows how long!" he lied. Then before she could prompt him again, he forced himself to talk about the mundane. "Terra as a whole views cities as a triumph over nature, not a complement. We build them as our monument to progress, in a way, but it's a haphazard exercise. There's no true order to the founding or creation of such a thing. It rises, lives, and falls as an entity within itself."

"Do Terrans pride themselves on competition with nature?"

"I would say Terrans pride themselves not in competition, but in mastery of nature. It is altogether a fleeting and false pride."

"That's surprising, especially considering Terra has no weather control, no geophysical stabilization system and no planetary protection screens. You are subject to the whims of nature, yet you build monuments to false beliefs. They are monuments destined to perish."

"Perhaps we simply want the comfort of the moment. Terra is a dynamic world, and thousands upon thousands come to grief because of it every year. We fear nature, and with good reason: we can't control it. That in itself isn't new. We've invented a host of Gods and Goddesses to explain the mysteries of nature, but in the end we fear it because of our own physical inadequacy. Of all the creatures of Terra, we are least physically able to cope. Without our minds we would not exist." They were halfway across and Alexander began searching for the stairs at the other end. There didn't appear to be any. Surely she didn't expect him to climb that sheer face?

"You can't understand the irony of your statement, Alexander," Nazeera smiled. "Among sentient beings none are more physically evolved than Terrans. You are stronger, faster and hardier than any other sentient. You are also the most barbaric. That piques our curiosity, but it's the brilliance with which you make technology serve your destructive nature that shakes us to our very cores."

Alexander sighed, and said, "You're not alone. We fear ourselves more than any other danger, even a hypothetical alien invasion. We've lived with the very real possibility of self destruction for almost fifty years. I thought we'd won over it, but I suppose in the end it will be our fault after all," Alexander said. "We are not completely hopeless, though. We learn and grow in maturity, and as we do our benevolent side becomes more dominant. I can't compare Terrans to other cultures, but I know of no other creature which can be so self sacrificing. There is nobility in us that I think must carry on. I would hope, after all is said and done between us that Terra has nothing to fear of Chem. Yet if I fail, and if Terra falls it will be our own undoing. It has long been said amongst us that we are our own worst enemies."

"What a tragic philosophy."

"Not nearly as tragic as this ending when I fall from that cliff!" Alexander mused, and so engrossed was he in the possibility of climbing that cliff he didn't mind where he set his foot. His boot slipped on the side of the rope bridge where the spray from the river made it slick. His left foot plunged into space and he straddled the narrow catwalk. A sharp stinging blow hit his groin. His hands slipped on the rope. Alexander fell.

CHAPTER 17:
EVOLUTION

In the backwater Terran system, the sensational phenomenon of contact with the Scythians erupted into a chaotic profusion of activity. The arrival of the Scythians caused a sensation to be sure, but it was news of the imminent Chem invasion that set off a near panic. When the Scythians offered to arm Terrans, however, the ancient Terran ability to adapt to change asserted itself, and panic gave way to single minded effort.

That effort was evident everywhere, except in the small ante-chamber adjoining the CODOTS council room. Admiral Augesburcke sat quietly, listening to the discussion of his four department heads. Roshani Darya was a beautifully aristocratic politician from Egypt, and headed the state department of CODOTS. She was never at a loss for opinion, and never fearful of voicing it.

"We must, I think, continue to try and discover the motive behind the arrival of the Scythians. Their dubious desire to arm us as their protector is suspicious at best. I abhor the thought of Terra entering the company of galactic civilizations as a mercenary state; especially in concert with the Scythians. Despite their apparent concern, I don't think they're being honest about the situation. If there's a possibility of a diplomatic avenue out of this we must investigate it. Perhaps we can still contact the Chem through diplomatic channels."

General Sampson, formerly of the US Army, agreed. "The explanation of Scythian benevolence as a driver for their actions is completely transparent. They're hiding something. No doubt, it would help us to know exactly what and why they're here. However, there is also no denying the fact that the Chem are coming. It's all over the ethernet, and it's not just Chem broadcasts."

Sampson punched up a display on his laptop and transferred it to the main screen. A half dozen different feeds with different alien broadcasters popped up. They all spoke in translated English, and the agitation in their voices was obvious. He turned the sound down. "As you can see we've intercepted broadcasts from all twelve identified cultures outside our system. To our distinct disadvantage there is one common link: the Galactics, all of them, look upon us as the aggressors. I must admit I was surprised.

"Somehow I expected we'd come on the scene as unknowns. The opposite seems to be the case. Everyone from the military controlled Chem to the obscure Hederans think they know everything about us and our aspirations. Every other broadcast on the ethernet is about the "Legend of Alexander," and the violent ascension of the Terran species into the galaxy. It's incredible!"

"It's insane, this Alexander the Great business," Darya nodded. "Who could imagine such an idea capturing the populace of a civilized galaxy?"

"It's certainly unfortunate, but it's not an irrational conclusion based on their limited knowledge of us," Doctor Juhma Koto, a Psychologist from Zambia interjected. "Much of what I can conclude is based only on conjecture, of course. Building psychological profiles for the Galactics cannot be done without some comparison to our own Terran psyche, which we understand imperfectly at best. Still, according to our observations, given the information supplied to the Galactics by the Scythians, and according to what the Galactics have broadcast compared with what the Scythians have admitted to us, it is quite possible, even probable, that the Galactics could paint just such a picture of us. Think of the data we made available to a race of beings desiring to portray us exactly as the Galactics now see us. You don't need to sift through Terran history very carefully to amass evidence which would be patently insurmountable."

"By which you mean to say that you consider diplomatic channels as impossible at this time?" Darya asked.

"You ask for a sure answer where there is insufficient data, Ms. Darya," Doctor Koto said.

"I have come to regard your opinions as rational, Doctor, despite my own desires. I would accept your guesses at face value."

"Then I'm afraid I would agree with your assessment, but for more than one reason. You see, the Galactics view us as barbarians. They justly fear us even as Rome feared the barbarians of Europe despite the disparity in technology and civilization. More than that, however, they fear Alexander. I use the name because to the Galactics it's more than a name. However it may have occurred, the Galactics have turned Alexander the Great into a half mythical, half real hero who will one day lead Terra to the stars. That journey will have one easily defined purpose: a continuation of Alexander's conquests. To the Galactics the natural aspiration of all Terrans is the continuation of Alexander the Great's conquests, and in their opinion, he is what we accept as the ultimate pinnacle of the Terran condition.

"We all strive to be like Alexander, but even if we cannot be Alexander we can still take part in attaining his goals. It's a form of bonding and identification that all civilizations must have in one shape or form if they are to advance. It's tragic that this mechanism is so damning; still, it's understandable considering the data available. The Galactics formed their opinion of us from a limited and focused source of data supplied exclusively by the Scythians. Although the Galactic opinion is without foundation that fact is, unfortunately for us, irrelevant. Nothing we can do or say will easily change it Ms. Darya."

"Why is that? Propaganda is a well documented tactic both politically and militarily. Why can't we put our own spin on this—we've an army of political advisors and handlers who live for this sort of thing?"

"Two reasons," Doctor Koto replied. "First, the accumulated evidence is already out there and second because it's factual. Propaganda based on falsehood is difficult enough to combat, but propaganda based on facts, even incomplete facts, is entirely different. We'd have an extraordinarily difficult time refuting it. We're not just another galactic civilization; we're outside their norm. They are bound to have a significant level of paranoia about us—even under the best conditions.

Remember we're dealing with a galaxy that's been at peace for almost thirteen thousand of our years. They're not used to war, and even if they were to recall their past wars they would remember that those wars were intercultural."

Koto accessed a file on his laptop and sent the information to the room's viewer. The numbers caused an audible gasp in the audience. "The last civil wars on record, the last intercultural wars that we have been able to access I should say, were the Chem civil wars which led to the Chem Wars of Expansion. Even those conflicts were tame in comparison to our own, however. Galactic warfare evolved long ago into a conflict which excluded the civilian population. A warrior caste is responsible for military operations, and has been for the entirety of recorded history as far as we can tell. Casualties were therefore limited to combatants. Let me put this in perspective; the casualties suffered in the three days of the Battle of the Somme, in World War One, are roughly equivalent to the total casualties suffered by the Galactics in the entire millennia of the Chem wars. Terran casualties for this century are greater than the casualties of all the Galactic wars on record for the last one million years combined."

"Are we really that brutal a people?" Darya exclaimed.

Koto sighed, and said, "War is very civilized in the present day galaxy, though it appears to have been otherwise at some time in the distant past. From what we can tell several of the civilizations in the known galaxy are close to ten million or so years old. It's difficult to say without full access to the Galactic's records. The Chem are one of the oldest cultures but also one of the most warlike."

Ms. Darya asked the obvious question, "Doctor Koto, what would it take to change the opinion of the Galactics, or modify it into a less harmful image of ourselves?"

"That addresses perhaps the most difficult aspect of the Galactic paranoia," Doctor Koto admitted. "This is because the portrayal of Terra in this aggressive manner persists for generation after generation. Literally since the time of Alexander the Great, the Galactics have expected this terrible invasion from Terra. It's now a palpable part of their psyche. The Legend of Alexander transcends our definition of legend and enters into what we would call psychosis. This is as absolute and real to the Galactics as their morning meal. It's ingrained into their military, their political debate, and even into the education of their children. It's impossible to combat a base of knowledge so thoroughly entrenched with a propaganda campaign."

"How do we combat it?"

"Somehow, we must mollify the Galactics. Perhaps, if we can gain time by bluff, using the Legend of Alexander to our advantage, we can gain enough respite to allow the Galactics to realize we're not the threat they think we are."

"That would be difficult, at best," Ms. Darya conceded. "Considering the numbers of our own people slaughtered, enslaved, and impoverished by our own hand how can they expect rational behavior from us? Damn, my own people from the Middle East are still stoning women—the backwards, ignorant bastards. If we're so capable of heinous acts how can they even expect mercy? I don't see the prospect of diplomacy bearing any substantial fruit at the time being. It seems I am superfluous."

"You are many things, Ms. Darya, but never superfluous," Admiral Augesburcke chortled, entering the discussion. "However, Doctor Koto makes his point poignantly. We are reviled throughout the galaxy, and whatever the Scythians' motives we can expect no help from any other quarter. If there were a way to show the Galactics our Humanity, for lack of a better term, I would welcome it and put Ms. Darya on the ethernet. As things are, however, the less said the better. We are unacceptably vulnerable, but we carry the brand of a bully amongst the Galactics. I agree with Doctor Koto's assessment. If we can put any semblance of a facade together to go with the fear the Galactics have of us we may be able to bluff our way out of this. It's a small chance, but it's better than coming to blows."

"To that end you are correct, Admiral," Doctor Koto agreed. "Our primary weapon is the psychosis of the Galactics. Fear is an age old weapon. The idea of the "paper tiger" has merit."

"To that end we need a "paper fleet." How is that part of our effort coming along?" Augesburcke asked, addressing General Sampson.

Sampson shrugged, "We've just started to tear into the "Iowa," but beyond that I'm afraid this is Doctor Hashimoto's territory."

Hashimoto cleared his throat uncomfortably. He was the obvious choice as head of the science department, but as a native of Japan, there was an unspoken schism between him and the Admiral. Augesburcke's father fought in the war against Japan, and scant months prior to "VE" day he'd been captured and executed in a prison camp.

"Well?" Augesburcke demanded.

"Thus far, I think we've done well," the scientist told Augesburcke, bringing up a hologram of the "Iowa" in the center of the conference table. It was a piece of technology only days old to the Terrans at the table, but they already took it as a matter of course.

Harsh white lights illuminated the battleship against the black night; a bulbous Scythian tender floated overhead. Hashimoto continued, illuminating features of interest with a laser pointer as he talked. "Ingenuity has made a seemingly mad scheme, excuse me Admiral, annoyingly practical. While it is true the requisitioned hulls are not space faring ships but naval warships there is surprisingly little difficulty in adapting them for space flight using Galactic technology. In fact, the vessels of Terra's blue water navies, which are of course ridiculously antiquated by Galactic standards, are strangely well suited to the task, with some slight modifications. In some instances our lack of advancement has actually proven to be an advantage. Galactic warships depend a great deal on structural integrity fields for their structural strength. Our navies, bereft of this advancement, are naturally designed to endure a constant and significant pounding at sea. They're far superior in structural strength to any galactic space vessel."

As they watched, a Scythian tender tried in vain to raise the "Iowa" with its blue anti-gravitational beam. The bow of the great ship began to rise, but the stern stayed firmly planted on the dry-dock. The Scythian ship started to wobble under the strain, and the "Iowa" started to shudder. Klaxons sounded all over the shipyard, and workers scurried away from the leviathan. The "Iowa" began to list to port and fall out of the air.

Augesburcke shot out of his chair. "Bloody Hell, we're going to lose her!"

CHAPTER 18:
THE TROUBLE WITH MEMORIES

Instinctively Alexander wrapped his legs around the rope bridge. His body swung wildly beneath the span and all he could see was the brown water below pocked with innumerable slimy boulders.

"Blast!" he cursed, trying to stem a rising tide of panic.

"Alexander are you trying to escape?" Nazeera asked, seemingly unconcerned. "I should tell you, I can shoot you just as easily in the river as from here."

Alexander cursed again, crunching to get a grip on the rail rope. With a Herculean effort he pulled himself back onto the bridge and stood up, sweating and clutching the ropes.

"If that was an escape attempt it was clumsy."

Alexander bit back an angry reply, and said, "Clumsy is the word for it, all right!" He stifled his racing heart, but he couldn't do anything about the sweat streaming from his forehead—he could feel the beads of perspiration literally popping from his pores.

Nazeera turned around and danced the rest of the way to the cliff. She stepped light as a feather, unconcerned with the rickety bridge, the precipitous heights or the possible enemy at her back.

Alexander couldn't have caught her if he wanted to. He labored the rest of the way, clutching tightly every step of the way. When he reached the cliff his worst fears were realized. There was no door. There was no stair. There was only a hundred meters of cracked, wet, vine-clad, black rock.

"I do hope you've no more displays of clumsiness, Alexander," Nazeera smiled. "A fall from here would be truly damaging—even to a Terran's physique. We might not be able to repair you, or think you worthy of the effort!"

She leapt up the cliff like a spider. She stopped ten meters above him and looked down at him. With a ferocious smile, Nazeera drew her gun. "Just in case you get any ideas, there's no going back Alexander."

Whoomph! Whoomph!

Each shot parted one of the cables that formed the hand rails. Alexander scrambled onto the cliff face before he fell again. He looked up to see Nazeera laughing.

She holstered her gun, and said, "You Terrans don't scurry very well despite your brawn. I wonder if you can climb at all." Without waiting for an answer she flew up the cliff as if it were a ladder.

Alexander glowered at her. At this moment, he truly hated her.

Alexander followed in a more sedate manner, but he kept climbing and he didn't look down. He took some comfort in his Viking ancestry. Often as a child he climbed the cliffs of his family's fjord. That is, he belatedly remembered, until he fell and broke his legs on the rocks below.

Perhaps that's why he was afraid of heights. Yet in his last incarnations he'd attacked that fear by flying. He shook his head and grumbled, "How are the Chem supposed to understand me; I don't understand me!"

By the time he'd finished his short psychoanalysis Alexander was at the top. He stepped onto a flat verdant mesa, trying to hide his immense relief of being on level ground again. To do this he turned and looked around at the vistas. What he saw caused his breath to stop in his lungs.

The rolling plains and ancient mountains of Chem stretched out to a distant line of green capped peaks. It was a dryad carpet of emerald forests and misty rivers under a pale blue sky. From every pocket Chem skyscrapers lunged for the sky like living things. It was awe inspiring and breathtakingly beautiful.

"Well, that was a proper work out! I've not climbed like that in years. We Terrans aren't spiders you know!"

Nazeera looked at him with a strange expression, as if she knew his thoughts were along a different line, but she couldn't guess what. At length she beckoned him, and he followed her into what appeared to be a park.

Alexander was about to question her about this newer and safer turn of events when they happened upon a Chem mother walking with a small boy and pushing the Chem version of a stroller.

Alexander stopped suddenly, no less surprised than the Chem woman. That Chem security should allow such an unwarranted meeting was unthinkable, but the expression on the woman's face was unmistakable. At first all she saw was an alien, and the unusual occurrence registered only slightly. Then the process of identification went further, and in a moment there was no mistaking just what alien was on the path with her and her children. She reacted with shock and dismay, pulling the interested young boy next to her and standing between the hulking Terran and her infant.

Her expression struck Alexander forcibly. He remembered coming home a fugitive in his life as a pirate. Unannounced, dressed in his barbaric garb, he snuck onto the grounds of his house and surprised his sister as she took a walk with her children—in almost exactly the same circumstances. She didn't recognize him at first and was equally as concerned over her children's safety.

Alexander raised a hand up, palm outward, instinctively. Giving the woman a sheepish smile he assured her of his harmlessness. The woman was unconvinced, and Alexander turned to Nazeera and said, "This is the real tragedy in of all this. On Terra, at this moment, are millions of children just like these. They are as ignorant of evil and prejudice as is this little boy. They don't care about the political boundaries of Terra, or the presumptuous military conquests of Alexander. They are innocent.

"It may be fitting for adults to reap what they sow, but that our children should suffer for it is perhaps the greatest crime in all our history. If we could learn to see our actions in that light maybe Terra could overcome her adolescence and make a positive contribution to the galaxy. Certainly we have that potential. Beyond all the glory and horror of our past we always had the choice of which way to go. I want to think that somehow Terra's children will still have that choice."

Nazeera touched the screen at her wrist.

A silver automaton appeared out of the sky and shrouded Alexander in a blue beam. It sped back over the river, dragging a helpless Alexander away.

✠   ✠   ✠

A day later Nazeera was in her holographic lounge. A holographic data tape was playing, but Nazeera wasn't watching it. She was in the middle of it.

She was dressed as Alexander was in a purple uniform with a pair of horns painted on the purple helm, and she mimicked his actions. Standing stolidly, hands on hips, her breath steamed from her lips as the line of white-clad warriors with the hated star on their silver helms approached. Alexander lowered himself into a three point stance, and Nazeera did likewise.

The warrior in front of Nazeera launched the dark spheroid to the Captain behind him and Alexander rushed forward like a charging bull. Nazeera launched herself into the melee. Instantly she was in the midst of thrashing, crushing, whirling behemoths. She fought, writhed, wriggled and thrust but she was crushed under the mountainous men.

Then it was over. The warriors stopped suddenly and left for their own sides of the field; they prepared to start it all over again. A programmed Alexander helped her up.

"Don't think about the man in front of you," he said, voicing a relevant point gleaned from the data tapes. "You goal is to get the ball carrier—not beat your opponent."

Nazeera shook her head in frustration. "Computer, lower the size and mass of the players another ten percent."

The door to the lounge slid open and Nazar sauntered in. His usual bright smile gleamed as he said hello to his sister and surveyed the scene.

"Playing with the gladiators are we?" he said, cocking his head to the side with interest. "I can't say whether I enjoy their modern games more than the more fatal games of the last periums, but they are definitely entertaining. What are we doing, trying to delve deeper into our inimitable Alexander? I can't say you'll get much out of this. Terrans enjoy violence for violence's sake. There's not much mystery in that."

"Actually, this is from a special program on Alexander. He was a football gladiator, you know."

"No, I didn't, but I'm not surprised. What else is he suitable for? He's a warrior and intelligent. He may even be the Alexander we've all been anticipating, or dreading, depending on your point of view. I've already conceded my admiration for him."

"Yes, he is admirable as a warrior," Nazeera agreed, taking off her helmet and walking toward Nazar.

"Nazeera!" Alexander called, "Are you in or what?"

"Go on without me for a few plays, Alexander," Nazeera told him.

"I'm already double teamed!" Alexander complained with a huff, but it didn't stop him. It seemed to motivate him even further.

Nazeera punched up a regenerative drink from the server. She sipped it, and said, "I don't really need to watch the games to know that, but this was in the Scythian data files we captured. It is a summary of his short, but noteworthy career. Alexander was in the arena for five periums before becoming a military officer. Injury may have played a part in his transition as much as reward for his performance. I've asked Alexander his version of his career. It is fairly consistent with what I've seen here."

"He's forthcoming then in your interrogations?"

"He is."

"Yes, but?"

"Things have grown interesting in the last few days."

"Do tell!"

"Don't get your hopes up, Nazar! I mean something entirely different—I've been running Alexander through the trials."

"At what level?" Nazar asked, obviously surprised.

"My own—the levels required for the Triumvirate and the seat of the Elder."

"That's classified—how has he performed?"

"He's done well, Nazar, he's done very well," she said. She stretched her arms as if they pained her. "It's been all I could do to endure the same trials—I spent all of last night in a recuperation chamber. Alexander was no worse for wear this morning."

"What about the mental aspects?"

"Impressive."

Nazar whistled.

"And the time spent outside the compound is, well, unexpectedly intriguing."

"Indeed and where did you go today?"

"I took him to the historic district of the city," she said, and she ordered the hologram to show the recording of their visit. It showed Alexander and Nazeera walking the streets. The throngs parted as they noticed him, but then they grew curious and approached him.

"That created a stir."

"Yes, it did. The people were almost as interested in Alexander as he was in them. I could read the surprise in their faces when they spoke to him, finding out he wasn't just a mindless barbarian. You know some people even remembered him from his career in the games."

Nazar gasped in surprise. "Good grief, they're having their holograms taken with him! He seems quite gracious in answering their questions and granting their requests. He's working the crowds. That sounds dangerous."

"Alexander is not a politician, but he is genuine. The people see that, and are surprised by it."

"Are you? That seems to me to be the primary question. Alexander may be admirable to the people, but how does he seem to you? You've had three decurns of interrogation with him, and I note that these last sessions were of a more personable manner than I would expect. What is your opinion of him? Do you believe his story?"

"I have come to think of Alexander as a genuine being," Nazeera said carefully.

"Really, Nazeera," Nazar said, and his smile grew conspiratorial. He nudged her in the ribs. "That is as guarded an opinion as I've ever heard from you."

"I've grown to respect him, Nazar," she said, and then she hesitated, adding somewhat thoughtfully, "I must admit, though, that I look forward to our sessions."

Nazar's eyes brightened with interest, but he avoided the obvious question. Instead, he announced, "Alexander is on one hand a stereotypical Terran: strong, fast, large, and as the files show, ferocious. On the other hand he's a disturbingly charming individual. Alexander is more of a paradox than ever. We need to be very careful how we use him, or abuse him."

Nazeera switched off the tape and left the room, Nazar in tow. She went into her private office and poured drinks. Handing one to Nazar, she said, "I spoke with the Elder this evening. He wants you to command the cruiser which will take Alexander to Pantrixnia. Congratulations."

"That will be a dubious honor," Nazar replied, raising his glass to hers. "Whatever his position with the Terrans I cannot bring myself to dislike this fellow. If Alexander is truly representative of his race it seems to me that we should take a less fatal tact. Duty is binding, however. When am I to leave?"

"Tomorrow evening."

"Indeed, he's going that quickly. Does Alexander know?"

"Not yet. I shall tell him tomorrow."

"You are comfortable with the Pantrixnia decision?"

"The decision is final, Nazar. Watching Terran games is satisfying, but it is a field of play which we cannot compare ourselves. Pantrixnia has had many Chem combatants, now it shall have a Terran combatant. We will compare the data."

"You are trying to justify your decision, Nazeera."

"There is nothing I could do about it even if I would."

"Would you, though, if you could?"

Nazeera opened her mouth as if to answer, but stopped. Without a word she got up and left the room.

CHAPTER 19:
PAPER TIGERS

A Scythian voice came over the feed, saying excitedly, "We have to cut the anti-gravitational beam or we'll risk losing the ship."

"Belay that!" roared an obviously Terran voice. "Scythian tender two and three get your asses over to the "Iowa" now and put your anit-grav beams on the "Iowa." Stabilize the ship if you can't hold her aloft. Do it now!"

Two Scythian tenders turned towards the "Iowa" and in a few seconds they surrounded the huge battleship. They added their anti-gravitational beams to the "Iowa" and the battleship stabilized. Slowly it floated into the air.

Augesburcke, who'd been holding his breath, let out a whistle. "It looks as though our ships are a helluva lot heavier than Galactic vessels—that was a close one."

The Terran yard foreman agreed, and over the airwaves he was yelling, "Who do you people have doing your calculations? I thought you were advanced; that was just plain stupid! Don't you ever put one of my ships at risk like that again!"

The Scythian's reply was terse, which only prompted more yelling.

"At least our people aren't intimidated by the Scythians or their technology," Augesburcke smiled. "Go on Doctor."

"Another advantage we have is our naval vessels were built to be sealed against the elements, specifically water. Their compartmentalized layout and limited necessity for having any crew topside makes the modifications relatively simple given the Scythian resources. The process has not been as labor intensive as might have been thought at first glance, but it is extensive, and time consuming.

"The old American battleship "Iowa" is the initial test project. What we see here is a "tritanium bath;" i.e. a Scythian tender irradiates the warship with an energy bath infused with tritanium. This changes the molecular structure of the ship's steel hulls into a tritanium alloy, making the ship even stronger than it was to begin with. We've already gutted the engine room, the equipment there being, of course, quite useless. The enormous size of the compartment works greatly to our advantage and we've used it for every type and description of Galactic equipment. The equipment comes in largely self contained units and takes up much less space than the ships original machines, while doing far more for us."

Hashimoto clicked the display to one of the engine room. In the abandoned space were ten rows of fifteen minivan sized units. "Here are the graviton generators; they generate the necessary gravitational fields which enable the ship to maneuver in an atmosphere, create artificial gravity and dampen the enormous accelerations associated with space flight. You'll notice they look almost exactly like all the other units, which though ridiculously small, are actually life support units, fire control units, and replication/regeneration units. Even the heart of the ship, the superluminal matter-anti-matter core, looks like anything but what it is. That's it in the center of the bay, looking somewhat like two garage sized cathode ray tubes placed vertically and back to back.

"Fortunately, all the units are designed to be completely self contained, and little more is necessary than attaching the equipment to bulkheads and control boards. Power is supplied through from the engines through conduits, but that was not a serious engineering problem, and the enormous volume of the engine room made this relatively simple. The translight engines are mounted externally. We did this consistent with the Galactic technique, and frankly it makes our job easier. Despite their internal complexity they come intact, no assembly required so to speak, and all we needed to do was to weld them at the aft of the ship, one on either side, and attach them through energy conduits to the core."

"What about control for the equipment?" Augesburcke asked.

"We've kept with tradition and practicality by keeping the nerve center of the ship on the bridge. The entire ship can be controlled from the bridge, but manual overrides and redundant controls will be available on location as well as on the battle bridge, which is deep in the hull of the ship. The new consoles, as well as every other station on the ship, will use the ship's hull to transmit orders. The technique is elegantly simple. Each control board sends out pulses of code attuned to the molecular tritanium structure of the ship. The pulses actually make their way naturally through the metal lattice of the hull on the sub-atomic level. An engine command from the bridge will leave a coded transceiver as an energy pulse and travel by shortest pathway to a similarly coded transceiver. Should battle damage occur the signals will automatically travel to the receiver via the path of least resistance, so long as a path remains. It's ingenious, and frankly it's all that allows us to tackle this problem at all. There's no need for the miles of slow electronic wiring, and the millions of connections and switches that conventional controls would require."

"I'm impressed, Doctor, I am genuinely impressed," Augesburcke admitted. "How soon can we make her fly?"

"Fly? That's not such a problem; two days. However,"

"There's always a "but" with you people," Augesburcke sighed.

"I'm sorry Admiral, she'll fly but she'll be a true "paper tiger," at least for the moment. We have a problem with the armament."

"I thought the Scythians had more than they thought we could ever use?"

"They do. It's all stockpiled in the navy yards; everything from small caliber weapons to battleship rated blaster projectors. We've got the weapons. We even have a practical method of mounting the projectors: our rifled turret guns are perfect mounts for them. The rotation and elevation of the guns in turrets is something we take for granted terrestrially, but it's not found on Galactic guns. All Galactic projectors are stationary. Therefore, if we ever get them working it will put us in a situation similar to the United States Civil War clash between the "Monitor" and the "Merrimac." Only this time the "Monitor" will have the same number of guns as its adversary."

"What's the problem then?"

"Energy transfer, Admiral," Hashimoto said. "Galactic design uses the energy conduits to transfer the energy of the engines directly to the weapons. These conduits are laid down as the structural backbone of the ship due to the sheer size and mass of the conduits. It would take weeks to cut out enough of the "Iowa" to put in the framework of the conduits and then we'd have a mess putting her back together. There's got to be a better way. We're working on it, but the Scythians are no help. They know one way to do things, and if it doesn't work it's considered impossible."

"I doubt if they really want us to arm these babies all that badly," Augesburcke admitted, warming somewhat to the Doctors efforts. "Well done, well done, I may have spawned the idea, but if you pull it off I'll make sure you're known as the Physicist who taught a battleship to fly!"

"Thank you, Admiral but we've got a long way to go," Hashimoto told him.

"How long until she's ready for trials," Augesburcke asked.

"We're about halfway complete at this stage, so another week at least. With what we've learned, however, I think we can eventually hone the process down to six or seven days."

"A week to a space ship, not bad, but a warship is what I could really use," Augesburcke said.

"If we can figure out the energy problem, Admiral, you'll have more than a warship. I'm not a military man, but when we're done the "Iowa" will outclass any Galactic battleship in space."

Augesburcke's brows rose and Sampson chimed in. "The good Doctor is right. One of the advantages we have, Admiral is the homogeneity of the Galactics technology. This includes military technology as well. A Chem battleship and a Syraptose battleship are virtually interchangeable. Although Galactic technology is many years ahead of us it has remained at the same level for hundreds of thousands of years. The result is there are no secrets left. Everyone out there knows exactly what to expect from everyone else."

"And here we come with something based on our warfare, but with their experience; something completely new. That will be quite unsettling to their military commanders," Augesburcke mentioned, thinking hard on the matter.

"We'll have quite a different fleet of ships than the Galactics," the General continued. "We've over built our ships because we meant them for the rigors of sea duty, and the pounding of combat. The Galactic ships are like eggs, held together with energy fields. With a tritanium steel hull one hundred times thicker than any Galactic hull underneath her shields the "Iowa" could theoretically take punishment the Galactic battlewagons could only dream of. In addition, if we get the blaster problem worked out the "Iowa" will carry nine level thirty-seven blaster projectors, the largest ever designed. A standard Galactic battleship carries fourteen, but because they're in fixed batteries the most they can ever concentrate on a target is five, only half our broadside."

"The rifled turrets will also gain us a measure of efficiency over the Galactic projectors," Dr. Hashimoto added, laying a square metal case on the table. Opening the top, he took out a basketball sized sphere that looked like a huge translucent ruby. A metal flange fitted around the bottom of the sphere with a square cutout in the center roughly six inches to a side. Hashimoto explained, "This is a level seven blaster projector, roughly what you would find on a tank, or a tertiary battleship projector. The way the projector works is elegantly simple. Energy enters through a conduit connected to the metal flange and is focused by the projector—which is essentially an artificial lattice. Through manipulation of an electromagnetic field, the blaster beam can emanate from any portion of the projector along a path perpendicular to the surface. In other words, the beam has a range of travel of about fifteen degrees from the center axis. This gives the Galactic blasters enough versatility to be operated from fixed mounts, but there is a price. The "sweet spot" of the projector, that is where it emits its most powerful beam, is directly along the axis from the energy conduit. A radial interference pattern is set up in the projector which focuses the beam and the wider that pattern the more coherent and powerful the beam. As you focus the beam further from the center this pattern becomes asymmetrical. The Galactics have alleviated this problem to some extent by enlarging the projector to as near spherical as they can manage, but the fact of the matter is that the power of the blaster degrades along a curve as you progress from a firing angle of zero degrees to the maximum of fifteen degrees. Hopefully, we won't have that problem. Our projectors can remain fixed, firing from the "sweet spot" at one hundred percent efficiency at all times while the rifled turret aims at the target. While it sounds good theoretically this concept also adds another technical problem."

"And what is that?" Augesburcke sighed.

"It's the energy conduit tie in, Admiral. The Galactics gave up on the problem. That's probably one of the reasons they opted for a fixed projector. Their energy conduits are fixed paths from the engines to the blasters. That's a fairly simple concept which we can probably emulate fairly soon. Somewhere along the line we're going to have to get that energy from a fixed conduit to a projector that is moving around on the back end of a rifled gun barrel. We can't just strap on an accordion frame and the mathematics involved in creating a moving magnetic bottle is frankly beyond our capability. At the moment we're stuck."

Augesburcke sighed and shrugged. "I have every confidence you can solve the problem, Dr. Hashimoto. Do you have any other good news for me?"

"There are the engines," Sampson chimed in. "We got fleet salvage and surplus for all the rest of the gear, but the superluminal and sub-light engines are state of the art spares for the Scythian merchant fleet. They're pretty much brand new, and there's nothing faster. This is especially good because our ships are so much more massive than the Galactic warships. If we had equivalent sub-light engines we'd be a great disadvantage in maneuverability, but with these we'll at least be able to keep up with them."

"Well that is better news," Augesburcke grinned. "It's a pity we've so few of them though, battleships, that is. The American Navy is the only one that kept any around. There's only eight out there as either reserves or museum pieces. Now the Galactics built them in a ratio of five to a hundred. That would give the Chem Armada about thirty-seven or thereabouts to our eight."

"Forty-two actually, discounting the Homeworld Guardian Armada," General Sampson chimed in. "But things aren't quite that gloomy, Admiral."

"Forty-two to eight, I would like to know why not?"

"We've found out quite a bit of unexpected information on our own stockpiles since this Chem threat emerged," Sampson smiled, and he changed the holographic display to a satellite view of remote northern

Canada. As he zoomed in on Hudson Bay, he explained, "Immediately following the Second World War there was a strong public outcry for disarmament. The powers at hand realized a need to address the public desires, but at the same time the realities of the Cold War meant that we couldn't afford to get rid of our hard to replace assets. To address this paradox the powers that be fell back on a tried and true method: they lied. We ended up putting our high visibility assets on the chopping block. On paper, that is."

The hologram centered on an orderly group of dark specks against the blue water. As the camera zoomed in the specks grew into ships. "In reality, all the old battlewagons, heavy cruisers, carriers and the like went into mothballs in the fjords of Norway, the bays of Canada, the inlets of Western Australia, etc. They've been sitting there just waiting for a day like this."

"Why those sneaky bastards, I didn't even know about that. How many does that give us?"

"We can give you thirty-nine battlewagons for modification, Admiral. That should give the Chem something to look at!"

"Hot damn, we'll build a real damn fleet out of this yet!"

"May I interject a point?" Darya asked.

"By all means," Augesburcke told her.

"I share your enthusiasm for an aggressive deterrent, Admiral, but I feel I must point out that any deterrent, no matter how fearsome, must also be creditable. We may be able to build the ships, and even outfit them with armament, but how are we going to actually use them? The Galactics fear us for what we might become, and though we would have gone a long way towards realizing that fear we've still never fought a space battle. I don't pretend to know the business of the military, but do we think we could win such an engagement against a warrior race to which space is second nature?"

"Ms. Darya makes an excellent, if sobering point," Augesburcke admitted. "Could we win such a battle—doubtful? The learning curve in war is very steep very quickly, but the cost of experience is always casualties. I don't think we have that luxury."

"Maybe, but we do have the "Legend of Alexander," Doctor Koto reminded them. "Faced with a Terran fleet led by the heir to Alexander's throne who knows what the reaction of the Galactics would be?"

"We'd need an heir to that throne, Doctor. What do we do, hire an actor? Still, it's a course of action, and I think we're at a point where things could go either way," Augesburcke said. "That is a far cry from a few days ago, ladies and gentlemen. I commend you on a job well along the way. I think we can agree that bluff and bluster are our best options and we should pursue that route, maintaining our military battle option as a fall back plan. I think, Doctor Koto that Ms. Darya and you had best brainstorm with me on that very issue. As for Doctor Hashimoto and General Sampson, well gentlemen, you've got a fleet to build."

The meeting began to break up when an aide entered the room. "I'm sorry for the interruption, Admiral, but we thought you better see this." A feed appeared on the hologram. It was a dark amphitheater within which a single naked Terran male stood illuminated in a pillar of light. "We just picked this up off the ethernet. It's apparently a rebroadcast. The Chem have captured a Terran and are putting him on trial."

"Well, well, this gets more interesting every day. Roll the tape!" Augesburcke ordered, and the five most powerful people on Terra watched the trial of Alexander.

CHAPTER 20:
CONTENTION

Nazeera ushered Alexander into the small interrogation room for one last time. She informed him right off about his impending departure, but Alexander simply smiled at the information, and repeated the old adage of all good things coming to an end. Nazeera simply shook her head and pressed on ahead with business.

Their sessions could not truly be called interrogations, as Alexander was never asked to reveal information he wasn't already willing to give. The two shared a mutual respect and after the ground rules were worked out they could even admit to enjoying each other's company. There was a clear gulf between them created wholly by their particular duties and the conflicts therein, but it did not make them openly regret the opportunity before them. The conflict of their interests was an unpleasant reality to deal with, and it might have been made easier if not for a burgeoning electricity which slowly crossed all cultural, rational and practical divisions.

To make Nazeera's job more difficult, or at least more uncomfortable, the Elder tasked her with certain questions to ask the prisoner. They were subjects which tread on the line Nazeera and Alexander had established, and on the level of trust in their rapport. Nazeera was proud, and quite conscious of the agreement she made with Alexander, but she could not persuade the Elder that an agreement with a prisoner was one which should be honored. Alexander was Nazeera's charge in so much as the

Elder was satisfied with her progress. Nazeera was more concerned with understanding Alexander and his people than discovering the nuts and bolts of their status. The Elder, however, had a more practical view of the situation. In truth, if Nazeera had disagreed strongly enough the Elder would probably have relented, but secretly the questions to be asked dogged her as well. It was a short and unsatisfactory debate within herself, but there was really nothing for it. Still, when Nazeera brought an image up on the hologram it was the special of Alexander she studied the night previously, and nothing particularly momentous.

Alexander was used to Nazeera producing tapes of his memories, mostly of past lives, and having him explain the circumstances, emotions and motivations behind what he saw and what he remembered. It was surprising how quickly he'd been able to adapt to the flow of all the new memories. In the first day he doubted he would ever get a handle on it, but by the second the new memory files were no longer haphazardly forcing themselves upon him at the slightest prompting. Now they took their place amongst his established memories, waiting until they might prove useful. What Nazeera showed him now was completely different, however. It was an interview, the only interview he'd done after announcing his retirement from the NFL. He thought it irrelevant, but even more he wondered just how Nazeera had gotten a hold of it.

Nazeera brushed off the question, saying instead, "Let's talk about this, Alexander. We've discussed your career briefly, but now I would like to revisit it in more detail."

"Very well, it is your dime. What do you want to know?"

"I'm intrigued by your transition from a gladiator to a military officer," she told him, and as she spoke the metal interrogation room transformed. They were on a mountaintop. It was as if the Chem sheared off the last few meter of the peak to leave just enough room for their table and chairs.

Alexander glanced down from the dizzying height. He stomach tightened. He guessed that Nazeera's medical equipment was registering his responses, and his focus.

"Such rewards must be rare on Terra," she continued. "I would like to know how you managed it. Did you have a political sponsor?"

"No, I was never politically adept," Alexander said, trying to ignore their nest in the clouds. "That failure in my character was the primary reason I eventually left the military."

"We'll get to that," Nazeera said. The wind blew and it grew uncomfortably cold. She didn't seem to notice. "I want your comment on this portion of the file. The interviewer prods you about what could have been a "Hall of Fame" career, and presses you as to whether you are frustrated that injuries prevented consideration for such an honor. You're most combative."

The hologram centered on a younger version of Alexander. His hair was longer and not yet streaked with gray. The eyes were the same shade of volcanic green, though, and this younger Alexander flashed them with clear impatience. His bassoon voice barked at the interviewer, leaving no room for argument, "Am I frustrated to have to leave the game?" he asked, and then he threw his brawny arms in the air. "I suppose I have a right to be, but I can't really say that I am. I was an undersized nose tackle who lasted a good deal longer than anyone could have anticipated, but less than I could have hoped." Alexander clenched his teeth, but the cold bit him with a sharp stabbing pain. He began to shiver. "I had a good run, even if it was only for five years. You can't mention my name in the same breath as Page, Marshal or Eller; but I think my peers can appreciate my play one way or another. That lessens the impact a bit."

The interviewer leaned forward, saying, "Certainly playing for a smaller market team like the Vikings didn't help your notoriety, Alexander, but I think it only fair to remind you, and our viewers, that in five short seasons you accomplished a great deal. It was enough to earn you the title, "Alexander the Great." That's not a moniker lightly bestowed. Let me run down a list: five straight Pro Bowls; Rookie of the Year honors; led the Vikings in sacks and tackles behind the line of scrimmage five straight years; and most sacks in a five year period in NFL history. Some of the words that your adversaries used to describe you: "ferocious," "relentless," "the perfect predator," and "the most terrifying presence since Butkus." Not too bad. Doesn't that accomplishment count for something?"

Nazeera smiled and asked, "Why do you refute your accolades, Alexander? From where in that ambitious breast does your humility spring?"

"There's always someone bigger, faster and stronger," he said gruffly, trying to keep his voice from shaking.

"That's a strange answer coming from Alexander's heir," Nazeera replied, and touched her wrist. The mountaintop scene changed to them sitting on a wide plain. It was night. Lightning flashed all around them.

Alexander relaxed. Lightning didn't bother him; even when, as now, it hit scant feet from him.

"Before you answer, Alexander, let's watch your file," Nazeera said, her eyes on the screen at her wrist.

A purple garbed Alexander battled through the snow, the mud and the rain. The record was brutal, even for those accustomed to the sport, and Alexander watched Nazeera unconsciously wince at each concussion. The effect of the programming was so calculated, and in that manner both the interviewer and Nazeera hit their mark. Alexander pummeled his opponents. He threw them aside like rag dolls or simply ran over them, treading on their chests with his cleated feet. Then he crushed his enemies mercilessly. They were images of primitive destruction, and Alexander dominated the scene, his grim visage setting fire to the torn field before him, inviting the carnage.

Still, it appeared that Nazeera wasn't seeing what she wanted in him. From a lightning storm the scene shifted underwater; Alexander sat in chains on a sandy bottom. The surface was tantalizingly close—only ten feet away. Shafts of sunlight glinted on him and Nazeera, and the water was pleasantly warm, but it was water and Alexander instinctively held his breath.

"So Alexander, you were the dominant male in your sport," Nazeera said in a normal voice. "Is a military commission the common reward for such accomplishments, or was there something else behind this?"

Alexander fought the urge to breath. Logic told him this was a hologram, Nazeera was breathing and he needn't worry. But instinct was a powerful controller, and he couldn't make himself ignore the water.

"Well Alexander?"

Alexander's lungs burned. He was blacking out. With every ounce of willpower he had he opened his mouth and breathed. Heavy, warm, viscous water flowed into his lungs. He immediately coughed and choked, but with each cough he inhaled more water. The feeling was dreadful, painful and frightening, but his mind cleared as Oxygen once again flowed to his brain. The choking subsided, and he growled, "There was nothing of the sort, Nazeera. There is no such tie between the games and the military."

He settled down, slowly getting used to the sensation. The panic stricken fear of drowning dissipated. Then he saw the sharks behind Nazeera, dozens of them.

They were small four and five footers—reef sharks. Alone they weren't anything to be afraid of, but in a pack they were as deadly as a Great White. They ignored Nazeera and swam around him, bumping, nipping and rubbing.

It irritated him. "The game's not working Nazeera."

"Let's try a different sort of stimulus then, shall we?" she smiled.

Alexander was in a cabin, sitting on a fur rug in front of a fire. Nazeera approached him, a glass of wine in each hand, wearing nothing but a purple silk teddy. She bent over to hand him his wine. Her breasts strained at the teddy. Only her erect nipples kept them from bobbing out.

Alexander took the glass dumbly, knowing that the instruments the Chem had monitoring him were going wild. She curled up next to him.

"Let's watch your TV, shall we?" she asked, sipping her wine.

The screen above the mantle went on, and the Terran interviewer said, "I don't believe I can name anyone since Butkus who instilled such respect or fear amongst his peers. There wasn't much question as to why your nickname became "Alexander the Great" was there? You played the game with a certain ferocious élan, uncompromising to the ideal of the game. You were so infatuated with what was right, and how the game should be played, that you threatened to leave if the roof to the Metrodome wasn't torn off and the field be returned to grass. You were prepared to sacrifice your career in Minnesota for the betterment of the game. There was more, though. You were the real leader of the team, and the elected Captain in four of your five years. That's not a position that falls to someone in the trenches all that often. To me that says a great deal about the player and the man."

"I appreciate the compliment," the younger Alexander said, "but it stops there. I gave it a go, and maybe a few quarterbacks will breathe a little easier, but really that's all there is. Next year someone else will be stronger and faster, with better media presence. By the end of next season no one will remember the name Alexander."

Nazeera stopped the tape, her voice deep with gravity. "An interesting statement, don't you think? No one will remember the name Alexander!" There is the crux of your desires, Alexander."

"What?"

"Alexander are you paying attention?"

"Alright, you win; you've discovered how to break my focus Nazeera. Can you blame me? You look enchanting in that negligee!" He reached for her.

They were back in the interrogation room. It felt especially cold and bleak now.

"Damn!" Alexander cursed. "That's bloody low, Nazeera!"

"Thank you, I'll take that as a compliment."

"I meant it as such," Alexander growled, but he grinned wolfishly. "Whatever you do to me you can't take away the image of you by the fireside—I'll keep that one locked away!"

Nazeera shook her head and leaned back in her chair. "Back to your desires, Alexander; you've exposed yourself. Modesty does not become Alexander the Great, past or present, and yet you downplayed yourself as the warrior. Why? What was your real reason for leaving the games Alexander? From all indications you were having an extraordinary career, but that wasn't enough was it? It was not enough for you to be a star in the spectacle, and you were too rare a prize to leave lying on the shelf. You left, or were pulled from the games for a career in the military. I can only conclude the decision was dictated by others, but what others? Someone very important must have had their eye on you Alexander."

"You're reading far too much into this, Nazeera. I was on my third knee operation in two years, my fourth overall. It was time to leave. I didn't want to end up a cripple. I barely passed my flight physical as it was. In the end all I got out of it was some money, some fond memories and an artificial knee."

"Really, Alexander, I'm not naive. This interview is intriguing, and telling. I've used the same methods myself. Nothing is as newsworthy as the thought of a leader turning down the laurels of victory. Caesar of Roma Terra did it. I expect you, as did he, got exactly what you were looking for at the time: increased responsibility, and your name in the hall of heroes."

"Caesar, if I remember correctly, did not live to reap the rewards of his ambition," Alexander chimed in. "Remember also, Nazeera, that when I went into the military I was only a lieutenant. I advanced only to Captain. That's not very successful in the grand scheme of things, especially when you're trying to work out an intergalactic conspiracy. Even if the opportunity existed, Nazeera, I was entirely too inconsequential to take advantage of it. Face it. As difficult as it is for me to admit, I was no-one."

"That is the crux of my argument, Alexander," she smiled. "I can see and understand your frustration, Alexander. Your transition into the military is predictable and transparent, Alexander, especially in as the Terran system, as we understand it, is designed to find and develop leaders. A warrior-caste society has no room for individual concerns. You were identified as a potential leader, but of course you entered a military system as just one of many such officers. Still, there was something about you which set you apart. You were marked for great things."

"That's not how it turned out," Alexander said, and he was immediately sorry he did so. Nazeera was ahead of him now—she was dictating the interview. The fireplace seduction was genius; he'd lost track of his necessity.

"The Scythians followed your career very closely, and you advanced initially as expected, but when you should have made the leap into the upper echelons of the command caste something happened. What happened to your patronage? Can you illuminate me?"

"Again you're reading too much into my career, and into the Terran political system." Alexander was in a difficult spot. He either marginalized himself to the point of being inconsequential, or he entered a lie. He couldn't do either. Growling, he said, "I had no sponsor; I played no political games. That's your answer; I wasn't willing to be an ass kisser. The next step was inevitable. That's all there is to it."

"Is it? I cannot quite believe that you are as insignificant as you claim to be, Alexander."

Nazeera pressed the screen at her sleeve, and Alexander tensed, ready for another change. It came, and it was absolutely contrary to the fireside with Nazeera.

The first thing that hit Alexander was the smell: sickly sweet blood, rank unwashed leather, rotting fish and slimy stone. He knew exactly where and when he was—bound to the block awaiting the headsman.

He opened his eyes. Nazeera stood over him dressed in black holding a huge axe. Behind her was a retinue of men in sober robes.

"Your retirement interview was an obvious stage, Alexander, but it tells me about the political strength behind you at that time."

"I liked you in the negligee better."

Nazeera ignored his remark, and knelt next to him. Her face was almost touching his. It was a strange mixture of emotion, the visceral horror of impending death and the growing desire for this woman.

"I understand your politics and their intrigues perhaps better than you can imagine," Nazeera said, unaware of the conflict within Alexander—intent only on emotionally prying out the information she needed. "Though you may not know it-or would not admit it-Terran politics grew from the roots of the Galactics Rome. The Galactics, with very little Chem input, founded your own Rome, providing Terrans with the Galactic model of government, law and society."

"I didn't know that," Alexander told her, testing the bonds on his wrists and finding them just as tight as they were five centuries earlier.

"Maybe not," Nazeera smiled, "I wouldn't to expect you to admit it if you did. Terrans have, of course, altered the Galactic model to accomplish the realization of Alexander's dream. The Galactics abandoned their attempts to control Roma Terra long ago, but what remains is still recognizable. I can read it, Alexander, and despite the gaps and your own vague references your career is something I can read as well."

"Then maybe you can explain it to me," Alexander told her with a wry grin.

Nazeera laid a hand on his shoulder, and he trebled at her touch. "I've seen your kind before, Alexander. The brevity of your career is not so strange. The Scythians were right to recognize you as Alexander's heir. I saw it in your trial. You are strong willed, aggressive, and intelligent. That was undoubtedly what your superiors noted in your gladiatorial career. It is no surprise to me that they drafted you into the military for the purpose of developing you for their regime. That is the common way of political ascension, Alexander. I've recruited many of my supporters in a similar manner. Like your superiors, though, I would have eventually realized that I had recruited not a supporter, but a usurper. You're dangerous, Alexander, too dangerous and too ambitious to be trusted as an underling. There was nothing else to be done. You couldn't be controlled, so you were surreptitiously cut loose before you could be a threat to your sponsor."

"Nazeera, you are again reading too much into this."

Nazeera grabbed Alexander's long locks, pulled his head up, and said, "Then there is the Scythian connection."

"You've lost me, Nazeera," he said, grimacing at the discomfort of the position.

"Why were the Scythians still interested in you if your career was over?" She tightened her grip.

"Ask the Scythians."

"Perhaps your career was not as dead as you would have me believe." Nazeera set down the axe and took out a pair of long iron shears. She sliced his hair off at the nape of his neck and let his head fall to the block.

"It was dead, Nazeera. You can abandon that train of thought," Alexander insisted, turning his head to the left so that he could see her.

Nazeera picked up the axe again.

"The Scythians offered you a way to bypass the Terran political hierarchy." She laid the edge of the axe on the bare skin of his neck. It felt cold, and to his disgust it felt dull, as if it hadn't been sharpened in countless strokes—just like the last time. His gut twisted into knots. It took all of Alexander's self control not to lose his composure at that moment.

"They knew your aspirations, Alexander, and I understand them. You desire something more, some higher pinnacle to achieve. I agree with you. You are meant for more than a gladiator, or a minor officer. When denied by the jealousy of your superiors, the Scythians offered you their throne."

She withdrew the axe, allowing the edge to grate against his flesh, just as before, and bent down to whisper at last word in his ear. "Scythian control would be temporary, of course, and you'd soon have your dreams of ultimate command realized. You would then, in truth, be able to bear the name of your predecessor, Alexander the Great."

"That scenario does not even bear comment, Nazeera."

"Why were you in the company of the Scythians when our raiders boarded the scout ship?" Her voice was insistent. Her eyes reddened.

Alexander was silent.

"You were found with the Scythians prostrated before you, begging for your mercy and protection, Alexander! Obviously you were communing with the Scythian Council, but apparently their offer was not satisfactory to you. You broke the telepathic connection and assumed control of their ship. I can only conjecture that Scythian control of you was very brief indeed."

"I did not negotiate with the Scythians! I have nothing but contempt for them. I would get my revenge if I could, but as it seems I will not have that opportunity. My only comfort is that the wrath of Chem will fall upon them, if the revenge of Alexander does not."

"There you speak as Alexander of Terra!" she said triumphantly. She stood tall and placed the dull, cold, hard edge of the axe against his neck. "Once and for all, are you the Alexander of legend?"

Alexander glowered at her—he couldn't refuse without groveling and he couldn't say yes without admitting the complicity of Terra. He clenched his teeth, and said, "Do what you have to do Nazeera."

"Very well, Alexander of Terra!" She raised the axe. Her mouth opened wide, showing her sharp gleaming platinum teeth as she started the heavy blade on its fatal plunge. Alexander heard her cry of effort as if from a great distance, but the whoosh of the blade sounded as if it were inside his head it was so close.

He tensed. The edge of the blade filled his sight. The metal creased his skin.

CHAPTER 21:
POLITICAL AND PERSONAL
INTRIGUE

They were back in the interrogation room.

Alexander stood abruptly, and Nazeera stepped away from him. Her involuntary reaction to his fury had the opposite effect—it drained him of all anger.

He turned away from her, trembling at the re-enactment of his execution, and at his rage of her using it against him. Yet he knew why she used that moment and his other lives—in her position he'd have done the same.

"I'm not the Alexander you think I am," he said softly. He glanced back at her, and his eyes lost their hard edge. "I've a great deal of respect for you, Nazeera—you're an extraordinary woman. What you just did took guts. Therefore, I'll tell you this: whoever I am, whoever you think I am, I have no malicious intent for you or for Chem."

It was a true statement and Alexander wanted to say it, but he also had an ulterior motive. It wasn't what Nazeera expected. Her shocked expression told him he once again had the initiative. He was out of the emotional trap Nazeera put him in, and once again he could take an exterior view of his situation, analyzing it almost as if it were one of his past-life memories.

Nazeera could obviously see that he was no longer controlled by his emotions, and she sighed.

"Come on, Alexander, I think we both need a walk in the park after that."

Alexander had a multitude of questions spinning in his head, but conflicting motivations stilled his tongue. As they flew in her aerocar to the park, sitting next to each other in uncomfortable silence, the calculating side to him weighed what he needed to know with what Nazeera's impressions might be. The Terran side felt an inner need to part with Nazeera on amicable terms. It was one of those ironic quandaries. Alexander would much rather debate the Chem Assemblage than fence with this extraordinary and enthralling woman.

It was a misty afternoon in the park. The air was heavy with the scent of rain and wet earth. The fern shaped leaves dripped on the sodden path, but the rains were gone and the Chem sun sent golden shafts of light through rents in the clouds. Alexander and Nazeera walked in silence for a time. He couldn't read her thoughts, but he was wondering how to say good-bye. Despite the difficulty of the circumstances he held no animosity for her. He was cognizant of the uneasy closeness in their brief relationship; something more than mutual respect and different than friendship.

Nazeera broke the silence.

"Alexander, I realize today was difficult. I want you to know that despite my misgivings I would rather have spent it in a more sociable manner. I have, I admit, enjoyed my time with you. I know I've told you this already, but it bears repeating. Pantrixnia and all it entails is not a personal vendetta of any kind. It was a purely practical decision when I first made it, and even then-when I knew nothing of you-it was not made with animosity. These are extraordinary times. The tempest brewing in the galaxy is many millennia in the making. We would keep the status quo, if we could, but those days are past. Much of what we knew, and much of what we care about will be swept away.

"You lament that your life has no purpose. Well, Alexander, be comforted—you've changed the course of galactic history. If it is any consolation, you've already made your mark."

"It is not enough, I'm afraid, just to be a footnote in history," Alexander told her, happy to hear a more personable tone in her voice.

For some reason it mattered to him. "I've been that footnote often enough, Nazeera. Looking back on it doesn't satisfy me in the least. I'm not quite done yet, you know."

He stopped and picked a flower. It was similar in shape to an orchid. The petals were purple with streaks of what looked like flakes of gold. He sniffed it, finding the scent pleasant but not overpowering.

"I suppose I should've asked if it was poisonous or sacred first."

Nazeera laughed, sounding sincerely amused. "It's Vatalya, the Shield maiden's Flower. Legend has it that Vatalya decides a warrior's fate and guides the chosen spirits to their rest."

"Like the Valkries," Alexander smiled. "On Terra, it's customary for a man to present a woman with a flower, usually a rose, as a token of affection and esteem. I can't imagine a more suitable flower for the woman who will decide my fate."

"Alexander, I don't know whether you're being cruel or charming," she said, taking the flower.

"Take it in the spirit of our fireside rendezvous—which I'd like to revisit someday."

"Alexander," she began, sounding half scolding and half intrigued. She never finished. Quick as a snake Alexander's hand shot out, grabbed her jacket where it plunged between her breasts, and thrust her down to the ground.

As Nazeera took the flower Alexander saw a dark shape dressed like a Ninja swoop out from behind the foliage directly at her back. The Ninja rode a small oval platform, like a flying surfboard. He aimed a blow with his armored fist at the back of Nazeera's skull.

Alexander had no time to warn her. He pulled her down with his left hand and punched at the assailant with his right. His fist connected with the center of the Ninja's masked face, and there was a frightful crunching sound as bone snapped. Blood spattered Alexander. The Ninja flew off his board and rolled in the wet earth. He came to a stop down the trail—a motionless heap.

Two other Ninjas flew out of the forest. One carried a sword in one hand and a knife in the other. The other carried a long forked spear and whirled a set of bolo balls. Before Alexander could react the bolo spun through the air and the balls whipped around his legs. The balls thumped painfully on his thighs, binding his legs. Fortunately,

Alexander stood ready for conflict after the first attack, and his legs were planted firm and wide—he didn't fall. The Ninja charged with his fork.

Alexander ducked beneath the spear, but just barely. The fork missed his head but creased his shoulder. Alexander thrust forward with his legs, throwing a shoulder block into the Ninja's knees as he flew by.

The Ninja cried out as Alexander cut his legs out from under him. He tumbled over his shoulder and the board went flying off into the trees. The Ninja landed a meter behind Alexander, and he whirled and dove on the injured attacker. The Ninja tried to draw his knife, but Alexander pinned that arm to the ground and struck him once, twice, three times on the jaw. The Ninja went limp.

Alexander snatched up the knife. There was a whoosh behind him. Without looking he dove aside, but he felt the cut of a blade on his back even so. Ignoring the burning pain he cut the cords of the bolo. He got out of it just as the third Ninja turned backed toward him.

He snatched the spear and held out the forked tines as the Ninja charged. The Ninja thought better of the attack and pulled up and over Alexander, but not quite out of reach. Alexander jabbed upwards, catching the Ninja between his legs. He missed piercing the Ninja's flesh, but the fork got caught in between the Ninja's legs and sent him flying off the board. He tumbled into a tree, and struggled groggily to his feet.

Alexander pounced on him like a lion, lifting the Ninja off the ground. Viciously he tore the mask off, leaving a bloody weal across the dark flesh. His hand went to the throat, and then he stopped, frozen. The Ninja was a woman.

Her face transformed from surprise to fury, and she cried out. Her knife flashed. Alexander saw that it was going to penetrate his stomach—there was nothing he could do.

Something hot swept past Alexander's ear and forehead. Then he heard the "Whoomph!" A deluge of hot charred flesh rained on Alexander's face. He looked up to see half the Ninja's head blown clean off. The knife fell from her twitching hand.

He let her go. She fell with a rumpled clatter.

Alexander turned to Nazeera, a stern gleam in his eyes. "Well, did I pass that test too?"

Nazeera holstered her gun, but shook her head. She touched the screen on her sleeve, and said, "I'm sorry Alexander that wasn't my doing. I told you things have changed; this is part of what I spoke of. There are elements of Chem society that don't want this to go any further."

Alexander sighed, and winced at his cuts—they burned. "Your world is beautiful, Nazeera, but dangerous. I hope the next time I come back here it's as a tourist, not a brigand."

Nazeera laughed, as a trio of aerocars descended on them. There were military people and a medical team. They saw to Alexander's wounds. He endured the attention stoically; more interested in what Nazeera was doing with the single surviving Ninja. Nazeera killed the one, and Alexander's blow to the face killed the other. As it was, the medical team had to give a shot to the last Ninja to revive him.

When he came to he simply glared at Nazeera and refused to answer any questions.

"Very well, it's Pantrixnia for you. Take him away!"

She came over to Alexander and got the report from the doctor.

"I'm phasing the dorsal wound now; it won't be but a moment," the doctor said. "He's not seriously damaged; he'll be fine for Pantrixnia."

"Silence!" Nazeera roared, catching Alexander and the doctor off guard. The doctor actually dropped his instrument in his surprise. Before he could retrieve it Nazeera clutched him by the collar, and said in a venomous voice, "You are speaking of the Warlord of Terra—you will display the proper reverence! If you utter another word beyond the duty of your office you'll join that other vermin on Pantrixnia, do you understand?"

"Yes, Lady Nazeera," the doctor said in a shaky voice. He knelt before Alexander. "Accept my apology, Dread Lord, I mistook myself. May I finish my duties?"

"Get on with it," Alexander frowned.

The doctor picked up his instrument and finished his work.

Nazeera ushered Alexander into her aerocar and they left the park with an escort.

"Thank you for saving my life, Alexander," she said when they were alone again.

"You can thank me by having dinner with me this evening. Consider it a farewell gesture of respect to a formidable adversary, if there is no other proper way of accounting for it."

Nazeera smiled, but told him, "I'm afraid I couldn't consider it in any such way. You can be far too charming for your own good, Alexander. I can't say more, except that as I'm married it would be socially unacceptable for my station. I'll leave it at that. It was a good barb, though, Alexander, and well aimed. I'm justly chastised for my verbal dissections. Is that a product of your awakened memory, or did you always have that skill?"

"I don't know that my past-lives have so beneficial an effect, Nazeera. I have a few pirates leering at you, a statesman admonishing them, a king too gloomy with guilt to care, and a Prussian too noble to whisper anything but attention to duty in my ear."

"You have your own Assemblage trapped in your skull, I pity you, Alexander."

"Don't pity me, Nazeera. It's been an extraordinary adventure. I count myself fortunate, not only for the opportunity history offers me, but for meeting you. You've made a grim adventure a wonderful experience."

Nazeera smiled, but turned her eyes from Alexander, a deep blush flushing her features. "Alexander," she said finally, "you are no doubt the strangest man I've ever met. You speak as though you're looking back, with the full knowledge that somehow you'll prevail in the terrible trials to come. I can't fathom what's going on in that Terran head of yours, but whatever it is, I'm one step behind. It's my task, I remind you, to probe and interpret your reactions, not the other way around."

"Don't worry, Nazeera, if you knew everything about me you'd probably be even more confounded!"

Nazeera dropped Alexander off at his cell and left abruptly. It was a thoroughly unsatisfactory goodbye.

Alexander lay down on the simple bed drained and dejected. He regretted that his time on Chem was now at an end. What troubled him was that it was a personal regret, not a regret that he'd failed in his self appointed task. Beyond his limited ambition there was the hauntingly fascinating persona of Nazeera. The desire to know her better preoccupied him, making Alexander angry with himself for wasting what little time he had to mentally prepare for his coming ordeal.

He fell into a restless slumber.

Alexander snapped awake. Something or someone was in the darkness of the cell with him.

CHAPTER 22:
CONSPIRACY

The Chem clock told him he slept for only a few minutes.

He didn't move or alter his breathing. His senses told him what he needed to know without the requisite civilized responses, and rather than give his awareness away Alexander stayed still and listened to his senses.

A foreign scent drifted in the air from behind. A soft footfall scuffed the metal floor, experienced rather than heard. His senses told him the position and the movement of the threat, and when it passed a certain point he acted. Alexander's actions were half planned, half instinctive. He lay on his side with someone advancing behind his back. In one spasmodic thrashing he twisted and turned, lashing out with his leg in a wide sweeping slash. His sweep caught hold of someone's legs, taking them out from under them.

Alexander leapt up, eyes wide and seething, even as a dark shape crashed to the metal floor. He lunged towards the figure to tackle and hold, but the figure was swifter than he. It recovered, scrambling to the side with a roll and a lithe leap. The shadow of a gun stopped Alexander from further advancement.

"Good evening, Alexander," exclaimed a voice, at once Chem and male. The lights snapped on to reveal a Chem, as tall as Alexander, handsome and lean, perhaps three-fifths his weight.

The Chem smiled and applauded him, "Well done!"

Alexander relaxed, crossing his arms over his breast. "I'm so pleased I passed your little test. Is there anything else, or are you disturbing my slumber for sport alone?"

"Not at all, not at all my worthy charge," the Chem laughed. "I'm here for a reason. Let me introduce myself, I am Nazar, and I'll command the ship which takes you to Pantrixnia. I understand you're prepared?"

"As well as I shall ever be."

"Really, have you no unfinished business on Chem then?"

Alexander's eyes narrowed, wondering whether the question was a trap.

"Indeed, Alexander of Terra, you spoke better before the Assemblage," Nazar told him. "In that hall you proclaimed how honorable your folk were, and how steadfastly you met peril. I even recall anger when you thought yourself insulted. Are your words simply words, or is there resolve behind them?"

"I do not hide behind my words, Commander Nazar," Alexander told him. "Have a care lest I make you put that gun to use. What's your game?"

"I merely question the temerity of your word," Nazar told him.

"That is enough to tempt me," Alexander told him, moving forward.

Nazar held the gun up and said, "It's your own silence, Alexander of Terra, which incriminates you."

"How so, what are you talking about?"

"Why Bureel's challenge to you, of course," Nazar told him.

"Who is Bureel, and what is this of a challenge?" Alexander asked viciously. There was something smelling of intrigue to Nazar's game, something which must have advantage to both Alexander and the Chem, so he played along. It wasn't so difficult to act enraged at the thought of insult, as it was essential to Alexander's present character. What made it unconsciously easier to react, as opposed to act, were the personas of days past which every hour became more and more a part of the instinctive Alexander.

"Hasn't Nazeera told you?" Nazar asked him. Alexander's response was exactly what Nazar apparently expected, and desired, as he continued in a more pleasant manner. "Well, then, my sister is at times more concerned with affairs of state than minor items such as points of honor. Yes, Nazeera is my sister, and the head of our house. Bureel, by the way, is her husband, though not of her own choosing. That is another story, however. It occurs to me, if you're truly ignorant of Bureel's challenge, that I have wronged you; if I've done so you have my sincere apologies."

Nazar was circumnavigating a point he wanted to get across, and Alexander was beginning to see that there was more to his position than that of a gladiator awaiting execution. Nazar obviously had no love for his brother in law, and Alexander was not above helping Nazeera out of such a situation, especially if it furthered his cause.

"I have immense respect for Nazeera, and I wouldn't consciously take any action to cause sorrow to her or her house. Yet I cannot overlook a point of honor, especially if I'm slighted behind my back. What of this Bureel's challenge to me?"

"Bureel is an interesting sort of fellow in the most despicable sense," Nazar told him, adding, "That is a personal opinion of my own. My sister and I, however, agree on many things, the soul of honor being one of them. To make a challenge is a serious act, don't you think?"

"None more serious."

"Perhaps I exaggerate my brother-in-laws measure, but where the honor of one's family is concerned I must be exacting, and stringent in my regard."

"A despicable act brings shame on not only the offender, but the whole house. In my view, it is often better that the offending member settle the matter honorably than to blight the family with shame. Sometimes, however, there are practicalities which prevent even these things from happening. A House will hide its embarrassments for the greater good."

"At times, however, such attention to detail can be to the benefit of a house. At other times such self reflection can benefit both houses of the conflict, and their empires."

"Say on."

"Allow me to show you something, Alexander of Terra, which you may find interesting." Nazar played a tape of the Assemblage. The camera zoomed in to display the discussion of Nazeera, Nazar and a Chem identified as Bureel. Nazar watched, needing to add no narrative to the scene. As the Chem warrior and statesman expected Alexander said nothing. He simply glowered, his scowl deepening with every word from Bureel.

CHAPTER 23:
A FAMILY SQUABBLE

The setting sun suffocated all levity in Nazeera's great hall. The thought of the meal made her think of Alexander. She cursed herself. Despite her best efforts at distancing herself from the man, he'd become more than a nameless being to her. Alexander was an extraordinary man with personality and ambitions—ambitions she dashed.

The thought of his inevitable death dampened her spirits. She would like see him again, and ignore the impending destruction of his Homeworld, but he was teaching her too many things she did not want to know about himself, his people and Nazeera the woman.

The meal looked even more distasteful than usual. She would just as soon forget this day. She'd definitely tried already. After her meeting with Alexander she delivered her final report to the Elder and thought her part done. Later, somehow, she found herself locked away, again reviewing the data tapes captured from the Scythians. In Alexander's memories she found all the facets he had shown her; the curiosity, courage, honor, humor, and even the taciturn stubbornness that could engulf his personality when pushed.

His lives were violent but without the malignant tendencies she associated with criminals. He was a merciful victor even against enemies who personally wronged him. His actions lacked the wanton cruelty, and the joy of cruelty, she'd expected. There were many more memories of a more compassionate nature than there were of glories won, or violence accomplished. This no longer surprised her, and it lent credence to the strength of his character. As she watched the tapes again she felt all the pieces of her suspicions, especially the ones concerning her personal opinions, neatly falling into a very restless picture.

Alexander grew and matured into a being at once vibrant and wise, as their elders. Watching him was almost as if recalling memories of someone she knew, or should know. She did not find that feeling comfortable at all, but at the same time it stirred a great regret towards her actions. In an attempt to purge herself of unwelcome feelings she drank more wine than usual; she'd lost an opportunity to explore a man who might mean a great deal to her empire, and possibly, just possibly, to her as well.

"Nazar, would it be too much to ask for you to find a house of your own," the smooth voice of Bureel whined, waking her from her thoughts. "Really, welching off your sister and I is beneath someone of you stature, not to mention your age. Might I advise you to take a wife and make a life of your own?"

"What and miss time with my melancholy sibling, as well as your inestimable charm?" Nazar entered the dining room with a flourish, kissed his sister on the forehead and seated himself. "What's for supper, I am understandably famished? I've just finished arranging transport for Alexander to Pantrixnia. As you know I shall have the honor of accompanying him to that planet of endless pleasures!"

"Oh, please Nazar, don't joke of it," Nazeera asked limply, pouring another glass of wine. It was bold and heady, dulling the growing pain in her consciousness.

"If only I'd been there to watch him plead for his life," Bureel grinned in between his more measured sips of wine.

"Now there's a being who wouldn't stoop to pleading. I would stake my life on it!" Nazar retorted.

"That would be an interesting wager," Bureel mused. Then he smiled his best snake's grin and added, "He doesn't deserve a warrior's death. Slit his throat and be done with it."

"And who will take the knife to him, Bureel, you?" Nazeera asked, her voice taking on a dangerous tone. When he didn't answer she laughed. "I thought as much!" Nazeera filled her glass and Nazar's as well. She did not fill Bureel's. "You know, in one life Alexander held an army at bay on a bridge alone and armed with only an axe. He kept them from crossing that bridge for a full quarter decurn, suffering wound upon wound, but he would not fall and he would not yield. Finally an enemy ignobly stabbed him from beneath and he was overwhelmed, but the mounds of dead were a testament to his courage."

"What's an axe, some form of primitive energy weapon?" Bureel asked.

Nazeera leaned forward with a sneer, "No Bureel, it is a semi-circular metal blade mounted on a wooden handle. It's used in hand-to-hand combat. It shears off limbs, and heads, quite effectively."

"Distasteful," Bureel said.

"Barbaric! What a splendid way to die!" Nazar exclaimed with a smile, fully versed in the story but well prepared to delve into Alexander at Bureel's expense. "I do think I'm beginning to like this fellow more and more all the time. He's certainly more of a model male than many a pretender I know. Though I know much about him from your interrogations, my dear sister, I can't pretend the intimacy to which you've studied his lives. What else has he done?"

Bureel complained, "Oh please, do we need to talk of the Terran during dinner. The mere thought of his pallid skin and lizard's eyes takes away my appetite."

Nazeera ignored him, "He was a king, but he didn't fare so well in that role; too young in experience I think, or maybe the realm was too small for his aspirations. Thereafter, he was a statesman, a pirate, and in one of his more interesting lives a general. It was in a cold land where snow, such as we have on our outer worlds, laid on the ground throughout much of the perium. He commanded a primitive civilized army, one in which they used single shot projectile weapons and beasts of burden for transportation. A great conqueror at the head of a vast army invaded his land. Overmatched, he decided not meet the invader in open battle. He stood when he could inflict damage, and then withdrew. He burned as he fell back, sacrificing even his cities."

"Coward," Bureel spat.

"It's a general's task to seek victory, not just a glorious death Bureel," Nazar said. "I suspect that's what occurs, as otherwise the story would lack relevance. It's difficult to accomplish a more admirable death than you've already described. Anything else would be redundant."

"Truly, Nazar, you have the makings of a general yourself," Nazeera told him. "He fell back repeatedly, burning his own cities until the snows came. When the winter sapped the strength of the enemy he attacked and destroyed them. The great conqueror never again led his army abroad. The victory changed the course of history on his planet."

"You see, sometimes, Bureel, it is better to be a living hero than a dead martyr," Nazar said, sipping his wine and pointing a long finger at his despised brother-in-law. "The fellow has pluck, and guile. We could use a friend like that on Terra, as opposed to sending him to Pantrixnia."

"We've covered this territory before, Nazar. I couldn't change it even if I wanted to."

"Which means you've thought about it already," Nazar replied, and he glanced at Bureel. "Too bad, really, he's not bad looking, for an alien. He's got enough bravado to stand up to you, Nazeera. He'd make you a good husband, if you were free."

Nazeera stifled an exclamation—too surprised to respond.

"You have the gall to insinuate such a thing!" Bureel scowled.

"Pure practicality," Nazar smiled. "Think of it, a union between Terra and the Chem; the debate about this Terran threat would finally end!"

"Really, Nazar, that's just about enough," Nazeera said, but without any real enthusiasm. With the wine in her head Nazar's idea almost sounded logical, if not desirable. She couldn't actually marry Alexander, of course, could she?

Nazar ignored her and addressed his plan to Bureel, "Consider it Bureel, you could repeat your challenge to the Terran, he'd kill you and marry Nazeera. The threat to Chem would be over. You'd be a hero, well; actually, you'd be a martyr. Think of it! You'd have done the state a great service and died a good death! What more can one ask for?"

Bureel stomped away from the table enraged. He stopped, however, at the entrance to the dining room. A figure blocked his way; a very large muscular figure. It was a figure that could only belong to a Terran.

CHAPTER 24:
DINNER, A GLASS OF WINE, AND MOONLIGHT

"Good evening," Alexander smiled evilly, his voice hardly above a growl. "May I assume that I'm addressing Bureel?"

"Terran dog, what are you doing here?" Bureel exclaimed, his light flesh turning dark red.

"Don't worry, Bureel, I have two guards and an automaton watching me. I am, of course, unarmed. That's indeed a fortuitous precaution for one of us."

Bureel interrupted, and motioned to the automaton floating behind Alexander. "Take this carcass away! Bring him back to his cell to await transport. Then report to me, I want to know under what authority this dog was allowed to leave his cell!"

"Under my authority, Bureel," Nazar chimed in. "At sunset the charge of the prisoner, Alexander of Terra, was transferred to me. Alexander is on his way to my ship, but we have unfinished business here, don't we Alexander?"

"We do indeed," Alexander smiled, then he turned to Bureel and his voice grew grave, but he didn't display any emotion. "Your challenge to me, Bureel of the Assemblage, is accepted. It will be answered at what time you wish, at what place you name and with what weapons you may choose so long as I'm provided the opportunity to familiarize myself with them. I charge you to uphold your challenge before the noble Nazeera of the Triumvirate, Nazar of the Upper House of the Assemblage, and these excellent witnesses. How do you answer?"

Bureel emitted a guttural cry of rage and attempted to force his way past the Terran. When Alexander did not budge he turned on his heel and left the room in another direction.

"May I take that for a yes?" Alexander called after him.

"Come in, come in Alexander," Nazar told him. He got up and went forward to meet the man.

"You're just in time for dinner. Now that nasty business is over please do come and sit down," Nazar ushered Alexander to a chair next to Nazeera and then sat down.

Nazeera attempted to hide her surprise, with limited success. She didn't need ask the obvious question, however, as Nazar explained presently. "I paid Alexander a visit, in preparation for our little excursion. He informed me that on Terra it's the custom for a condemned prisoner to be granted a final wish: a "last request," that's what you call it isn't it?" After an assenting nod the Chem continued, "The request seemed reasonable, especially for one going to Pantrixnia, and so upon hearing it I took it upon myself to grant it."

"And this request was for me?" Nazeera exclaimed.

"Dear me no, my sister, would I sell you so cheaply?"

"I'm beginning to wonder."

"It was for dinner, and specifically, dinner with you, Nazeera. The request seemed reasonable."

"Oh, did it?"

"Yes, after all when will we get another opportunity to have such an interesting dinner guest?" Nazar said, and then he addressed himself to Alexander. "You may try anything you like; I don't think there is anything harmful to your physiology. I welcome you to our table, and I'm certain Nazeera is glad to see you as well. She is really quite extraordinary, and normally open minded. I have quite a high opinion of her, notwithstanding that she is my sister. Tell me, as guest to host, what opinion have you formulated over the last decurns? Do not feign ignorance or courtesy Alexander, I warn you. You've spent too much time in each other's company not to form at least a professional opinion of her."

Alexander smiled at the flush in Nazeera's cheeks, but he answered diplomatically, "I find her remarkably suited to the responsibility of her position. She is highly intelligent, insightful, and can even be understanding, when she desires. I would not wish to number her amongst my adversaries."

"A fair assessment, considering the politics of the situation," Nazar said, filling Alexander's metal goblet with a fragrant red fluid. "Now, you don't have to answer this, it's a dangerous question, Alexander, and I shall know a lie when I hear it. Still, I'm curious. As a male, and male-to-male, tell me what you think of my sister."

Nazeera didn't protest, but Alexander saw that she was holding her breath. He tilted his head slightly to the side, his hand lightly cradling his wine, and smiled. "When the beauty and power of a woman carve her image forever in the mind of a man, then she is nothing less than an enchantment. If this be the price for your prison planet then I am well paid."

He raised his glass and drank to her.

Nazeera's jaw dropped in surprise.

Alexander smiled at her.

Nazar laughed and exclaimed, "Marvelous, how paradoxical, a warrior-poet! That was well-answered, don't you think, Nazeera?"

Nazar's pleasure was interrupted by a low gong. A message addressed to him instructed him to take command of the cruiser "Shen Fuur" immediately. The Chem sighed, and told Alexander, "Your transportation to Pantrixnia, I'm afraid."

"Well, at least I will not be bereft of civilized company," Alexander answered, "Unless, of course, I'm to be put in isolation."

"There is no requirement for it," Nazar said. "You have only a short time, Alexander; enjoy it, but not too much. My dear sister I shall see you upon my return." He kissed Nazeera's cheek with a wide grin, and happily left the two alone.

Nazeera cradled her brow in her hands, massaging her temples.

"Does Nazar do this to you often?" Alexander asked.

"No, you're the first Terran that he's brought home to dinner," she laughed nervously.

"Good, I then stand in unique company," he laughed in reply. "Seriously, though, I must apologize to you Nazeera."

"Apologize, for what?" Nazeera glanced up at him.

Alexander smiled sheepishly and sipped his drink. Tasting it produced a gratifying expression, and a comment on its excellence, but it only served to lengthen the uncomfortable moment. How much to admit? He asked himself. Then he reminded himself that he'd never see this beautiful, amazing, intriguing, powerful woman again.

"I find myself in perhaps too many unique positions at the moment, Nazeera. I didn't want our relationship to end—at least not on so formal a note. You have your duty and I have mine, but there is a personal side to this adventure.

"I realize it may be against your customs, and your station, but I think I have the right to be a little selfish. The Pantrixnia nights will be somewhat shorter with the memory of my time with you. Despise me if you like, but I wanted my dinner date. Whatever roles reality may assign us to play, Nazeera, my imagination tells me things could have been much different if we met under different circumstances. Don't worry, though, my intentions this evening are honorable and quite easy to fulfill. A quiet dinner with you is all I ask for. Besides they've given me an implant. One wrong move and the automaton gives me some ungodly number of volts through my brain."

Nazeera started to smile, and even reached out to touch his hand, but suddenly, vehemently, she regained her perspective. "Alexander, I will not have this!" she told him, cradling her temples. "It was irresponsible for Nazar to bring you here tonight, as if it was some form of social event, and you're not making this any easier. When will you realize just what a sentence to Pantrixnia means? It's a death sentence, Alexander. It will be a violent and painful death without even the possibility of a decent burial. How can you sit here and want to have dinner with the woman who is sending you to this fate?"

Alexander smiled, "You are intent on spoiling my evening."

"Alexander!" she almost screamed his name at him. Then, as if all the energy drained from her she closed her eyes and said, "You're making this extraordinarily difficult. Is this your revenge? You make me actually care about your fate, knowing I have to watch your destruction and then live with the weight of it for the rest of my life?"

Alexander laughed, and said, "Nothing so devious, Nazeera. We all die, but how many of us get the chance to do something with our lives? I don't see the point in worrying about it. I'll deal with Pantrixnia when I need to. At the moment, however, I'm not on Pantrixnia. I am, amazingly enough, having dinner with the powerful, exotic, and beautiful Nazeera of Chem. The very reality of it makes my future adventures more than bearable. It's a bit of magic I could never have dreamed up, and one that no one would ever believe. Now come, you can treat it as a tête-à-tête between dignitaries if you like. I'm perfectly willing to be the captured Warlord of Terra if that's what the noble Nazeera of the Triumvirate of Chem requires to be sociable. Trust me. I promise I'll behave."

"In what way I wonder?" Nazeera smiled, and she finally allowed a trickle of laughter to overwhelm her. "Alexander, Alexander, how can I defy you? Your request is eloquent if not realistic, and I suppose you did save my life. If apologies are in order I must add my own. I enjoyed these last decurns no less and no more than you. If things are not as they could be, between yourself and Chem, I can only plead that I was doing my duty as best I could to my empire, and myself."

"We each have our duty, Nazeera; don't beat yourself up over it."

"I'm not certain what you mean, Alexander, but you've cajoled me into this little dinner of yours. Tell me, what can I expect? From your colorful past I should perhaps be prepared for some trickery or deceit. Is this how you drew in your cousin the King?"

"You cut me to the quick. That's not one of my shining moments. I was a noble lord and man succumbing to greedy opportunity, persuaded I might add by the wiles of my wife. She knew just what switches to throw to spur the dark side of my ambition! Ah, but I was much younger then, and she was not like you at all—it was an arranged marriage, rather like yours. I hope I've improved with age."

"I think you have, but I can't decide with whom I'd rather share this dinner."

"How do you mean?"

"Well, your Viking was somewhat too barbaric, though interesting. To sit at the same table as your King would not give me a moment's comfort, and to dine with Alexander the Chancellor would be tedious. The pirate Alexander is quite a close match to you at the moment, forgetting the fact that he was a scoundrel."

"An honorable scoundrel," Alexander corrected her. "As a pirate he didn't believe in some of the more heinous crimes of his peers; i.e. rape and the romantic practice of "walking the plank." To women he behaved with chivalry, and to his captured adversaries there was something positively Chem-like in him. He never could stomach the execution of a helpless being, so instead of feeding them to the sharks he had the habit of dropping them off in the wilderness. Not a charitable solution, but honorable, I think."

"So you've lived my side of this drama yourself have you?"

"Distantly, I don't recall marooning anyone I ever really esteemed."

"Then you haven't lived what I'm going through, Alexander."

"I'm sorry about that; it wasn't my intention. If it makes you feel any better I'm in the same boat; I wish there were more of me for you to dig up. I never thought I'd miss being interrogated, although to tell you the truth I won't miss your testing my fear of heights!"

Nazeera laughed, and patted his hand.

"Is there anything I should know about how Chem males socialize with females—within the bounds of decorum of course."

"By which you mean how do Chem men seduce women?"

"My goodness no, Nazeera, but now that you mention it . . ."

"You're doing quite well, Alexander," she whispered, almost to herself. She actually let her hand linger on his and squeeze it. Her eyes turned a warm shade of violet.

CHAPTER 25:
COMPLICATIONS

Nazeera abruptly pulled her hand away. Immediately she straightened in her chair and coughed, as if she caught herself doing something wrong. It was the most human and telling act Alexander had yet seen from her.

"Come, the dinners getting cold," she said, and attended to her plate.

Alexander fought himself during the entirety of the dinner, attempting to contemplate conversation, any conversation, which would not further his growing attraction to this woman. He laughed at himself and his own discomfiture. Should he live to old age he'd remember nothing of the dinner, but every detail of her form and figure, the scent of perfume, every different shade of her eyes would be indelibly etched in his mind.

Finally the silence became ironically unbearable, and Alexander knew his time was drawing to a close. Draining his goblet he refilled it, and then Nazeera's. Rising from his seat he approached her, and without asking or making any pretense that it was other than a normal act, he took the hand of the alien woman. "My time here is almost over. You know me, Nazeera, almost as well as any. If you would understand me, even a slight amount, then come with me."

Nazeera assented, a suspicious shade of violet in her eyes—or was it a blush of emotion? He led her to the end of the dining room where the doors opened onto a balcony. It overlooked the dryad jungle that was the Chem Homeworld. He opened the doors and went outside. Letting go of her hand he moved to the rail. Gesturing to the jungle beyond, he said, "Look about you, Nazeera, what do you see? Beyond your door is a jungle you've looked at a thousand times before. Look at yourself and what do you see? In the glass is the image of a being you've watched grow from a child to a beautiful and powerful woman. Look above you, and you see the stars which have watched you from the same constellations your entire life. What's more, there's life out there, and you have names for it all, images and memories which make the universe real for you.

"All of this is old and natural to you, but it's completely new to me. The wonders of my dreams now confront me as reality. It's marvelous and magnificent beyond my capability to ignore. Yet you ask me to push all of this aside and worry about a future which I cannot control? Impossible, I must live moment to moment, and look for enjoyment where I can. Certainly these few hours with you were more pleasurable than fretting my time alone in that cell, worrying over how I'm to die. If we were to say nothing at all from this moment, and I died a slow painful death the instant I set foot on that prison planet of yours, I'd still count myself fortunate. At least I've built some memories worth dying for. I haven't humiliated myself. I have, I think, reached a form of understanding with you. If all that remains for me are an honorable death, then I'm content."

"So you are content to die, Alexander?" she asked with a strange timber in her voice.

"By which you mean am I willing to die? No! I'm not willing or ready to die. You'll see just how hard a Terran can struggle for life, Nazeera. I promise you that. I have much to live for, but there are no ghosts in my conscience. In essence, I've already won my battle. Horace once wrote, "Happy is the man who seizes the day, who is content with what is within himself. Let tomorrow do its worst, for I have lived today."

"Who is this Horace, another of Terra's great warrior heroes?"

Alexander laughed, "Indeed not, though he belonged to one of the mightiest empires Terra has ever known. Horace was a poet, and a terrible soldier. You might have called him a coward if your sight was blind to the meanest interpretations of honor. Horace feared the din of battle, but he braved the baring of his soul in his poetry. It's easy to die in battle, Nazeera, but difficult to live in the face of ridicule. Horace and his words, even as he predicted, lasted long after the names of many a noble warrior were forgotten."

She moved over to him, standing so closely that they touched. Cradling her drink she looked up at him. "You've won, Alexander," she said finally. "You have, by your actions made the trial of Pantrixnia superfluous, but unfortunately that is only my opinion. Nazeera the woman believes Alexander the man, and she has no desire for conflict. Yet, Nazeera the woman is not Nazeera of Chem, of the Triumvirate; and Alexander the man may also be Alexander the legend. Nazeera of Chem cannot accept such a risk when the empire is at stake. How can one man wipe out the aspirations of generations? By my own estimation, Alexander, you've built your life for a grasp at immortality. How well that sits within the construction of Alexander's dreams! Who better to lead the race of Alexander to the stars, and to conquest than you?

"Yet when you speak to me as a man to a woman I don't see the general plotting over my empire or the pirate greedy for my wealth. I see in those saurian eyes sincerity, courage, desire and honor. How am I supposed to read this riddle? Does the culmination of the "Legend of Alexander" stand before me, daring me to disbelieve, or is Alexander simply an extraordinary man plucked from his world; bravely trying to make his way in the strangeness of an unknown universe? Nazeera of Chem still doubts that you may be anything but a marvelous actor, and a very dangerous adversary. Of only one thing am I certain: you are no mercenary of Scythia! No Scythian ever bred could heel you to their side. Oh, how you've addled my wits, I who abhor self doubt!"

He took her by the shoulders and turned her gently to him. "There are times, Nazeera, when all the pieces of the game are in motion and we must allow them to play their parts. Something tells me you and I are not finished with this drama. If by chance we meet again it will be on different terms, and who knows what may happen? For now let's leave the weight of the world on someone else's shoulders, and enjoy a drink on the edge of your wondrous planet."

"There is only one other certainty in this: Terrans are poets," she smiled. "Warriors, philosophers, and poets; what a fascinating combination, I should find it very difficult to be bored with you, Alexander."

"Well that is certainly an improvement," he said. "By night's end I hope to maybe we can strike a happy medium between the mercenary dog and the aspiring galactic despot. Neither is very probable. The truth, as usual, is somewhere in the middle."

She laughed, "Alexander, you speak as suitor would, with charm and wit. I wish I were indifferent to your fate. I admit that a further exploration of you would be stimulating. It's too bad you weren't born of Chem."

"You cut me to the quick yet again," he told her in mock lamentation. "Do you find my alien looks so ugly?"

"Oh no, not that at all," Nazeera told him. "My brother thinks you are quite acceptable, for a male. I must admit that I agree. While you're strange, with your saurian eyes and bulky musculature, I don't find you unattractive. Now if you were born of Chem, who knows? I might never have married Bureel."

"Ah, so I would have had to have been born of Chem!"

"Alexander, don't be so childish! Interspecies marriages are not so unusual amongst the Galactics, and there is no stigma attached socially or politically." Nazeera smiled, giving him a good natured prod in the ribs. "You infer my words in too personal a manner. I can't blame you, however, as Nazar isn't very careful about such things. I spoke only for the purpose of giving you an example. I didn't intend on personalizing our situation."

"I think you spoke to the point, to the moment, and to the crux of our situation," Alexander said. He lifted a hand to her cheek and gently stroked it. Her eyes flashed, but she didn't stop him. Alexander could feel the battle, and the uncertainty within her. She trembled ever so slightly. "I very much wonder what it would be like to kiss you, Nazeera."

"Alexander, I cannot and will not!" Her words were sharp, and their meaning was apparent, but they were hushed, as if spoken half against her will. She took his hand in her own, removing it from her cheek, but she didn't let it go.

Alexander grasped her hip with his free hand and pulled her to him. In that short second their bodies embraced; the suppleness of her form unleashed a rush of warmth through his body, and he kissed her. The kiss was fleeting, warm, effervescent, and for a brief instant returned with wonderment and interest. Then she pushed him away.

"No, Alexander, I cannot," she said, breathing heavily. "This is not acceptable, for me, or for my position."

"Indeed it is not," agreed the smooth voice of Bureel. "It is touching, but I wonder, if the Assemblage would see it so?"

"Bureel!" Nazeera gasped, angry that he should invade her privacy, and catch her in such a compromising position.

"Well, Bureel have you found the guts to return and fulfill your cowardly challenge to me?" Alexander growled, turning upon the smaller male with ferocity born of embarrassment. "If so you find me ready to wait upon your treachery!"

"How quaint, my barbaric friend, but I can't help but thank you. How else could I have revealed my wife's treasonous behavior?"

"Treason, how dare you to insinuate," Nazeera protested.

"In the arms of an enemy of Chem, my dear wife," Bureel interrupted, but the wolf-like leap of the Terran cut him off.

Alexander launched himself at the Chem male, hands grasping for his throat. Bureel gasped, but at the same moment he pressed a button on his belt. In mid leap, Alexander felt a terrible burning in his brain.

✠   ✠   ✠

Alexander convulsed in mid leap. His momentum carried him into Bureel anyway, knocking the lesser male sprawling. Alexander hit the floor as a lifeless mass and did not move.

Nazeera rushed to him, but there was no sign of life. "You fool, Bureel, he's dead!"

Bureel rose with a snarling laugh. "He's not dead, my dear wife. No, he's tied too closely to my plans. He must die on Pantrixnia, as you so wisely decided before your emotions overwhelmed your reason. Then, we shall launch our invasion of Terra, Scythia and the galaxy. You will now become my greatest ally, Nazeera. Even I couldn't have foreseen such good fortune! You will now use your influence at my bidding, at least until the point where you vacate your seat in favor of your husband, so that you may properly tutor my heir!"

"Never Bureel," Nazeera spat in furious disgust. "Never shall you see your heir spring from my loins, and you shall never have my seat!"

"Think again my lovely," he advised her. "Should I inform the Assemblage of your treason you'd be fortunate to join your Terran on Pantrixnia. It might be more difficult at this point for me to make such a leap of power. With Nazar out of the way, however, the task is much simpler!"

"Nazar," she breathed.

"Of course, being the loyal brother, and honorable son, he would have no recourse but to address his shame with suicide," Bureel grinned with nefarious pleasure. "That is how I would explain his untimely death."

"So you're behind the assassination attempt! Bureel you are a shameless cur with no sense of honor or loyalty," Nazeera told him.

"I wasn't found in the Terran's embrace. If that delicious tidbit is to remain a secret I will have your obedience, Nazeera."

Bureel grinned and rang for his henchman, who summarily removed Alexander. Then he poured himself some wine. Turning to Nazeera he said, "This is an exceedingly eventful night, don't you think? I can think of no better way to consummate it than for us to address the issue of an heir!"

CHAPTER 26:
PANTRIXNIA

Alexander's head throbbed with a sharp electric burn. He marveled that Bureel hadn't fried his brain completely. The familiar sensation of a cold metal floor brought his senses back into focus. He opened his eyes to the dull gray light of another dungeon, but one slightly different from his other cell.

On the wall was a flat gray screen, and beneath it was a series of icons. He got up to investigate. He was stiff, and the nerves of his hands and feet like live wires. The physical pain only served to heighten his own criticism of his behavior.

He was mad to compromise Nazeera as he did.

"Funny way to show her I care," Alexander scolded himself, looking around at his new prison. "This is Bureel's work. I guess he's calling the shots now, and I'm on my way to Pantrixnia. If I ever get out of this I'll finish the strangling of him!"

There was a thump, and he almost fell to the floor. A loud noise grew outside his cell. The screen illuminated and a female Chem appeared. It wasn't Nazeera. "Terran, we've entered the atmosphere of Pantrixnia! We'll be landing shortly. You may select whatever weapons you choose, and whatever clothing, but we will not wait for you. As we touchdown you will be discharged. That is all. Remember all the Chem Empire is watching you, may you die well!"

The picture changed. It now presented a table of weapons ranging from energy guns to edged blades. He chose what appeared to be an energy rifle, a pair of hand held energy guns, a long knife and a sword. He expected to be on the planet longer than the Chem did, so he didn't want to be entirely dependent on energy weapons.

A second screen showed a similar table of garments. These included all encompassing suits of armor, light clothing and combinations in between. He chose a suit of mixed protection and weight. The weapons were behind an automatic sliding hatch, as was the suit. Alexander gathered everything about his person and hurriedly dressed himself. He was none too quick. He'd hoped to go back and review the choices at a more leisurely pace, but just as he shrugged the sword belt over his shoulder the ship bumped to a landing.

He looked around for a door, but he saw none. Then the floor slid away beneath his feet. Alexander fell heavily to the ground. A hurricane of wind and debris surrounded him. Wet leaves slapped against his face and a rush of hot air pummeled him. Then, just a suddenly, the world quieted down and the sound of the jungle overcame the receding engines of the Chem ship.

He was alone in the misty daylight of the Chem prison planet Pantrixnia.

It was a jungle planet; that much was apparent. They set him in a small clearing. It had a dirt floor and was perfectly circular—obviously artificial. All around was a dense jungle, hot, moist and full of sounds. He wasn't alone. Already, eyes were upon him.

Alexander took out his pistol. With a cursory glance he guessed at its operation. There was a contact where the trigger should be. Aiming at a tree he pressed it.

Nothing.

Another glance and he found a latch that looked as though it moved. He slid it back and a red light illuminated on top of the gun. A small green light bar also illuminated in the handle. He aimed and pressed the contact again. A blast of blue energy erupted from the focus and the tree splintered and burned at the point of contact. The light bar in the handle shrank by a small amount, and gauging it he guessed there were fifteen to twenty shots left. Holstering the gun he drew the sword.

The blade was lighter than a steel sword, and roughly a meter long by three inches wide. It had a comfortable feel in his hand, and he had no doubt that he could use it with great effect despite the lives that lay between the present Alexander and the swashbuckler. He kept the sword out as he turned to the jungle.

Water must be his first order of business, and then shelter for the night—he needed to see the lay of the land. Through a gap in the canopy he spied a high crag roughly a kilometer distant. It was the obvious choice for a lookout, and might provide a defensible camp.

Paths left the clearing in three directions. Alexander turned towards the crag; he loosened the gun in its holster, and held the sword before him. His plan of action, such as he had, was to use the guns as a last recourse, relying heavily on the sword.

From what little the Chem told him of this place it was a twisted form of galactic coliseum intended for dispatch of criminals in an honorable way. If stocked only with animals, and no intelligent life, he hoped that sheer bluster would carry him through as much as his sword and gun. Animals on the whole, at least those of Earth, usually tried to avoid conflicts that would get them injured. Injury in the wilderness was a death sentence. Perhaps, he thought, bluff could go as far as combat. He hoped so. Considering the possible length of his stay the gun and the rifle would have frighteningly short lives, and swordplay would have limited affect on large carnivores.

He stepped onto the trail, instantly aware of two things. There was a piece of armor or clothing lying partially on the beaten path. It was ragged on the edges and stained. The other object of note was the wall of impenetrable foliage on either side of the track. It was the perfect place for an ambush. He crouched, waiting and listening. For the moment he was at a loss as to how to proceed. A barely audible whirring caught his attention and he whipped around to face it, backhanding his sword in a whistling arc.

A sharp metallic "thunk!" announced the collision between the sword and a floating metal automaton. His expectation of danger turned to surprise as the automaton, jumped upwards several meters at the impact. Shortly, however, it steadied and floated back down to him. It stopped slightly out of range of his sword and hung in mid air.

"Edgy already, eh Terran," said the automaton in a high pitched sing-song voice. "Welcome to Pantrixnia! I'll be following your progress for our intergalactic ethernet broadcast, so no need to be alarmed at my presence. I see you've found our last participant, or what they left of him. He didn't get very far. It was a very disappointing performance."

Alexander tried to hear over the artificial buzz of the automaton, but it was difficult, and that was making him nervous. "I'll try to improve on that, now if you don't mind,"

"Let's hope so," the voice cut in. "After all we've a vast audience. Over fifty billion people of eleven different species are tuning into to watch you this instant. The level of interest is quite high. The Elder himself, and the entire Assemblage, is now watching you live on the Chem Homeworld!"

"They honor me," he said sarcastically.

"By the way, that's an interesting choice of weapons you have," the automaton said. "Would you mind explaining your rational. We've never had a Terran participant before."

"Maybe later, if you don't mind, I'm busy," Alexander told it with finality. He'd finally made up his mind as to how he would progress. He made his way alertly over to the tree he'd blasted. As he crossed the clearing there was a slight tremor in the muddy earth, followed quickly by the heavy breathing of some cavernous breast and the sound of undergrowth being trampled. It reminded him vaguely of a dog trotting through tall grass, a very large dog.

"We have our first guest of the day," exclaimed the automaton. "You guessed it, the Banthror! As always he's attracted by the sound of our drop ship. He knows what that means!"

Alexander cursed, but he held his ground next to the charred tree. The sound grew louder, and suddenly a bright orange and purple striped head burst out of the jungle wall. It was conical, as if shaped for penetrating the dense jungle, and contained the requisite maw filled with tusk-like teeth. The head joined a muscular body, tall in front and low in the back like a hyena, but more the size of a large rhino with eight legs.

The Banthror stopped suddenly and leapt sideways. The move startled Alexander until he realized the creature had done this before. It expected to get shot at. In mid leap it sighted him. The Banthror landed on all eight feet at once. Immediately it sprang for the spot where Alexander stood, mouth agape and the four front feet splayed, claws springing to ready.

Alexander expected as much, or rather his instincts expected it. The Banthror was too fast to think of a plan of action. He leapt to the side, swinging the sword in a wide defensive arc as he did so. The blade caught one of the paws flush at the ankle, and with a "chunk!" the member flew off. The Banthror scrambled to a stop just to the side of Alexander, one claw catching the shoulder of his armor. The claws skidded off the plate without penetrating the armor, but it spun Alexander about. Alexander didn't try and resist the force of the Banthror's blow, but used the impetus to turn and strike at the same time. As the Banthror snapped at him with a mouth large enough to bite the man in two, Alexander's backhanded slash cut deeply across the creature's snout. Blood spurted as the blade parted the sensitive flesh and raked across its skull. The Banthror snapped its head back with a yelp.

Alexander ducked behind the tree, but the Banthror moved swifter, despite its wounds, and cut him off. The leering bloody face loomed directly in front of him. The mouth opened, and the four hind legs gathered themselves in the soft soil to leap. Alexander drew his pistol and shot straight into the slavering maw. Burned flesh and blood showered him in a crimson haze. The Banthror dropped like a stone.

"Well done, well done!" the automaton exclaimed. "What an exciting way to begin! Tell us, how does it feel to defeat one of the lesser scavengers of Pantrixnia?"

Alexander ignored the remark, but he did reflect momentarily on how well his past-life experiences served him in the combat. His fight with the Banthror could have been choreographed with pistol and cutlass, or knife and sword. Alexander didn't think; he simply acted. The reality of his theory was comforting, but the sounds of the jungle reminded him that there was much still to do.

He turned his attention to the fallen Banthror. The carcass would soon attract other predators. Cutting a long swath of hide, about six feet wide and six feet long, he folded it in two and draped it over his shoulder, tucking either end into his belt. His idea was to carry the scent of the Banthror with him. The creature may be in the lower echelons of the food chain on Pantrixnia, but it was still a step up. Hastily cutting a few strips of meat and securing these to his belt Alexander left the clearing.

"Ugh! You're not planning on eating those are you?" the automaton asked. "I doubt if it will harm you, but Banthror is at best unpalatable."

"I like my Beef Wellington medium rare with a flaky crust if you care to send down something a bit more civilized!" Alexander snapped, as he worked his way through the hole the Banthror made in the jungle and on to the round bole of a tree.

"That wouldn't be fair. This is, after all, a party of your own making, Terran. We must all lie in the bed we make."

Alexander reached the tree and grappled one of the thick vines that grew up the trunk. The trees grew to over forty meters, with the top half being composed of a matte of thick branches. The canopy of trees looked to be interwoven, and might provide him with a quicker, and safer, route than along the jungle floor. It was a long climb, but the bark was rough and gave his boots good purchase. In a few moments he was twenty meters above the jungle floor, and none too soon.

Several other carnivores already gathered to feast on the Banthror's carcass. Some were larger, and some smaller, but they were all strange to his eyes. He sat in a crotch of the tree, watching. Half dozen animals were pulling and tugging at the Banthror when a large black and green lion creature made its appearance. It was half again as large as the Banthror, and its presence made the other beasts shrink back snarling to the edge of the clearing. The monster deposited itself over its meal and soon the sound of crunching bones and ripping flesh drifted up to him. Alexander thought he'd seen enough, but then something caught his attention.

Not one hundred meters from him, just at the edge of his sight, a huge saurian shape stalked silently through the jungle. It led with its enormous head, parting the foliage and carefully placing each of its taloned feet into the damp earth. Its tail moved in concert, floating far behind as a counterbalance to that two meter set of jaws.

The sight of this ancient Earth creature on this alien world stunned Alexander with delight. The automaton floated next to him, and whispered, "You have the rare privilege of watching the greatest carnivore of our galaxy on the hunt. He comes from your planet,

Terran. We theorize that some ancient race transplanted them here, and on other worlds. That was many lost civilizations ago when the galaxy was adolescent. We found them here on Pantrixnia, and that gave us the impetus to build this world as you now see it. In all the galaxy, though, there is nothing like this creature!"

"It's a Tyrannosaurus," Alexander breathed, "an honest to God real Tyrannosaurus!"

"What did you call it, Terran?" the automaton asked.

"Tyrannosaurus Rex: King of the Tyrant Lizards."

"An admirable name."

The Tyrannosaurus wormed its way to the edge of the clearing with no one the wiser. It chose just the right vantage point, whether by instinct or cunning, at the hindquarters of the lion creature. The lion creature munched contentedly, unaware that the Tyrannosaurus was gathering itself for a leap. Alexander held his breath, but when the leap came he was altogether unprepared for the suddenness of it. The Tyrannosaurus covered twenty meters with two strides and a lunge. Despite its bulk it was almost graceful, but the violence of the charge destroyed whatever beauty it had. The enormous head stretched out to bite and hold, but so quick was the lion creature that it escaped the six inch teeth. Unfortunately for the lion, the direction of the Tyrannosaur's attack propelled its panic stricken escape straight into the tree.

Frantically, it scrambled to get up, but the jaws of the Tyrannosaurs shot down at the exposed spine. The huge teeth found purchase in the soft flesh; the grip of the terrible vise drove the moist air from the creature's lungs with a terrible fatal gasp. Lifting the enormous mammal like a doll the Tyrannosaurus shook it, showering the glade with blood and fur. A rending snap signaled the parting of bone, and the Tyrannosaurus threw the carcass to the ground, bellowing a challenge through the jungle. Then, with what could only be a growl of satisfaction, it settled down its feast.

"Amazing," Alexander breathed.

"Yes, indeed, but the wonderful thing about Pantrixnia is not the sheer power of death, but the subtlety of it."

A thrill of fear shot through him, and Alexander turned just in time to see the blur of the snake as it struck. It aimed for his neck, but his sudden movement caused it to strike his back. The force of the blow nearly catapulted him off the tree, but his left hand blindly clutched for, and desperately held on to a thick vine. He swung into space, hanging there twenty meters above the forest floor.

CHAPTER 27:
SURVIVAL

Alexander clung desperately to the vine with one hand while clawing for a hold with his other hand. His momentum carried him out and around the tree, twisting and turning. He smacked against the trunk or a thick branch, he couldn't tell which, and the stiff vine propelled him back whence he came. Back he swung, the jungle whizzing by below in a green blur. He turned half around when he landed back in the crotch in the midst of the snake. Coils as thick as his waist looped over him.

The snake's head, nearly half a meter wide, separated itself from the snarl and lifted above him. It struck for his face, but Alexander let go of the vine and blocked it with his armored left arm. The armor saved his life. The fangs failed to penetrate smearing venom on the hard surface. The snake didn't let go, and tried to inject its venom into the captured member. It champed, but to no effect. The Chem armor was simply too tough to pierce.

Alexander's right arm was free, and as the snake sought to deliver a mortal bite he clutched for a weapon. The first thing his groping fingers found was the haft of his knife. He drew it, slicing a wide gash in the snake's body. Red blood oozed out of the deep wound, but the snake didn't let go.

With its head locked on his arm Alexander set the point in the beaded scales of the lower jaw and shoved. The eighteen inch blade plunged through the jaws until the point sprang from the top of the skull smeared with gore. The jaws opened, releasing his arm, but the crotch of the tree became a writhing mass of muscle and scale.

The death throes of the snake pummeled Alexander mercilessly. The knife was torn from his grasp, still transfixing the skull. With a final spasmodic jerk the snake shuddered and slowly slid out of the tree. The snake was still looped around Alexander. As if to gain a final measure of revenge the heavy carcass began to pull Alexander out of the tree. He clutched for the closest vine, frantically wrapping it around his arm. The snake slid out of the tree, coil by coil, stretching him like a rack. Finally, the last coil slipped off and the carcass thumped to the forest floor.

Alexander watched it fall, and so did the Tyrannosaurus. The snake dropped not five meters away.

"You'll have to be more careful in the future," the automaton advised him. "We wouldn't want to waste such a promising start! A pity about your knife though, I've a feeling you'll be missing it!"

Alexander settled himself back in the crotch of the tree and caught his breath. He cast a sour glance at the floating silver ball.

"Just how many people have you talked to death down here?"

The Tyrannosaurus looked up at him and snarled. Then it returned to its business, ripping huge chunks of flesh and bone from the rapidly disappearing lion creature. Alexander surveyed the scene. All the other carrion creatures scattered during the attack, and none had returned. His knife was still lodged in the snake's head, tantalizingly close, and yet impossibly far away.

If he waited for the Tyrannosaurus to finish and leave, the scavengers would be on the snake in no time. They would dissect the carcass and carry the head away to some dark den, and the knife with it. At the moment the Tyrannosaurus seemed unconcerned with anything or anyone. There was nothing for it. Alexander took a deep breath, questioned his own sanity and began to climb down the vine.

"What are you doing?"

"No one takes what's mine," Alexander said gruffly.

"You can't be serious. A knife can't be that valuable. Think about this. You've already made a wonderful beginning, don't spoil it now."

Alexander ignored the rest of it. Cautiously he made his way down, keeping an eye on the Tyrannosaurus. He didn't want to surprise it, so he climbed down in full view of the leviathan, not trying to hide or do anything else which would arouse its suspicions. It watched him for a short time. Then apparently deciding he was too small to be of concern, it turned back to its meal. It continued to feed as he passed the ten meter point. Now it could pluck him from the tree if it so desired. His heart beat palpably in his breast as he reached the ground.

There was no use of stealth now. If the Tyrannosaurus wanted him he'd have to shoot it and hope for the best, there was no way he could climb the tree faster than the dinosaur could move. Alexander stepped boldly to the body of the snake, going straight to the head.

"Excuse me Rex, I'll just get my knife and be on my way. There's a good boy," Alexander said, trying to bolster his own courage. As he stooped to pull out the knife the Tyrannosaurus raised its dripping head from its meal and snorted. The fetid breath, heavy with the smell of fresh blood, rolled over him. He ignored it and went about his business of pulling out the knife. The Tyrannosaurus snorted again, but then returned to its meal.

Alexander took the opportunity to cut snake's tail off, it was right there within arm's reach, giving him a meter long piece of meat—just in case the Banthror was as bad as the automaton said. Without further notice from the Tyrannosaurus, he climbed back into his perch in the tree. The automaton was waiting for him.

"In all my decurns on Pantrixnia that's definitely a first. Terran, either you are the most foolish form of intelligent life ever spawned in this galaxy, or, well, I can't actually think of another option."

Alexander caught his breath, and let his heart rate settle to an acceptable level, but while he rested he scanned the trees. He wouldn't be caught by surprise a second time. Alexander didn't hurry, but was content to recover from his exertion and watch the Tyrannosaurus. After fifteen minutes the Tyrannosaurus gave a bellow, picked up the remains of the carcass and stalked into the jungle. Alexander got up and climbed higher into the canopy. The automaton followed him, floating annoyingly close to his head.

"What now Terran?"

He stopped, glancing at the metal ball with blatant irritation. "If you're going to tag along you might as well start calling me Alexander. "Terran" is growing tedious."

"Unfortunately, Terran, we do not typically allow our participants the honor of being named until they've distinguished themselves in death."

"Very well, have it your way then." He pulled out his gun and shot the automaton. The ball burned and fell from the air, careening off a number of branches and scattering the scavengers that were already gathering at the carcasses.

"Waste of a round," Alexander observed, and he continued to climb. His goal was a level of matted growth thirty meters above the forest floor. Years of undisturbed growth allowed the branches from different trees to intertwine. Vines and creepers made the matte impenetrable in places. Old leaves and other debris collected in the densest spots. In this decaying mass other plants took hold, adding their stems and roots to the weave. Another layer of the canopy spread overhead and another after that. A perpetual twilight hid these secondary worlds from the sky, and the darkness of the forest floor below, but they were far from empty.

Alexander gained the first level of the canopy and gingerly started in the direction of the crag, vague comparisons with Tarzan of the Apes flitting though his head. He hadn't progressed more than fifty meters before he saw he was not alone in the trees. In the glooms were tall insect-like creatures shaped roughly like a praying mantis, but like everything else on this planet they were far larger. There were a number of them, and they seemed to be foraging along his trail. Carefully, Alexander stepped off the matted vegetation and onto one of the larger branches. Footing on the undulating canopy floor was treacherous. Hidden holes and snags forced him to use vines and branches for support and pay close attention to each step.

He took a direction leading led away from the creatures. He stayed low, almost moving on all fours, and crept along quietly, hoping they might just miss him. He'd only gone another twenty meters when one of them sprang suddenly upright, its antennae waving in the air.

The mantis emitted a loud staccato clicking that attracted the attention of the others. The mantis turned towards him. Alexander stood upright, facing them openly. He hoped his size might cause them to lose interest and seek easier prey. Their answer was one of great excitement and chatter. Like crabs they scuttled over the matt toward him, clacking as they came. As they approached the insects fanned out with the obvious intention of encircling him.

Alexander cursed. His sword would be next too useless against this many creatures. He took out his gun reluctantly. Perhaps if he killed one the rest would retreat. If they did not, however, he'd use up half his remaining charges defending himself. He hesitated.

"Who makes an energy gun with so few shots!" he cursed aloud. Then it occurred to him that no one would. Swiftly he scanned the device. There were no buttons or controls that he could see other than those he'd already found, but the muzzle had a notched projection on the ring immediately behind the focus. He'd have guessed it was a sight. At the moment, though, it set upon the side of the barrel. He turned it and the light on top of the gun dimmed. He turned it all the way around until the light went out, and then back up a few clicks. The light was dim but apparent. He shot the foremost mantis.

A thin beam scorched its abdomen, and it beat the air with its forelegs. Alexander turned the gun on the next, and the next, and so on until each mantis had a taste of it. The insects, with much clicking between them, beat a hasty retreat. They gathered at the edge of his visual range, and then disappeared.

Alexander didn't like the look of the insects. They worked together and they were too numerous to beat back with a sword. With a greater sense of urgency he worked his way towards the crag. He'd not gone more than a hundred meters, however, when he caught sight of movement behind him. It was the mantises. This time they'd returned in greater numbers. Scores of the huge insects scuttled across the canopy at an alarmingly swift rate.

Alexander's gun was useless against such a horde. He headed for the nearest hole in the canopy. The mantises were scarcely ten meters behind when he came to a spot where he could see the forest floor. He didn't wait but jumped through and caught hanging vine. The vine hung in a great loop thirty meters above the forest floor—he swung to and fro. Alexander made his way hand-over-hand away from the hole as quickly as he could. A quick glance behind did nothing to ease his nerves. As he feared, the mantises were scrambling out of the hole after him. Their articulated appendages made maneuvering upside down on the canopy as easy as walking.

"I see you've found the Remvalix," said a familiar voice, and another silver automaton floated by his right shoulder. "They are perhaps the most intelligent of the transplanted species of Pantrixnia, and they've claimed the canopy as their territory."

"Really," Alexander grunted. He was too busy to comment further. He wasn't going to make it to the trunk of the tree before the mantises caught him. He switched tactics, wrapping his left arm around the vine and drawing his knife. As the first mantis closed in he slashed at the vine. The vine parted and he fell just beneath the cut of a mandible.

He fell ten meters before the vine jerked him up and swung him towards the tree, but not quite to it. Alexander swung back and forth in space, ten meters below the matte of the canopy and twenty meters above the forest floor.

"You're in a spot now," the automaton told him. "Your present predicament looks fairly bleak; any ideas?"

"One," he gasped. He sheathed his knife and started to swing on the vine. He couldn't reach the trunk of the tree, but five meters to the other side was another vine that hung straight down from the matte to just above the vegetation of the forest floor. The mantises were now gathering above his haven. One was quickly starting to come down the vine towards him.

He took a moment to shoot it. It squealed and fell by him, crashing into the undergrowth of the forest floor. He did the same to the next mantis that dared the vine. This one flailed as he fell, reaching for him with its hook-like hands. A mandible caught his shoulder and only the raised lip of his cuirass kept it from sliding into and slicing through his exposed neck.

Alexander holstered his gun. Fortunately the Remvalix were now wary of his gun. They skittered around the vine clacking excitedly; apparently, they didn't want to give up on him, but they didn't want to climb down the vine either.

While they hesitated Alexander swung himself on the vine and launched himself into space. He caught the other vine several meters lower than he started. It jarred him, but he hung on. The mantis scuttled over to his new hanging spot intent on repeating their strategy, but before they could get there a thin dark shape shot out and caught one of them.

It was a tongue.

The tongue belonged to a ten meter monstrosity that lurched out from behind the trunk of the nearest tree. It hung upside down from great hooks that plunged into the tangle of vines and branches. The tongue drew the struggling mantis into its long tubular mouth where its jaws ground the insect to a pulp. No sooner had the first mantis disappeared then the tongue shot out again. The procedure repeated many times as the creature ambled towards the hole. The mantises fled back into the canopy, but it followed them; it poked its head through the hole it, adding a few more to its colossal stomach.

Alexander made his way down the vine before the anteater, or whatever the thing was, decided to try him as well. He would take his chances in the jungle. There, at least, he could maneuver naturally.

It was a severe blow to his hopes. The trees on Earth were man's ancestral haven, but he should have expected as much. The Chem were clever, and it wouldn't surprise him if every nook and cranny of this world had its own unique representative among the galaxies most fantastic carnivores. He returned to the forest floor with the grim realization that he could still see the burned tree of the clearing. His afternoon thus far included three close brushes with death in a hundred meters of travel. He was growing thirsty and tired; he'd yet to find water or a place of relative safety to hide.

He was alive, though, and that alone made up for all his misfortunes.

The automaton bobbed up in front of him. "That was another narrow escape, Alexander of Terra. Nazeera of the Triumvirate authorized us to use your given name during your adventures. You've been remarkably lucky so far. Do you have anything you wish to pass on to the many who are watching you now?"

"My thanks to Nazeera of the Triumvirate for her noble gesture," he said, moving on into the jungle. "I count myself fortunate to have had the honor to meet her. She is well worthy of your praise. I send her greetings, as I do all Chem but one."

"And who would that singular Chem you spurn be?"

"To Bureel of Chem I send nothing but scorn and contempt for his cowardice," he said harshly. "When I leave here I will return to Chem, not for conquest, but for Bureel. I repeat my challenge to him: Bureel you are a cowardly cur! I will meet you at any place, any time, and in any honorable manner. Will you satisfy honor? Upon your answer does the honor of all Chem rest before the eyes of their brethren on Terra. Yet will you or nil you, Bureel, one day I shall have the satisfaction of strangling the miserable life out of your wretched carcass! Then I shall have rid an otherwise august body of a worm!"

Alexander stormed off into the jungle, leaving the automaton speechless before over fifty billion beings.

CHAPTER 28:
THE PAPER TIGER GROWS TEETH

It was three days travel from Chem to Pantrixnia, and during that time work on Terra progressed at a feverish and increasingly organized pace.

Everywhere there was preparation, but the greatest hive of activity centered in Terra's port cities. Scythian tender ships floated over the dry-docks. Terrans teemed by the thousands over the beached hulls of ships. Terran engineers worked side by side with Scythian engineers. They were, to be certain, awed by the technology and the reality of what they were trying to accomplish at first. The Scythians placated their charges in their desperation, but never expected the hodgepodge navy they were building would ever do anything but orbit Terra harmlessly.

The Terran idea was surprisingly workable, but the reality of Terrans being able to adapt to the new environment of space was unthinkable—to the Scythians. The Scythian attitude, so justified during the first few frantic days, endured something of a change as Terrans soon grew accustomed to the miracle they created. Terrans morphed from obedient drones to the imaginative power and energy behind the magic they made.

The turning point was the armament problem. For simplicity's sake the Terran engineers had the Scythians mount the energy weapons in the "Iowa's" turrets, which they found surprisingly well suited for the task. The ability of the guns to maneuver gave the Terran Fleet an advantage over the fixed blaster projectors found in all other galactic fleets. The power required by the blasters, however, proved to be a problem.

The ship's engines had more than enough energy for the purpose, but it required a daunting network of shielded conduits to transfer power to the respective weapons. The Scythians had no easy engineering solution, and suggested that the Terrans be satisfied with the appearance of a well armed fleet.

That response was wholly unacceptable, so the Terran engineers tackled the problem themselves.

The crux of the problem was size. The conduits were massive. Installing them required ripping the ship apart. There wasn't enough time for that, so Terran engineers came up with a solution of their own. They mapped the nearest corridors from the weapons all the way back to the engine room. Then by sealing and strengthening them with another more concentrated titanium bath they turned the corridors themselves into energy conduits. Conventional conduits connected the corridors to the engine junction boxes and the weapon transfer boxes, thereby getting the energy in the proximity of the projectors.

The second problem was that of transferring the energy to the blaster projectors. The solution was another example of absolute simplicity. The projector spheres focused energy in a coherent beam manipulated by electromagnetic fields. Blaster capacitors fed raw energy to the projector spheres after they were charged up with energy supplied by the energy conduits through junction boxes.

There was no way to maintain a connection between the blaster capacitor moving on the end of the projector sphere, the junction box, and the energy conduit—therefore, the Terran engineers simply removed the junction boxes altogether. They sealed the turrets into three separate chambers, one for each gun. An electromagnetic valve opened between the chamber and the energy conduit, allowing energy to flood the chamber and charge the blaster capacitors. The valve closed and the gun was free to maneuver. When the electromagnetic field around the projector opened the high energy plasma flowed from the capacitor to the lowest energy point in space; i.e., the energy well of the projector spheres. The projectors promptly funneled the energy outboard in an appropriate and devastating manner.

The solution to the armament problem cost the engineers double the time they anticipated, but the "Iowa" experiment paid far more in dividends. By the time the "Iowa" was nearing completion a miraculous transformation occurred in the ship, and in the people who worked on her—what Scythians began Terrans finished.

What Scythians considered impossible Terrans solved.

The Terrans quickly took the technology for granted and put it to work for them. By the time the "Iowa" was ready to cast off Terran engineers were in charge of every phase of construction. The grand old ship gleamed with new life under the floodlights; it was a portent for what was soon to be a fleet of well armed modern interstellar warships.

In the thirteen short days of the colossal "Iowa" experiment, Terra underwent a metamorphosis from a planet bound people into a race of fledgling galactic warriors. By midnight on the thirteenth day the "Iowa" would be in orbit. The construction of a Terran battle fleet was already underway, using the principles developed in the "Iowa" experiment. Engineers felt the next wave of ships could be completed in only nine to eleven days, and in a few weeks the process could be honed down to only a week.

By time Scythian intelligence estimated the Chem Armada could enter Scythian space, Terra could theoretically mass over seven hundred warships able to meet them. They would comprise a rag tag fleet to be certain, but each vessel would be capable of delivering the most prevalent weapons in the known galaxy. Even the Chem would view the Terran Fleet with respect.

In a gray office overlooking the dry-dock the Scythian Liaison watched the frantic work below, fully cognizant that in the space of two Terran weeks it had lost control of its charges. It was night, but floodlights illuminated the enormity of the "Iowa" and the army of dockyard workers swarming over her, getting her ready for her first flight.

As if to further the Scythians' new found concern the indomitable lines of the "Wisconsin" rose in the dry-dock next door, and beyond that were the "Missouri," and the "New Jersey." As the Scythian watched it listened with intense concentration to a transmission from the Scythian Council. It was disturbed. By all accounts the arming went remarkably well, but even at this early stage the Scythians were becoming observers and advisors, not controllers.

The Terrans absorbed the data the Scythians presented them and disposed of the constant influx of supplies with a rapidity that confounded the Galactics. The Scythian theory of a "paper" fleet was rapidly melting away; it disappeared along with the Scythian hope that Terrans simply could not handle the paradigm change inherent with this incredible leap in technology. Less than a week after first contact with the species Terra already sprouted planetary defenses and now it was plotting its strategy for using a translight capable fleet of warships.

The thoughts of the Council representative were upbeat, but still concerned. "We understand by your reports that the Terrans will be capable of a significantly greater response than originally anticipated. You have done well, Liaison, though, the numbers you quote have, I admit, alarmed some members of the Council. With seven hundred warships the Terrans could do quite more than just defend themselves."

"That is true, Council," the Liaison answered. "It is the crux of my complaint. Even with the primitive vessels they are using as hulls their fleet will have relatively modern engines and weapons. As you know there has been very little real advancement in warship technology in the last two thousand millennia. There is, therefore, little or no difference in the performance of the Terran equipment and the modern fleets of Chem, Golkos or Seer'koh. I have complained that the Terrans needed only a deterrent fleet, yet they will accept no argument.

"They informed me that if we wanted Scythia protected we would have to supply them with anything and everything they need."

"Inform them we are short of the necessary materials," Council said.

"Unfortunately our earlier negotiations gave the Terrans quite the opposite impression. We did not anticipate how quickly they could assimilate to their new circumstances," Liaison told them. "The Council made the decision to arm Terra shortly after the Chem boarded our science vessel and took the Terran subject prisoner. The Terrans responded with amazing promptness. We already have several hundred thousand Terran troops enroute to our Homeworlds, and Terra sprouts defenses, rivaling those of any Galactic Homeworld. In less than a decand the Terrans began construction of their first warship. It will be ready for trials in less than a decurn. We estimate, at this rate that the Terran Fleet will number between seven hundred and nineteen and seven hundred and thirty-one vessels of various armaments."

"That is roughly three quarters the size of the Chem Armada if it sailed in its entirety," Council mused. "How well are they armed?"

"The vessel that will launch tonight will have a total of thirty-three blaster projectors ranging from level thirteen to level thirty-seven weapons. In addition there are provisions for two batteries of matter-anti-matter torpedoes."

"Incredible! That is in the same class as a Galactic battleship. How is this possible? Can we allow this to continue, even to buy the Terrans aid? Perhaps we can persuade the Terrans that a smaller fleet is practical. Can you slow them down?"

"In their paranoid state it would only cause suspicion, which might have dangerous repercussions."

"Well, what about our request for Terran troops?"

"The Terrans have already designated five million troops for transportation to Scythia, however, they demanded that the families be allowed to join them," the Liaison told them. "Their argument is that if the Chem destroy Terra their race would survive elsewhere. I saw no counter argument to their logic."

"Very well, we understand the situation," Council answered. "Continue as you are. Ingratiate yourself with our new Terran friends. Help them as much as you can. If we cannot keep them harmless we must direct their passions to the correct purpose. The Chem have sentenced the captured Terran to death on Pantrixnia. Make the broadcast available for distribution through Terran communication channels. Play this up as typical Chem justice. We shall make the Terrans hate the Chem."

"It is an apt suggestion. However, the Terrans have already accessed those Ethernet channels. They are fully aware of the Chem atrocity. In that respect, at least, we need not worry over Terran ingenuity. They are thalamus driven, as are the Chem, and shall easily be turned against them."

"Very well, we shall pursue that avenue. Our goal must now be to ensure that if Terra indeed builds a fleet that she uses it against the Chem. Our cursory estimate is that in the aftermath of such a titanic battle neither the Chem nor the Terrans will be in any position to threaten Scythia. In their weakened states we shall be in a prime position to reap the predictable rewards."

CHAPTER 29:
ANOTHER FIGHT FOR SURVIVAL

Nazeera closed her eyes and allowed the slight hum of the anti-gravity disk to wash away the memories of the day. She leaned forward ever so slightly and the disk rose and accelerated. Crouching increased her speed and stopped her climb. She leaned to the left, turning that direction in a long curve. It took her around the tree cloaked finger of a ridge and into a misty valley.

A gushing river churned beneath her, brown foam bubbling around the smooth chocolate backs of slick rocks—like the humps and knobs of half-submerged monsters. Nazeera drew her gun.

She dialed the muzzle back so that the intensity indicator barely showed in the shadowy-misty light. The sound of a waterfall grew in her ears, and Nazeera followed the winding course of the river until she entered a circular amphitheater surrounded by thousand foot cliffs.

A white lace waterfall fell down the slick stone into a lake about two hundred meters wide. The river left the lake through a cleft in the rock. Nazeera scanned the air. She wasn't alone. At least a dozen brightly feathered birds as large as her but with wingspans four times her height, cruised the lake. Their cries and squawks echoed along the cliffs, filling the amphitheater with a raucous deluge of noise that vied with the roar of the waterfall. They were hunting for fish, and they ignored Nazeera. She smiled and pressed a switch on her wrist.

Nazeera couldn't hear anything, but she knew the transmitter was working, because the effect on the birds was immediate. The birds wheeled up and around, squawking angrily, and turning toward Nazeera. The cliff face erupted in a profusion of color as scores of other giant birds left their perches. They made for her, talons glinting in the fading light, half meter beaks snapping in fury.

Nazeera crouched and gained speed. She slalomed through the whirling flock, shooting as she skidded over the brown water. Her shots scorched the birds, but the beams only maddened the birds—the setting wasn't strong enough to drive them off.

A mass of seething, screeching, color enveloped Nazeera. She could only react, darting into patches of clear air, firing from pistols in both hands as she twisted and turned through the feather strewn air. It was wild and perilous. A hum whooshed by her, and she turned hard toward it, surprised by the unwelcome sound, but it was only Nazar.

"By the Moons, Nazeera, are you trying to do Bureel's job for him?" He was riding a similar antigravity disk, and he was armed as she was—but the beams from his guns were brighter. When he shot a bird it squawked and flew out of the fight. "Relax! He's still alive, and quietly bedded down for the night in a niche in the cliff—as you should be! This is insane!"

"Then go home and go to bed, Nazar!"

Nazeera was just beginning to find release of the tension of watching the drama at the Assemblage. She'd convinced herself that she had no true feelings beyond respect for Alexander; the kiss they shared was a natural reaction to the time they'd spent together—yet each new peril had her holding her breath. She watched his trials alongside her peers wearing a mask of cold interest, but beneath her armor her gut was churning with intimate disquiet. Bureel's political and personal schemes did not help matters any. This perilous exercise was pure joy in comparison.

Nazar pulled up next to her, firing as he flew. "Alexander's safe, Nazeera, and that's where you should be—safe and at home!"

"He's safe for the moment, but I've let an opportunity slip away. You were right, Nazar," she admitted, stealing a glance at him. "He's masterful being. We face the prospect that Alexander's death will hurt the Empire in ways we can't imagine, when his friendship might have ended an era of fear and anticipation."

Nazeera shot at three birds closing in on Nazar. He ducked as the beams sizzled by his head.

"It's not the Empire I'm worried about, it's these blasted cormantars you've enraged, and Bureel!" Nazar said with a grimace. He slid behind Nazeera and shot a bird coming up from underneath her. "The birds are sneaky, like your current husband! Don't worry; Alexander's built himself for this moment, Nazeera. Destiny is on his side."

Nazar pulled alongside Nazeera again, trying to keep his antigravity disk steady enough to talk to her while avoiding the cormantars and Nazeera's shots. "I only hope we're still alive when he returns!"

Nazeera grimaced, flipped upside-down and fired at the roiling flock below. One of the cormantars took advantage of her maneuver to dive on her. Nazar saw it before Nazeera did and shot the bird in the wing; its momentum carried it right into her. It hit Nazeera hard, knocking the wind out of her and sending her spinning into the humid air.

Nazeera was too low to retrieve her disk in time. She hit the emergency button on her belt and a microscopic antigravity generator sprang to life. It didn't stop her fall, but it slowed her to a survivable speed—that is, if the cormantars left her alone.

They didn't.

The giant birds must have sensed her helplessness, for they dove on her with renewed vigor. Nazeera increased the energy level of her gun, but she couldn't maneuver herself to see all the cormantars.

A pair of claws ripped at her back, tearing through the thin armor and gashing her flesh. She dropped one of her guns as it sent her flying, but it was a strangely fortunate thing—a huge cormantar sped by—its beak snapped in the moist, empty air where her head used to be.

Nazeera steadied herself, swearing mightily, and shooting as fast as she could. It wasn't enough. Another bird wheeled on her—claws outstretched. Thump! The breath left her lungs in a great rasping gasp, but it was Nazar. He wrapped his arms around her.

"Hold on!" he said, as he accelerated out of the angry flock. He had to make several hasty turns, all that more difficult with Nazeera's extra weight, but momentarily they were out of danger.

Nazar flew to the top of the cliffs and set down on a rocky promontory next to the waterfall.

Nazeera stepped off, saying, "Thanks, Nazar, I owe you that one."

He waved her thanks aside, getting the medical kit out of the disk. "I'd be happy if all we had to worry about was birds." He opened the kit and scanned her back. "There are no infectious bacteria, just some lacerations. The scanner can close them up—just stay still for half a moment, if that's possible."

"I wonder, is there support in the Assemblage for the accomplishment of Bureel's challenge?" she mused, as if the fight never happened— completely oblivious to their perch overlooking a thousand foot waterfall in the emerald green Chem forests. "I'm beginning to think Bureel and his scheming are a greater threat to the Empire than Alexander."

"Finally coming to that conclusion, eh? Well, unfortunately that will take time," Nazar sighed, finishing the medical scan and fusing her clothing back together. "When Alexander challenged him over the ethernet Bureel had no choice but to reiterate his challenge in public. He could never have backed down in the open Assemblage. That you brilliantly made it a motion of Assemblage Procedure makes it official. A pity you wouldn't support the idea when Alexander was on Chem. This would all be over by now. Bureel would be dead, and you would be happily married off and on vacation producing what can only be described as interesting heirs."

"Please Nazar; don't twist the story into an undeserving and unrealistic drama."

"As you wish Nazeera, but remember Alexander is on Pantrixnia fighting for his life while Bureel is after our heads. I don't know what he has over you, but I can guess Alexander fits very neatly into that puzzle. For that I'm sorry—it's my fault for compromising you."

He punched a code in his control pad. Nazeera's antigravity disk obediently climbed up to them and landed next to Nazar's. He punched another code, and they heard the whine of an aerocar approaching. "I put it to you, what better way to solve the collective problems of Bureel and the Terran threat? Bring back Alexander, have him kill Bureel, and marry him. I'll pay for the honeymoon."

"I'm the one with the fortune, Nazar."

"A technicality," he shrugged, as his aerocar landed. He opened the trunk and took out a bottle of wine and a basket. "Looking after you is hungry work," he told her, and he poured them each a glass of wine. There was food as well. Nazar handed Nazeera a drumstick and then munched on his own.

"You've got to stop being so blasted liberal, Nazeera. You know as well as I that cementing empires through marriage is a time honored tradition. Nor is this problematic—we both know Alexander has more than a passing interest in you."

"Which you know a good deal too much about," Nazeera interrupted.

"If I hadn't been distracted by duty I'd know even more—we wouldn't be in this mess." The sun set over the verdant mountains, turning the sky red. Nazar elbowed his sister playfully, "I know enough be certain that Alexander would find the concept intriguing, and why not? He's Alexander, and it's the Chem who concern him above all other people. Without an armada of his own, however, Chem is unassailable. Let the other Galactics fear his legions. Chem doesn't fear Alexander, but we can use him for the greater good of the Empire."

"This is all moot with Alexander on Pantrixnia," Nazeera growled, looking up at the brightening stars. She found the slightly golden pinprick of light that was the Pantrixnian sun, and looked away, unable to contemplate the man as practically as her brother.

"All is not lost," he said. "There's a good chance that we can get him back, and that he would be willing to work with us. Many of the younger members who support Bureel are clamoring for a vote. They want Alexander returned to Chem to undergo the challenge, and for once I agree with them. Be patient."

"A few more decurns and he could be dead. Bureel and his cronies will have all the more reason for a war of aggression, and our position could well be untenable."

"Have some faith in Alexander. His survival this decurn was not entirely due to luck and that fact didn't go unnoticed. Give Alexander a decand and he'll have the Assemblage looking for a way out of this thing; they'll be ready to go and get him just to avoid a war with Terra."

"Or they'll vote for the immediate extermination of all life on Terra, as a precaution," Nazeera replied, finishing her wine and pouring herself another glass. She got up and paced the rock next to the roaring river. "As brave as Terrans may be they have no armada. Our ships would be able to stand off in orbit and bombard the planet into rubble."

"That's a possibility, but don't discount the media," Nazar told her, settling back on a moss covered bank. Something caught his attention and he glanced at the display on his sleeve. "Dear sister, would you mind coming my way about three meters—be quick but not too quick please."

Nazeera knew her brother well enough not to argue. She did as he asked, making her movements as casual as she could muster. She watched Nazar, who seemed unperturbed by whatever his display told him; slide a half meter long black mechanism from the basket. He clipped this into a rod tucked in his boot, and pulled the telescoping tube out to a meter in length.

"Right there is fine, Nazeera, now drink your wine and don't move!" Nazar checked his wrist again, and manipulated his remote, muttering. "There's no courtesy amongst this new generation—our generation. Here we are having a nice quiet picnic and they're intent on spoiling it. Bloody bastards—they're good though!"

Nazeera wasn't sure what Nazar was talking about, but she trusted his judgment.

His aerocar's engine started, and it revved up.

"I don't think they'll notice that, but I can't take the risk," he said, again sounding as if he were talking to himself. He attached his remote to the top of the black mechanism and flipped the screen up. Then he withdrew another bottle of wine from the basket—at least Nazeera thought it was a bottle but it was slightly flattened and concave at the broad end. Nazar shoved it into the back of the mechanism.

It wasn't until he did that the Nazeera realized he'd put together a rifle. He smiled.

A shot split the air.

Nazeera flinched despite her monumental self control and dove for the ground. The air rang, and out of the corner of her eye she saw an angry splash of energy spread out in a golden blaze two meters behind her.

Nazar rolled himself prone, and raised the rifle to his cheek. He looked into the screen of the gun, and said, "The next one's going for the car—and that one, my friend, will fry you!"

Sure enough, another shot sounded, and Nazar's car erupted in flames.

"Got you!" he said smoothly, and he shot once. "Oh my, that one hurt—right down your sight! That won't leave much to look at for the funeral. Oh, you have a partner, run rabbit run!"

He shot again.

"Anyone else?" he smiled, checking his screen. Nazar turned to Nazeera, and said, "That's all of them." He got up and walked over to his smoldering car, shaking his head. "Damn! It's brand new, and bought with your money, Nazeera. Too bad, but I needed the extra power for the defensive screens." Nazar picked up his wine and took a long swig. "The gunner used an express rifle—same one Alexander picked for Pantrixnia—nasty weapon."

"How long did you know about them?" Nazeera asked.

"They followed you here," Nazar told her. "I thought they were after me initially—why take you out now Nazeera? Bureel wants an heir first doesn't he?"

"He has my eggs, Nazar," she growled. "As much as he might like to consummate the act physically he knows he has legal access to my eggs should I die."

"We need to get Alexander back here," Nazar said, and his expression was deadly serious.

"Is that what is best for Chem, though?"

"What? Do you really think that Terrans pose such a threat to Chem?" Nazar asked, obviously startled by her response. He pulled up a tape of Terrans on the screen of his sleeve. It was footage intercepted by the Chem scout ship that kidnapped Alexander.

There were two Terrans—they were painting the interior of a house. He grimaced. "Look at them. If they're going to waste time and effort broadcasting programs on habitation remodeling I wouldn't say they're on a war footing! I may have a high opinion about Alexander, but I'm not so certain of his people. I think they're ignorant, as Alexander said they are, to all that's gone on. Oh they still have their aspirations, but that's for the future. The Scythians, for all their treachery, have succeeded in keeping their word and bottling up the Terrans."

"That line of reasoning only works if the Terrans stay ignorant, Nazar. If you were a Scythian, with some semblance of common sense, what would you do? Consider your millennia long lie revealed, and the talk of alliance against the Chem is just that, talk."

"I would plead like the worm I was."

Nazeera shook her head, "No Nazar, you would run helter skelter to Terra with stories of the evil Chem who are intent upon their destruction. You would arm Terra with your ample supply of weapons. You would, in essence, make your lies the truth. I raised my concerns with the Elder today. We've dispatched another spy ship to Terra, but it will take almost nine decurns to reach Terra."

Nazar thought a moment, "Decurns are roughly one Terran day-night cycle. I assume that our Armada will be ready on time another one hundred and twenty decurns hence, and it takes twenty decurns at fleet speed to reach Terra. The Armada will enter the Terran system approximately one hundred and forty Terran cycles from today. What could the Terrans possibly hope to accomplish in that amount of time, even with Scythian help?"

"It depends on how motivated they are," Nazeera replied.

"Maybe, but the best thing we can do for ourselves, and Chem, is to wait. Let Alexander do our work for us. In the end we shall gain support for bringing Alexander back to Chem. He'll kill Bureel and marry the honorable Nazeera of the Triumvirate. At one stroke we shall gain peace with Terra, and joy for ourselves. The disciplining of Scythia can then take place at our leisure, success assured. Remember, Alexander has no liking for them either."

Nazeera smiled weakly, "Another arranged marriage, Nazar?"

"Don't worry, Nazeera, at the worst our Armada will arrive at Terra and find a planet-bound populace without enough defenses to be worthy of bombing. If there is no threat there is no reason to make war upon them. Given a thousand decurns, maybe, but one hundred, it's not possible. What could they have to put against us at ten decands?"

Nazar smiled, scoffing at the idea, blissfully unaware that the Terran battleship "Iowa" was, at that very moment, lifting off out of Newport News. She was heading for orbit, and her guns were pointing into space.

CHAPTER 30:
WILD KINGDOM

Dawn found Alexander chilled and painfully stiff. The first day on Pantrixnia demanded more from his body than he'd thought possible, especially after so many years of relative inactivity. He didn't hurry himself, therefore, as the morning brightened. He stretched leisurely and looked about.

The tiny cave, a crack really, offered just enough room for him to set his back against the wall and stay out of the rain. He stayed dry so long as the wind didn't drive the rain into the cliff. The cliff itself was his primary protection. It was almost one hundred meters high and not quite vertical. The wall was cracked and pitted so climbing wasn't difficult. The jungle improved matters even more. It grew back on a shelf behind the cliff's edge. The trees leaned over it, sending vines and creepers down the steep slope. Alexander amused himself with the thought of his sleeping in this bird's nest. A month ago he'd not have climbed such a rock face for any reason. Heights made him nervous if he didn't have an airplane strapped to him. Events now made the aerie quite attractive, and he was quite pleased that he found a place at once so safe and accessible.

He looked out over his new world, sipping fresh water from a concave leaf that he left at his feet during the night to catch rainwater. The morning mists steamed from the jungle as the land fell away into a broad depression. The cliff was at the edge of a roughly circular depression. Mountains rose in the haze maybe sixty or seventy kilometers distant. The sun rose from that direction so he named it east.

The mountains swung north and south, disappearing into a jumble of rolling forest. To the North they left the jungle and made a chain of emerald clad islands in a sea glittering with the morning sun. There was no sign of any other landscape besides jungle. At its closest point he guessed the sea to be at least thirty or forty kilometers away. There was a white ribbon of mist, probably a river, which wound southwest towards his haven. It passed behind the ridge to his left, and it looked to be only a kilometer or so distant. He was just thinking he'd have a look at it today when a movement caught his eye.

He looked to the sky and saw a bird circling overhead. It seemed to be watching him, and trying to decide just how to go about plucking him from his perch. The animal was certainly large enough to carry him off, but Alexander was in a well protected position. The bird circled for a few more minutes and then descended. He drew his sword and backed into the crack. The light disappeared as the bird hovered just outside the crack, blindly grasping inside with its claws.

Alexander was not so much worried as irritated. The bird had an unenviable task, considering his position. He, on the other hand, just had to wait for an opening. When the bird drew close enough he lunged forward, plunging the blade into the feathered belly. He withdrew the weapon quickly to keep the crippled bird from wrenching the sword from his hands.

Squawking in pain the bird flapped wildly away. Laboriously it tried to gain altitude, but blood and entrails streamed from the wound. Slowly it sank to the trees below and finally crashed into the upper canopy.

It struggled feebly for half an hour before a disturbance in the trees caught Alexander's attention. A flurry of mantises boiled up through the canopy and immediately attacked the wounded animal. The fight was brief and one sided. Razor sharp mandibles quickly cut up the corpse, and the insects took it, piece by piece, into their shadowy realm. The display was sobering, but also enlightening. It took the mantis some time to find the stricken bird. It was very possible that his encounter with them was bad luck, and not due to the canopy being infested with the creatures. It was a point he'd remember, but it didn't make him any keener on returning to the trees.

The chore of self protection complete, Alexander turned to more mundane matters. He used the gun to start a fire and cook the snake meat. The automaton was right, the Banthror was unpalatable. He tossed the greasy strip of meat into the forest. The snake, on the other hand, was fine. The meat, once cooked, reminded him of something not quite like chicken. He washed it down with rainwater, and pondered his next move.

The cliff hole was fine for a night, or an emergency, but if he was going to spend and extended period of time on the planet he needed something more permanent. A cave or grotto that was defensible would be perfect. He expected to find such a place, if it existed, near the river. The river in its rush from the hills might very well have cut many such places. So, throwing the Banthror hide over his shoulder, the smell of which he was mercifully unaware, he quit his sanctuary.

Predictably, the automaton waited for him outside. He glanced at the metallic ball with ill concealed contempt. "Well, what clever remarks have you for me this morning? Will I have to put up with you every day from now to eternity?"

"Eternity is a long time relatively speaking, though on Pantrixnia we measure it in decurns, at the most."

"We'll see," Alexander replied. With a parting growl he grabbed a vine and climbed up to the top of the cliff. The cliff itself was a massive shelf of broken rock which ran towards the river. Behind was dense jungle leading into a craggy series of broken hills. He set off at a good pace across the edge of the cliff and headed toward the river. The cliff gradually sank towards the jungle floor but streams from the hills carved sheer chasms which lay directly across his path. His only choice was to climb down the cliff and back into the jungle. When he came to the first chasm, this time from below, he explored it. Unfortunately, there were no caves or cracks that would provide more suitable shelter than he already had.

"What are you looking for?"

"A hotel," was his terse reply.

He continued to work his way towards the river, poking into every chasm he came across. The small streams wound their way into the jungle, fed by the torrential runoff from the heights, but none of them provided suitable shelter, although one gave him his biggest surprise of the day.

It was a rather wide chasm, surrounded by sheer black cliffs thirty meters high. Vines and creepers gave it an ancient appearance. A clear stream bubbled out of the center from an oval pool at the end. The back of the canyon echoed with the rush of an energetic waterfall. It was a pleasant backdrop to the otherwise deserted place. There was unfortunately no cave behind the waterfall, only a shallow scoop in the cliff. It was a pleasant enough, though, and as it was empty of anything else he took it to be the perfect place to bath. The pool of water was only a couple of meters deep at most, and he could see the bottom. There was nothing lethal waiting for him in the water, at least nothing he could see, so he shrugged off his weapons and armor.

The armor was a one piece coverall that included boots and gloves as well as integrated armor plates, so it went on and off quickly. Underneath he wore only a light coverall. He took that off, washing it at the edge of the pool, and then laying it by his weapons to dry. Then he showered under the waterfall.

The automaton hovered nearby. "You wouldn't have any soap would you?"

"No, Alexander of Terra. We don't provide our participants with anything other than what they carry with them. The vast majority have no need of such things."

"The vast majority, are you telling me that I may meet up with someone else in this place?"

"Oh, don't be foolish. The longest period of survival on record for Pantrixnia is six decurns. I understand the odds makers are giving you a fifty percent chance on making it three decurns, which is very respectable."

"Three days, that doesn't sound very good to me."

"The odds would probably improve if you weren't so reckless."

"You usually mean something gruesome when you make a comment like that," Alexander said, taking it seriously and ending his shower.

Hurriedly donning his wet armor and strapping on his weapons Alexander started back up the canyon. The place lost its innocence. Now it was a trap whose only escape was its entrance, and the precarious vines that hung over the edge of the cliff.

That thought, of course, triggered his fear into reality.

A tremor shook the ground, and a familiar snort rolled along the walls of the canyon. He cursed to himself. A quick glance revealed no reachable vines in this end of the canyon. The canyon itself made a dogleg to the north, so the entrance was hidden from him, and he from it. The closest vines were on the south wall, in full view of the entrance. Carefully, but quickly, he went to the curved edge and peered around the corner.

It was the Tyrannosaurus, of course. The huge carnivore stopped twenty meters into the canyon and sniffed at the ground. He cursed again. The vines were twenty meters from him, the Tyrannosaurus maybe forty. He'd never win that race.

Back up the canyon he went. There was no better place to hide than just behind the waterfall. It would obscure him from sight and hopefully cover his scent. There was nothing else he could do.

Alexander took out his rifle, set it on full power and stepped behind the waterfall. He stood stock still on the slick rock with his back to the slimy cliff wall. In the midst of the spray he waited. After what seemed an hour he saw movement through the cascade.

The Tyrannosaurus stalked heavily up the canyon. He could feel its progress as easily as he could see it. It stopped once, and again sniffed at the stones, but only for a moment. Then it growled irritably and walked straight towards the waterfall. It waded through the pool, seeming to be in no hurry. The creature's entire demeanor indicated a complete lack of concern or interest in the strange scent it picked up; rather it just seemed to be weary after a long day and somehow pleased to be back in its private lair.

The Tyrannosaurus halted in the pool with the cool water rising to its belly, and Alexander watched with a curiosity mixed with awe as it dipped its enormous bulk into the water and bathed. The Tyrannosaurus was obviously enjoying itself. It snorted and sighed as it wormed its way around the pool, at one point scratching its back against a familiar and well-placed rock. For a while it just lay still, head resting on the cool rock of the bank, until Alexander thought it was asleep. He began to wonder about the possibility of escape when it raised its massive head and looked around.

Alexander stiffened. The Tyrannosaur's head moved around as if watching something, but he couldn't see from his vantage point what that might be. The Tyrannosaurus itself was large enough so that he could gauge its actions from behind the imperfect screen of water, but he saw little else. The head followed the hidden object to his right and growled. Anger made the cords stand out in Alexander's neck when he caught a glimpse of the automaton whirring around the canyon. The automaton flew behind the waterfall, hovered for a moment above his contorted features and then flew off again.

The Tyrannosaurus got up. The head followed the automaton into the sky. It expressed its irritation with a raspy bark, and another discontented snort. Alexander watched in horror as the huge carnivore stalked through the pool and up to the waterfall. Without hesitation it put its two meter head into the cascade of water.

CHAPTER 31:
ALEXANDER, THE GALACTIC
SPECTACLE

The sharp intake of Nazeera's breath was clearly audible in the Assemblage chamber. She glanced around to see if her colleagues noticed her attention. No, all eyes were on the huge screens that showed Alexander retreating back into the trap that was the Tyrannosaur's canyon and attempting to hide under the waterfall. Only one set of eyes, bright with malignant intent, watched her; the sneering glance of her husband, Bureel.

"It seems that my challenge may go unfulfilled after all," he leered smoothly.

"You'd like that wouldn't you, Bureel," she whispered. "It would be too dangerous for you to face him alone and on equal terms."

"Careful, my dear wife," he told her. "My patience is short. It would be a severe blow to my heart if I thought your interests in the Terran were greater than those of Chem. I would have no choice but commit the sad duty of exposing you before your peers."

"If I connect you to last night's assassination attempt you'll join Alexander on Pantrixnia; and woe to you if he finds you before the scavengers do!"

"Hardly likely, seeing as I'm in charge of the investigation," Bureel smiled. "Don't worry, Nazeera of the Triumvirate, I've already got some suspects in mind—peaceniks, desperately trying to halt your push to war and glory! Have no fear, even should they succeed I will carry your banner forward."

"You're playing a dangerous game, Bureel."

"Any risk is worth the prize I'm after," he told her, and then his eyes turned to slits of displeasure as her brother approached them. "Well, well, if it isn't Nazar. Your service in the government's counter-terrorism corps apparently went unnoticed by the assassins—how fortunate for Chem."

"Meaning you didn't expect me to interfere with your little scheme, Bureel?" Nazar whispered, nodding to several of his peers.

"It seems they, whoever they are, miscalculated," Bureel noted. "I'll make sure they don't do it again—try to deprive Chem of you or your inestimable sibling, that is."

"Bureel, you cold calculating worm I never thought even you were capable of such a despicable act!" Nazeera trembled in cold rage.

"Why Nazeera, I'm shocked insinuation. It is doubtless your concern for the Terran's trials that has you upset. Things have grown rather stale for the moment on Pantrixnia, and there is an alarmingly small amount we can gleam from things. I shall leave you to calm yourself."

Nazeera fumed and Bureel slunk away with an evil smile. Nazar put a finger to her lips, "Careful Nazeera, don't worry yourself; I've put my people on his people. We should have ample warning the next time he tries something." Nazar turned to the screen to watch the Tyrannosaurus bathing in the pool. "How are things going? Is the day so uneventful that the Assemblage is watching a carnivore take a bath?"

"He's behind the waterfall, Nazar."

"Alexander? Oh my, how did he get there?"

Nazeera explained the sequence of events to Nazar, who could only shake his head. Suddenly a gasp and a rumbling murmur in the Assemblage caught their attention.

They turned back to the screen. The images came directly from the automaton, which was hovering overhead unobtrusively. Now it buzzed the resting Tyrannosaurus, flitting about its head. The carnivore blinked in irritation, and followed the path of the little metal ball. With a groan it rolled its heavy bulk out of the water and shook.

"What's going on?" Nazeera wondered.

The ball's commentary explained it. "Apparently the Assemblage is curious to see how the Terran is reacting to this stressful situation. By order of Nazeera of the Triumvirate we are going to get a look at the Terran as he attempts to elude the greatest carnivore the galaxy has ever known!"

"What? Who dares usurp my name," Nazeera breathed, and all eyes of the Assemblage turned to her, including those of the Elder. She fought for self control, and just about lost, when the soothing voice of her husband announced his return.

"Your pardon, my dear wife," he whispered venomously. "I felt it necessary to insulate you from your own emotions; you've been far too open with them thus far. Members were beginning to talk. Bringing our friend's hiding place to the attention of the carnivore was genius. It should quell any rumors of a soft spot in your heart for this enemy of Chem. Don't you agree?"

Nazeera shook with an absolute and helpless rage. Her nails dug into her own fists, and blood dripped to the floor. Bureel turned with an amused smile and left his wife with images of murder filling her beautiful head.

Nazar touched her and motioned to the screen. The automaton floated behind the waterfall for a moment, capturing the furious face of Alexander. His eyes burned like green witch fire. There was a palpable silence in the Assemblage. Then the automaton drew back through the water and rose into the air with the comment, "I don't think the Terran appreciated our curiosity, and you can see why!"

As the automaton withdrew to its former position the Tyrannosaurus stalked to the waterfall and poked its head through. The Assemblage gasped, and again all eyes turned to Nazeera. She stood stone faced as the automaton said, "That looks like it will just about do it. A disappointing end to a noble effort, I must say."

"Why the cold blooded bastards," Admiral Augesburcke exclaimed. He was watching the pirated Chem broadcast in the CODOTS chambers at the United Nations building. "It wasn't enough that they put him in that infernal place, but now to goad a Tyrannosaurus Rex after him. My god! Who is this Nazeera of the Triumvirate? I'll remember her name to be sure!"

Augesburcke's swarthy visage creased into furrows of disdain as he witnessed Alexander's plight. He pulled at his thick mustache and directed his remarks at Doctor Hashimoto.

"It is certainly not consistent with a "hands off" approach to experimentation," Hashimoto said. "I don't know how they expect to get accurate results if they're manipulating things."

"They're not looking for results," Augesburcke told him. "The damn thing's a spectacle, it's purely for entertainment. If this Alexander fellow does well enough they'll probably want to use Terrans as gladiators down there!"

"Many of us wouldn't fare so well," Doctor Hashimoto said.

"I can't disagree with you there, Doctor." Augesburcke turned to his aid, and asked, "Colonel Sandberg, any luck on who this fellow is?"

The Colonel responded in the negative.

"Keep them working on it," he said brusquely, and then he moved on to the next item on his mental agenda. "Have we gotten the hourly updates yet? Let me have them." The Admiral almost tore them out of the Colonel's hands. He scanned the reports, muttering aloud, and turning through the pages with a vengeance.

"Superluminal trials with the "Missouri" completed this morning, out to Alpha Centauri and back in a little over three days. What would Nimitz have thought? He took the Jap surrender on that deck, and now it goes out to Alpha Centauri and back!"

He looked up; belatedly realizing his comment attracted the attention of his colleague, Doctor Hashimoto. Two weeks past he might have made the same comment on purpose, but today he said, "My apologies, Doctor, the reference was uncalled for. I suppose we all have some growing up to do."

"No need, Admiral," Doctor Hashimoto replied, "I believe we all, as you say, have some growing up to do before we can properly be called "Terrans." Concerning the gunnery trials, everything checked out surprisingly well on the "Iowa," engines, scanners, and weapon systems all performed up to or in excess of specifications."

"Excellent! I especially enjoyed the video feed of the blaster tests. Now that is what a broadside should look like!"

"I'm afraid the astronomers won't be very happy," Doctor Hashimoto said. "We left some good sized holes in Charon, Pluto's moon. We got good pictures though."

"This makes all the difference in the world. I'd much rather defend Terra in open space than from the ground. It's amazing that this crazy scheme of ours is actually working. Who would have ever thought a salt water navy could fly, not to mention go into space? Crazy idea," Augesburcke shook his hoary head in wonder, belying the fact that he'd originated the idea.

"Still, it looks as though folks are getting the hang of this. We expect three more launchings today, five tomorrow, twelve the next, and so on. We've got enough equipment for three hundred ships, and if we can get the Scythians moving we could add another twelve hundred, if we had the ships."

"The Scythians assure us that another convoy is on the way," Doctor Hashimoto told him.

"Yeah, like I really trust those bastards," Augesburcke mused, and then his aide handed him a file. "We have something? Is this our boy? Excellent, let's see here, Alexander Thorsson. Here's something you don't see every day: he was an NFL nose-tackle, then an Air Force pilot, and now he's an airline pilot. I should say he was an airline pilot. What do you call what he's doing now? I suppose he's the poor sidekick on some form of galactic "Wild Kingdom," but I'll be damned if he can expect Marlin Perkins to lift him out of there! This would be a helluva thing to put on a resume. What else has he done?"

Augesburcke perused the record, and a frown spread across his face. Eventually he put the record down. "I can't figure this, Colonel. This man had an outstanding record. Why did the American Air Force let him go?"

"Didn't make the next rank," the Colonel told him. "Though from what I saw there was nothing in his record to warrant that."

"No, looks like a damn fine record," Augesburcke said. "Typical military; kick out the good people to make room for the ass kissers. Well, what's our boy up to now? Has the dinosaur eaten him yet? I haven't been watching."

The television showed nothing but the Tyrannosaurus standing under the waterfall. "No, as far as I can tell he's still under there."

"What's he doing, taking a shower with it?" Augesburcke remarked as if there was nothing whatsoever which could surprise him.

CHAPTER 32:
PLAYING DANIEL BOONE

Alexander watched the massive head thrust under the waterfall, scarcely a meter above him. The Tyrannosaurus turned its head this way and that, allowing the rushing water to douse its considerable skull. The huge mouth yawned open and the head tilted upwards. The Tyrannosaurus messily drank from the descending fountain. The backwash from its effort drenched a patient but disconcerted Alexander with the remains of its most recent meal. It drank and drank with the man standing directly beneath it. He was so close he could've touched the greenish-purple scales of the neck.

Alexander found it easy to resist the temptation to do so.

After what seemed an eternity the Tyrannosaurus, its thirst sated, simply stopped drinking and allowed the water to cleanse its mouth. The water gathered inside the Tyrannosaur's maw before overflowing onto the stone and Alexander. This continued for quite some time, and the Tyrannosaurus appeared in no hurry to stop its hygienic exercise. Evidently this was a habitual routine for the dinosaur, and Alexander was in no mood to interrupt it.

He wasn't certain whether it was sight, sound or a combination of both by which the Tyrannosaurus hunted. Earlier it discovered the tiny automaton, which was obviously the automaton's intent. The automaton, he figured was quieter as well as smaller than he, so he doubted whether he could successfully skulk away, even with the Tyrannosaurus in its present relaxed state. He decided to continue to wait. It proved to be an excellent decision. A moment later the Tyrannosaurus backed out of the waterfall. It shook itself free of excess water and stepped gingerly to a smooth expanse of rock that was warming in the sun. After an enormous yawn it settled itself down on its bed. For an hour or so it basked, blinking its eyes every so often or swishing its tail. Finally the unmistakable sound of a snore rumbled through the canyon.

Alexander waited another half an hour before he ventured from behind the waterfall. The dinosaur's snoring was comfortable and rhythmic, signaling a deep sleep, or so he hoped. Carefully he made his way along the opposite side of the canyon, a watchful eye on the Tyrannosaurus. It continued to sleep. Then a sudden growl startled Alexander. He froze, but the Tyrannosaurus didn't rouse.

It continued to growl, and he could see spasms flexing the arms and legs. The tail swished back and forth in quick tense jerks. Alexander wondered what it was all about, thinking perhaps the Tyrannosaurus could sense him even in its sleep. Eventually he realized that it must be dreaming. He shook his head, thinking maybe now he'd truly seen everything.

Alexander worked his way to the canyon's end and turned towards the river. A familiar whirring alerted him to the presence of the automaton.

He ignored it.

The terrain became more chaotic the closer to the river he got. The cliff walls grew more and more broken, and he was able to find some cracks and tracks by which he could make his way to the top of the cliff again without climbing. This gave him a better vantage point for the river and the lands below. The sun was at its zenith and burned off all the morning mists. Below he could see the river winding through the jungle, brown waters glittering in the sunlight. Five kilometers distant there was a vast flood plain, previously hidden in the morning fogs. Even at this distance he could see enormous herds of animals wandering across the green grasses.

Herd animals. Herbivores! Of course, the planet must operate on an ecological balance. That required a greater number of herbivores than carnivores, but his experiences hadn't highlighted this. As if in answer there was a great thundering in the jungle behind him, and Alexander had just enough time to scramble behind some rocks. Peering through a gap in the stones he watched an enormous shape trot out of the trees. It looked vaguely like a long legged rhino, excepting that the bone upon its nose and brow was blunt and it stood a full six meters high at the shoulder. It crashed through the foliage; a pack of Banthror's nipping at its heels, and looking incredibly small beside its bulk.

That question settled he turned back to the river. It wound down the uplands to the sea in long lazy loops, but not a kilometer away he heard the rush of a waterfall. That was his target.

It took two hours to get within fifty meters of a raging cataract. His languid pace was not due to distance, but rather to the ridge trail being a well used avenue to the water. Twice, curious carnivores forced him to seek cover in the rocks at the cliff base. On the second occasion one of the green-black lion creatures actually stopped and sniffed him out. It lost interest, however, when Alexander slashed it heavily across the nose. Coughing and sneezing it loped towards the river, shaking the sting off as it ran.

When he finally reached the water Alexander saw the cataract plunge from the mountains over a wide notch in the cliff. The river dropped twenty meters in a luminescent green curtain forming a small lake in its shadow. Below the lake the land fell away to the flood plain. The lake emptied through a notch in the shoreline and through a short stretch of rapids before becoming a wide meandering ribbon of brown water. The chute of these rapids sprouted innumerable sharp black teeth; numerous rocky projections and boulders interrupted the normal flow beneath the lake, sending frothing fountains of white water exploding over the landscape. Amidst the boulders shaggy bear-like shapes crouched on the rocks and snagged fish with their paws. Next to them, in the midst of the torrent, two reptiles that looked very much like plesiosaurs planted their round bodies in the waters as if they were huge stones. Their whip like necks propelled bullet heads to snatch fish out of the air. The carnivores seemed content to ignore each other so long as the fish were plentiful.

Making his way upstream Alexander explored the enormous waterfall. It was like a jade wall a hundred feet long. Perhaps, there was a cutout behind the water that would be dry enough to serve him as a shelter.

First he had to bypass a plethora of enormous herbivores, and some additional fish catching plesiosaurs. Alexander gave them a wide berth. It took some time to get around the lake and he had two encounters, neither of which he thought much of. One was a dinosaur, an ankylosaur that he surprised coming out of the tangle of foliage. It was a quadruped slightly shorter than he was at the shoulder, but very heavily armored with bone scales and spikes. It stumped around on short thick legs that despite their stoutness still looked too small to carry its weight. They looked at one another for a moment, and then in one motion the beast swung its tail around and bolted into the trees. Alexander ducked as a slab of bone and spikes whistled over his head. Then it was off, bowling over small trees and shrubs in its haste.

"I must be gaining a reputation," Alexander said to himself. His second encounter was with a log; or rather, what he thought was a log. He'd set his foot on a fallen log when suddenly it took off under him. He never did find out whether it was a tail, torso, or neck he'd trodden on. Regardless, he made his way without further adventure to the falls.

After poking around for a while he found a small cleft that led beneath the falls. Behind the cataract was a grotto that wormed back into the rock at least thirty feet in places—enough to keep him dry. A verdant light filtered through the cascade giving the grotto an eerie look.

It was too much to ask that the cave be deserted, and indeed it wasn't. Inside, Alexander found a fascinating species of spider. They were roughly the size of large dogs. The spiders were busy spinning nets and casting them into the falls. Dark shadows in the green wall betrayed the fish that, every few minutes, would mistakenly stumble into a net. The webs caught the fish, which the spiders withdrew, stung, and wrapped up for further disposal. It all seemed very innocent, except that some of the fish were as big as Alexander. Knowing the planet as he did he had no desire to cohabitate with anything.

He used the low setting on his gun to wound the spiders, and then he dispatched them with the sword. He discarded their bodies, and their prey, into the river. Then he gathered some dry wood and made torches by splitting and feathering the ends. Using his gun to light the torches, Alexander burned every inch of the cave. This got rid of the webs and hopefully any eggs the spiders might have lain.

He was just starting to feel content with himself when the automaton appeared from the shadows. He pretended to ignore it, but as soon as it was in range he lashed at it with his sword. There was a sharp clang as metal rang on metal and the ball spun back a few meters, momentarily wavering in the air.

"I see you haven't forgotten the Tyrannosaurus incident," it said.

"It's not bad enough I have to listen to your squawking or have you watching my every move, but now you're aiding the beasts of this planet!" He advanced on it. "What's the matter, have I survived too long? It's only the second day. I can't be wounding your precious Chem pride yet!"

"I had no choice," the automaton told him. "The order came to me directly from the Assemblage. I'm not told why these things are done. I only follow my programming."

"Who gave you this order?"

"I'm told it came from Nazeera of the Triumvirate," the automaton answered.

Alexander didn't answer, but his rage abated when he saw the automaton wobble. It was only a few centimeters at the most, but his senses began to attune to the needs of this world. Without thinking about it he ducked and rolled to his right, but as he hit the rock floor something grabbed him by his armor and started to pull him toward the cataract.

CHAPTER 33:
BEHIND THE TRAPPINGS OF ROME

The known galaxy boiled with anticipation and fascination. The galaxy depended upon official Chem releases for Chem intentions, but like the Chem they watched the ethernet transmissions from Pantrixnia with a growing sense of admiration and trepidation. Alexander's exploits were at once marvelous entertainment and a cold slap of reality. To watch Terran gladiatorial games was one thing; they were remote, even alien, quarantined from the known galaxy as they were. Now, however, they watched a man who journalistic rumor built into Alexander of Alexander's lineage run amuck in their own Galactic forum. It was an ascendancy of Terrans to a level closer to the Galactic hearth, which was frightening, but it was also the first opportunity of the Galactics to watch an individual Terran with any sense of intimacy, which was enlightening.

Journalists, being who they were, took great leniency on filling the gaps in actual knowledge, and rumors flowered into accepted fact with great rapidity. The Chem were becoming remarkably tight lipped and grim concerning their intentions towards Terra, and that was a bad sign. Galactic journalists correctly interpreted this as a mood of extreme disquiet amongst the normally decisive Chem. To spice the drama were the reports of the Chem Armada massing for the first time in thirteen millennia, and Scythian hints that the Terrans were far more capable of defending themselves, and Scythia, than the Galactics believed.

Nothing like this had happened in the known galaxy since the last of the Chem Wars of Expansion. The populace of the known galaxy waited, not able to come to any conclusion on either the Chem threat of genocide or Alexander's place in their universe.

During this agonizing time the ten civilized cultures outside Scythia, Chem and Terra met routinely on Rome. The gleaming marble of the city lost its luster in the gloom of the times, and the Galactic politicians lost their nobility to their fears. Still, there were some who were more confident about the coming war than others. The Golkos saw advantage in the clash of the titans. They bore little love and much jealousy for the Chem, their historic rivals. Now they faced the prospect of being bettered by the Terran mercenaries as well. Like the other Galactics, however, the Golkos were cautious. It was a far cry from their wilder days. The ancient reputation of the Golkos was as a warrior race, and they still bore the appellation with pride. But the Golkos were not as old as the Chem, and had expanded into empty space for several millennia before coming into contact with the Seer'koh, the Kempec and finally the rest of the civilized galaxy. Their immediate reactions were militaristic, at least until they met the Chem. The Chem were far older, more honorable and deadly. It was probably the best thing that could have happened to the Golkos, to be put in their place by their cousins, but not stripped of their empire.

The resultant peace, maintained by an ever watchful Chem, allowed the Golkos to mellow somewhat. They were still petty, ruthless and antagonistic, but they were a marked improvement over their ancestors. In their hearts, however, the lesser cousins of the Chem continued to dream of being the Galactics dominant warrior race, and with this in mind, they saw the coming war between Terra and Chem in a greedy light. To this end, Grand Admiral Koor accosted She-Rok after the Galactics daily conferences.

"Tell me, She-Rok; is it difficult for the Hrang to be so wholly dependent upon Chem and Scythian information?" She asked the Hrang, joining him as they walked a back corridor. It was gloomy and dark, meant to allow dignitaries to traverse back and forth between meetings without having to deal with the press. Her manner was more demonstrative than her words. She smoked a long black cigarette, punctuation her words with streams of green smoke. "The rumors of Terran preparedness are certainly revelations of the most trying sort. I do not doubt that had the Hrang known of them they would have reported the details to the Senate. I cannot help wondering why, however, we have so little information from your people in this crisis. It is in all of our best interests to pull together in whatever way we can. The times are too dangerous for selfish actions."

"I don't understand your accusation, Grand Admiral," She-Rok answered, perturbed. "We have been most forthright in all of our intelligence gathering. Everything that is known about this crisis we volunteered to the Galactic Senate, and confirmed the veracity through Scythian and Chem channels. We cannot gather that which does not yet exist."

"Please don't consider this an accusation, She-Rok," Koor assured her compatriot smoothly. "I am simply surprised at the passive manner in which the information is collected. After all, we can all listen to the ethernet. If the Hrang are more adept at breaking Chem and Scythian code, well that is to our advantage. Yet the Hrang are remarkably suited for more energetic methods of obtaining information as well. Your reputation is greater amongst the Golkos even than our cousins, as we have had the opportunity to use your special talents on more occasions."

"Such occasions as these are extraordinarily dangerous," She-Rok informed Koor.

"And they deserve special reward," Koor assured him. "The price is yours to name."

She-Rok's brows knit with doubt, but he told her, "The price would depend on the specifics of your need."

"Our need," corrected Koor. "The Golkos are willing to be the leaders in this, and to pay the price for it. Our need is similar to that of Chem, but I think on an amplified scale. We do not necessarily need Terrans in the flesh, but Galactics among the Terrans to ascertain just what we face."

"It is possible, though difficult. The Scythians use a number of Galactic underlings on their freighters and in their depots for engineering functions; especially people from the wandering races. I might have trouble finding operatives with the required motivation, however. As Alexander wins galactic renown for his exploits on Pantrixnia there is as much admiration of Terrans as there is fear. My people are not in any way excited about the prospect of conflict with Terra."

"Do you propose to sit by-and-by and hope to win the conqueror's friendship when he comes to your Homeworld, Master She-Rok?"

"I stated that we're not excited about the idea of conflict, Grand Admiral, I did not say passivity was a viable option. We are taking this development very seriously, and we shall proceed very carefully. That said your request is not the first time we've discussed the subject." She-Rok stopped and checked the security display on his sleeve. Someone was listening, or was trying to. He activated a security screen on his belt. A hum surrounded them, and Admiral Koor's smoke drifted through the field with a slight crackle. "That's just the screen re-phasing the molecules of the air and your smoke; otherwise audio sensors could decipher our conversation through the molecular vibrations. Now, Admiral, in our opinion, it's possible to infiltrate Terra, but it will have to wait until the Chem-Terran conflict is decided. The Terrans are dangerous, and we're willing to accept that risk, but that is all. I will not put my people on a planet that is about to be destroyed."

"Certainly not," Koor agreed. "Regardless, we will not need them until that time. If the Chem take care of the Terran problem then so much the better. Yet if the Terrans triumph, or if the Chem-Terran conflict becomes a stalemate then we must make it a priority to get a clear picture of events on Terra."

"It will still entail some expense to preposition operatives, in case the latter scenario becomes necessary."

"Of course," Koor smiled. "You will be reimbursed for your labors."

"Very well, we will make everything ready," She-Rok bowed stiffly in agreement and cut off the security screen. Admiral Koor left the hall, apparently satisfied with the arrangement.

She-Rok smiled, knowing full well that Hrang operatives were even now trickling into the Terran system despite the peril.

The Hrang turned back the way he came. He stopped abruptly. Perowsk, the Syraptose Ambassador, barred his path. He held a blaster in his pallid, soft, shaking hand.

CHAPTER 34:
GETTING OLD

Alexander rolled onto his back and cut blindly with his sword. The blade skipped off the hard skull of one of the plesiosaurs. It bellowed and let him go. The head disappeared into the falls.

"That was close," Alexander breathed, picking himself up and moving away from the falls. It was none too soon. Without warning, the head of the plesiosaur appeared in the grotto again, this time followed by the entire body.

"Damn it Nessie!" he exclaimed, skipping away from the plesiosaur, which did indeed look like something from Loch Ness. Fortunately, the animal was as ungainly on land as it was graceful in the water—its four large, flat flippers gave it a lurching awkward gait over the rock. Still, the plesiosaur's head had quite a range on the end of its long neck, and it used this to great advantage, snapping at Alexander.

He bobbed and weaved, trying to swing at the head without losing his footing on the treacherously slick floor. He cut the plesiosaur a couple more times, but it was too fast to get a good hit on it. Alexander backed away from the falls, trying to get to the dry rock in hopes that the plesiosaur would give up the chase. In his retreat Alexander bumped his head against something metallic. It was the automaton.

"Damn it, can't you see I'm in the middle of something!" he said angrily, taking a swipe at the ball. He struck it flush, sending the automaton careening toward the plesiosaur.

The automaton bumped it in the nose, and hung there.

The plesiosaur barked at the automaton, and then it snapped at it. The automaton disappeared into the plesiosaur's mouth. The plesiosaur shook its head, and then, seemingly unable to bite down on the automaton, it tried to swallow the ball whole.

Alexander watched the plesiosaur try to force the ball down its throat, a noticeable lump appeared behind the jaw, but there it stopped. The plesiosaur's neck undulated repeatedly as it tried and tried again to swallow the automaton. That didn't work. The plesiosaur convulsed, obviously trying to spit it out, but again no matter how hard it tried it couldn't dislodge the automaton. It was too big to go in and too big to get out.

The plesiosaur went into a panic, thrashing around madly, eyes staring wide as it desperately tried to get the automaton out of its throat. Alexander stepped away, not wanting to get beaten to death. He was safe now, and it was obvious that the plesiosaur was going to choke to death on the automaton—but he was struck with pity. It was a horrible thing to watch, and he completely forgot the plesiosaur was trying to eat him a moment prior.

The plesiosaur was weakening.

He should dispatch it, he thought, and put it out of its misery. The plesiosaur was nearly prone now, its thrashing growing weaker by the moment. The long neck lay on the grotto floor as if on the block. It would take just one stroke and he'd have meat for a year.

He approached the plesiosaur. The animal's eye rolled back and looked at him—it couldn't have looked more like a seal's expression of pleading. It didn't make any move to defend itself, it just kept choking weakly.

"Damn me for an idiot!" Alexander cursed, and he sheathed his sword. Moving over the plesiosaur, he straddled the waist-thick neck. Reaching around he placed his arms below and behind the lump where the automaton lodged and heaved upward. The plesiosaur gave a strangled bark and the automaton bounded across the rock floor with a clang.

Alexander leapt away from the plesiosaur.

The automaton struggled back into the air, its red eye turning this way and that.

The plesiosaur lay there wheezing; but its eye remained fixed on Alexander. For a full minute it just lay there breathing. Finally, it raised its head and turned toward him, barking furiously.

"Haven't you had enough, Nessie?" Alexander shouted, and he drew his sword.

The plesiosaur barked at him, turned around, waddled like a huge seal to the falls and dove into the water.

"Are Terrans always this magnanimous?"

Alexander looked at the automaton. "What are you squawking about now?"

The automaton floated upward—Alexander interpreted it as the equivalent of a shrug.

"You could have killed it easily enough; it was near death already."

"Why kill it; it was helpless at that point and no danger to me," Alexander said, taking advantage of the encounter to make a point. "Terrans don't kill for the sake of killing, if that's what you're asking."

"But it could have turned on you after it recovered."

"Plenty of time to kill it then," Alexander said, and he retrieved his torch and relit it. He went to the rear of the cave, getting back to the business of survival, wondering whether there was some defensible nook he could use for a bedroom.

"If Nessie betrayed my magnanimity, as you put it," he said, turning the encounter into the galactic situation in microcosm, "I'd hunt her down and kill her. As it is, she hasn't betrayed me, so I expect we'll get along just fine."

"Nessie," the automaton mused. "Do Terrans always give personal names to their adversaries?"

"This animal reminds me of a creature we have at home in Loch Ness, we call her Nessie—it's natural transference or something like that."

"And Terrans are familiar with this Nessie?"

"Of course," Alexander smiled. "She's something of a pet."

"Terrans keep fearsome pets."

"Remember that if you try and settle our planet," Alexander muttered, as if to himself, but so the probe could plainly hear him. Then he found what he wanted. It was a round niche about three meters in diameter hollowed out by the river. It was small enough so that he could build a barricade, but large enough that he wouldn't suffocate in his sleep.

"It's going to get cold in here," he said aloud.

The cave explored, Alexander had some ideas. A first thing first, night was coming on and fire would give him some measure of comfort and protection. He collected wood from outside the cave. Getting it back in gave him another idea, as the longer branches kept getting wedged in the rocks. He collected enough wood for a fire, and then gathered together some long branches, small trees, and some vines.

As he was doing this he heard a commotion in the lake. He hopped up onto a rock, being careful to scan the area around and above him. A hundred meters away three of the plesiosaurs were fighting. It soon became apparent that two were attacking the third—it was the wounded plesiosaur Alexander fought.

"I'm not going to waste the energy of saving you just to let a couple of bullies kill you!" He swung out his express rifle and set it as low as it would go. He took two quick shots. Crack! Crack! A blossom of dim flame impacted each of the offending plesiosaurs. They screeched and dove into the waters.

Nessie looked his way, and seemed about to swim away. He lowered his gun and waved. She swam off into the lake, glancing back at him now and again as if she wondered what in the world he was doing.

Alexander enjoyed the moment, if for no other reason that he hated bullies. He'd grown into his NFL frame late, and spent most of his school years as the smallest guy on every team; the little Napoleon with a chip on his shoulder. When he grew to manhood and came into the NFL he was playing against all the boys who'd beaten up on him in his youth—figuratively, at least. It was payback time. It was still part of his character.

"So you enjoy interfering with the laws of nature; is that another Terran trait?"

"I made an investment in Nessie," Alexander told the automaton. "We Terrans like to give other beings a second chance, and see if they've learned from it."

"Altruism seems out of character."

"Then you don't understand us," Alexander said. The sun was setting, and the chorus of howls welcoming the coming night began. It was time to get indoors.

One of the bear creatures thought so too and apparently its cave was close to Alexander's entrance. They approached the same area, and as they drew closer to each other the bear became increasingly agitated. Alexander didn't bother with the sword. This animal was larger than a grizzly and with an extra set of claws. When it approached within twenty meters he yelled at it.

It stood and bellowed.

He approached it, trying to be the aggressor and scare it off.

It charged.

He shot it, but the shot didn't stop it, it made it angrier.

"Damn!" Alexander cursed; he'd forgotten to reset the rifle! He shoved the intensity lever forward and shot again. Crack! The rifle discharged into the bear's chest and it skidded to a stop a meter away. "Damn me for a fool! I'm too busy talking to a bloody piece of metal to pay attention to my business! Damn!"

"I suppose I don't warrant a name," the automaton said morosely.

Alexander glanced at it, and said, "What? You want a name?"

"It's not in my programming, not specifically, but I am programmed with certain emotions so that I may better communicate with the gladiators. I'm intrigued by the idea. What would you call me?"

"Bob."

"Bob?"

"Yes, Bob; you remind me of a game show host—in a good way."

Alexander skinned the bear as quickly as he could, taking the head and cutting off the paws. He dragged the skin into the grotto and returned to the carcass for meat. Several scavengers were already at the carcass. He shot the first on low and they scattered—this time he remembered to return it to high.

He didn't waste time cutting steaks but lopped off one of the hind legs. It was getting dark. Alexander grabbed the lower end of the leg above the ankle joint and heaved the hundred pound leg over his shoulder. Then he heard a low growl. He looked up to see an enormous shadow not twenty meters away.

It was the Tyrannosaurus.

Alexander had the leg over one shoulder, and his express rifle, the only weapon that might harm the Tyrannosaurs, was slung over the other shoulder. He drew his blaster pistol with his free hand—though he doubted it would do anything but irritate the Tyrannosaurus. Slowly he backed away.

The Tyrannosaurus stepped toward the carcass, or him, he couldn't tell which.

Alexander shuffled backwards, but he couldn't be sure exactly where the entrance to his grotto was—it was deep twilight and several of the deep shadows behind him could be the entrance.

The Tyrannosaurus reached the carcass and sniffed at it.

"It's all yours, big fella," Alexander said. "I'll just take my little morsel and leave you alone—if that's alright."

The dinosaur growled at him, and then sniffed the air. He cocked his head, as if Alexander's scent was familiar. Could it possibly remember him from the scent in the canyon? Alexander stole a glance back. The entrance was a black slash of shadow hidden amongst the spray. He saw it about five meters to his left—at least he thought that was it.

He wanted to dash for it, but running from a predator was a sure way to be chased. If he was wrong about the opening he'd be dead.

The Tyrannosaurus stepped over the carcass and took another step toward him.

"Eat it, Rex; consider it a gift!" Alexander said loudly.

The Tyrannosaurus took another step toward him, and then another. It was ten meters away.

"This had better be the door," Alexander whispered as he reached the shadow.

CHAPTER 35:
MORE POLITICS

"Ambassador Perowsk what can I do for you?" She-Rok asked soothingly. The Syraptose were not the most aggressive of species, and Perowsk was particularly squeamish. The gun shook violently in his hand, and She-Rok's greatest concern was the Syraptose discharging it accidentally.

"You were talking with Grand Admiral Koor; I saw you!"

"Isn't that what you want us to do—to talk?"

"It's the plotting that has us worried. We know you're up to something. Left to yourselves that's not so bad, but the Golkos want hegemony. They want the Chem out of the way."

"That's between the Golkos and the Chem; it's certainly not in the interests of the Hrang."

Perowsk wiped the sweat from his clammy forehead, waving the gun around erratically. "You don't understand, She-Rok, they're using you to get the Terrans to beat down the Chem."

"Your point?"

"If the Chem are neutralized that leaves us alone in space against Alexander," he said firmly. "Terra lies between the Syraptose Empire and the rest of the Galactics. No one could come to our aid. You'd leave us to die!"

"Calm yourself, Ambassador Perowsk," She–Rok smiled. "Nothing could be farther from the truth. Besides, isn't it the Syraptose philosophy that any issue can be resolved by dialogue regardless of the nature of the parties?"

"That is true," Perosk admitted, lifting the gun. "Five hundred millennia past when the Golkos Armada swept into Syraptose space we sacrificed a dozen worlds before finally reaching a dialogue with them."

"As I recall, the Golkos ships could carry no more plunder and they'd expended all their fuel in destroying and plundering and entire sector. The Golkos Armada was stranded in space and lost. It was a testament to exhausting your enemies to death—if nothing else."

"There is a great deal of debate about that, but I happen to believe appeasement and dialogue were the correct strategy then, and now."

"Then why worry?"

"Under the Golkos lead there will be no dialogue, and the Syraptose will be left hanging on the vine alone!"

"My friend, I've already spoken to Kvel Mavec. The Kempec will be instrumental in our strategy—they share your desire for dialogue, and the Golkos trust them."

"Then you aren't trying to undermine our position?"

"Quite the contrary, the Hrang are simply trying to gather as much information on Terra as we can—we can't trust what the Scythians told us all these periums."

Perowsk holstered his gun, and nodded. He disappeared without another word, hurrying down the corridor as if the Golkos were after him.

"It's a wonder that species still survives," She-Rok sighed.

The Elder drew a crystal decanter of wine from the cabinet in his office. He poured two glasses and handed one to Nazeera. Then he turned away, sipping at the wine. "I'm old Nazeera, not blind. Tell me what just happened in there."

Nazeera took a deep breath. She'd composed her answer some time ago, and it came easily from her lips, "Unfortunately Bureel misconstrued a comment I made. He acted on his own, but with the belief that he was acting in my name. I've counseled him on it. It won't happen again."

"I told you I was not blind!" the Elder said vehemently. "What's going on in your House Nazeera? I know you too well to think this is some sort of misunderstanding. You expect me to believe that Bureel would even consider using your name? It's unthinkable, unless he has something over your head. He's a conniving devil, that one. I was angry with your father when he sanctioned this marriage, and I'm still angry! I knew trouble would come of it.

"Bureel's influence grows daily. The populace enjoys talk of expanded horizons, and a return to Chem's ancient glories. What he failed to mention in his speeches was the nature of the galaxy then, wild and uncivilized, with half a dozen new space faring races fighting for hegemony. The galaxy is a very different place now. War brings a greater price with it today, if only because we have so much more to lose. I won't drag Chem down such a road without great need.

"That is, however, Bureel's purpose, as I read it. Dynamic times are ripe with the opportunity for meteoric gains in power. I know he has his eyes set on your seat, and I have a feeling he's been eyeing my own. I expect you to one day assume the High Chair of the Elder, Nazeera. You are the best and brightest Chem can produce, but what goes on with you now?"

"You ask a difficult question, Elder," she told him. "As you know I have dealt with the Terran almost exclusively."

"Yes, yes I've read your reports," he said impatiently. "They are at once most thorough, and completely devoid of information."

"In what way," Nazeera asked in surprise.

"I asked you to interrogate the Terran because of your insight, your ability to see through the mask to the truth." He said. "I didn't find that in any of your analysis. Your facts are most thorough. Your conclusions are most vague."

"That was my conclusion as well, Elder," she said. "My reports reflect my opinions. I am not certain what to make of this Terran, whether to believe him or not."

"Rubbish!" the Elder snapped. "You have your mind made up. I can see it in your eyes. I won't delve any further. I'm afraid of what I may find. This situation is growing far more complex and fraught with dangers than even I could foresee. The Chem Empire looks to your House to stabilize us in these times of upheaval. We can afford no more distress, and certainly no scandal, on the part of the House of Nazeera; is that understood? See to it, but be discrete, even beyond what is expected in politics!"

"Might I suggest a course of action, Elder?" Nazeera asked.

"Go ahead," he said grimly.

"Allow Bureel's challenge to go forward," she said gravely, "What's more make a point of parliamentary honor and hold no vote. Bring the Terran back from Pantrixnia and hold the challenge before the Assemblage."

"Absolutely not," the Elder thundered. "Have you forgotten Chem law? If a mortal challenge is undertaken by the male of a house, even if he is not considered master of the house, it can result in the complete loss of your lands, wealth and even your position. Your entire family would be destitute at a time when Chem needs the strength and wisdom of your House, Nazeera. I cannot allow such a possibility!"

"There is another possibility, Elder, one which has interesting implications," Nazeera offered.

"Maybe so, but I will consider no challenge, or any other course of action, until I know more," the Elder told her emphatically. "You stated so yourself in your final report. Although the Terran's story is consistent with the current evidence we have there is nothing to disprove the notion that the Terrans and Scythians are in collusion. At the moment, we help ourselves with the pragmatic course you've chosen. The Armada will continue to mobilize and arm. In the mean time, we have a scout ship dispatched to Terra, on your advice. It should report within the decand. Then we'll have the true status of Terran preparations for war. We can afford no guesswork in this.

"If, as you suspect, the Scythians are arming a previously ignorant Terra then it may then be to our advantage to bypass the Terran system and strike directly at Scythia. I see no advantage in destroying a race seeking only to defend itself. If there is evidence of Terran preparations for aggression, meaning we've been right all along, we'll have no choice but to destroy the Terran system while we can, and then move on to Scythia. Either way we shall teach the Scythians a painful lesson, and if necessary we will rid the galaxy of a dangerous tool by destroying Terra!"

"How shall we know for certain if the Terran lied and a Scythian-Terran connection exists? If the Scythians plan was to use them as mercenary troops, and their link to Terra is as ancient as they say, what will we find on Terra that will illuminate us?"

"Meaning an ignorant Terra may well appear similar to a guilty Terra," the Elder said. "Both versions would be planet bound, but arming, and likely shipping out troops to Scythia for Scythian defense. The motive on the guilty hand would be a long-standing agreement between Scythia and Terra. The motive on the ignorant hand would be that the Scythians would not agree to arm the Terrans without a price. It is an important distinction. The Scythians, worms that they are, are the finest liars in the galaxy. How do you tell when a liar is lying? In this case the fate of a race hangs in the balance. I can see no clear-cut answer, Nazeera, except to continue on our present course. We shall prepare for war. Hopefully, our scouts will be able to provide us with definitive evidence, one way or the other."

"So it is your opinion that the challenge of Bureel must wait," Nazeera asked.

"Yes, absolutely," the Elder nodded. "If our reports indicate that Terra is no threat to us or the rest of the galaxy I will allow the challenge of Bureel, loath though I am to see your house ended. I don't see Bureel as being successful in that suit."

"I will deal with that problem when it arises. Still, the delay will mean at least another ten decurns for the Terran on Pantrixnia," Nazeera noted.

"A small matter considering the importance of everything else," the Elder told her. "I'm not blind to your regard for the Terran, Nazeera. You've had a great deal of contact with him and his conduct is admirable. It will be all the more painful, and dangerous, if we find that this admirable character is wrapped in a package of deceit."

"There is nothing in his memory patterns to indicate any such thing," Nazeera reminded him. "He has a rather vindictive attitude towards the Scythians, and his memory patterns give him good reason for this."

The Elder looked troubled, saying, "Memory patterns are powerful drivers in emotional beings such as the Chem, or the Terrans. The Scythians admit being able to repress them, but are they capable of manipulating them?"

"You think Alexander might be altered, and planted? That is giving the Scythians a great deal of credit for cunning." Nazeera replied.

"How can we know? That is what we are faced with, Nazeera, uncertainty at every step. Alexander is making this a difficult and dangerous decision. It's his potential I fear. From what he's shown us he'd make a difficult adversary, just by his resourcefulness and prowess, but there's more. You've already noticed in your personal contacts that he can be charming and persuasive. A formidable foe that is openly hostile, or at least predictable, is dangerous. A formidable foe that is neither is deadly. How do we answer this riddle? How do we read Terrans when by all the accounts of his own memories they cannot even read each other? They are to be feared."

"There is that in them, Elder," Nazeera said gravely, "but I trust my Chem instincts, at least as far as Alexander is concerned."

"Well, then you will be perfect to lead the Armada," the Elder told her. "If he is true then Terra will have nothing to fear from their cousins of Chem. If he is false then their many gods will not help them against your fury."

"We may never know the truth of Alexander," she reminded him. "A decand on Pantrixnia is a long time."

"I shouldn't wonder that by that time he'll have the entire populace won over and calling for his return." The Elder told her, and then he chuckled. "Don't worry over the Terran, Nazeera. Give him a decand and he'll make a pet out of the King of Carnivores!"

CHAPTER 36:
THE FRONTIER LIFE

The shadow turned out to be the entrance to the grotto. Once inside, Alexander sighed with genuine relief. He succeeded—he thought—in hiding his very real fears from Bob the automaton. To be honest, the encounter scared the crap out of him.

The Tyrannosaurus poked its nose into the entrance of the grotto, but that's as far as it could go. Alexander slapped it on the nose with the flat of his blade. Rex retreated and feasted on the rest of the bear.

Alexander was too wound up to sleep for a long time. He built a fire and roasted some meat. The rest he cut into strips along with the snake meat and tried to smoke them.

When he was too weary to continue he dragged the bear rug into the bedroom. Then he put a pile of long branches and small trees in front of and over the opening. If anything came into his grotto it would wake him up as it made its way through the barrier—so he hoped. Then he dozed off.

Alexander awoke to a dazzling green light.

His first thought was the Scythians or the Chem, but then he realized it was just the sunrise through the green curtain of water.

There was a present in his living room; a fifty pound fish laid on the wet rock of the grotto. It wasn't there by accident. There was a large semi-circle of teeth marks on the flank of the silver fish.

"I think I've made a friend," he said, and then he sighed. "It's a shame I hate fish."

Alexander's "house" was coming along nicely. It took many risky forays for him to get the wood and vines he required but when that chore was complete he started construction. He wanted to accomplish three things initially with his work: safety, comfort and food. The food was the easiest. There was plenty of game to hunt, but he didn't need to—every morning he had fresh fish waiting for him in his living room.

For comfort he rigged a rude hammock, again out of small vines. He hung it in the rear of the grotto between two tripods of sturdy branches. He walled off his bedroom with sturdy branches. They wouldn't keep a large carnivore out, but they'd slow it down enough so he could shoot it at his leisure.

His primary, and most challenging, problem was now that of safety. He needed something that would block entrance to the cave. Doors were the answer, but they were impossible to engineer, so he set about to build a barrier and gate. He cut logs thick as his leg with his sword and then lashed them together into a wall. He wedged one side of this wall into a crack at the entrance to the grotto. The other end was kept in place by braces wedged into the stone. He made the door of smaller branches lashed and woven together. When placed against the wall he braced it from the inside with logs. The first project took two days. The last took a good deal longer, but as Alexander soon learned he had plenty of time.

The grotto became the center of his new existence, and theoretically he'd never have to leave it. He had food, water, shelter and sometimes even company.

Nessie appeared every once and a while, poking her head through the curtain of water to see what he was doing. He threw her some bear meat and she seemed to like it. On his third morning in the grotto he woke up to find the plesiosaur snoring on his living room floor like an enormous seal. Thereafter, Nessie spent her nights sleeping in the safety of his grotto.

Still, as safe as his new residence might be compared to sleeping in the jungle it was as good as a prison. Therefore, even when he had projects unfinished, he left the confines of his haven and explored.

His explorations had their own rewards far beyond what he could have imagined in his former, duller life. The one adventure he recalled for the rest of his days happened on his sixth day on Pantrixnia.

Alexander now knew the land thereabout well. He returned to the Tyrannosaur's canyon, arriving just in time to watch the Tyrannosaurus wake from its afternoon nap. He sat down with his constant companion, Bob the automaton, on the edge of the cliff and watched. From his vantage point at the bend he could see both the waterfall and the jungle below. It was an awe inspiring view. The Tyrannosaurus looked very different in the full sunlight of noon, when the rays penetrated the high walls of the canyon. Its coloration changed, reflecting the magnificence of evolutionary perfection. In the shadows its hide disappeared into mottling bands of dark shiny greens. Yet now, revealed by the sunlight, the hide glistened vibrantly with an overall winter sea green cut with swaths of bright purplish banding. Alexander was enthralled. From his perspective there could be no argument. The King of the Tyrant Lizards was indeed the pinnacle of galactic creation.

The Tyrannosaurus was just stirring. Lifting its muscled bulk from its sun baked rock it stalked over to the falls and stood under the shower of water for a half hour, drinking deeply. When it left the waterfall it shook. Thus far he'd seen nothing new, but he was simply enjoying watching the leviathan. Then the Tyrannosaurus did something extraordinary. It stretched, and then started to go through the motions of stalking, lowering its head and raising it feet in exaggerated steps. It went back and forth in the hidden end of the canyon, stalking and pouncing.

Then it made a mad dash down the canyon, but it stopped at the bend and ran right back, leaping feet first into the pool. There was an enormous splash, and when it settled the Tyrannosaurus sunk into the water, alligator-like, with only it's the top of its skull showing. It lay there, breathing silently, for several minutes. Slowly the massive head rose out of the water—a leering grin of teeth and scales.

It erupted from the pool and dashed back to the bend, only to again turn around and plunge madly back into the pool. Up to this point the entire performance was silent, except for the sounds of the enormous body bounding across the stone and into the water.

Alexander was mystified.

He watched the Tyrannosaurus repeat the same procedure in the pool, lifting its dripping head slowly out of the water like some ancient dragon about to pounce upon an unsuspecting knight. Again the Tyrannosaurus burst from the water and ran with incredible speed down the canyon. This time, however, it did not stop at the bend. It continued full force down the canyon and began to bellow. It leapt head first into the jungle roaring and bellowing.

The jungle exploded. Animals from kilometers around trumpeted and screamed in sheer unadulterated panic. Flocks of birds sprang from the canopy as far as the eye could see, their squawking adding to the already rising crescendo of the forest. The sound of trampled undergrowth, the shaking of the earth beaten under heavy feet, trumpets, honks, roars, and screams all preceded the bassoon bellows of the mighty lord. The Tyrannosaurus kept it up for a good five minutes. Alexander could occasionally catch glimpses of it in the forest, but it was primarily by following the aural catastrophe by which he kept track of the king of beasts.

The bellowing finally ceased and the Tyrannosaurus returned, leaving its kingdom in fear and confusion. Panting with obvious pleasure it stalked back up the canyon and placed itself under its waterfall. After another half an hour it shook, and went back to sleep, leaving Alexander in jaw hanging wonder.

Alexander finished the gates on his ninth day on Pantrixnia. His establishment in the grotto signaled the beginning of a relatively routine existence. Pantrixnia abounded with dangers, but Alexander was beginning to gauge the limit by which he could live. He could move about during the day with a reasonable amount of security, but venturing out at night was completely out of the question.

Alexander learned that the hard way after being careless enough to watch the Pantrixnia sunset from the ridge above the Tyrannosaur's lair. It was a wondrous evening with the sky dying through crimson, purple, and finally a velvet black studded with jewels. There was no moon on Pantrixnia, and the heavy air allowed only the brightest stars to twinkle through; as soon as the sun slipped beneath the ocean, blackness overtook the world.

Alexander was only a half mile from his grotto, but it may as well have been the other side of the planet. He scrambled with difficulty over the ridge, which in places was dangerously narrow. During daylight hours the precipice was no great problem, but there was no darkness that equaled the night on Pantrixnia, unless it was the perpetual night in the deepest caves of the world. Alexander had been under the midnight of Mount St. Helen's eruption and he remembered the eerie pitch of that world, but there the ash also absorbed all sound.

Pantrixnia at night was a symphony of a planet gone mad.

Alexander picked his way slowly over the slippery rock, ever mindful of the twenty to thirty meter fall on his right. He took enormous care, but was saved twice only by the clinging vines that hung from the slope to his left. The anxious moments occurred when he traversed two of the innumerable small waterfalls. Moss and slime coated the rock beneath his boots. The moss afforded him specious purchase at best, and on both occasions it gave way suddenly beneath him. In the first instance he suffered only from the face first fall to the stone, but the second time he lost all footing. He slid uncontrollably down the muddy rock until he caught blindly at a tangle of vines, his legs dangling into space.

"Third time's a charm, Alexander, this is a mess of your own making! It does no good to be complacent about this place. It's unforgiving to the stupid!" he said, berating himself after climbing back up to the trail. He persisted across the ridge. As he neared the ridge, sounds in front and behind brought him to a halt. In the gloom his inadequate eyes discerned shadows slightly darker than the shadow of the rock. They were roughly man size, and several were before and after him. Without waiting, he raised his gun, wrapping his left arm around a nearby vine. Blindly he fired a volley of shots ahead of him, being rewarded by the momentary sight of half a dozen wolf-like shapes barking and writhing under his fire.

He swung back to shoot those behind, feeling them nearing his unprotected flank, but too late. Just as he pressed the contact a heavy body slammed against him, tearing the vine out of his hand and crushing him against the rock. The creature was easily his own mass, and Alexander felt the breath forced out of his lungs as he crashed against the ridge. A slavering jaw closed about his armored arm, and he continued to fire blindly. There were grunts and growls, and the smell of burned flesh, but they dimmed as heavy talons raked his forehead. Then the ground beneath him moved.

He fought desperately and viciously, beating, firing, even feeling the heat of fur and blood between his teeth; then the ground gave way and they were in space, locked in a life and death struggle.

Alexander fell from the trail and into the inky darkness of the Pantrixnian night.

CHAPTER 37:
ADVENTURE TO EXILE

Somehow, fortune didn't quite desert Alexander. The twenty meter plunge landed him on top of the beast, and its body provided a cushion for the impact. The splintering of bones beneath him and the popping of soft flesh signaled the end of the carnivore, and Alexander's salvation. Dazed, but otherwise conscious and alive he staggered up, slipping on the mush that was now the carnivore's corpse. As he reached his feet an assembly of howls broke all around him.

Blindly he fired in the most strident direction of the cacophony. Both blasters spat time and again, burning into the angry pack, but the beams began to dim almost immediately. In a moment's time Alexander's two blaster pistols were useless.

He drew his sword.

The carnivores were on him. He hacked and slashed at the shaggy shadows and gleaming eyes. Twice the beasts knocked him from his feet, but each time he forced his way up through the writhing tornado of blood, fur and teeth. Alexander instinctively returned to that inner world of red icy rage which served him through so many lives. It was rage at his stupidity, and an egotistical primal rage aimed at any creature that dared threaten his right to live.

Alexander's strength burst forth like water through a dam and he shouldered his way through the lanky shapes, slashing limbs, and spraying the canyon with showers of blood from his sharp Chem sword.

He didn't think. Time was too precious for anything but instinct in the melee. The fight whirled around him like a fog, but he saw every beast, knew every intended move and acted instinctively before necessity made it too late. Alexander reached a rhythm in his slaughter, where the cold calculation of the mind becomes a detached master guiding the body's future movements and leaving the present to the flesh.

Then, just as terribly as it began, it ended. Alexander was alone in the canyon, with only the fading yelps of the maimed and defeated. Shaking the blood from his eyes he slowly came down from his mountain of fury. As he did so his senses expanded their range of attention, heretofore shortened to the immediate necessity of the battle.

The forest was alive with his raucous activity, and by the sound of it carnivores were searching out the battlefield, intent on the spoils. Alexander growled to himself, still angry that his complacency had landed him in such a spot. He didn't have much time for self reflection; however, as once again he'd forgotten his location. The fight was only two hundred meters from the Pantrixnian Lord's lair, and the enormous shadow looming at the canyon entrance was as unmistakable as it was unwelcome.

"Well, what do you want, Rex?" Alexander demanded, and not at all pleasantly. He shook his sword. "Don't even think about it, I'm not in the mood; if you need a snack take one of these curs! I'll not sleep in your belly tonight!"

Alexander grappled and then heaved one of the wolves down the slope at Rex, who growled menacingly at his tone and action. Still, the dinosaur did not charge, rather its dark shape, stunningly huge in the glooms of the night, padded forward to the corpse. It snuffed at it and then snorted. Another low growl emanated from the cavernous throat and suddenly those two meter jaws plunged down and plucked the carnivore from the stones like a doll.

Alexander watched in awe as the Tyrannosaurus shook the corpse so violently that the body separated with a resounding snap, showering him with bloody chunks of flesh and innards. Then, as if in disgust the dinosaur tossed the remains high into the night air where it landed at Alexander's feet.

Rex roared at him.

"Very well, you've made your point," Alexander admitted. "You're not a scavenger."

Rex snorted so hard that Alexander caught the warm wind of its breath. Then it turned, bellowing, and plunged into the forest with the obvious intent on wreaking havoc.

"Touchy!" Alexander told himself, though, of course, he was not the only audience to his night's adventures.

"You seem rather certain of your superiority, Alexander," Bob noted. "This was quite an evening. You dare the Pantrixnian night, slaughter thirteen Kalvrones, and insult the galaxy's greatest carnivore. Tell me, and the galaxy, Alexander, are you that arrogant or are you simply extraordinarily lucky?"

"Sometimes I am simply extraordinarily stupid, Bob." He started carefully down the jumbled slope of the canyon.

"That's an interesting comment, considering it comes from the longest lived nonresident of Pantrixnia. Indeed, this night you add to your record by a full fifty percent, completely eclipsing the mark set by Zunthrug the Bold. That's a significant accomplishment, Alexander of Terra, and one which has not gone without notice."

"What do you mean? Am I to be granted a reprieve? Better yet, has that sniveling worm Bureel finally remembered his noble heritage and agreed to my challenge?"

"Nothing so staggering," Bob admitted. "I apologize for getting your hopes up. My intent was merely to inform you that you have ranked amongst the highest rated personalities on the ethernet, not just in Chem but throughout the galaxy! You are on everyone's after dinner schedule."

Alexander stopped suddenly, and turned to the automaton. "I had no idea," he mused. "I send greetings to all who watch, both from me and from Terra. Take from my trials what you will, but I will offer you an ancient Terran saying for your reflection, "Don't tread on me."

"Treat us as your equals and we will enter the Galactic family peaceably and with reverence for your accomplishments. Threaten us, and we will respond in kind with ferocity you cannot imagine. Think carefully how you treat us. You do not understand your peril."

"That is a dire warning, Alexander, and I expect the majority of the warning is directed towards the people of Chem."

"Don't misunderstand me," Alexander cautioned. "I have a great deal of respect for the people of Chem. Yet the course of an honorable people can often be twisted by ignorance and trepidation. If my sacrifice on Pantrixnia can ease the transition of Terra into the Galactic neighborhood, and do so in peace, then I shall die well."

"You speak with great finality, Alexander."

"I'm banished here," Alexander said in the darkness, making his way with difficulty through the jungle. "Unless I discover how to build a starship out of vines and logs this is the veritable definition of finality."

"Is that regret?"

"Certainly," Alexander replied gruffly, striking a path toward the river. He was seemingly unconcerned about the noise he was making, and for good reason. In the not so distant jungle Rex was still raising Cain in its kingdom.

Alexander knew the way, but it still wasn't easy. Mother Nature was especially stingy when she designed Terrans for coping at night. Compared to the denizens of the jungle he was stone blind. Night was where his grotto really made the difference between survival and death. He was sure that other beings, equally capable of surviving on this world as he, failed simply because of protracted exhaustion.

Bob stayed with him, finally asking Alexander to expand on his last comment. Alexander growled, "What do you think? A planet bound people are suddenly informed of the civilized galaxy through threat and intrigue? We have dreams and aspirations of the wonders which you take for granted. We are warriors, yes, I readily admit that. We have our faults, but we are not without virtue. I regret that the galaxy decided its opinion of us before we could debate it. I shall die with that thought on my head; I shall most probably die with the slight of that dog Bureel rattling in my ears, without any chance for satisfaction! Regrets? Yes, I am full of them, but there is also contentment. I got to know the noble Nazeera, and in her I saw understanding and wisdom; so I'm not without hope of justice for my people, even though I shall never see it."

"You wander with great facility between the brusque and the eloquent, Alexander." Bob answered, and then maintained its silence throughout the rest of Alexander's trek through the jungle.

The way wasn't easy, especially when he came to the river. Alexander had to shoot his way into the grotto. A dozen huge crocodiles smelt him out. They forced him into a tree, and it was there that he discovered the rifle had a night scope. It was possibly the only pleasant discovery of the evening, and it was the only reason he was able to get to the grotto at all. He picked off four of the massive creatures before the rest scattered into the water. Minutes later Alexander barred the entrance to the grotto, and heaved a sigh of relief.

Nessie barked her greeting and lay back down to sleep.

"Congratulations, Alexander of Terra. The populace of Chem passes on their appreciation for an exciting evening. There is one other message I am to pass on. It is my honor to relay a message from Nazeera of the Triumvirate of Chem."

Alexander looked up with renewed vigor at her lovely face playing on small hologram transmitted by the automaton.

"Greetings and congratulations Alexander of Terra, it has been some time since I enjoyed our meeting on the Chem Homeworld. I see now that the honor and resolve which you displayed before me and the entire Assemblage was genuine. Your exploits earn you renown amongst the most extraordinary figures of our time. We rejoice at your courage and prowess. You have our best wishes for continued success."

Alexander read between the lines. Nazeera still believed in him. He knew that she hadn't betrayed him at the Tyrannosaur's canyon; it was simply another trick of Bureel's. He didn't wonder that they had spent so short a time together. The feeling was right, somehow. Marooned on this hellish planet he cherished that sentiment, as it was the only comfort he had.

Alexander awoke the next day with renewed spirits.

Nessie poked her head into the grotto and tossed him a fish.

He cleaned it, humming to himself, almost happy. He was putting the fish on the fire when he noticed something was different. Bob wasn't there.

Alexander ate, and afterwards went outside. Perhaps the more mundane activities of his existence were wearing thin on the audience. The day wore on; Bob was nowhere to be found. The next day was the same, and the next. On the fourth day Alexander lost all hope of Bob returning or being replaced.

He was alone on Pantrixnia. Exiled. He'd spend the rest of his life on the hellish planet with no hope of ever seeing or talking to another sentient being again.

CHAPTER 38:
THE ARMADA SAILS

The lights of Nazeera's office were low. The ethernet was broadcasting a special on Alexander. It was a documentary with the title "Alexander of Terra, Conqueror or Friend?" It was typical journalistic sensationalism. They sought to weave a connection between the ancient Alexander of galactic legend, and this new Alexander. There was little real information available on either Terran, so it was amusing in its conjecture.

She smiled. The ordeal was almost at an end. Once the scout ship sent its report Alexander would be retrieved. She'd command the ship herself. Within a decurn Bureel would be dead, and she would be . . .

There was a light knock on the door and Nazar poked his head in, telling her earnestly, "The Elder has called an emergency meeting of the Assemblage."

They left immediately, arriving at the Assemblage hall in a few minutes. Nervous talk pervaded the chamber, but no one knew what it was about. When the Elder finally appeared everyone went dead silent.

"Nine decurns past, I dispatched a scout ship to the Terran system. The purpose was to determine whether the Terrans were arming for war, or defense." His voice was heavy with gravity. "The scout ship entered the Terran system this evening. It sent a transmission that I will play in its entirety."

The viewers brightened all around the room. A blue and white planet came into sight with a companion planet in near proximity. The image jumped in size to show a quarter of the planet. There were tiny bright lights orbiting against the velvet of space. The view magnified again and they lights turned into ships—ships unlike anything they'd ever seen.

A voice joined the tape, and the Elder explained, "That is Captain Terval, commanding the twenty member crew."

Terval said, "As we noted earlier there are a large number of scans taking place in this system, most emanating from the planet itself. Therefore, this is as close as we can get. The scan system indicates an advanced planetary defense, but what's interesting is the presence of ships. We've identified one hundred and thirty-seven vessels thus far, of which the majority are Scythian cargo freighters. We must assume the rest are Terran, and are obviously warships. The particular vessel in our viewer is in the process of forming a squadron."

The picture revealed a large vessel coming around the night side of the planet. Unlike the smooth shark-like shapes of galactic warships this ship brazenly sprouted sharp metallic superstructure and weaponry. It made no pretense at being anything other than a warship.

Two other ships of equal size and twenty smaller ships were all in formation. The ships moved slowly away from the planet and into space. Their course would take them past the scout ship, and quite close.

"We have our screens up so they shouldn't be able to detect us," the Captain said. "We should get a very good look at them."

They did indeed. The battleships paraded majestically across the viewer as it closed in. They made an impression on the Captain.

"Incredible! I'm reading a full array of weapon systems, defense screens, scanners and superluminal engines. The design is certainly not that of any galactic civilization we know of, so I must assume it's Terran. I have no definitive analysis on the ship's complement, the formation is loose and of strange configuration, but as to the ships themselves they are definitely comparable in weapons and defense. Wait a moment. We've been spotted!"

A transmission interrupted the picture. It was a large Terran in a black uniform with silver decorations.

"Alien vessel, this is Captain Thomas of the Battleship "Iowa." You're in Terran space. Maintain your position and prepare for escort. Please acknowledge."

The Chem Captain gave several curt orders to the crew, and the Assemblage heard the surge of the engines. The Terran squadron was breaking up. Initially, there seemed to be no method, but in a moment it became apparent that the Terrans were attempting to block the Chem escape. Another message came over the Chem's video ordering the ship to halt or the Terran's would open fire.

The Chem ship turned away from the squadron, though the viewer still showed the Terran ships. The battleships spread out with a halo of other ships around them.

"Prepare to engage superluminal engines!" Captain Terval ordered. The viewer showed the battleships close behind. Suddenly six enormous flashes of flame erupted from the lead ship. The screen went dead.

Silence filled the hall. At length the Elder said, "No further communications were received from the scout. None are necessary. Captain Terval and his crew did their duty honorably. His ship was well armed and fast but was nonetheless destroyed. Terran intentions and capabilities are, I think, self explanatory. We are now in a struggle for the very existence of our Empire. I ask for no debate. I put forth a motion of war against the Terran system, and the Scythian Empire. What says the Assemblage?"

A chorus of "yea" greeted the Elder. "The Armada will sail at the earliest opportunity. Nazeera of the Triumvirate will command the Armada. May fortune follow us," he said, and he left the chamber.

The hall burst into a cacophony of conversation, but Nazeera would have none of it. She stormed out of the building, Nazar at her heel, and Bureel watching in evil pleasure.

At home Nazeera raged, "How could I be so blind, Nazar? I shall take a ship to Pantrixnia and blast him myself before we destroy his precious planet!"

"He may not have betrayed you, Nazeera," Nazar told her.

"How can you say that? You saw the Terran Fleet. They've been mobilizing for years with the Scythians graciously providing cover!"

"That may be so," Nazar replied, "I'm not speaking to that. I'm merely saying that Alexander may be telling the truth, at least as he knows it.

His memory tapes give no indication of an advanced Terran space faring capability, or modern technological war fighting capability."

"Memory tapes can be altered."

"But why alter the tapes and not the memory? If he was so important that the Terrans purposefully put him in our hands then why leave his memory intact? Chances are we would discover the inconsistencies, and fairly soon after that, the truth. Alexander is a pawn in all this. He was truthful about everything to you; to the extent he was able."

"Let him live his life out on Pantrixnia then," she said bitterly. "He is a symbol of my shame and foolishness. I want nothing more to do with him!" When Nazar attempted to protest she cut him off, "I mean it Nazar, nothing more! I could not live with such shame around me."

"I can understand your bitterness, dear wife," Bureel told her as he entered the room. "We must forget such petty thoughts, however, in view of our greater purpose. Once the Terran system and Scythian Empire are under our sway, then there will be time to turn our attentions to smaller matters."

"What is it you want Bureel?" Nazeera asked dangerously.

"What does every male Chem want, an heir. I've let the subject lie far too long. Before I allow you to go into battle I want an heir. It is a valid request, and a legal one."

"Leave it alone, Bureel," Nazar cautioned. "I'm in no mood to listen to your legalities today. The subject can wait until after the war. We are far too concerned with the survival of the Empire to deal with this."

"How patriotic of you Nazar," he said. "I am touched with your far sighted duty to the state. However, this is a personal matter between my wife and me. You would do well to leave it alone. The tribunal does not take kindly to interference in these matters."

"He's right Nazar. You should go." Nazeera told him.

Nazar left, but not before he planted himself in Bureel's face, "This will be settled between us one day." Then he stomped out.

"Well, what of my request?" Bureel asked. "I'll take it to a tribunal the moment I leave this room, if you don't agree. That would likely result in a rather compromising scandal."

There was a long pause. Nazeera had no doubt that Bureel would do exactly as he threatened. It was the Empire that made the decision for her. "I have conditions, Bureel," she told him with finality. "You will leave Nazar alone. You will in all appearances, no matter how small, support and conform to the policies of the House of Nazeera. There will be no undermining of my position in the public eye, is that understood?"

"Understood and accepted," Bureel smiled.

Nazeera never claimed any memory of the act, when Bureel finished she showered—she over-rode the computer safety and tried to scald away the stain—then she returned to the Assemblage. She avoided Nazar that entire day, and their dinner was silent. The next day she went to the physician and had the fertilized egg removed. They put it in an incubation cell, and she forgot about it.

CHAPTER 39:
WHO IS TO BE THE NEXT CAESAR?

Admiral Augesburcke turned off the tape of "Alexander of Terra, Conqueror or Friend?" and addressed the assembled CODOTS team. "Ladies and gentlemen, this broadcast aired within the Chem Empire two days before we blew their spy ship out of space. We seem to have answered their question, any thoughts?

"It was an unfortunate incident, Admiral, but hardly uncalled for," Admiral Sampson replied.

"Maybe, but the timing couldn't have been worse," Doctor Koto said. "You see, Alexander single handedly built a bridge of communication between the Chem and Terra. Indeed, he'd been our representative to the galaxy, and we couldn't have chosen a more effective one.

"He won their respect, and even their admiration. I'm not blaming the military. Their actions were logical and well justified. The question we now face is, do we give in to the prospect of total war or is there a way to rebuild this bridge of communication?"

"They've stopped transmissions from Pantrixnia," Roshani Darya pointed out. "I can't say that Alexander is portraying the best of Terra, but I must admit it fulfills the need of the situation admirably. If his actions are calculated then he's an astute individual, if not then we're very lucky indeed. Either way this is an unfortunate turn of events. We need him whoever he is. However, I don't see how he can help us anymore."

"The Chem cut the transmissions after their formal declaration of war," the Admiral told the assembly. "They wouldn't let the media build their adversary into a hero."

"But they've already done that to a certain extent," Doctor Koto said. "There is, perhaps, a way we can use that."

Augesburcke spread his arms wide in resignation. "I'm not sure how we can, Doctor. The Chem's association with Alexander was quite specific. I don't think they're going to transfer his qualities to our Fleet. Just because I'm a flag officer and I've driven a tank doesn't make me Rommel. That is our biggest problem, as Ms. Darya has previously pointed out: our complete lack of legitimacy. We'll have the ships to face the Chem, but that's not the point. The military might of Terra is a legend, and we've no way to flesh it out."

"You've hit upon a possible solution, though, Admiral," Koto told him. "We must associate ourselves with the legends of the galaxy. The Chem must believe that they face the Fleet of Alexander. If their psychology is anything like ours it would be an enormous advantage."

"Doctor I hear what you're saying and I don't disagree," Admiral Augesburcke told him. "We'll put up a good fight, but we've got the most inexperienced military in the history of the galaxy. We may be all right in the planetary battles, but in space? I can't promise any military genius there."

"Admiral, you miss my point entirely," Koto smiled. "We don't have to do any such thing. The Chem have already done it for us."

"What do you mean?"

"We should use Alexander." The room went silent, and everybody wondered whether Koto had gone mad. The Doctor stood up and paced around the table. He was excited, as if he'd just discovered the answer to all things great and small. "The Chem have already drawn the parallels between our Alexander and Alexander the Great. Look at the past life memories they've shown. He's a violent and powerful man. All of his history confirms this. The Galactic legends say that one day Alexander will return and Terra will conquer the stars. It's grown into a phobia for them. They're wondering whether this Alexander is the incarnation of Alexander the Great, and our Alexander has done nothing to make them doubt this.

"On the contrary he has caused them great doubt and consternation, and at the same time he fascinates them. He's become a counter culture hero to the galaxy because the establishment fears him. We need Alexander, here, and in command of the Fleet," Doctor Koto told them, and he pounded his fist on the table. "This one man can give us legitimacy. Even if he's a figurehead, Alexander may be able to bluff the Chem out of battle. If we offer them an honorable way out they may very well forego a battle with Alexander, and who could blame them?"

"And what would this honorable way out be?"

"For that answer we must go to the expert," Doctor Koto said. "Alexander's been dealing with the Chem from the beginning. Ms. Darya is quite correct when she says Alexander is an astute individual, but she doesn't realize how astute."

"In what way, Doctor," Darya asked. "He's the prototypical American "Rambo." No doubt he was impossible to be around on Terra, but now he's found his niche and he fits in it quite well."

"You're usually a better guesser, Ms. Darya," Doctor Koto told her colleague, and then he took his seat and elaborated. "Alexander Thorsson on Terra is very similar to what we've seen, but much more subtle and well rounded."

"Explain," Augesburcke asked.

"What we are seeing, ladies and gentleman, is not a new man—it's a makeover. Alexander is Scandinavian and Scottish by birth, areas with rich warrior traditions that Alexander was very proud of. He was also highly intelligent and widely talented. He participated in professional sports and the like, but he was also a painter, a pianist, an avid reader of the classics with a thirst for Shakespeare."

"Doesn't sound like his cup of tea," Augesburcke barked.

"No it doesn't; does it? You don't see those qualities in him now, except possibly for the Shakespeare which makes its appearance in his verbiage now and again. What does this mean? It's actually quite simple. Alexander examined the need at hand and molded himself to meet it.

"Remember his first experience in Chem hands, the trial, where the Chem proclaimed Alexander as the representative of all Terrans. He tried to argue his way out of it, but failing that he gave the Chem exactly what they were looking for."

"You mean he's portraying a Terran as the Chem wish to see us, or think to see us?" Darya asked. "That is taking a huge gamble."

"You are not quite correct," Koto replied, bringing up two slides showing personality traits along the bottom and columns above them. The traits were common to both charts, but the columns varied in height. "This will explain, somewhat. On the left is a personality profile of Alexander before his capture by the Chem, built by myself from interviews from friends, colleagues, family, etc. On the right is Alexander's personality profile now. All the traits are still there. It is only magnitudes which have changed. We see the character of Alexander change from a well balanced individual to a person with very singular purpose."

"He's adapted to his environment," Darya commented. "Impressive, and necessary, I would venture to say that's what's kept him alive."

"He's done so very quickly," Augesburcke noted. "It takes a great deal to accept so radical a change, and then adapt to it. It's a pity he's out of reach."

"You still don't quite see," Doctor Koto explained, jumping up again and striding round the conference table. "You don't fully appreciate Alexander's transformation, nor understand why he was able to accomplish it. Both are extraordinarily important points if you are to understand the man, and how he may still be of use to us. You see Alexander's adaptation didn't come through acclimatization. It was not, as is the classic scenario, the gradual emergence of survival instincts and traits over time. His change was sudden, indeed it was almost instantaneous. Let me show you the entirety of the Chem trial from the first moment of Alexander's appearance." Koto showed the hologram beginning with a naked Alexander awakening in the Chem cell.

"We see the humble beginnings of Alexander's emergence with his realization that he's not on Terra. He retains the memories of Scythian capture and swiftly ascertains his position. The trial begins and the new Alexander quickly emerges.

He's built upon the old Alexander, but stressing a new set of needs: strength, courage, a demand for respect. There's more. Alexander draws upon his ancestor's warlike nature but he tempers it with honor, a quality the Chem so obviously revere. He builds this new character very quickly, and I'm certain his intention was to portray himself, and Terra, not as we are but as we ought to be."

"That is not exactly as I would have chosen," Darya said.

"Nor is it what any of us would have chosen," Koto told her, "but Alexander had only himself and a few precious seconds to work with. In this new world, with no rules of society or law, he recreated himself as he would like to be seen. He is warlike, but driven by honor and justice. Think of what he portrays: Terrans as supremely powerful enemies if crossed, but trusted friends if respected and left alone. Alexander's purpose is completely transparent. He's calculated his position, and the Chem intentions, and is doing everything in his power to convince them that Terra is not worth going to war with."

"At what price though," Darya mentioned. "It seems that Alexander has compromised himself. He can't beg for a reprieve without destroying the image he's created. His only possible release from his death sentence is just that: death."

Koto's expression turned serious. "It's obvious that Alexander considers himself expendable."

Augesburcke nodded, and said, "He's a military man, Ms. Darya, and this is a one way mission—no return. He knows that it's not just his life that's at stake it's Terra. It's a fair trade."

"Until we shot the Terran scout ship out of space he may well have been close to accomplishing his goal," Doctor Koto said, and then he sat down. "However, despite the obvious fact that Alexander was willing to trade himself for Terra there are certain indications of a subplot. Alexander has had some contact with Nazeera of the Triumvirate, a person of some importance on Chem."

"She's leading the Chem Armada," Admiral Augesburcke told them. "We've built quite a profile on her through Scythian information and on the galactic ethernet. The Galactics don't take many pains at secrecy, and they're as ravenous about information as we are. Nazeera is certain to succeed as Chem's Elder. Without going into all the details I would hazard to say we have a very potent adversary."

"Yes, and Alexander has gone out of his way to mention her by name," Doctor Koto told them. "Nazeera, on the other hand, made the primary interrogation of Alexander at his trial and is the author of his exile to

Pantrixnia. She was also, as stated by the automaton on Pantrixnia, the one who tried to get Alexander eaten by the Tyrannosaurus.

"However, her latest involvement was a personal message, delivered directly to Alexander by the automaton praising his bravery and wishing him success. It's not entirely consistent with the Nazeera we've seen previously. There is a mystery there. Then there's Bureel, with whom Alexander has an open challenge of honor. That may be his attempt to get off Pantrixnia."

"Possibly, but there's another consideration," Sampson offered. "We found out this morning what now turns out to be an interesting point. We've been trying to identify all the players in this soap opera. Well, here's one. Bureel is, as we knew, a relatively minor member of the Assemblage. What we didn't know was how he got the position. He entered into a marriage arranged by his father who was owed a debt by the father of a current member of the Chem Triumvirate."

"Let me guess, our very own Nazeera," Augesburcke whistled.

"You bet. We got it from the Golkos, who are not big fans of the Chem and only too willing to cause them scandal or embarrassment," Sampson noted.

"This does paint an interesting picture," Darya mused with a smile. "Did Alexander and Nazeera get to know each other somewhat better than we imagined?"

"You're late, Ms. Darya," Sampson smiled, "the Golkos have already played up that line. Their conjecture is that Alexander is truly Alexander the Great's namesake. He will kill Bureel in a duel and marry Nazeera, joining the Terrans and the Chem as one. Then he will launch a galactic war of conquest."

"I like everything but that last part," Darya said.

"Well, it doesn't matter a wit," Augesburcke said gruffly. "Whatever personal schemes Alexander and Nazeera may have had are all a bunch of garbage now. We saw to it when we blasted the Chem ship out of space. If there was an understanding between them, which I hope to hell there wasn't, things are worse now. Alexander always maintained we were ignorant and planet bound.

"We've made a liar out of him, and I hate to sound sexist, but Hell hath no fury like a woman scorned, or lied to. Nazeera's either out to remove a threat to her people's existence, or out for revenge, or both.

From what we know, she's not a character you want to have hating you. Suggestions?"

"There's only one person we should be asking, and I would say we ask him," Koto said.

"I thought you would say something like that, Doctor," Augesburcke sighed. "Very well, I don't disagree, but how do we get him?"

Koto smiled, and said, "For an Overlord go to a man with delusions of grandeur; for a kidnapping go to the Scythians—they've been abducting Terrans for ten thousand years."

CHAPTER 40:
A NEW ARENA

When Bob left Alexander felt extraordinarily isolated. The full realization of what it meant to be marooned leapt upon him. During the next days, he did little but sit in the grotto and sulk.

He forced himself to go out once a day to check on Rex. Watching the Tyrannosaurus never got dull, and he and Nessie were now Alexander's only ties to Earth, and home. Now that his adventure was all but complete the idea of home grew important, more so than at any other time in his life. Time passed, but he was unaware of whether it was months or just days. On one of these days he was watching Rex's "romp," as he called the dinosaur's exercise of frightening the wits out of his jungle minions, when something finally occurred.

Above him there was a sound. It disturbed Rex as well. He jumped up in sudden hope that it would be Nazeera in a Chem ship. Disappointment hit him in the gut when he stared up at the brassy saucer shaped ship, knowing it for what it was, a Scythian scientific ship. Just such a ship plucked him from Terra three times before. This time, however, he remembered them. The horrible blue beam enveloped him, lifting him bodily into the center of the ship. He looked down to see Rex gazing up at him quizzically. Then Pantrixnia disappeared behind the sliding door of the hatch. The beam set him down in the middle of a hemispherical chamber. He wasn't alone.

"Welcome Alexander!" a cheery faced man with large mustachios told him. The man wore a black and silver military uniform, spoke with an Australian accent and was definitely Terran.

Alexander shook hands, though somewhat suspiciously, and he said, "I wouldn't have expected to find a Human out here, and in a Scythian ship no less."

"I imagine so. Let me introduce myself. I'm Admiral Augesburcke, Commander in Chief of the Council of Defense of the Terran System, CODOTS, for short."

"CODOTS, well you're definitely from Earth, and definitely military if you can make sense out of that gibberish, but go on."

The Admiral simply laughed and led him to a makeshift stateroom where there was a bunk, two chairs, and a table laden with Terran food and drink.

"Beer and pizza, eh, excellent, I've had nothing but snake and fish since I left Chem," Alexander said, still not overcome with joy at his rescue, but somewhat placated.

"I know," the Admiral told him, explaining, "I've seen most of the galactic broadcasts. Unfortunately I cannot say my sole purpose in coming here is to rescue you from exile. There's more to it, and as busy as you've been, Alexander, Earth, or Terra as we now recognize it, has been just as busy. Let me tell you what we're up against, and why we're here.

"It's the Chem. They're going to attack Terra. We're in the dark about these people. You are going to have to tell me all about them, that's one of the things that brought us out here, your knowledge of the Chem."

He sat down in one chair, and Alexander took the other.

"That's somewhat amusing," he smiled, sipping some beer. "The Chem kidnapped me to find out more of Terrans, and now you kidnap me back to find out more of the Chem."

"I wouldn't call our little foray out here a kidnapping," the Admiral told him. "Although, I mark that you don't seem particularly overjoyed to see me. I would have thought the possibility of going back to Terra, especially after what you've gone through, would provoke a somewhat more enthusiastic response."

"I wasn't really expecting Terran's to pick me up," Alexander told him. "Now that you're here I can't say that the prospect of returning to my life on Terra excites me a great deal."

The Admiral leaned forward in earnest, and said, "What would you think if I told you that you have been and you still are a central player in all this? Would you be game, or are you ready for a vacation?"

Alexander looked straight into the Admiral's eyes. "Augesburcke, in the last months I've done more and seen more than I could ever have dreamed of. If you tell me I've nothing more to look forward to on Terra than flying for the airlines than you might as well put me back on Pantrixnia. If you've got something more to put on the table then all you have to do is tell me what you need."

"I expected, or hoped you would say as much. Well then, here it is," and he told him everything that happened in the last months since Alexander's capture. It was a thorough brief, and it took several hours. It fascinated Alexander, and he felt a twinge of pride at the way Terrans dealt with the situation. Just as he had realized what needed to be done and rose to the occasion, so had Terra. What he accomplished in microcosm they accomplished on a planetary scale. They were becoming a power to be reckoned with. If war came the galaxy was in for Terra at its most creative, and at its worst. They would make a good showing for themselves.

Augesburcke told him, "There you have it, that's pretty much what's been going on. We're not done with you. As I said before, you are a central character in all this. You have a unique understanding of the situation. The Chem, well let's just say they have a unique understanding of you. We want to take advantage of both of those viewpoints as well as the Galactics interpretation of Terran history. We are offering you an equivalent to a five-star flag rank in command of the Terran Fleet. The position is a visible one, though not equivalent in power. We want the Chem to see Alexander at the head of his Fleet, but the actual command of the Fleet will be mine. Being a former military man yourself I expect you understand the limitations of such a position."

"I understand them all too well, Admiral," Alexander said gruffly.

"I didn't expect you to like it when I said it, Alexander but it had to be said," the Admiral told him. "I've taken the liberty of reading your record by the way, and I must say I was impressed. You had every right to think you would have a very promising career. I can't change that. I hope you won't bring that baggage along with you. We need your help."

"Consider the subject closed, Admiral," Alexander said, waving his arm as if to brush the past aside. "I was reacting more to the prospect of being a figurehead under the control of politically motivated military officers. You don't strike me as that kind of man, so I hope you will understand. I don't give my respect to brass insignia anymore. I give it to people. That's one point this ordeal's driven home. Don't worry Admiral. I won't let my pride get in the way of Terra's future. I'm not that petty."

"I understand you, Alexander, believe me. For an Aussie like myself to be in charge of this thing, that didn't happen easily. There are some fairly ruffled American and Brit feathers. I won't even mention the French, but we're doing fairly well at pulling together.

"I'm willing to do more. You see the Chem are not the only ones who were watching you. The entire galaxy's been your audience, including Terra. The whole planet's been watching, and they've seen what you've done. They've also heard everything the Chem media's said about you. The legend of Alexander the Great, as I'm sure you've heard, is now inextricably linked to you; and now the question is: are you the next Alexander? The Chem have shown the past life clips, and that's gotten everyone wondering about ourselves, our place in the galaxy, and about you. My crews are starting to ask the same damn questions about you as the Chem are.

"That's a powerful tool for an old commander like me who has to motivate an entirely green fleet. We know next to nothing about space warfare, but suddenly we have a fleet and we must fight with it."

"You want me to try to talk the Chem out of the fight?" Alexander mused, going further in thought along Augesburcke's line of reasoning. "That's what I've been trying to do all along. It's possible. They're already halfway there, and I'll wager the sight of the Terran Fleet surprised the hell out of them, but they're proud. They'll not back down just because it's a tough fight."

"That's your ballgame, Alexander," Augesburcke told him. "That's the real power that comes from your position. You'll be on the bridge of the "Iowa" parleying for the Terran race. You've done it once before.

They broadcast your inquisition before their Assemblage, as an opening to their special. You put on quite a show then. We want you to repeat it, with free reign to do what you will, short of surrender. If it goes badly we'll fight, but if we can we'd like to avoid showing just how green we are to all this."

"Understood," Alexander told him.

"The other portion of your real influence is in the CODOTS working group. Twenty-two of us answer for and advise the entire council. You make twenty-three, with full voting rights and privileges. In one respect you may be a figurehead, but you are also one of the twenty-three most powerful people on the planet, more so in fact, because of all of us, only you have the power to think on your feet when dealing with the Chem. Well, what do you think?"

"Agreed, Admiral," Alexander told him, and they shook hands on the bargain.

It took four days before they were out of Chem space. The "Iowa" with her full squadron met them on the border of Scythian space. Alexander transferred to the battleship, and the Captain met him at the airlock and had him piped aboard as a dignitary. As he walked down the corridor the crew lined up against the walls in salute. The reception surprised him.

"You've given us a measure of credibility in the galaxy, Alexander, everyone knows that much," the Admiral told him.

Alexander must have looked the part, for though shaved and washed his still wore the purple-black Chem armor and weapons. He refused to part with them while on the Scythian ship. Indeed he'd had as little contact with the Scythians as possible. Alexander did not illuminate his motives, and Augesburcke didn't ask.

The Admiral escorted him through the "Iowa's" labyrinths to the main conference room. Five members of the CODOTS group and the ship's senior officers attended. The rest of CODOTS attended via Ethernet secure links. After the introductions Alexander asked, "Are there any Scythians on board the ship?"

When Captain Thomas shook his head he sighed with relief. "Ladies and gentlemen excuse me, for not being absolutely candid with you aboard the Scythian ship. I was afraid of Scythian surveillance, so I was not thorough in my story to you, Admiral, but if we have a moment let me fill in the gaps."

"By all means Alexander," the Admiral nodded. He referenced Alexander not by his familiar name, but by his new title. They'd debated whether some grandiose title such as Field Marshal or the like would be appropriate, but Koto advised the simple name association of "Alexander." That, more than any title, would convey the message they wanted to send.

"Everything you've said to me about the Scythians makes me nervous," he told them. "From my personal experiences I think I've built a fairly good picture of their character, and I learned more from the Chem. The Scythians convinced me that benevolence is not an often used term word in their vocabulary. Let us take my experiences on the Scythian ship's first."

He went on to describe in detail everything he remembered about his abductions. Most of those present knew the general nature of Scythian incursions in Terra, but Alexander's knowledge was firsthand and specific. He went into his account on Chem again, in full, including the Chem accusations of collusion with the Scythians, and especially the Scythian use of the Terrans and the "Legend of Alexander."

"We had our suspicions, but now the pieces are beginning to fall into place," the Admiral said soberly.

"This is how things stand, as I see them," Alexander told them. "The Scythians have been amplifying the legend of Terran ferocity, using Alexander as a focus, throughout the galaxy for the last two thousand years. It worked until they used it on the Chem. They called the Scythian bluff and made a great deal of noise in stating their intentions to settle the "Legend of Alexander" conclusively. I don't believe it was their intention to exterminate us, unless we proved to be the mindless savages the Scythians portrayed us as. It was their intention, however, to ensure that we were not a threat to them. The Scythians would pay a very high price for their lies, though not as high as price as Terra. The Scythians didn't take these threats seriously until the Chem attacked their science vessel and captured a living Terran. Then they panicked.

"Their only recourse was to make the threat of Terran mercenaries into a reality. Even in that it seems they didn't learn much from their experimentation. They grossly underestimated the Terran reaction. They could not very well tell us that they would only arm us to a certain extent, that would be too blatant a lie, and they needed our friendship, because they desperately needed Terran troops who would fight for them. Originally they'd thought of arming Terra as a deterrent, and importing enough Terran troops to make Scythia too difficult a target. Even the Chem in their anger would not wish to bombard Scythian cities to dust, and that meant a planetary engagement, and required an army of Terrans. The Scythian strategy of containing our expansion failed, so they've done the next best thing. They've fed it."

"Why would that gain them anything," Hashimoto asked.

"You've estimated our Fleet at about seven hundred ships by the time we meet the Chem, who have around seven hundred and fifty by Scythian report, and another two hundred and fifty in reserve as Homeworld defense. The Scythians have been very careful to control the propaganda coming into the Terran system. They've tried their best to make us hate the Chem. They are counting on this upcoming battle.

"This will be the largest space battle in this age, if it takes place, and the Scythian hope is that we will both emerge weakened and relatively helpless." Alexander paused to let this sink in. "Afterward they, with the help of their neighbors, will feast on the scraps. It rids the galaxy of potentially tyrannical Terrans. It rids Scythia of the Chem, the single race that doesn't wear a set of Scythian made economic thumbscrews."

"What do you intend to do to stop the battle?" Augesburcke asked.

"Any sign of backing down, or weakness is out of the question," he told them. "Much will depend on the Chem Fleet commander. If it is indeed Nazeera, as I would expect, we will at least have a fair minded, but tough individual to deal with. Her level of trust in me may be small, especially after your encounter with the scout ship. It took some time convincing her that Terra was ignorant of all of this. However, no one expects a completely new fleet to be built in such a short time. I must assume that she thinks I lied to her, and I can't tell her the truth of the matter. If any commander found out what these ships really are they'd attack without a second thought, no matter how effective they might be.

"It'll be difficult, but not impossible. Nazeera understands command. She's astute, so I think I can tell you what her perception of me shall be when I appear on the bridge of the "Iowa." Could the Chem have possibly been lucky enough to capture Alexander in the midst of his negotiations with the Scythians? No. The only logical conclusion would be that I intended myself to be captured for the express purpose of studying the Chem, my greatest possible adversaries, just as she stooped to kidnapping to study Terrans.

"That, at least, will be a palatable reason for my perceived deception, and hopefully defuse her anger enough so that she will see reason. There's another possibility. If Bureel is in control he will have no thoughts other than attacking us. If I can avert an attack in that instance it will be by pressing my challenge. I will decry his cowardice and challenge him to formal combat. If he is pushed into it by his officers, as very well might happen, then I'll kill him and that will be that."

The group pricked their brows at Alexander's blatant manner. To threaten war and mean it was not an unnatural abstraction for them. The act of the duel, where one of the participants would surely die, that was a dim concept in the group's minds. What was unthinkable for the group, though, was now very natural for Alexander. A paradigm shift, partially caused by events themselves and partially formed by his perceived needs, sent Alexander back into time.

His concerns were amazingly different now compared to just a few month's past. Personal comfort, financial security and affability were all concepts that meant close to nothing to him now. His situations demanded that he thrust an image of courage and honor over any personal desires. In the social melting pot of invisibility Alexander was strikingly apparent. A fortress of self assurance, originally built by necessity but constantly added to by his successful adventures, cast a different light on events. Alexander's perception of the world, and the universe, was much different perception than that of the group. His mortal challenge to Bureel caused an instant assessment of the possible repercussions amongst the group, and instant concern. In Alexander the same event caused no emotional response whatsoever. It was required. It would happen. That was enough.

"Nazeera is married to Bureel we understand." Koto mentioned.

"Yes, the intrigue of Chem is somewhat of a soap opera," Alexander replied. "But we have bargaining power with this fleet. It is impressive in size and capability. It is a ghost fleet in that it should not exist, but it does. In history disinformation or simple lack of knowledge has proven to be a decisive player. I expect it will be so again. Now there are some specific military options I would like to discuss, they may be useful bargaining chips."

The discussion went on for some time, and many of the non-military members were obviously nervous, but Alexander was proving to be as dominant a figure in his people's councils as he was in alien councils. Augesburcke agreed to back his proposals with military might if it came to that, and they all agreed on a set of parameters within which Alexander could operate freely.

When Alexander went to bed that night it was with a different kind of exhaustion than that he faced on Pantrixnia. The dangers of that world were less harrowing than the power struggles in this. Still, he was satisfied with the day's progress. He'd time to think of the tactical situation ahead, and he brought facets of it to the CODOTS table that no one had considered. The options he presented were not easy ones for everyone to swallow, but in the end he was able to force them to accept their necessity. It was a hard won victory, but an important one to Alexander, and his future.

Alexander recognized he was at the crossroads of the future. The course of the galaxy was being decided here and now. He could remember his own past, where had once seen such opportunities, and where he had also missed them. The Alexander of by-gone days had just enough self doubt to have prevented his asserting himself. This new Alexander, borne of the trials of Pantrixnia and guided by the experience of centuries, cast aside all self doubt. Victory and defeat, errors of judgment and miscalculation were all a part of life. The real mistakes were in succumbing to such fears before they were manifested.

Alexander, for more than any other reason, saw himself with the opportunity to continue to affect and even direct the course of future events. To ignore such a chance would undo all he'd accomplished. He was determined not to let go the reins of life ever again. Alexander had a destiny to fulfill, and he forged ahead in this new arena with all the bravado and bluster he used on Pantrixnia to meet it. He had a clear vision of what was possible in the coming days, and he wanted to take full advantage of it. His motives were more than glory, or personal satisfaction, for this was the stuff of dreams, and such opportunities were extraordinarily rare. Having come so far he was not bashful about asserting his thoughts, and he used every inch the council gave him.

In Alexander's mind he had a vague position of power, and an enormous opportunity for the betterment of the Terran position in the galaxy. His task was daunting, but it didn't disturb him. The Chem didn't disturb him. The galactic situation, he was certain, would work itself out as he foresaw. Yet even with this self assurance of a great threat overcome he could not work himself out of a deepening mood. It was not a question of power, or of destiny. It was Nazeera.

With all the momentous events surrounding him it was the Chem woman who held the thought's of Alexander even after the head of the Terran Fleet drifted off to sleep.

CHAPTER 41:
THE PIECES ARE SET

Two light years from the border of Chem-Scythian space the "Iowa" hung like an apparition with five hundred ships at her heel.

Admiral Augesburcke paced the bridge like a Tasmanian devil, ceasing his endless roving only when the long expected message arrived. He dove for the communications console and read the message over the operator's shoulder, "Alexander, the latest intelligence reports show the Chem Fleet massing upon contact with our reconnaissance screen. That puts them roughly eight hours ahead of us, and seven days flight from Terra at flank."

The Admiral straightened with a concerned shake of the head, thinking.

Alexander nodded. It was as he expected, and the reality that the most powerful military man on Terra was briefing the explanation to him—who two weeks ago was foraging for food and wearing animal skins—didn't affect Alexander in the slightest. That Augesburcke, of all people, accepted the change in stature was possibly the most amazing event in the entire unlikely adventure.

Alexander showed himself as a shrewd leader, and the Admiral's equal in military strategy. To be certain Augesburcke molded the fleet, but the stratagem they took into this crisis was uniquely Alexander's. It hadn't begun that way, but over the last two weeks days the logic and ingenuity of Alexander completely transformed the Terran plans. As the

Admiral's respect for Alexander's capacity to contribute in their present situation rose, so did his respect for Alexander's position. Subconsciously, almost without his knowledge, the Admiral was viewing Alexander's position as less and less that of a figurehead.

When he turned to Alexander, the latest data on the Chem flashing upon his console, he addressed man as his equal. Gravely he told Alexander, "There are one thousand Chem warships waiting for us. You were right: they've committed their Homeworld Fleet. Our sub screens have moved off to their flanks, and they're maintaining their position outside weapons range. When we join them we'll have five hundred odd ships arrayed against them. That's not great odds, considering our experience in this arena. I wouldn't mind having the hundred ships that have been built this last week, but not with enough time to make it here."

"One hundred ships," Alexander mused, "They'll be all that stands between Terra and oblivion if we fail. I expect they know that, though, and if it comes down to it they'll put up a fight worth remembering. At the very least we'll whittle the Chem down so the odds aren't so bad."

"That we will," Augesburcke said. "Besides the backbone of that force are the carriers. They're loaded with all the nuclear warheads we could scrounge up. People have wanted them off Terra for a long time, and now they've gotten their wish. The carriers can launch hundreds of them in salvos. That's the last ditch plan."

"We still have the Scythian gambit, Admiral, and that at the very least will bear some positive dividends. We've done what we can to prepare. It looks as though that's about it then," Alexander sighed. "Shall we invite the Chem to the dance?"

"The best of luck to us, then," Augesburcke said. They shook hands and the Admiral gave the order.

Captain Thomas of the "Iowa" stepped up to the operations console. It was a broad graphite and metal construction. Its curving board encompassed nearly three quarters of the circumference of the bridge, and had a dozen stations. Above the board there were six large displays. Currently they emulated windows looking out into space. The Fleet sailed with them in every direction.

Close by was the "Wisconsin" squadron of three battleships, seven cruisers, and fifteen destroyers. On the other side the "Rodney" and her squadron floated. The ships were close enough for every detail to stand out sharply in space. The metal gleamed silver-white and the shadows were a deep impenetrable black. It made the ships appear even more strange and menacing. Other squadrons stood further out, like distant constellations, over five hundred ships. A hum rumbled through the "Iowa" as the engines engaged. The ships of the squadron started to move back in the screens as "Iowa" took the lead.

"Prepare for superluminal speed," the Captain ordered.

Alexander sat in his designated chair, a high backed seat behind and above the Captain's chair. From there he had a perfect view over the bridge. It was an imposing position, especially considering he had no real decision making capability for the ship. His time would come, however, and unlike the crew he had nothing to do to take his mind off the waiting. It would take eight hours or so to intercept the Chem Fleet, and then what? There was no way he could prepare for the coming trial.

The words would either come, or they would not.

He would have to be as sharp as he was back on Chem, ready to react and interpret the Chem's replies and demands. This would not be a game of diplomacy. It would be a game of nerve and patience. It was strange how little that bothered him. His greatest concern was of Nazeera, for Nazeera? In some ways she would be the most difficult of the Chem to face, especially if her opinion of him differed from before. She would be shocked to see him. No doubt this would be a difficult thing to explain. When she saw him on the bridge of the "Iowa" there could be only one answer in her mind: Alexander the Conqueror, himself journeyed to the Chem Empire to study his adversaries, and then submitted himself to their greatest tests.

That's how the Chem would see it, that is how she would see it, and that had its advantages. It would also make it very clear that he had consciously betrayed her. He hoped she would understand the need as a commander in her own right. If she viewed him otherwise, however, his deception might drive her to fury. She would be more dangerous than ever. If roused, she was capable of cold, heartless and thorough actions.

He looked up, finally aware that the sounds of the ship were different. On the front screens, the stars coalesced into a dim blue tinted ball. Single stars separated from the center and slowly floated by the ship. The cruisers and destroyers sailed overhead, to the sides, and underneath. They advanced slightly staggered, above and to the left the "Wisconsin" and her screen, below and to the right the "Rodney" and hers. It was remarkably quiet and peaceful. The bridge was a wonderful place to be when sailing through space, he thought to himself, but it was lonely. He was as lonely now as he had ever been in that cell on the Chem Homeworld.

✛   ✛   ✛

Nazeera was all but unapproachable. Even Nazar could scarcely communicate with her. Almost one thousand Chem warships spread out across space with deadly intent, every warship in the Chem Armada including the two hundred and fifty ships of the Guardian Armada. She'd taken them across the Scythian frontier with no more opposition than the crackling ethernet. The news spread swiftly across the galaxy. The time of rumor and innuendo was over. The Chem Fleet departed Chem space with hostile design for the first time in over thirteen millennia.

There was giddiness in the ranks that Nazeera found unpleasant. The ill fated scout ship reported a Terran Fleet of scarcely squadron strength. If logic followed, those ships sighted comprised a significant portion of the Terran fleet. Conservatively then the Chem should outnumber the Terrans at least ten-to-one. That numerical superiority, taken as truth, had the crews singing in the mess halls, and eager to be on the first watch that sighted the Terrans. That glut for battle did not affect the Armada Commander though, and the bridge of the battleship "Kuntok" was a somber place.

She accepted that the Scythians and the Terran's altered Alexander's memory, and he'd been left by his planet, as much as the Chem, on Pantrixnia as a sacrifice to strategic policy. She wondered if the loss of memories affected the man. Nazar didn't seem to think so. He thought that only those memories recent enough to be of particular value to the Chem changed. To completely reprogram a being and expect them to be sane was beyond any race's medical skill.

Nazeera confided to herself that once this distasteful business was over she'd take the "Kuntok" to Pantrixnia. If Alexander was still alive she'd bring him back to Chem, the last of his people. Bureel's feelings about the matter never entered the picture for her. He would die soon after this was over, either by Alexander's hand or hers. Perhaps she would leave him on Pantrixnia in Alexander's place. The thought brought the only glimmer of joy to her this entire voyage.

Nazar approached her. He did not look pleased. It couldn't be about Bureel. Nazeera had him confined to quarters as soon as he set foot on the ship, quietly, of course. Her brother stepped up to the command dais and whispered, "Armada Commander, we have just received scans of the main body the Terran Fleet."

"Very well, and how close were our estimates?"

"Scans pick up over five hundred ships, Armada Commander!" he said as if it caused him great pain, "Once again it appears we underestimated the Terrans."

The news didn't surprise Nazeera, and she sighed, "Certainly if the Terrans fight as did Alexander we have reason for concern. The Terrans are honed for war, Nazar. They toughen their brows by beating upon each other. Yet what of the Chem, does fortune desert us Nazar? Even now when we are at our zenith, something reaches out to strike the Chem. Why? Have we been too bold, or have we been soft for too long? We depend on ourselves to be the warriors our grandsires were, but we learn too late that we must fight with rusty swords and weakened thews."

"At their present course and speed we will engage them in slightly over one twelfth of a decurn," Nazar told her.

"Very well, I shall inform the Armada. It's better that they hear it from their commander than through rumor," she said. She flipped a switch on her panel, "To all warriors of Chem, this is the Armada Commander. Brave news of the Terran Fleet; they come to honor us with battle, instead of denying us glory. Our scans show five hundred of their number enroute to battle. We shall engage them shortly. This will be a glorious chapter in the history of Chem. Rejoice that you can now speak to your ancestors with pride of the coming day!"

She clicked off her mike and felt the mood of the Armada shift unmistakably into a grim pessimism. Turning to Nazar she patted his hand. "I am glad you are here with me brother."

"Glory has many faces, Armada Commander," he told her, his voice carrying an uncharacteristically serious timber. "So long as Nazar is considered worthy enough to be at your side he has gained glory for a lifetime. I am satisfied whatever the outcome."

✠   ✠   ✠

The members of the Scythian High Council met on their primary Homeworld. The five sat around a low table of gray metal. There was silence in the room, but not between the minds. Indeed, though these five beings sat alone in their chamber all Scythians were with them in thought. It was the way of their people that at momentous occasions such as this that all Scythians shared their thoughts simultaneously. So it was that when the Chem boarded the Scythian experimentation ship all of Scythia heard, felt, and saw the outrage. Now their revenge was at hand.

The first of the five to transmit a thought was the Council who dealt with the Terran Liaison. "Liaison has accomplished its task well. The two fleets shall meet with equivalent strength. Everything is proceeding according to plan. The results have a ninety-three percent chance of falling within the desired categories."

"The Chem disregard for our need of efficient trade routes should disappear along with their power and influence in this sector."

"I foresee even greater benefit; there are over four million Terran troops and ten million civilians on the four Homeworlds at this time. After the fall of their world to whom can they turn but us? With careful consideration and patience we may well be able to manipulate them into the mercenaries we have envisioned all along—obedient and self sacrificing to the greater good of Scythia."

"Indeed, whatever the outcome I see profit in this for us, and the triumph of the superior intellect over the violent savage."

"True, but I will allow myself the thalamic enjoyment of watching them destroy each other. Especially since the Terrans, conscious of their promise to protect us, have placed themselves only light hours from our systems. They mean to ensure that no Chem renegades engage us. They have as a result given us a wonderful seat from which to watch them."

"Long will this day be remembered by the Scythian Empire, and the galaxy. Let them tremble at the power which will awaken this day, renewed and terrible to behold! Then let the new age of the Galactics begin!"

CHAPTER 42:
TITANS CLASH

The Terran Fleet slowed as they came into communications range. Alexander watched from the bridge as the sensors picked up the Armada. He wore a specially crafted uniform of purple, gold, and black made from the Chem cuirass and armor; it gave him a distant resemblance to his forefather, Alexander; which struck at the heart of their intent.

His Chem knife hung from his belt, blade naked for all to see, as a reminder that he still had an outstanding challenge with a member of the Assemblage. It was a point he would remind the Chem. He also had the Banthror pelt properly tanned. He wore this as a sash across his chest, as another reminder to the Chem of his exploits on Pantrixnia. It was the uniform of an Overlord, and he was prepared to play the part. When the two fleets stopped and arrayed in battle order, Alexander rose from his seat.

"Wait for them to call us first," he said, and turned his back on the main viewers, expectant.

Captain Thomas announced, "Admiral, Alexander, a ship is detaching itself from the Chem Armada. Its course is directly towards us, and it is not slowing!"

"Shields up," the Admiral ordered.

"Hold position Captain, order the Fleet to hold their fire unless fired upon," Alexander said.

"Sir," Thomas queried.

"Follow his orders Captain," the Admiral said.

The Captain nodded as the smaller ship barreled in on the "Iowa." Alexander didn't look up. The bridge crew clung tensely to their seats until the Chem ship suddenly pulled up and around and headed back to its Fleet.

"No Chem would commit suicide before battle."

The Admiral leaned over to Captain Thomas, "It's his show now. Unless the shooting starts, Alexander is in command of this whole damn Fleet."

"Aye, aye, Admiral," the Captain replied nervously.

"Don't worry, Captain," the Admiral smiled, "I've learned quite a bit about Alexander over the last few days. Besides, at one time or another in his past he's commanded more men and ships than this. If nothing else he's a ruthless bastard. I think we're in pretty good hands."

"I hope you are right, sir," the Captain nodded.

"Communications coming in, sir," a sailor informed them.

"Put it on the screen," Alexander told her without turning around.

The picture of an aristocratic woman with shining blue eyes appeared on the main viewer. "This is Armada Commander Nazeera of Chem. I address whosoever commands the Terran Fleet before me to identify yourself, and prepare for subjugation!"

Alexander turned around, a grim smile upon his lips. "Hello Nazeera, it's good to see you again."

"A-lex-ander!" She breathed venomously, spitting out each syllable as if it were a delicious poison. Nazeera had no reason to be anything other than shocked at the sudden appearance of Alexander, but he was impressed with the speed at which she composed herself.

She put on a haughty mask of indifference, but her words carried more emotion and meaning to Alexander than any other being there could recognize. "I see Pantrixnia was no more a prison to you than Chem. This was a wonderful play, to be sure, Alexander. What part are you playing at now? Is this the real Alexander, the Overlord at the head of his Fleet, or have you another mask to wear before me? It's a pity, in truth; for I came to respect the Alexander I met on Chem. I suppose I should have known, but my you are a good actor!"

"Quite the contrary, Nazeera, I'm good only at playing myself," he told her. "Certainly you couldn't expect to see me again, and my return can only pique your suspicions. Then again, why should I be anywhere else? I'm Alexander of Terra. Where should I be but in the center of the maelstrom? That's where Overlords tread, Nazeera, you no less than I. Events cannot avoid us. You are as central to this, Nazeera, as I, and so here we are again, at a critical point and time in the histories of our two peoples. Two peoples who are very similar, almost kindred. Speaking of kindred, is Nazar with you?"

"Of course, but do not try to twist this into a personal discussion, Alexander," she cautioned him, "Such tactics will not work again. We have business to attend to. Do you wish to hear my terms?"

"Not in the least, but offer my greetings to Nazar anyway will you?" He turned and paced, in this instance he was controlling the conversation and Nazeera was still trying to piece events together. It was a reverse of their last such encounter, but now they were both of equal strength.

"To business then, I know why you're here, Nazeera, and you know why I'm here. In space we sit, glaring across the battlefield; the two greatest fleets in the galaxy. Does honor dictate we fight, and if so, what are our reasons? Even honor must have an argument.

"Is this war over territory? Terra does not wish territory from Chem, and what would Chem do with one star system? Do we then fight for glory alone, to beat each other to a pulp so that we may sing our own praises to our grandchildren, what of that? I'm not ignorant of the valor or prowess of the Chem, Nazeera and you should not doubt the resolve of the Terrans. What is there to be gained then from a pitched battle where the conclusion leaves us each the weaker?

"Shall we fight for glory, only to diminish in stature and power, allowing the lesser cultures of the galaxy, such as the Golkos or the Scythians, to clean up the scraps? Ah, the Scythians, I had almost forgotten them."

Alexander walked to the front of the bridge and looked into Nazeera's eyes. He planted himself firmly on the tritanium alloy deck and clasped his hands behind his back. Cocking his head to the side as if he'd struck an interesting thought, he said, "Isn't it interesting how the Scythians always find a way to bring us together?"

"What is your point, Alexander?" Nazeera asked.

"I have a very simple point, one which you of all people should remember. I once told you I harbored no ill will towards Chem. I spoke the truth. I don't see why we should be angry with each other. It's the Scythians, who manipulated us both. I'm not overly fond of being used, Nazeera, and I've had my fill of it lately. I'm also not fond of destroying that which I respect and admire. I say again, I'm not angry with you, though from some viewpoints I should be.

"If Pantrixnia was not a luxury hotel I'm willing to forgive that. If being pulled naked before your Assemblage and sentenced to exile and death was an injustice then I am prone to forgive that as well. I will not, however, forgive or forget my duty to defend my planet, and my people. I will forgive the threat made upon the belief of false accusations, but I will not forgive the cause. That cause was unique and well thought out, and greed was its fuel.

"It should be as apparent to you as it is to me, Nazeera; this is a Scythian war: staged and promoted by the Scythians. We are here because the Scythians cause us to fear each other. This is not a war over the grievances of Chem and Terra. This is not our war. This is not necessary, Nazeera."

"Your words are hollow, Alexander," she said gravely. "You plead an eloquent case, but you are a conqueror. I can see it in your eyes. You will not add Chem to your list of glories."

"If I wanted Chem, it would be mine, Nazeera! You know this better than anyone. Chem would fall to me, not due to weakness or lack of honor, but to destiny. Whether it's in this lifetime or the next, if I wanted the Chem Empire I could have it!"

Alexander paused, and there was not a sound on the bridge. He let the moment draw out and fade from the threat it was to a more subtle and diplomatic point in time. He spread his hands out wide. "The Chem are a people of honor whom I have come to respect and admire. A people whose dedication to honor can soothe the terrible wrath of my own unrequited people. I don't wish the Chem Empire as conquered adversaries, but as allies, friends and teachers."

"I listened to your lies in the Assemblage, Alexander," Nazeera told him. "I have no need to listen to them now. You are bold, to allow yourself to endure capture and exile thus, but I finally see through you.

You are here, even as the legends said you would be, but I will stop you if I can."

Alexander walked to the rear of the bridge and sank into his seat, a grim look coming over his strong features. "Very well, I expected some stubbornness; let me give you some truths to consider. Listen to your communications channels. I would like to demonstrate something to you."

He turned to Augesburcke, and said, "Admiral put me on all assigned Fleet frequencies."

"You're hooked up Alexander," Augesburcke answered.

"To all Terran ships and troops outside the Fleet of Alexander, you may proceed according to plan with the following restriction: no Terran warship shall violate Chem space except under my expressed orders. Proceed with operation "Overlord." You may commence to subjugate the Scythian Empire!"

"You have no right to interfere with our quarrel with the Scythians!" Nazeera protested.

"I have every right!" Alexander thundered, bolting upright and catching everyone off guard, including his own crew. "I have the right after two thousand years of having my name bandied about the galaxy as a murderer and a conqueror! I have the right after ten thousand years of experimentation on my people! I have the right after having my civilization constrained and manipulated!

"I speak for Terra, Nazeera, because I am Terra, and I seethe with the dishonor heaped upon me! The Scythians wanted me as a conqueror and I'm giving them what they wished for! Yet I am no chattel to do their bidding. I am Terra, and equally as proud as Chem! Does your complaint for a single snub carry more dishonor than the millennia Terra endured under an unseen puppeteer? The Scythians hid in the shadows poking and prodding us, pruning the branches by which we might grow, and all the while sowing lies about us to our cousins in space. Do you have the right to interfere with our vengeance? Answer me honestly Nazeera!"

"In that you have struck a chord of logic," she said, in a more diplomatic tone. Then her demeanor took on a renewed air of gravity and she asked, "But should I not now fear you more? Whether the Terrans attack from under the Scythians wing or on their own makes no difference to Chem, even if I do not fight for revenge upon Scythia my primary care is the protection of Chem."

"Well said, Nazeera, but there is a difference between Chem and Scythia. The Scythians wronged us. They wronged me. The Chem, thus far, have not. I've had the opportunity to learn of you, under dire circumstances, and still I came away with admiration, no, much more so than that. Earlier I said we were almost kindred, and I stand by that. We are so very much alike. We will go to enormous extremes and great personal risk to ensure the safety of our civilizations. If we insure that safety, you and I, then our people are capable of respect for each other and perhaps eventually trust.

"The protection of Chem is your concern. The protection of Terra is mine. It seems to be my task also to dispel the rumors of two thousand years of Scythian treachery. The only way I can do that is to somehow prove to you that my Fleet is here in defense of Terra, and not in aggression towards Chem. That proof is now in the transmissions taking place throughout the Scythian Empire. I'm certain Nazar is keeping track, and even now has something to report to you."

Alexander saw Nazar approach her, and he didn't need to hear him to know what he said. The reports were coming in from all over the Scythian Empire. Over the few moments both fleets listened. He'd already heard the important news he wanted: the four Homeworlds of Scythia fell almost instantly to the four million Terran troops supposedly there to protect the Scythians from the Chem.

His second objective was the capture of the twelve habitable systems on the Scythian-Chem frontier. His remaining two hundred and fifty ships accomplished this by cutting the two major trade routes and advancing on the planets. The Scythians surrendered before the first warship fired a shot. A week before he'd convinced Admiral Augesburcke that a charitable action and a well-defined threat were essential elements in convincing the Chem he was sincere. To accomplish this dual objective Alexander sent elements of the Terran Second Fleet around in a sweeping right hook to land four days behind the Chem Armada. It hung in space between the Chem Homeworld and its Armada, but when Alexander's order came the Second Fleet attacked the Scythian frontier instead of the advancing into Chem space from behind.

After the loss of the Homeworlds and the Chem frontier Scythian offers of surrender poured in from every corner of their Empire, even areas not attacked. A moment later a general offer of surrender communicated directly to Alexander on the "Iowa" arrived from the Scythian High Council. The Scythian Empire, which spanned two hundred and seventy-three habitable star systems and over two million years of history, fell in sixty-three Terran minutes.

Nazar confirmed everything with Nazeera, not bothering to conceal his communications. There was no need. The results in Scythia were too obvious to be denied.

"Listen to him, Nazeera," Alexander told her, "You are flanked. If it was my intention to attack the Chem I could send two hundred and fifty ships to the Chem home world, but that is not, and never was my aim."

Alexander went to the front of the bridge, and paced, as if lecturing. "You are an honorable people. We are an honorable people. We have no basis for disagreement; I will therefore build a basis for friendship and trust."

He selected his mike switch again. "Alexander accepts the unconditional surrender of the Scythian Empire. From this day onward the Scythian Empire is dissolved. I claim this space in the name of the Terran Empire. To all ships in the Second Fleet on Scythian-Chem frontier, your commanders are to inform each populace of the twelve frontier planets that they are now part of the Chem Empire."

He let the proclamation sink in, enjoying the expression of surprise on Nazeera's increasingly beautiful face. "Occupants have one Galactic decand to decide to leave or to stay. Secure the frontier planets for our neighbors the Chem, and then withdraw to Terran space according to doctrine. Alexander to the Fifth Fleet, upon my order all squadrons are to withdraw to pre-designated stations except the "Iowa." Secure our holdings in this space, including a star system wide buffer between the Terran Empire and the Chem Empire. Stand by."

Alexander turned his attention back to Nazeera, and his eyes hardened. His voice was commanding again, as he told her, "It's up to you, Nazeera. Upon your word this conflict shall either end amicably or begin in grim resolve. I shall give the order to my Fleets to secure their new holdings, yours included, upon your word."

"What act of assurance do you require, Alexander of Terra?" Nazeera asked him with a mixture of curiosity and suspicion.

"The word of the Armada Commander of Chem is the only guarantee needed by Alexander of Terra."

"The Chem have no wish to fight another's battle, especially those of Scythia!" Nazeera told him. She leaned back in her command chair and for the first time since she saw him she relaxed, and that feral grin returned to her face.

"I'm satisfied that the Scythians shall receive their just deserts from you Alexander, for I know too well the cruelty of your humor! Very well, then the situation is acceptable to the Chem. When your Fleet departs the Chem will not violate our agreement in the interests of galactic amity. The person of Alexander, your flagship and your space will be respected by your neighbors, the Chem."

Inwardly Alexander smiled at the victory, but to his crew and the Chem he merely inclined his head to Admiral Augesburcke. The Admiral gave the order for the Fleet to deploy and secure its new won empire. Alexander watched his screens as the Fifth Fleet wheeled and broke up. Within moments the five hundred odd ships disappeared over the superluminal horizon, leaving the "Iowa" and her squadron alone against the Chem Fleet.

"You are magnanimous in your victory, just as your own memories dictated, Alexander," Nazeera said. "I see no reason to pursue an unnecessary conflict, at this time. We will be watching you Terrans with excessive scrutiny, though. I, especially, shall be watching you."

"I desire more than that, Nazeera," Alexander told her.

Her expression turned noticeably grim again, "Are you baiting me, or do you really have the ignorance and impudence to demand terms for peace with the Chem? I can't believe that you, who have dined at my table, could win such a victory over enemies and then squander it by insulting those who might one day be your friends! What is it you are up to now, Alexander?"

"You've answered your own question, Nazeera," he smiled. "I have dined at your table, and I would do so again. It's not my intention to allow our peoples to come to the brink of war, and then withdraw to become distrustful neighbors suspiciously eyeing each other over a fence. My desire is to establish a dialogue so that one day there is trust and friendship between us. It is my intention that one day the rights of Chem and Terra are mentioned in one breath throughout the galaxy."

"An interesting concept," Nazeera replied. "How do you propose to begin this dialogue?"

"As a gesture of good faith I will agree to give myself as a hostage, under two conditions."

Nazeera settled back again in her chair. The suspicion left her voice. She allowed a ghost of a smile to play upon her blue lips, as she said, "I think that the center of the Chem Empire may be the most dangerous place to put you. What are your conditions Alexander?"

"First, on the threat of disgracing his people in front of the eyes of Terrans, Bureel must answer my challenge," he told her grimly.

"An honorable request, Alexander of Terra," Nazeera smiled maliciously. "As the Armada Commander of Chem, and Nazeera of the Triumvirate, I vouch that Bureel of Chem will answer your challenge, or he shall forfeit his heritage. What is your second condition?"

Alexander almost allowed himself to grin, but with the strictest gravity, he said, "Dinner and I wish to finish it with you this time. These are my conditions. Are they agreeable to you?"

Nazeera leaned forward, a wicked grin lighting her face. "Agreed," she said pounding her fist on her console. "I expect your shuttle promptly. I shall see you shortly, Alexander, Nazeera out."

The screen returned to stars, and the entire bridge crew breathed again. The realization that Terra escaped a deadly danger and that there was now a Terran Empire in space dawned on them all. There were cheers, back slapping, and an excited din of conversation. Alexander sighed and made his way to the bridge hatch, ignoring the hubbub. He was going to his stateroom to fetch his gear, but Augesburcke intercepted him, "Alexander! Well done! Well done man! But we've won, why sell yourself?"

Alexander smiled, crossing his arms contentedly, "This part of the mission is done, Admiral but we've both got more work to do. I've got the opportunity to cement our friendship with Chem, which we need to do while we get our space legs, so to speak. That's your responsibility. If you want my advice I'd allow the Scythians their four Homeworlds. The rest of the habitable worlds, aside from the twelve along the Chem frontier should be used for immediate transplantation of Terrans from the Terran system. We must never again be caught on a single planet, Admiral."

"Sound advice," the Admiral replied. "But let me ask you, again, why are you doing this? It was a brilliant strategy, Alexander, and yet after the victory you are willing to disappear? Man, you have an entire planet ready to honor you. You are also a member of CODOTS, Alexander, and are now in a position to make your mark. I know of no one more capable. Think of it man! You are at the pinnacle of fame, why leave now when we can use you?"

"Isn't that the time for conqueror's to disappear, Admiral—while they're still conquerors and not despots? I have no political agenda. I haven't the patience for it, or the desire. I have some unfinished business with Nazeera and a worm. It is my business to finish, but if I remain in CODOTS and as Ambassador to Chem so much the better."

"I'll guarantee it, Alexander, good luck!" The Admiral said, extending his hand.

"Providing I survive my challenge, that is. Still, space is a very large place and I daresay there's room for Terrans to expand and explore. If you need me you know where I am, Admiral," Alexander shook his hand. "You have the bridge Captain, good luck!"